WILD ABANDON

The sight of Fantasy in the low-cut gown, her exposed skin even creamier next to the black silk when bathed in the soft glow of lamplight, sent Jesse's pulse into another wild rhythm.

Never taking his eyes from her face, Jesse approached Fantasy with slow, measured steps. Stopping directly in front of her, he cupped her chin with one hand. "You're so beautiful, Fancy. I want to kiss you. I've wanted to kiss you all evening, and now I'm going to."

As Jesse lowered his face to Fantasy's, her eyes fluttered shut. Pulling her fully against him, he explored her mouth, nipping with his teeth, then soothing with his tongue.

Fantasy felt herself slipping away, completely powerless to do anything about it. She found herself transported to a world she knew little about—a world of sensual pleasures like nothing she had ever imagined—a world where Jesse reigned as undisputed master. Acting totally on instinct, she pressed closer.

"Slow down, Fantasy," Jesse whispered. "Much more of that and I might carry you to my bedroom."

She stared up at him. What she wanted became crystal clear. Her voice was very low when she spoke. "I *want* you to carry me to your bedroom."

Jesse studied her through narrowed eyes for several long moments. "Do you know what you're saying?"

Fantasy nodded and with a growl, Jesse swept her up into his arms. . . .

TODAY'S HOTTEST READS
ARE TOMORROW'S SUPERSTARS

VICTORY'S WOMAN   (4484, $4.50)
by Gretchen Genet
Andrew—the carefree soldier who sought glory on the battlefield, and returned a shattered man . . . Niall—the legendary frontiersman and a former Shawnee captive, tormented by his past . . . Roger—the troubled youth, who would rise up to claim a shocking legacy . . . and Clarice—the passionate beauty bound by one man, and hopelessly in love with another. Set against the backdrop of the American revolution, three men fight for their heritage—and one woman is destined to change all their lives forever!

FORBIDDEN   (4488, $4.99)
by Jo Beverley
While fleeing from her brothers, who are attempting to sell her into a loveless marriage, Serena Riverton accepts a carriage ride from a stranger—who is the handsomest man she has ever seen. Lord Middlethorpe, himself, is actually contemplating marriage to a dull daughter of the aristocracy, when he encounters the breathtaking Serena. She arouses him as no woman ever has. And after a night of thrilling intimacy—a forbidden liaison—Serena must choose between a lady's place and a woman's passion!

WINDS OF DESTINY   (4489, $4.99)
by Victoria Thompson
Becky Tate is a half-breed outcast—branded by her Comanche heritage. Then she meets a rugged stranger who awakens her heart to the magic and mystery of passion. Hiding a desperate past, Texas Ranger Clint Masterson has ridden into cattle country to bring peace to a divided land. But a greater battle rages inside him when he dares to desire the beautiful Becky!

WILDEST HEART   (4456, $4.99)
by Virginia Brown
Maggie Malone had come to cattle country to forge her future as a healer. Now she was faced by Devon Conrad, an outlaw wounded body and soul by his shadowy past . . . whose eyes blazed with fury even as his burning caress sent her spiraling with desire. They came together in a Texas town about to explode in sin and scandal. Danger was their destiny—and there was nothing they wouldn't dare for love!

Available wherever paperbacks are sold, or order direct from the Publisher. Send cover price plus 50¢ per copy for mailing and handling to Penguin USA, P.O. Box 999, c/o Dept. 17109, Bergenfield, NJ 07621. Residents of New York and Tennessee must include sales tax. DO NOT SEND CASH.

His Wildest Fantasy

ARLENE HOLLIDAY

ZEBRA BOOKS
KENSINGTON PUBLISHING CORP.

ZEBRA BOOKS are published by

Kensington Publishing Corp.
850 Third Avenue
New York, NY 10022

First Printing: November, 1994

Printed in the United States of America

*He was a kind, gentle man, always ready
with words of praise and encouragement. We
shared a love of reading and the Old West, and
he proudly awaited the release of my first book.
Sadly, he was taken from us a month too soon.
This book is dedicated to my father.
I love you, Dad. I miss you.*

Chapter 1

FANTASY'S.

Bright red letters curlicued across the sign on the front of the white clapboard building.

Withdrawing a slip of paper from his pocket, Jesse McAllister checked the address he'd written down. Two-sixteen Fourth Street. He had the right house.

Now why the hell would John tell me to keep an eye on a sporting house? He'd expected what his boss described as the major link in his assignment to be a more reputable business.

Looking back across the street, his gaze traced the name on the sign one more time. FANTASY'S. Unbidden, his mind filled with carnal images. For a moment he gave one particularly erotic scene time to play out, then shook his head to chase away the thoughts playing havoc with his concentration.

As the front door swung open, his gaze dropped from the red letters to the doorway. A nattily dressed man stepped through the door into the stifling heat of the Tombstone afternoon. He started to walk away, then turned and hurried back to the young woman who'd followed him onto the boardwalk. Jesse's attention instantly shifted from the man to the woman, drawn by a magnetic force he couldn't break. Even from his poor vantage point across the street, her auburn hair and heart-shaped face took his breath away.

Through narrowed eyes, he watched the man pull

the beauty against his chest, lower his flushed face, and plant a kiss squarely on her lips. An immediate tightness gripped Jesse's groin.

He knew why the man's face was the color of the sign above his head and why he kissed the woman with such enthusiasm in view of the entire town. Obviously the man had just come from the *lady's* bed and was thanking her for time well spent.

Jesse's temper rose at the thought of the lovely young woman taking men to her bed to make a living. Why he should care how a woman he didn't even know earned her money was beyond him. But he did. And worse yet, an emotion, irrationally close to jealousy, twisted his insides. While he hadn't been with a woman in a very long time, he'd never reacted so strongly to one he'd never met and only seen from a distance.

Leaning against one of the posts supporting the boardwalk's wooden awning, Jesse scowled fiercely at the couple across the street. When their kiss ended, the woman stared after the man for several seconds then slipped back inside the house, forcing Jesse's intense stare to shift to her departing patron.

Jesse watched him walk away in what could only be described as a swagger. *Arrogant bastard.* When the man disappeared around the corner, Jesse turned back to the white building with its brilliant sign.

If John wants me to keep an eye on a whorehouse, then by damn that's what I'll do. Jesse pushed away from the post. *But from the inside. Starting right now!* His sudden decision propelled him across the dusty street and onto the opposite boardwalk.

With determined steps, he approached the doorway that had given him a glimpse of an angel—a bit tarnished, but an angel just the same. He opened the door and stepped inside. Pausing to let his eyes adjust to the dim interior, he found himself in a small foyer at the head of a long hallway.

The air was blessedly cool compared to the arid heat outside and held the tangy scent of lemon oil. A staircase hugged the wall to his right, and two doors opened off the hallway to his left. From the doorway closest to him came the clear, sweet voice of a woman singing.

It was his auburn-haired angel. Somehow he'd already come to think of her as his. Just looking at her sent another rush of need surging through him. The fact that a lady of joy was doing such a mundane task as dusting didn't seem incongruous to his desire-ridden brain. His thoughts were centered completely on the lovely woman across the room, and her finely sculpted profile.

Jesse's gaze drifted down her smooth forehead and slightly upturned nose, then lingered on lush lips. Forcing his gaze away from the temptation of her mouth, he focused on her glorious hair. Gathered in a loose knot on top of her head, a few unruly strands had escaped and dangled down her back in long silky curls.

She stretched to dust the top of a picture frame, pulling his gaze to the ripe bosom pressing against her dress bodice. Her narrow waist and rounded hips sent another flash of desire slicing through him. He wanted to rush to her, take her into his arms, but for some reason his feet didn't respond. Feeling as if he were moving in slow motion, he approached her with silent steps.

Fantasy Williams stopped singing, straightened and rubbed the small of her back with one hand. Of all her chores, she hated dusting the most. With the dust of the Arizona desert continually coating everything with a layer of yellowish-white dirt, it was a neverending job.

The hair on the nape of her neck suddenly prickled with apprehension. She had the distinct feeling she was no longer alone.

Dustrag clutched in her hand, she whirled around. A

man she'd never seen before was moving slowly across
the parlor toward her. As he drew closer, the intense
look on his handsome face kept her feet rooted to the
floor.

"Hello, gorgeous," he murmured, his deep voice
sending a ripple of apprehension up her spine.

"Who . . . ? What . . . ?" She snapped her mouth
shut, dismayed that this man's brazen greeting had
robbed her of her ability to put two words together.

Before she realized his intention, Fantasy found herself locked securely in his arms, her breasts pressed
against his muscular chest. When she started to voice
her outrage, he covered her mouth with his.

She couldn't believe what was happening. A total
stranger had pulled her into his embrace, molded her
body intimately against his, and was kissing her sense-
less. For a moment she allowed herself to enjoy the feel
of being wrapped in his arms, the pressure of his firm
lips, the heady mixed scent of his heated flesh and
shaving soap.

As his mouth and tongue explored hers totally, thoroughly, a deep groan rumbled in his chest. The sound
brought Fantasy out of her momentary lapse with a
flash of shame.

What was she doing? She didn't indulge in such
wanton behavior. Bracing her hands on his muscular
arms, she tried to free herself from the man's embrace.
The best she could do was pull her mouth from his.

"No," she croaked, her voice raspy from both an
unwanted awakening of her long-buried female needs
and fury at the man's bold-as-brass behavior.

Jesse lifted his head and let his eyes slowly drift
open. Taking a deep, shaky breath, he tried to regain
his composure by focusing on something, anything but
the temptress in his arms. Through glazed eyes, he
looked around the room. The upholstered settee,
matching chairs, and pair of wooden rockers all facing
the marble top coffee table indicated he stood in a
parlor. His brow furrowed when he noticed the muted,

pastel print of the wallpaper and the fine lace curtains at the window. The walls weren't covered with gaudy, flocked paper; the windows weren't hung with heavy, velvet drapes. Not how a bordello's supposed—

The woman's renewed efforts to wrench free halted further thought about the room's decor. When her wiggling pressed her belly against his groin, Jesse felt his manhood spring to life with such force he inhaled sharply. All he'd intended to do was kiss this beauty once, then make arrangements to enjoy more of her charms later. Now he felt as if he hadn't had a woman in years rather than months. Although nightfall was only a few hours away, it was much too long to wait.

Sweeping her up into his arms, Jesse murmured in a thick voice, "Where's your room, honey? Upstairs?"

Shocked by his continued forward behavior, Fantasy shook her head mutely. Casting a frantic glance toward the open door leading to the back of the house, she prayed he wouldn't find the small apartment she shared with her five-year-old son.

Jesse hadn't missed her gaze darting across the room. Thinking her behavior a coy way of answering his question, he flashed a smile then carried her effortlessly toward the doorway.

"Stop! What are you doing?" Her legs thrashing wildly, Fantasy tried to twist out of his arms.

"Shh," Jesse crooned, crossing the threshold and nudging the door shut with one foot. "Don't worry, I'll pay double your usual rate." Taking her shocked silence for acceptance, he pressed his mouth to hers again.

For a second Fantasy forgot what was happening, forgot she wanted desperately to end this man's assault. As his kiss worked its magic, she felt almost faint. Never had she experienced anything so wicked— or so wonderful.

No, nothing in her twenty-three years had prepared her for her body's response. Although she'd believed Thomas had taught her all there was to know about kissing, she now knew she was a novice. This man's, *this stranger's,* kisses transported her to a world where only physical pleasure existed. A world she had only glimpsed when Thomas had held her, kissed her, loved her. The passion Thomas had never been able to stoke beyond a tiny spark had easily been fanned into a raging inferno by the man holding her.

Just as quickly as her desire flared to life, reality flooded back. Mortified with guilt for responding in a way she never had with her husband, Fantasy stiffened in the stranger's arms.

Pushing against his chest, she tried again to wiggle out of his embrace. For all her efforts, the only thing she accomplished was an unintentional exploration of the rippling muscles beneath his shirt. He moaned at the contact, instinctively tightening his grip to pull her more snugly against him.

"Please, put me down." Her voice lacked the volume and force she wanted to project.

"Soon, my gorgeous angel, soon," Jesse promised, taking her softly spoken words for encouragement. He trailed lazy kisses across her cheek, then nibbled his way to the heated, creamy skin beneath her jawbone.

"Momma, Momma!" A child's piping voice came clearly from the other side of the door.

Robby's call from the parlor galvanized Fantasy into immediate action. She struggled harder to break the man's embrace, bucking and twisting against him. At her son's second call, she increased her efforts.

A child's voice and the woman's frantic wiggling penetrated Jesse's passion-fogged brain. With a grunt of exasperation, he halted his attempt to explore her silky neck. Breathing hard, he kept his eyes tightly closed, trying to cool the blood running hot and thick through his veins. When his senses returned, he realized the child was calling to someone in this room. Based on her reaction, that someone had to be the spirited wildcat caught in the snare of his arms.

Afraid of what he'd find, Jesse slowly opened his

eyes and allowed his gaze to settle on the woman still cradled against his chest. As he stared at her, she ceased fighting. Her energy spent, her breathing labored, she watched him warily.

This time when he looked at her, he noticed her clothing wasn't the usual skimpy, silk variety most prostitutes favored. Made of a pale blue, lightweight material, her simply tailored dress was very proper. Attractive and flattering, but most definitely proper.

Taking a deep, shuddering breath, Jesse forced himself to finish his analysis. His gaze moved slowly to her left hand, still balled in a fist over his hammering heart. The gold band winked up at him, its brightness silently mocking.

"Dammit," he growled.

He dropped his arm from beneath her knees, letting her slide down his body until her feet touched the floor. As she brushed against his arousal, a moan of half-pain, half-pleasure escaped his tight throat.

When she made a move to go around him, Jesse grabbed her arm. "Hold it, I wanna talk to you."

Her head snapped up. Green eyes, as dark as the deepest jade, searched his face.

His features were rigid with anger, and fear of the man's intentions formed a lump in Fantasy's throat. She swallowed hard, then asked in a shaky whisper, "Can I see what my son wants first?"

At his terse nod, she opened the door a crack. After listening to her child's excited chatter, she said, "Momma's busy now, sweetheart. You go back outside, and I'll come out later."

By the time she eased the door closed and turned to face him, Jesse had riled himself into one hell of a temper. Whether his anger stemmed from allowing his passion to soar out of control, from being forced to put a cap on it before finding relief, from the realization he'd apparently made a serious error in judgment, or from a combination of all three, Jesse wasn't sure. However, he was sure of one thing—the blame for his present mood rested squarely on this woman's shoulders.

How could she? How could a married woman, especially one with a child, run a whorehouse? Though he knew women were often forced to take up work they normally wouldn't consider because of unfortunate circumstances, his reaction to this woman's profession was irrational condemnation.

When he realized she was waiting for him to speak, Jesse exhaled slowly, trying to tamp down his towering fury. "That man I saw you kissing—" Her sharply indrawn breath halted the question he started to ask.

"Kissing?" Her voice was a weak croak.

"Yeah, kissing. Right out there on the boardwalk," Jesse said, pointing to the front of the house.

Her cheeks burning, the lump in her throat dropped like a stone into her stomach. She'd been afraid this would happen—this man, and Lord knew how many others, had witnessed the shameful scene of less than half an hour ago.

She had just finished sweeping the parlor when Garland Baxter, one of her boarders, rushed into the house.

"Mrs. Williams, I'm glad you're here." His voice had been louder than usual and slightly slurred.

"What is it, Mr. Baxter?"

"Ben Goodrich offered me a junior partnership in his firm this morning."

"Oh, how wonderful. I'm so happy for you." Fantasy moved closer to offer her hand in congratulations. Catching a whiff of his breath, she abruptly changed her mind and stepped back. Obviously he'd already begun celebrating.

Baxter pulled his watch from his vest pocket, snapped open the cover and checked the time. "I just stopped by to tell you my news. I have to be going. I'm supposed to meet someone at the Crystal Palace."

Replacing his watch, he turned to leave. Fantasy followed him into the hall and through the front door.

"The Crystal Palace? Don't you have to go back to the office?"

Considering his ruddy complexion, glassy eyes, and unsteady gait, the last thing he needed was more whiskey.

"No, Ben gave me the afternoon off."

There was nothing she could say to change his mind, so Fantasy nodded absently. "Well, congratulations, Mr. Baxter."

He started to walk away, then paused. It must have been his immense excitement and inebriated state that made him shed his usual reserved demeanor. Before Fantasy could anticipate his actions, she found herself in Garland's arms and on the receiving end of an exuberant kiss. Although she hadn't responded, she'd been so taken by surprise she hadn't stopped him either. And worst of all, they were standing in the middle of the boardwalk where passersby couldn't miss the disgraceful display.

With an exasperated sigh, Fantasy looked up at the second man who'd forced an unwanted kiss on her that afternoon. He was glaring at her, his cold blue eyes accusing and judgmental. Although she longed to set him straight, she figured she'd be wasting her breath. Clearly the man was like her mother-in-law, ready to believe the worst. In his surly mood, nothing she could say would make any difference.

Seeing the emotions flit across her face, Jesse knew she had recalled the incident he mentioned. "I see you remember that touching farewell," he said, his voice heavy with sarcasm. "Was that man your husband?"

"Husband?" Her auburn eyebrows shot up.

Jesse's fists clenched and unclenched impotently at his sides. He wished he could punch something to ease his growing frustration.

"Yes, husband! That is a wedding band, isn't it?"

"Yes," she answered quietly, dropping her gaze from his glowering face.

"So was that man your husband or not?"

She peeked up at him through partially lowered lashes. His face could have been made of stone, so harsh and forbidding were his features. "No, he isn't my husband."

Expecting her reply to be affirmative, it took Jesse several seconds to realize what she'd said. A muscle jumped in his cheek. "What did you say?"

Lifting her chin defiantly, she looked him straight in the eye. "He isn't my husband."

Jesse squeezed his eyes shut for a second and sucked in a deep breath through clenched teeth. *Not only does she run a whorehouse, she's also a cheating bitch.* "So who was he? A customer?" He couldn't leave well enough alone. His training as an investigator compelled him to dig deeper, or was it the feelings she stirred in him?

It was apparent by his cold attitude he believed she'd betrayed her husband. Yet Fantasy was stumped why it mattered to him, or why he insisted on knowing the identity of her supposed paramour.

"I guess you could say he's a customer," she finally replied. "He pays me for the service I provide, just like the others."

Although not pleased with her nonchalant attitude about the *service* she was paid for, her last word kept echoing in his head. *Others!* A terrible pain wrenched his chest. The thought of this beauty with the man he'd seen her kiss was bad enough. But her matter-of-fact mention of her other customers cut him more deeply than he could have imagined. Then he realized something pained him even more—her marital state and her apparent refusal to take her wedding vows seriously.

"And what does your husband say about that?"

"My husband is—" she halted her retort when she realized what she'd almost revealed. "My husband doesn't say a word, not that it's any of your business," she finally said, growing irritation clear in her voice.

One of Jesse's eyebrows arched. He couldn't help wondering what kind of monster would allow his beautiful young wife to share her charms with other men. The very idea made his insides roil. "Just where is this husband of yours?"

"Well . . . he's . . . uh . . . he's around . . . um, somewhere," she stammered, dropping her gaze once more.

"I don't understand. You're married, and your husband isn't concerned about you running a bawdy house? What—"

Eyes blazing, she lifted her head. "A *bawdy* house?"

Now all of the man's little innuendoes and strange comments made sense. Never had she suspected he had mistaken her business for a whorehouse. *He thinks I'm one of those . . . those women.*

All at once it was too much: her husband's abandonment of her and their newborn son to seek his fortune in the mines of Colorado then Arizona, his death just before their reunion in Tombstone, her struggling long, hard hours to make a decent living for her son, and now the horrid accusations of this ignoramus. A gentle-natured woman, Fantasy seldom lost her composure, but this man's ill-bred treatment was the proverbial last straw for her slow-to-rouse temper.

"Anyone with a lick of sense knows all houses of ill fame in Tombstone have to be east of Sixth Street. That's by town ordinance, in case you're interested. Secondly, does this look like a house that entertains men?" She gestured around the room. Not waiting for his reply, Fantasy continued. "No, it damn well doesn't."

Grabbing a handful of her simple cotton dress, she shook the rumpled material at him. "And do I dress like a woman who sells herself to men?" Once more she didn't allow him time to get a word in. "I should say not! How *dare* you accuse me of raising my son in a house with such goings on!"

Quivering with rage, she drew a deep breath before making her final statement. "This is a *boarding* house, not a *bawdy* house!"

Undaunted by her considerable display of temper, Jesse refused to relent. "Then why the hell is a boardinghouse called 'Fantasy's?' Do you have any idea what a name like that implies?"

"You have a filthy mind," she retorted, her back ramrod stiff, her delicate chin lifted defiantly. "My boardinghouse was named for its owner."

In spite of the heat still flashing in her eyes, Jesse felt the chill of her icy voice. "Who are you trying to kid, sister? No one has a name like Fantasy."

"Don't call me sister, you ninnyhammer." Eyeing him scornfully, she continued. "Of all the nerve, criticizing the name a mother gives a person. Contrary to your opinion, which isn't worth a hill of beans, my name is Fantasy. Fantasy Williams. Not that I give a tinker's damn what you think."

Straightening her spine still more, she drew herself up to better meet his gaze. "Now, I'd appreciate it if you'd take yourself, along with your disgusting slurs, out of my house immediately."

Though he towered over her, Jesse felt like a school boy receiving a lecture from his teacher. He looked around the room for confirmation of her claim.

Nothing in the sparsely furnished sitting room suggested it belonged to a prostitute. Neat and spotless, it spoke of respectability. Then something else niggled at him—the outer room and the way it was decorated. Now he knew why it had disturbed him. This *wasn't* a whorehouse!

His anger vanished like air escaping a punctured balloon. *Aw, shit. Now I've done it. Not only did I try to have my way with her, but I insulted her twice in less than two minutes, accusing her of running a house of prostitution, then finding fault with her name.*

Keeping his gaze downcast, Jesse gave her a courtly bow as he murmured, "Please accept my apology, Mrs. Williams. It was my mistake, on all counts."

With that he turned on his heel and walked out of the room. When she heard the front door click shut,

Fantasy released the breath she hadn't realized she'd been holding.

"Mattie said it would never be dull in Tombstone," she mumbled, thinking of her only close female friend in town. *I sure hope I don't have any more afternoons like this one.* She walked back into the parlor and looked out the front window. He strode down the boardwalk toward Allen Street, his tweed jacket thrown across one arm, his light brown hair brushing his collar, his wide shoulders filling out his cotton shirt perfectly.

Closing her eyes, she allowed herself a moment to bask in the memory of being held in his arms. She could still smell his wonderful scent—the pungent odor of heated skin and the spicy aroma of sandalwood shaving soap. She could still taste his exhilarating kisses. The memories sent a tingling down through her belly that settled between her thighs. It was a sensation she'd never experienced, not even with her husband.

"You're working too hard, Fantasy," she muttered, retrieving the dustrag from where she'd dropped it on the floor. While she finished the dusting, she realized she didn't even know the name of the man who'd come storming into her parlor like a dust devil swirling off the desert.

What does it matter? He's obviously looking for the kind of woman he accused me of being, so I'll never see him again. The thought was a relief, or was it? Shaking her head to clear her conflicting emotions, Fantasy remembered she told her son she'd come out to look at the bird's nest he found.

Before leaving the parlor, she looked out the window one last time. He was out of sight. I don't need a man anyway. But her body told a very different tale.

Nursing his battered ego, Jesse stomped down Fourth Street. He crossed the first intersection, turned

east, then marched down the south side—the respectable side, he figured, since only the north side sported
saloons and gambling halls—of Allen Street.

"Women!" he muttered aloud, drawing a strange
look from the couple coming toward him. Nodding his
head politely, he smiled a silent greeting. He hoped he
didn't look as much like an idiot as he felt. He kept
trying to thrust Fantasy Williams from his mind. But
the green-eyed beauty continued to haunt him, each
time searing him with her fiery gaze, calling him a
ninnyhammer with her lush mouth. The ridiculous
word brought a smile to his face. Amusement quickly
turned to annoyance. He *had* acted like a fool.

Pressing his lips together in fierce determination and
hoping he could force thoughts of Fantasy from his
brain, Jesse entered the Grand Hotel on the ground
floor of the Ritchie Building. Crossing the lobby, he
paid little attention to its sumptuous furnishings. He
moved up the wide staircase, barely noticing the elegant carpet beneath his feet, the black walnut bannis-
ter beneath his hand.

Once inside the Tombstone Club on the second
floor, Jesse looked around for Nick Trask. They'd
made arrangements by telegram to meet here as soon
as Jesse arrived.

His arrival at the men's club had been delayed by his
disastrous visit to the house on Fourth Street and his
even more disastrous confrontation with its owner.
Intent on finding Nick, Jesse walked purposefully into
the main sitting room. He gave the rich Brussels carpet
and tasteful furnishings only a cursory glance. His
mind was still too occupied with trying to evict the
lovely Fantasy Williams from his thoughts to be impressed by the posh interior of the club.

He finally spotted Nick in the far corner, engrossed
in a newspaper. As he approached his friend and co-
worker of nearly six years, Jesse saw the intense concentration on Nick's face—a handsome face the ladies
loved. Jesse grinned. How many Tombstone women

had Nick captivated with his devilish good looks and quick, easy smile? Erasing his grin, Jesse stopped beside Nick's chair.

"I see you're still interested in the state of the world," Jesse said with a chuckle, noticing the European masthead of the publication.

"Why not?" Nick replied, his voice muffled by the paper. "The Club gets something like sixty magazines and newspapers. That's one of the reasons I joined." Lowering the paper, Nick's smile of greeting abruptly changed into a frown. "Just where the hell have you been? Your stage should have gotten in long before now."

"It did," Jesse replied. "I took a walk to stretch my legs." Nick should accept his excuse of wanting to get some exercise. It was a long trip by train from northern California, followed by a cramped stage ride from Benson, twenty-five miles north of Tombstone.

Nick nodded, searching Jesse's face for a sign that there was more to the explanation. Though his friend's words made sense, it wasn't like him to shirk his responsibilities, even briefly. Smiling, Nick rose from his chair. He pumped Jesse's hand, then gave him a rough hug.

"Damn, it's good to see you, Jesse."

"Good to see you, too, Nick. How about a drink to celebrate my arrival?" After his humiliating experience at the hands of Mrs. Fantasy Williams, he needed the fortification of strong whiskey.

"Sure thing." Nick headed for the magnificently carved sideboard, stocked with every possible liquor and a fine selection of choice cigars.

Once they had settled into comfortable chairs located a good distance from the other men in the room, Jesse and Nick spent a few minutes catching up on where they'd been for the last two years. Finally the conversation turned to the reason both men were in Tombstone.

"So what did you and John come up with as a

cover?" Nick asked, curious to learn what excuse their boss, John Valentine, General Superintendent of Wells, Fargo and Company, had decided to use for Jesse being in town.

"I'm a land speculator." Jesse stretched his legs out in front of him then crossed one ankle over the other. "With all the mining around the area, property seemed like a good reason to be in town. There's always money to be made from buying a piece of land in a boomtown, then selling it at a profit a few months later when the value goes up."

Nick nodded his agreement, knowing others had done exactly that. "Did John tell you about Jack Lawson?"

"Yeah, he said you sent word you think he's head of the gang people here are calling the *cow-boys.*"

"Actually, the folks around here first gave the name to the cattle rustlers working between here and Mexico. Now they're using it for all law-breakers."

Jesse nodded. "I remember reading a newspaper article you sent John. I think the headline read 'The Cow-boy Scourge.' "

"That's right. The article called the stage holdups by the so-called cow-boy scourge the greatest outrage ever perpetrated against the citizens of Arizona." Chuckling, Nick scrunched down in his chair.

"Anyway, Lawson works as a night bartender at the Oriental Saloon. And though I can't prove it yet, I'm sure he spends some of his days holding up stages with the rest of his gang—not holed up in his room like he wants everyone to think. I struck up a friendship with him and started spending time at the Oriental until he got edgy about the questions I asked. I think he was beginning to suspect I'm more than a gambler. I've had to lay off him for a while. Now that you're in town, maybe you can dig up the evidence we need to send the bastard and his partners to prison."

They sipped their drinks in silence for several minutes, until Jesse could no longer contain his curiosity.

"John mentioned a place on Fourth Street as a possible connection to the stage robberies. Do you know anything about that?" He kept his voice purposely bland.

"Yeah, the boardinghouse where Lawson lives." Noticing how Jesse's lips flattened into a thin line, Nick wondered briefly at the cause. "I haven't been able to find out if anyone else in the place is involved. None of the other boarders associate openly with Lawson. 'Course that doesn't prove anything; they could still be part of his gang."

Nick burst into deep rumbles of laughter, bringing Jesse out of his brooding thoughts. "The boardinghouse is called Fantasy's. Isn't that one helluva name?"

When Jesse didn't respond, Nick went on. "But the name sure fits when you see the owner of the place. Yes sirree, Fantasy Williams is one beautiful woman."

Jesse jerked upright, leaning forward to brace his elbows on his knees. "Just how well do you know this Fantasy Williams?"

Nick realized he'd been wrong. His friend *was* keeping something from him. Nick also knew no amount of badgering would get Jesse to loosen his tongue until he was good and ready.

"I don't know her personally," Nick began. "She keeps pretty much to herself, but I've heard she attends the Episcopal Church, works with its Ladies Aid Society, and helps one of the doctors in town. Beyond that, there isn't much I can tell you about the Widow Williams."

Jesse's eyebrows shot up, then immediately pulled down in a frown. Blinking at Nick, he sat back in his chair, grasping the upholstered arms in a fierce grip. *Widow!*

Chapter 2

Nick's revelation rang over and over in Jesse's head. *Widow.* That one word wrapped itself around his windpipe, squeezing unmercifully until breathing required every ounce of his concentration. For several seconds he stared at Nick in total silence.

"Widow Williams?" Jesse finally managed to say.

"Yeah, she's from back East somewhere," Nick said, crossing one ankle over the opposite knee, pointedly ignoring Jesse's strange behavior.

When Jesse said no more, Nick continued with what he knew about Fantasy Williams. "Her husband worked in one of the local mines—the Goodenough, if I remember right. Anyway, after a couple years he decided his family should join him, so he sent for his wife and son. I'd say she got here six, eight months ago. Turned out she made the trip for nothing. Her husband got himself killed in a saloon fight two weeks before she arrived.

"Although Williams had bragged his beautiful wife was coming, no one knew exactly when she was expected. The undertaker couldn't very well wait for someone to claim the body, so he had no choice but to bury Williams in Boot Hill."

Nick paused to light a cheroot. Taking a puff and blowing the smoke out leisurely, he added in a low voice, "It's a damn shame, such a good-looking man having to work so hard running a boardinghouse. But from what I hear, she's doing a fine job."

By the time Nick finished, Jesse had snapped out of his stupor and right into another prize-winning fit of temper.

Damn her hide. Now everything fell into place. At the time he'd been too full of anger to recognize Fantasy's strange reaction to his questions about her husband. But in retrospect, he recalled how she'd kept her gaze carefully averted, how she'd stuttered her answer about her husband's whereabouts. *Around somewhere, indeed.* He cleared his throat to cover his harrumph.

Nick watched the emotions passing across Jesse's face through the smoke of his cheroot. He realized his friend was struggling with some inner battle and wondered again what had him so tied in knots.

Shifting his gaze to Jesse's empty glass, he said, "Ready to head for the room I rented for you in the hotel?"

A sudden flash of inspiration cooled Jesse's anger. "No, I've decided on a different plan of attack. I'm going to take a room at the Widow Williams's boardinghouse," he explained, warming to the idea more and more as he spoke the words aloud. "If I live under the same roof as Lawson, I can find out what we need to know faster than if I stay in the hotel."

Nick ground out the butt of his cheroot in an ashtray, then rose from his chair. "Getting closer to Lawson could speed up this damn investigation. I've been in town nearly a year, and I'd sure like to get back to California. So what should I do about the room I rented?"

"Nothing. Keep it until I find out whether the boardinghouse is filled." Silently, he hoped that wouldn't be the case. "Then if I don't need the room, you can settle up with the hotel."

After agreeing on their next meeting, Nick bid Jesse a good afternoon.

For several minutes Jesse sat quietly, reviewing what

had taken place in the last hour. Somehow it seemed much longer. With determined strides, he left the Tombstone Club and retraced his steps to the boardinghouse on Fourth Street.

When he saw the painted sign on the front of the building, his mind was again besieged with a bevy of tantalizing pictures. Only this time the woman in his erotic imaginings had a familiar face. The *Widow* Williams. In spite of the humiliation she'd caused him, she was the woman whose mouth he wanted desperately to taste again.

As Jesse entered the boardinghouse the second time, he heard a low murmur of voices coming from the parlor. Moving silently down the hall to a spot where he could see into the room undetected, Jesse peered inside.

Fantasy stood near her desk, talking with a man. Jesse had only a partial view of him, but from Nick's description the clothes—Prince Albert coat and checked pants—and the black hair and sweeping moustache suggested the man was Jack Lawson. Wishing he could hear what they were saying, Jesse maintained his vantage point. What could hold them in such deep conversation?

His curiosity increased when the man withdrew his wallet from inside his coat, pulled out several bills and handed them to Fantasy. Jesse was too far away to make out the denominations, but it sure looked like a lot more than rent money.

Their business apparently completed, the man turned to leave, heading toward the hallway and Jesse's hiding place. Jesse eased farther down the hall, hoping the deep shadows would conceal his presence. As the man passed through the parlor doorway, Jesse flattened himself against the wall.

"Thanks, Mr. Lawson," Fantasy called from the parlor. "You're very generous."

"Think nothing of it, Mrs. Williams. You're doing a fine job, and I like to see my money put to good use."

"Well, thanks again."

"You'll keep this our little secret, won't you? Like the other times?"

"Of course, Mr. Lawson. Mum's the word."

"Good, I knew I could count on your understandin'. Have a nice evenin', Mrs. Williams," the man called over his shoulder before opening the front door and stepping into the fading afternoon light.

Jesse relaxed his pose. The man *was* Jack Lawson. But what did the tail end of that conversation mean? Was it hush money? Then another question popped into Jesse's head before he could stop it. Was Fantasy renting her favors along with her rooms? As his temper started climbing again, he wondered why he couldn't keep a cool head where Fantasy Williams was concerned.

He forced himself to think rationally and realized his last question wasn't a viable explanation. A lover wouldn't compliment his partner on a job well done. Lawson and Fantasy weren't lovers—or at least he wasn't paying her to share his bed. *Dammit, McAllister, knock it off.*

As he lectured himself on controlling his overactive imagination, Jesse slipped back to the parlor door. He had a horrible suspicion the beautiful Fantasy Williams wasn't the fine upstanding citizen she wanted everyone to believe she was. If the money he'd seen changing hands was any indication, he'd better keep a close eye on her as well as Lawson.

He peeked into the parlor. Fantasy was washing the front window, her lovely face streaked with dirt, her dress clinging to the most delightful places. Jesse hadn't noticed her disheveled state when he'd first seen her talking to Lawson. But it didn't make any difference. He still found her truly beautiful, and again she affected his senses instantly. As he watched her work, the heat of desire swept over him.

His body reacted as strongly as it had earlier, though now there was a subtle but very distinct difference. He still wanted her, yet this time his need was deeper, more substantial than just the physical urge to find release in her sweet body. There was a thirst in his soul longing to be quenched. A thirst he'd never known and couldn't explain.

Such feelings were foreign to Jesse. He'd never given any thought to experiencing more than fleeting desire for a woman. Oh, he was a considerate lover to be sure, pleasuring his partners as much as he took pleasure from them. And for that reason, the women he'd known always welcomed him with open arms, several even hinting they'd like to make their alliance permanent. But Jesse had never crossed paths with a woman who made him want more than a good romp in her bed. And besides, his career with Wells, Fargo had always taken precedence in his life.

Now here he was entertaining thoughts of permanency with a woman he barely knew—a widow with a young son, no less. And even worse, a woman who could easily be involved in the gang of thieves he'd been assigned to break up. Jesse forced his mind back to his reason for being at the boardinghouse.

Running a finger inside his suddenly tight collar, he squared his shoulders then stepped into the parlor. He moved across the room, taking care to stop a respectable distance from Fantasy. If he got too close, he might make a spectacle of himself again by pulling her into his arms. Or worse.

"Excuse me, Mrs. Williams." He grimaced. His voice sounded strangely husky to his own ears.

The deep voice made Fantasy gasp with surprise, jerking her out of the daydream she'd been having about a man with unusual blue eyes and lips that caused her self-control to melt like butter under the Arizona sun. Trying to slow her hammering heart, she pasted a bright smile on her face and turned. She hoped whoever had slipped silently into the parlor would take her mind off the bold stranger who'd refused to vacate her thoughts since his hasty departure.

"What can I—?" Her smile vanished when her gaze lit on the man standing a few feet away. Certain she was still caught in the tangle of her own woolgathering, she squeezed her eyes shut.

Inhaling deeply, she slowly allowed her eyelids to drift open. Through the thick fringe of her lashes, she was dismayed to see the face right out of her daydream. The corners of her mouth turned down in annoyance.

Recognizing her pique at his presence, Jesse decided his best choice was to go on the defensive. "I'd like to apologize again for my earlier behavior," he began, struck with the realization he wanted desperately to get into this woman's good graces—for his own personal reasons as well as for his assignment in Tombstone.

"The way I treated you, well, there's . . . there's just no excuse for what I did," he finished quickly, willing the honesty of his declaration to be reflected on his face. Working for Wells, Fargo had taught him the art of lying effectively when the situation warranted it. Hoping he hadn't lost his touch, he waited apprehensively for Fantasy's reaction.

She stared at him silently, studying his face for any sign of duplicity. This time her observation of him wasn't colored by her strong reaction to his kisses. This time she kept a level head while she searched his face. She found only genuine regret mirrored in the firm line of his lips, in the slight arch of his eyebrows, and in those beautiful eyes. She'd never considered anything on a man's face beautiful before now—not until she'd seen the eyes of this man. They were definitely blue, but distinct greenish flecks floated in their depths.

Only a few tiny lines surrounded his eyes, a sure sign he was new to the area. He hadn't yet acquired the habit of squinting into the bright Arizona sun. Men who came to this part of the country soon learned the best way to protect their eyes from the harsh sun reflecting off the desert was to keep them partially closed. The resulting crow's-feet made locals easy to recognize.

Yes, Arizona Territory was obviously new to Mr. . . . Realizing once again she didn't know this man's name, Fantasy puckered her mouth in a slight moue. Mentally chastising herself for letting her thoughts wander, she forced her attention back to the matter at hand.

"Apology accepted. Although it wasn't necessary to come back here to tender it, since you've already apologized once. Now if you'll excuse me, I have work to finish." Her cool announcement was accompanied by a jerky wave toward the partially washed window behind her. Water flew from the cloth still clutched in her hand, striking her full in the face and making her squeal in surprise.

Her face shining with rapidly shifting emotions: vexation, surprise, and finally embarrassment, Jesse stifled the urge to laugh at the careless dousing she'd given herself. He closed the distance between them and lifted a corner of the apron tied around her narrow waist. Using gentle pats, he dried the drops of moisture from her forehead, her nose, and finally her flaming cheeks.

"Apologizing was only one of the reasons I returned," he said, dabbing her cheeks one last time. "Now that you've forgiven me, I can get on with the other reason. I'd like to rent a room." His voice had turned husky, his throat clogged with a resurgence of desire. Her nearness was having a pronounced affect on his ability to think, let alone speak.

"A room?"

"Yes, a room. You know, four walls, a door, and a bed for . . . sleeping."

His husky whisper and the obvious double meaning of his words sent Fantasy's pulse thrumming wildly. Looking up into his amused eyes, she felt herself flush even more.

She swallowed with difficulty, forcing herself to look away. As she contemplated having this man as a boarder, her thoughts tripped over themselves. He'd be under the same roof, sitting in the same parlor, sharing the same breakfast table—so close to her. Too close? His voice pulled Fantasy from her musings.

"Do you have a room I can rent?" Jesse held his breath for what felt like hours while waiting for her answer. An icy fear she would send him packing surrounded his heart. *After all, it's what I deserve for my earlier treatment of her.*

"Yes, I have a room." Her voice quavered slightly in spite of the decision she'd made.

Lucky to have a group of long-term boarders, she only had a room available because one of the men had recently married. As much as she wanted to refuse to rent the now-vacant room to this man because of the potent effect he had on her, there was the very important matter of money. Money she needed to remain independent and support her son. Money she needed to keep her in-laws from—she slammed the door on that thought.

Suddenly all business, she dropped the wet cloth into the pail with a resounding plop. Ignoring the water that splattered on her skirt, she dried her hands on her apron and marched to the desk in the corner of the room.

"Rooms are fifteen dollars a month which includes breakfast every morning except Sunday. You'll have to take the rest of your meals at one of the restaurants in town."

Taking a seat behind the desk, she opened a ledger, picked up a pen and dipped its tip into the inkwell. Her gaze riveted on the page in front of her, she said, "I'll need some information from you."

"Of course," Jesse responded, his lips curved up at her no-nonsense tone. "What would you like to know? My age, my favorite book, how I like—"

"Your name will suffice," she snapped, cutting off

his attempt to tease her. Then thinking better of her petulant manner, she added in a softer voice, "If you please."

"My name is Jesse McAllister. I'll need the room for a month, perhaps longer."

When her back stiffened at his mention of a possible long stay, his smile broadened. *I can change that cool reserve into hot abandon, Fancy.* The shortening of her name came easily. He yearned to whisper it across her flesh. His fingers itched to bury themselves in her thick hair, and his lips longed to nuzzle her exposed nape. Forcing himself to stand stock-still while she completed her entry, his gaze drifted to where her left hand lay atop the opened ledger.

"Shouldn't you check with your husband before renting a room to me, Mrs. Williams? Perhaps he'll object to having me as a boarder." He knew he risked stirring her anger, but he couldn't resist the opportunity to let the auburn-haired beauty know he was aware of her ruse.

Her hands stilled in their task of cleaning the ink from the pen nib. Flustered, she forced herself to replace the pen and ledger, then rose from the chair. She cleared her throat and handed Jesse a key. "Your room is number five, upstairs, last room on the right. Rent is due on the first and, no, I'm certain my husband won't say anything about your taking a room here."

Jesse gently removed the key from her outstretched hand. "No, I should think not." In spite of feeling a momentary sorrow for her loss, he couldn't stop himself from adding, "It's kind of hard to say anything from Boot Hill."

His words were said without any apparent rancor, but Fantasy could tell he was rankled beneath his calm exterior. Lowering her head, she stared at the toes of his boots. She could feel the heat of his gaze boring into the top of her head. Wondering how he'd come upon the truth so quickly, she forced herself to meet his intense glare once again.

Though aquiver inside with her own confusing mixture of feelings about this man, she managed to find the strength to test his mood. "Indeed it is, Mr. McAllister. Don't expect me to apologize for pretending my husband is alive. What was I supposed to do when you marched into my house, accosted my person, then insulted my character? The protection of a husband, even a dead one, seemed a wise choice at the time. One I would make again."

While he chewed on those words, Fantasy took a deep breath before continuing. "Let me give you some advice, Mr. McAllister. I suggest you watch yourself in this town, or you may end up joining the others lying beneath Boot Hill."

Watching the pain flicker across her face, Jesse realized life hadn't been easy for the Widow Williams. Though he didn't want to, he again found himself feeling sorry for her. Ashamed of how nasty he must have sounded, he fleetingly wished he could take back his words.

Fantasy stepped around him and glided out of the room. In spite of her shaking knees, somehow she managed to make her exit without falling on her face.

Watching her retreating back, Jesse snapped out of his somber thoughts. He chuckled to himself, the stern demeanor he'd affected for Fantasy's benefit completely gone. Though he'd suspected it from the first time he'd laid eyes on her, he now knew it was absolute fact. The Widow Williams was some woman.

Not afraid to speak her mind, she intrigued him more than any woman he'd ever known. Then there was his intense physical attraction to her. He'd never experienced anything even approaching the desire that surged through him at her nearness. And if he didn't miss his guess, Fantasy was strongly affected by his presence as well. Yes indeed, whether brandishing words or exchanging kisses, Fantasy Williams was some woman!

Careful, McAllister. Don't get too caught up in your desire. She could be involved with Lawson's gang clear up to that pretty little neck of hers.

The thought instantly sobered his light mood. Walking into the hall and over to the staircase, Jesse decided to check out his room before going back to the stage depot to retrieve his luggage.

After a restless night filled with dreams of Fantasy, Jesse woke later than he intended. By the time he'd shaved, dressed, and made his way downstairs to the dining room, everyone else was already in attendance.

Fantasy's heart accelerated at the sight of her newest boarder standing in the doorway. She steeled her body to resist her humiliating physical reaction to him, then rose from her place at the head of the table.

Clearing her throat, she said, "Gentlemen, I'd like to introduce the newest member of our household."

The clinking of silverware on china stopped; the buzz of conversation ceased. All heads turned toward their landlady, then followed her gaze to where Jesse stood.

Suddenly the center of attention, Jesse forced himself to break his visual contact with Fantasy. A polite smile on his face, he quickly scanned the group sitting at the table. There were four men—none of them Jack Lawson—and a young boy, apparently Fantasy's son.

As Jesse took a step into the room, Fantasy began the introductions. "May I present Mr. McAllister."

She indicated the man closest to Jesse. "This is Nash Sparks. He's one of our town's finest schoolteachers."

Jesse cringed inwardly at her formal introduction, wishing he could hear her say his first name. Certain she wouldn't take kindly to a request to drop the formality, he dismissed the idea and clasped Sparks's outstretched hand. Jesse's first impression of the small-statured man as a sissified schoolteacher was erased when Sparks's firm handshake revealed his physical strength.

"Pleased to make your acquaintance, Mistah McAllister," Sparks said in a soft drawl. "I'd be pleased if you'd call me Nash."

"My pleasure, Nash," Jesse responded easily, "provided you call me Jesse." Cataloging the man's slim build, gray eyes, dark hair with silver at the temples, and impeccable black broadcloth suit, Jesse's gaze moved to the man to Sparks's right.

"And this is Gilbert Gunderson," Fantasy said.

"Nice ta meet y'all, Mister McAllister." The young man flashed an easy smile. "Everybody calls me Gil."

Jesse shook the hand of the lanky, blond-haired, blue-eyed youth firmly. "Nice meeting you, Gil."

"Next to Mr. Gunderson is Garland Baxter."

Jesse recognized him instantly. The man he saw Fantasy kissing the day before. He knew Baxter wasn't her husband, but was he something more to Fantasy?

As his gaze swept over Baxter's wavy brown hair, wide forehead, and astute hazel eyes, Jesse realized the man was older than he'd originally thought, probably in his late twenties. Just the right age to be the Widow Williams's suitor.

Seeing Baxter's face sported the same florid complexion as yesterday, Jesse glanced briefly at Fantasy. He couldn't help wondering if she had caused Baxter's flush this early in the day. Another kiss maybe, or . . .

Realizing he was being rude, Jesse halted his train of thought before he did or said something stupid. "Baxter," he said gruffly, trying desperately to be civil to the man.

Sensing Jesse's animosity, Fantasy immediately guessed its source. "Mr. Baxter shared some exciting news with me yesterday," she said, looking directly at Jesse although her words were meant for everyone in the room. "He was made a junior partner in the law firm where he works. I think that's wonderful, don't you?"

While the other boarders congratulated Baxter, Jesse didn't miss the spark of defiance in Fantasy's eyes.

When the clamor died down, Jesse's attention turned to the man sitting to the left of Fantasy's place at the table. He was considerably older than the rest of the boarders, in his sixties by Jesse's estimation. Though the man's heavy cotton shirt and corduroy pants had seen better days, they were clean. Jesse's silent study of the man's gray hair, equally gray beard, blue eyes and the leathery color and texture of his face was interrupted by Fantasy's voice.

"And this old codger is Fagen Fitzpatrick." Although her words were less than complimentary, Jesse didn't miss the note of affection in her voice.

The man stuck a gnarled hand—the skin rough and deeply browned from years in the sun—toward Jesse. "Howdy there, McAllister. Fantasy, here, is too fandangled formal for me tastes. Just be calling me Spud, that's what I answer to."

As they shook hands, Jesse was impressed by the older man's strength. A second look revealed the wide breadth of his shoulders and the bulge of muscles beneath his worn shirt.

"Pleased to meet you, Spud," Jesse replied with a smile. "Do I detect a bit of the old sod in your voice?"

"Aye, that ye do, laddy. You've a good ear. Ireland is the land of me birth," he answered, chuckling with delight. "I came to America when I was just a lad. Been here ever since, though I still long for the cool, green hills of the emerald isle every now and agin. Ye must have a bit of the Irish in ye, too, what with a name like McAllister."

"Aye," Jesse agreed with a laugh. "My grandparents came from Dublin and settled in Texas when my father was a boy."

"Did ye hear that, Fantasy? Jesse here is one of us."

"Yes, Spud, I heard," Fantasy replied. Meeting Jesse's questioning gaze, she explained, "My maiden name was Muldoon. My grandparents also came from Ireland." She shifted her attention to the boy next to her.

"This is my son, Robert Allen Williams, Mr. McAllister." Smiling at the boy, she smoothed an unruly lock of his deep russet hair.

The boy's face puckered with apparent displeasure at his mother's use of his full name. In his best imitation of the other men, he said to Jesse, "It's nice to meet you, Mr. McAllister." Then before Fantasy could stop him, he added, "Call me Robby."

Jesse checked the chuckle that threatened, then squatted down next to the boy. Shaking Robby's small hand, he ignored the stickiness of the fingers in his grasp. "It's nice to meet you, too, Robby. What's for breakfast? It sure smells good."

"Flapjacks," the boy announced merrily, picking up his fork and digging into the syrup-covered pancake on his plate. "Momma's flapjacks are the best."

"Don't talk with your mouth full," Fantasy admonished in a firm yet gentle voice.

Robby swallowed, then said, "Yes, ma'am. I forgot."

"That's okay, Buckshot, I forget sometimes, too," Jesse whispered near the boy's ear. As he rose from his crouched position, he looked at Fantasy.

"Where would you like me, Mrs. Williams?"

Although Fantasy knew he was referring to his placement at the table, she couldn't stop a flush from creeping up her face at the unwanted answer her body gave.

She simply pointed at the chair to the right of her son, wishing the only unassigned place at the table was farther from her.

Jesse sat in the chair Fantasy indicated and helped himself to bacon, flapjacks, and fried potatoes. When she set a cup of coffee in front of him, he thanked her in a husky whisper. He didn't miss her reaction to his voice: the faint shudder of her shoulders, the slight widening of her eyes, the increased throbbing of the pulse at the base of her throat.

He swallowed hard and forced his gaze back to his plate. Remaining silent while he ate the excellent food, Jesse listened intently to the banter around the table. He answered questions asked of him directly, but otherwise he was content to simply observe.

For Fantasy the meal was extremely uncomfortable. She had never felt this way around her boarders. They were the closest thing she had to family, and she usually enjoyed their time together over breakfast.

Jesse's intrusion into her usual routine was disconcerting. He filled the room with his powerful masculinity. She had trouble concentrating on the conversations around her or trying to plan her chores for the day as she normally did.

As Jesse cleaned his plate then filled it a second time, she couldn't help thinking how breathtakingly handsome he was. Of course she'd known that yesterday. But in the bright light of the new day, his freshly shaven face and less formal clothing—snug denim trousers and casual shirt opened at the neck—made him even more attractive. Although she fought against it, she couldn't stop her breathing from quickening or her body from throbbing in the most embarrassing places. She decided she'd best stay clear of Jesse McAllister.

When Jesse looked up and met her intense stare, Fantasy dropped her head instantly, embarrassed at having been caught gaping. Twisting her napkin nervously in her lap, she decided to use her obvious curiosity to her advantage. She lifted her chin and looked in his direction but focused her gaze over his right shoulder. She couldn't bring herself to meet those beautiful eyes. "You didn't tell me yesterday, Mr. McAllister, what you're doing in Tombstone."

Jesse swallowed a sip of coffee and resigned himself

to the fact that necessity forced him to lie to Fantasy. "I came here to look into the possibility of buying some property for my employer," he said smoothly.

"Employer?" she pressed, filled with fear her in-laws had hired another man to spy on her.

Noticing the pinched look on her face and how her hand tightened on her coffee cup, he wondered briefly at the cause of her uneasiness then said, "Yes, a land company in New York." Turning to the other men at the table, he attempted to shift the attention from himself. "I know how Nash and Garland make their living. What about you, Gil?"

"I came to Tombstone after hearing 'bout the silver strike nearly a year ago. I come from a big family in Texas, and there ain't much chance I'll ever inherit my Daddy's ranch. I decided to try my hand at minin' so's I could earn enough money to start my own place. I work as a teamster, haulin' ore from the mines to the stamp mills over on the San Pedro River. The pay's a whole lot better'n workin' underground in the mines, like I did when I first got here. In a few months I'll have enough saved so's I can settle down with Sue Ellen."

"I assume Sue Ellen's your gal and not your horse?" Jesse asked, unable to resist teasing the likeable Texan.

"Yes sir, she shorely is." A huge grin split the younger man's face. "She's back in Texas. I promised I'd be back in two years if she'd wait for me. The way things are goin', I should be headin' home a good spell 'fore those two years are up."

"That's great, Gil," Jesse replied, then turned to the crusty old boarder sitting by Fantasy. "What about you, Spud?"

"I'm in minin', too. But not makin' no bone-rattlin', nine-mile trip ridin' them ore wagons every day, like this rapscallion." He nodded toward Gil. "No workin' fer somebody else fer Spud Fitzpatrick, no sir. Got me a claim in me own name. Long's these old bones can make the trek inta the hills, I'll be workin' me pile of rocks all by meself. I been a prospectin' fer nigh onta forty years, and me and Con don't aim to change our ways none."

"Con?"

"Me pack mule. Full name's Contrary cuz of the ornery streak he has a-runnin' through him. But Con and me, we've knowed each other fer so long I kinda got used to his cussedness."

Jesse smiled. "If you've got your own claim, what are you doing at a boardinghouse?"

"If you'd spent as many nights as I have sleepin' on that durn hard ground with nothin' but scorpions, coyotes, and one stubborn ole mule fer company, you'd wanna nice soft bed to be restin' your weary bones on every now and agin, too. I ain't never found that glory hole, but long's Con and me keep findin' enough silver fer grub and rent money, I'm happy as a fat ole sow in a mud hole."

Jesse chuckled at Spud's colorful outlook on life. "How often do you get into Tombstone?"

"Every couple a weeks. Con and me don't like to be stayin' away from town for too long like we used to." He looked at Fantasy, then Robby. " 'Sides, I like to be seein' these two real regular."

Jesse didn't miss the affection in the old man's gaze, or the smile Fantasy flashed him. Spud clearly thought of the Williamses as family and the boardinghouse as home. When Spud shifted in his chair and turned to meet Jesse's gaze, Jesse was surprised to see something else shining in the miner's eyes. The fire blazing there shouted a warning not to hurt either of the two people the older man held so dear, or he'd have Spud Fitzpatrick to answer to.

Jesse swallowed the promise he wished he could make, praying he wouldn't have to ignore the silent warning the old prospector had given him. *I sure don't want to hurt her, Spud. But the decision may be taken out of my hands if what I suspect proves to be true.*

Chapter 3

Jesse spent his first few days in Tombstone acclimating himself to the town and wandering its streets at all hours. The saloons, gambling halls, and pleasure palaces never closed, so no matter the time of day, there was always someplace to go, something to do, someway to spend money. It soon became apparent to him why Tombstone had the reputation of being the toughest town west of the Mississippi.

Not a day went by without a murder, whether from an argument over a cardplayer caught cheating, an attempt to jump a mining claim, or the law fighting desperadoes. So common was the loss of life one of the town's newspapers, *The Tombstone Epitaph,* ran a column in each edition headed "Death's Doings."

Just that morning Jesse had read two brief reports under the heading. One man had met his demise when his neck was broken in a fist fight. The other, still unidentified, was found on the side of Naco Road just outside of town. The *Epitaph* devoting space in each edition for such untimely deaths and never lacking for reports to fill the space was testament to the extremely rough and tough nature of the frontier town built on a barren spread of desert once known as Goose Flats.

In spite of hotels with posh interiors, restaurants offering the world's finest delicacies and modern theatres presenting the latest in stage plays, Tombstone was still a wild, often violent place. Surprisingly, Jesse found he liked the town a great deal.

Priding himself on always learning his opponent's home ground, he made a point of walking each street. He located the Western Union office, the Sheriff's office, the Oriental Saloon where Lawson tended bar and other places that might prove useful in his investigation. After becoming familiar with the main section of town, he widened the area of his scrutiny.

He explored Hop Town, the Chinese section which encompassed several square blocks and housed several hundred Chinese, and he strolled through the red-light district, finding it exactly where Fantasy had told him it was located. The town council really had passed an ordinance establishing geographical limits within which houses of ill fame could be opened. The council also levied a ten-dollar-a-month fee on each house for a license to operate. Noting the number of such houses, Jesse figured the city must be making a small fortune off the soiled dove trade alone.

"Hey, darlin', wanna have Lola show ya a good time?"

The brazen words pulled Jesse from his musings. He glanced up to find a sultry, black-haired woman leaning against the second-story balcony railing of one of the bawdy houses. Her heavily rouged lips smiled widely, her dark eyes sparkled with invitation. A black corset trimmed with red lace pushed her amble bosom up so far it nearly spilled over the top. Matching ruffled drawers, black net stockings held up by fancy red garters, and a cluster of red feathers—drooping from the heat—pinned in her curly hair completed her attire.

"What'd you have in mind?" Jesse smiled back at the woman, thinking she might be very attractive if she hadn't been so generous with the makeup painted on her face. A few days earlier he might have accepted her offer. But since meeting Fantasy, other women had lost their appeal. His perplexing preference for his auburn-haired landlady wasn't something he consciously encouraged. Yet it was very real.

"Anything ya like," she drawled slowly, leaning farther over the railing and displaying more of her deep cleavage. The tip of her tongue moved slowly over her ruby-colored lips.

Jesse's smile broadened at her tactics to lure another customer into her bed.

"Lola knows many ways ta please a man. And you're definitely *all* man." Her dark gaze swept over him appreciatively. "What do ya say, darlin'?"

"Not today, Lola. Perhaps another time."

His refusal turned her smile into a pout of disappointment, making Jesse laugh at her ability to change expression so easily. Tipping his hat in farewell, he watched her smile return at his gallant gesture.

Heading back to the boardinghouse, Jesse decided to double his efforts to get to know Fantasy better. While she hadn't been openly antagonistic toward him, neither had she allowed him even a glimpse of the passion she'd displayed during their initial encounter. Instead, she'd continually maintained a cool, proper manner around him. Somehow her indifference seemed to fire his blood more than the overt behavior of the prostitute who'd just solicited him.

"Hi, Jesse."

The small voice jolted Jesse out of his musings. Looking around, he was surprised to find he'd walked from Sixth Street to the boardinghouse on Fourth without being aware of it. The realization that his usually sharp senses had been dulled by thoughts of Fantasy came as a shock. Proud of his investigative skills, he normally remained totally attuned to his surroundings when on a case. That one woman could change what had become second nature to him so easily was very unsettling. Jesse promised himself to concentrate harder on his assignment.

"Hi, Buckshot. Whatcha doing?"

"Nothin'. I got nobody to play with me."

"You don't?" Jesse replied, sitting down next to the long-faced Robby. "Don't you have any friends around here?"

"Yeah, but Willy had ta go home. His Ma needed him ta do somethin'." Robby scuffed the toes of his shoes in the dirt street, his mouth drawn into a frown.

"Oh, I see." Noticing the small cloth sack in the boy's hands, Jesse pointed at it. "What's in there?"

"Marbles. Me and Willy was gonna play."

"Marbles, huh? I haven't played marbles since I was a boy. I used to be pretty good." Jesse studied the boy's slumped shoulders and dejected face. "How about me taking Willy's place?"

Robby raised his head and stared at Jesse with wide turquoise eyes. Jesse wondered fleetingly if the boy's father had had blue eyes. Mixed with Fantasy's dark green, blue might produce the unusual color of Robby's eyes. Shaking off such thoughts, he waited for the boy to respond.

"You'd play marbles with me?" His voice sounded incredulous, yet his upturned face shone with hope.

"Sure thing. Where do you usually play?"

Jumping to his feet, Robby pointed down the alley next to the boardinghouse. "Out back. Me an' Willy have a place behind my house."

Standing up, Jesse chuckled at the boy's enthusiasm. "Okay, let's go. Lead the way, Buckshot."

Fantasy finished tucking in the sheet at the foot of the bed and ran her hand over the mattress to smooth out the wrinkles. Picking up the pillow, she held one end under her chin and worked the pillow slip over the opposite end. When the pillow slip was on completely, she shook the pillow to fluff it, then tossed it onto the head of the bed. She straightened with a sigh, grateful this was the last room.

She did half of the rooms on Saturday, the other half on Wednesday. The boardinghouse created enough work without having to change all the beds at one time. The schedule worked out fine, even if it did necessitate making extra trips to the laundry in Hop Town.

Gathering up the sheets she'd just removed, she couldn't resist pressing her face into the pillow slip on top of the pile. This was Jesse's room, the room she'd put off until last. Inhaling deeply, she filled her lungs with his scent, the mingled scent of sandalwood and male musk, the scent that did funny things to her insides. She pressed her lips together in annoyance. *Stop such foolishness, Fantasy. You know men can't be trusted. You give them everything and they repay you by taking off.* She had no intention of allowing another man to do that to her. She had a son to provide for, a business to run, and she must never let anything interfere with the priorities she'd set in her life—especially love.

Love? Where had that come from? Fantasy had learned her lesson about love and didn't intend to fall into that trap again.

She was brought out of her thoughts by the sound of her son's high-pitched squeals of delight followed by the bass tones of a man's rumble of laughter.

What in the world? That wasn't Willy. She crossed the room to the window which faced the rear yard of her house. Pushing the curtain aside, Fantasy peered through the glass.

She could see Robby on his knees in the dirt, a game of marbles apparently in progress. But she couldn't see her son's opponent. Holding the sheets in one arm, she opened the window with her free hand.

"Robby, who are you playing with?"

Before the boy could respond, his companion, crawling on hands and knees, moved into Fantasy's line of vision. Her eyes widened in shock. Jesse McAllister!

"Shh, Momma," Robby called in a loud whisper. "Jesse is gonna try a really hard shot."

Her heart pounding, she watched Jesse's back, buttocks, and thighs stretch and strain against his shirt and trousers as he maneuvered into position. She had the sudden unbidden wish to see those flexing muscles without the confining clothes. Gasping with embarrassment at her line of thinking, Fantasy tried to concentrate on Jesse's ability as a marble player. She watched in fascination while he lined up his shot, then expertly flipped his marble into the hole scooped out of the hard-packed ground a good four feet away.

"Wow, Jesse, ya done it!" Robby crowed, clearly in awe of the man's skill. "Did ya see that, Momma?" He looked up at her, his face glowing with excitement.

"Yes, Robby, I saw. That was a nice shot, Mr. McAllister."

Turning toward the house, Jesse sat down on the ground, draping his arms over his up-drawn knees. A wave of pleasure washed over him when he realized she was in his room. "Thanks. Don't you think it's time you called me Jesse?"

As his penetrating gaze met and held hers, Fantasy felt flustered, hot, ashamed all at the same time. She had purposely refused to use his first name because she'd convinced herself keeping it formal would put the kibosh on her thoughts about him. She now realized how ridiculous her idea had been. Whatever name she called him, it wouldn't make any difference. Her body still reacted in the same undignified way each time he was near: her respiration increased, her pulse throbbed in places too numerous to count, and her fingers itched to touch him.

Even now, wallowing in the dirt, his hair mussed, his face covered with dust, he aroused her senses to that same feverish pitch. Realizing she had ignored her own advice of not five minutes ago, her back stiffened. Why did this man make her forget everything except him?

"Yeah, Momma, call him Jesse." Robby's plea swayed her decision.

"All right, Jesse it is." Those words said, she pulled her gaze away from Jesse's face. But not before she saw his triumphant smile. Turning to leave the room, she silently chastised herself for giving in.

Jesse had been certain hearing Fantasy say his name would be sheer pleasure. Still, he wasn't prepared for the seductive quality it had in reality. Dragging his attention back to Fantasy's son, he noted the confusion on the boy's face and knew Robby was trying to figure out what was going on between the two adults. Unable to explain something he didn't completely understand himself, Jesse made no comment to enlighten the youngster.

"It's your turn, Buckshot," Jesse finally said in what he hoped was a normal voice. But nothing had been normal since he'd arrived in Tombstone and tasted the sweetness of Fantasy's kiss.

He looked back at the second story of the house. When only an empty window stared back, a strange hollowness filled him.

"Are ya okay, Jesse?" The boy's russet eyebrows were drawn together with concern.

"Yeah, I'm fine," he replied, knowing it wasn't entirely the truth. Then with sudden inspiration, he asked, "Do you like ice cream, Buckshot?" At Robby's eager nod, he added, "Would you like to get some later on?"

"Sure. Momma likes ice cream, too," he offered.

"She does?" Jesse responded, pleased with the boy's volunteered information. "Do you think she'd go with us?"

"Yeah, I think so. Want me to ask her?"

"Yes, why don't you." Jesse was confident Fantasy wouldn't turn down her son. "If she agrees, we'll go after supper tonight, okay?"

"Yahoo," Robby cried with delight, leaping to his feet then throwing himself toward Jesse.

Surprised by the sudden display of affection, Jesse instinctively reached out to grasp the thin body catapulting toward him. Robby snuggled closer and wound his arms around Jesse's neck in a tight hug, swelling Jesse's heart with unbelievable joy.

Jesse leaned back until he lay flat on the ground, the boy sprawled across his chest. Jesse realized his clothes were probably beyond cleaning, but he didn't care. The dirt was nothing compared to the wonderful time he'd shared with this young boy.

Robby heaved a contented sigh, then rolled off Jesse's chest and stretched out on the ground next to him. Jesse could smell the soap Fantasy had used to wash the boy's hair, could see the smattering of freckles on the bridge of his small nose, could hear his soft breathing. Jesse's heart swelled even more.

Lying side by side there in the dirt with this five-year-old boy, hands tucked behind their heads, Jesse studied the buildings surrounding them and the clouds scudding across the Arizona sky as if they'd done this many times before. He had never known such contentment.

After a long silence, Jesse said, "Besides ice cream, what else does your mother like, Buckshot?"

"Well, she likes flowers, and music, and picnics. And she likes dancin', but she don't go no more."

Smiling, Jesse turned his head to look at Robby. "Dancing, huh?"

Jesse pulled out a chair for Fantasy at a small table near the window of the ice cream parlor on Fourth Street, helped Robby onto another chair, then seated himself. After placing their order, Jesse smiled at Robby's bubbling excitement.

"Haven't you ever had ice cream, Buckshot?"

Robby nodded. "A few times. Momma always buys it for me on my birthday."

"Ice cream is a luxury we don't indulge in very often," Fantasy added. "We save it for special occasions."

Jesse nodded, certain luxury and special occasions

meant ice cream was too expensive to buy more often. Yet, why would a woman with the kind of money he saw her accept from Jack Lawson hesitate to buy something both she and her son enjoyed? He pressed his lips into a firm line. Obviously, she didn't want to call attention to her financial state. If she spent money in what some folks would call frivolous ways, like for ice cream, people might start wondering how a boardinghouse could make such good profits. A situation she no doubt wanted to avoid.

His thoughts were interrupted by the arrival of their dishes of ice cream. Watching the expression on Robby's face as the boy took his first bite, Jesse smiled, his somber mood vanishing.

He picked up his spoon, dug into his ice cream, then lifted it to his mouth. His gaze snared by Fantasy, he swallowed the frozen treat in one gulp. He watched her slip a spoonful of ice cream into her mouth, fascinated by the way her lips puckered as she savored the taste. He felt himself harden. Squeezing his eyes closed for a second, he hoped to halt the direction of his thoughts. Yet, his imagination continued to recall her mouth closing around the spoon, her soft lips puckering, filling his head with images that had nothing to do with eating ice cream.

Shifting in his chair, he tried to ease the tightness in his groin. Determined to gain the upper hand on his desire, he forced himself to concentrate on finishing his dessert and Robby's happy chatter. Still, he could not stop himself from sneaking occasional peeks at Fantasy.

Fantasy looked up from her dish and caught Jesse staring at her. There was something in his eyes, something powerful and magnetic tugging at the very center of her being. She dropped her gaze, a blush burning her cheeks. As much as she enjoyed ice cream, the frozen concoction suddenly lost its appeal. She felt alternately cold, then hot. The intense heat low in her belly was back again, as well as the insistent throbbing even lower. She pressed her knees tightly together, hoping to stop her body's reaction to Jesse's nearness. She didn't want another man in her life, yet she couldn't seem to control her physical response to the man sitting across from her.

Looking up at him through partially lowered lashes, she wished she knew more about the man she found so attractive. Was he here to spy on her as she feared? She prayed that wasn't true.

Fantasy stepped into the dress shop on Safford Street owned by her friend, Mrs. Mattie Moreland. The tinkle of a tiny bell hooked to the top of the door announced her arrival.

"I'll be right with you," came a voice to Fantasy's right. Turning, she spotted Mattie's petite frame arranging one of her creations on a mannequin in the front window.

Mattie straightened from her task, then turned around. Brushing back a lock of dark brown hair, surprise registered on her elfin face when she saw who had entered her shop. She blinked her dark eyes once, then said, "Well, hi, Fantasy. What brings you here in the middle of the day?"

"Oh, nothing, I guess. I just felt like stopping by." Fantasy winced, her answer sounded lame even to her own ears.

Mattie stared at her friend with an amused smile. Ever since her newest boarder had moved in, Fantasy had been preoccupied.

"How about something to drink? I just had a block of ice delivered, so the cider's good and cold."

"Fine," Fantasy replied absently, idly fingering one of the samples of lace Mattie had displayed on the counter.

"Well, come on then," Mattie urged, giving Fantasy a gentle shove toward the curtained doorway at the back of the shop which led to her apartment.

As she sat in Mattie's tiny parlor, Fantasy fiddled with the crocheted doily pinned to the chair arm, fussed with her hair, and made a half-hearted attempt to carry on a conversation with her best friend.

Setting her own glass down, Mattie took the barely touched drink from Fantasy's hands. "What is it Fantasy? You've been acting jumpy as a frog in a lake full of hungry bass since you got here. Are you gonna tell me what's bothering you?"

Fantasy met Mattie's concerned gaze and sighed heavily, unaffected by the other woman's attempt to lighten her mood. "I'm afraid Mother Williams has hired another man to poke around in my life."

Mattie eyed her friend silently for a minute, recalling the first man Henrietta Williams had hired to dig up dirt about her daughter-in-law, apparently in an attempt to have some bargaining power to get Fantasy to return to St. Louis.

After Fantasy had notified her husband's parents of their son's death, her mother-in-law had taken ill from her grief. Several months passed before Fantasy heard from Frank and Henrietta Williams, then the first letter arrived. It was a terse missive from Henrietta asking Fantasy to return Robby to civilization, claiming Arizona Territory was no place to raise her grandson. There was no mention of wanting Fantasy back in the Williamses' home, only Henrietta's desire to have her only remaining blood relative under her roof. Fantasy knew that meant under Henrietta's control.

Mattie remembered her friend's reaction to that first cold letter and to the succeeding ones. Fantasy had been outraged that Mrs. Williams would callously ask, just short of demand, she give up her new life and scurry to do the woman's bidding.

Fantasy had answered each letter with the same cool response—she liked Arizona and intended to stay. In deference to the fact they were her son's grandparents, she invited them to come for a visit. But Fantasy emphatically refused to return to the oppressive Williamses' household and her tyrannical mother-in-law.

Mattie vividly recalled the story Fantasy had told her about living with the Williamses. From the time she joined the Williams household as their adopted daughter, she had been treated little better than hired help. Even marrying Thomas had apparently brought no change in her treatment. Fantasy worked from dawn until well into the night, sometimes until bedtime, doing whatever Henrietta demanded.

No task escaped the list of chores Fantasy was given each morning. Added to the daily cooking, cleaning, and laundry might be polishing the silver, waxing all the floors, weeding the flower beds, or anything else Henrietta might think of. Fantasy was even relegated to the insulting position of waiting on Henrietta's friends. Like a lowly servant, Fantasy served the gossiping women tea and whatever sweet her mother-in-law had insisted she get up before dawn to bake.

Pressing her lips together in disgust, Mattie knew there was no way Fantasy would return to that house, back under the thumb of Henrietta Williams.

A month after Fantasy had mailed her last letter of refusal, a man showed up in Tombstone asking questions about the Widow Williams. He asked about the business she ran, the way she raised her son, how she conducted herself in town, and who her friends were. Fantasy hadn't known many people in Tombstone then, so for a few weeks she wasn't aware she was the object of the man's investigation.

When Mattie finally came to her and told her about the man's snooping, Fantasy confronted him directly. Cowed by her unexpected directness, the man reluctantly told her why he was in town and who hired him.

Recalling the man's hasty retreat from town, Mattie stifled a smile. Fantasy was a formidable opponent when it came to protecting Robby. Her thoughts returning to the present, she wondered if Henrietta Williams had really sent another spy. "Do you have a suspect?"

"Yes. I think . . ." Fantasy's voice faltered sightly. Clearing her throat, she rushed on, "I think it's Mr. McAllister. He's always asking me questions, and he's started spending a lot of time with Robby. The other day I found the two of them crawling around in the dirt playing marbles. Why would a grown man play with a child he barely knows unless he has an ulterior motive?"

Now that she'd said the words aloud, they didn't sound quite so condemning. As much as she wanted to believe Jesse's behavior stemmed from another purpose, deep inside Fantasy was grateful for the attention he gave her son. Undeniably, Jesse was good to the boy. Never having known his father, Robby needed a man's influence in his young life. But she wouldn't allow the man to be one Mother Williams had sent to discredit her.

"That doesn't mean he's here to investigate you," Mattie answered carefully.

"I know. But there's also the way he makes me feel when I'm around him."

"How's that?"

"Oh, I don't know. Like I'm off balance all the time, I guess. My insides get all quivery-like, and I feel flushed whenever he's nearby."

Mattie hid her smile behind her hand. Fantasy's description of the way she felt around Jesse McAllister sounded more like attraction to the man, rather than nervousness about his reason for being in town. Although Fantasy was physically no innocent—after all she'd been married and had a child—Mattie knew from their previous discussions that Fantasy was extremely naive about the chemistry between a man and a woman. Mattie cursed Thomas Williams silently for not showing his wife how fulfilling an intimate relationship could be.

"Didn't he tell you he was in town to look at property for a land company?"

"Yes, but he could have made that up. I don't see

how he'll ever buy any property when he's constantly underfoot at my place."

"Really? He never goes out?"

"Of course Jesse goes out," Fantasy snapped, immediately contrite for her sharp words. "I'm sorry, Mattie." She rose from her chair and moved to stare out the small window into the side yard. "I don't know what's wrong with me lately."

Jesse? Mattie wondered at Fantasy's use of the man's first name, something her friend had never done before. "So, it's Jesse now, is it?"

Fantasy cringed, wishing she hadn't impulsively stopped at Mattie's shop. "The day I found the two of them playing marbles, Jesse asked me to call him by his Christian name. Robby wanted me to, so I agreed. Then he took us out for ice cream that night after supper." Fantasy could have bitten off her tongue for making that last statement.

Thinking Mattie's silence signalled her disapproval, Fantasy added, "I couldn't disappoint Robby, could I? He had his heart set on ice cream, and I certainly couldn't let him go with Jesse alone. Besides, it's been a month of Sundays since I had ice cream, and I figured as long as I went with Jesse, he couldn't ask people questions about me."

"Has he been asking the townsfolk questions?"

Fantasy's brow puckered. "I honestly don't know."

"Well, seems to me," Mattie began, rising from her chair and heading for the kitchen, "you could keep a better eye on Jesse if you spent more time with him. You might find out his real reason for being here, find out if what he told you really isn't the truth."

Mattie had met the man and didn't think he'd been sent by Henrietta Williams. He just didn't seem the type to jump through hoops like the woman would expect. Perhaps he hadn't told Fantasy the real reason for his coming to Tombstone, but Mattie would bet her last dollar he wasn't here at the request of Fantasy's old harpy of a mother-in-law. Mattie also knew her friend wouldn't listen to a defense of Jesse McAllister, so she figured getting the two of them together would either make or break any relationship in the offing.

Fantasy contemplated Mattie's words for several seconds, then turned away from the window. "I hadn't thought of that. But I don't have time to play games while I'm trying to figure out what Jesse McAllister is up to."

"I know running that boardinghouse of yours and helping Doc McKee takes up a lot of your time. But you have an occasional free afternoon or evening. If I was you, next time Jesse hints at spending some time in his company, I'd accept. Ya never know what you might learn about the man."

"I suppose I could, for Robby's sake," she hedged, uncomfortable with Mattie's advice, but also recognizing the merit in the idea.

"Ya know anytime you want to go out at night and Spud isn't in town, I'll keep Robby."

"Yes, I know that." Fantasy smiled warmly at her friend. Spud took care of Robby whenever she had an occasion to go out in the evening, though such times were few and far between. Other than Mattie, there was no one in Tombstone she trusted with her son more than the cantankerous old miner. "Robby thinks of you as his Aunt Mattie, just like he thinks of Spud as his grampa. We're so lucky to have you two." She crossed the room and gave Mattie a quick hug.

"I love that boy somethin' awful. I wish John and me could've had a child before he died." Mattie's eyes suddenly filled with tears.

Mattie and her husband had arrived in Tombstone from Pennsylvania in 1880 after Ed Schieffelin, the founder of Tombstone, had sold his holdings to mining companies from the East. John had worked for the Tombstone Mill and Mining Company until his death a year after their arrival. Mattie liked the desert of Arizona and had decided to stay, just as Fantasy had.

Planning to use her sewing skills, she'd rented a small store front with attached living quarters and opened a dress shop. The quickly growing town had brought in plenty of customers, providing Mattie with a comfortable living.

"You'll meet another man, get married, and have children someday, Mattie." Fantasy squeezed her friend's hand in encouragement. "Besides, aren't you seeing Nash Sparks?"

Mattie's cheeks flushed a bright pink. "Yes, Nash and I are keeping company. But, even if I did get married again, I'm too old to start a family."

"Oh, Mattie, that's nonsense. It isn't too late for you to have babies. You're not thirty yet. My mother was over forty when I was born." At the mention of her mother, Fantasy's heart contracted with pain. It hurt to think about it, yet the memories came flooding back.

Charlotte Muldoon had believed God was punishing her for some unknown sin by refusing to answer her prayers for a child. Then finally when she had given up on getting her wish, she found herself pregnant at the age when most women had long since had their last child. At forty-five, Charlotte had a relatively easy pregnancy, but the birth of the child she wanted desperately was long and difficult.

Although she delivered the child safely, the effort greatly weakened her and she never fully recovered. Grateful God had answered her prayers, Charlotte believed her resulting poor health a small price to pay. As long as she had the daughter she'd named for her long held fantasy of bearing a child, Charlotte was content.

Then tragedy struck. Fantasy was four when her papa died, and only two years later her mother followed him to the grave. With no other family to take her in, she was placed in an orphanage in St. Louis.

Mattie's sniffles pulled Fantasy back to the present. "I know women have babies at my age and older,"

Mattie said, dabbing her eyes with a handkerchief. "But I'm not sure I can have children. All the times John and I were together never created a babe." Shaking off her morose thoughts, Mattie gave Fantasy a watery smile. "Enough of that. I best get back to my shop. Mrs. Lamb is due to arrive for a fitting soon. And you know how she can be if she's kept waiting."

Fantasy nodded, moving toward the door. "Yes, I know how impatient Mrs. Lamb is. I have to be going myself. I promised to take Robby to the circus and I have a million things to do first."

"The circus?" Mattie's smile widened, her earlier idea resurfacing. "Why don't you ask Jesse to go with you?"

"I . . . I don't think—" The look on Mattie's face, halted the protest Fantasy was about to make. "I'll think about it."

"Good, now git, I have work to do."

"Yes, ma'am," Fantasy said with a laugh. "I'm going. See you at church on Sunday."

As Fantasy walked down Safford Street and turned south on Fourth, she pondered Mattie's advice. Ask Jesse to go to the circus? She wasn't sure she could do it even if she could convince herself it was the smart thing to do. Mattie might think so, but she certainly didn't.

In the end, Fantasy didn't have to worry about asking Jesse. When she arrived back at her boardinghouse, Jesse asked her if she and Robby would accompany him to the circus that evening. Momentarily startled by the turn of events, she said yes before the potential consequences she had so recently analyzed could still her tongue.

But as they walked to the edge of town where the circus had set up, Robby skipping along merrily in front of them, Fantasy's doubts about accepting Jesse's invitation came flooding back. Jesse affected her much more than she wanted to admit and in ways she wasn't prepared to deal with.

All her self-condemnation about allowing herself to be attracted to this man had somehow been shoved aside. She couldn't completely squelch the premonition she was setting herself up for another dose of men's perfidy.

Glancing up at Jesse, she wondered what he wanted from her and her son. Surely he wasn't interested in a widow who would only disappoint him if their relationship were to become intimate.

Robby's laughter jarred her from her thoughts. Smiling at her son's obvious enthusiasm, she tried to forget her misgivings about Jesse's intentions. Her efforts were only partially successful. Fantasy still couldn't shake the feeling she should have her head examined for agreeing to this outing.

Chapter 4

"Know what, Jesse?"

"What's that, Buckshot?" Jesse slowed his pace even more to match Robby's lagging stride. Exhausted from their evening at the circus, the boy struggled to keep up with his mother and Jesse.

"I liked the tiger best."

"Did you? What about the lions and the trained bear? Didn't you like them?"

"Yeah, but the tiger was the prettiest."

Jesse chuckled. "He was pretty all right. How about you, Fantasy, what did you like best?" Looking over at her, he tried to make out her features in the poor light cast by the gas lamps along Fremont Street.

Though she couldn't see Jesse's eyes, she felt the warmth of his gaze, making her heart pound wildly. "I guess my favorite was the trapeze act."

"Yes, I liked her performance, too." The flash of white teeth stood out clearly in his otherwise shadowed face. "That was quite a costume."

Fantasy's cheeks warmed at Jesse's remark about the scrap of cloth worn by the female trapeze artist. She'd been too enthralled by the daring tricks the woman performed high above the circus ring to be embarrassed by the small, frilly costume.

When Robby's steps slowed even more, Jesse bent down to the boy. "Why don't you let me carry you?"

Robby was reluctant to accept the offer—being carried was for babies. Glancing wistfully at his mother then back at the beckoning comfort of Jesse's arms, he gave up trying to act grown up and nodded his agreement.

As he lifted Robby, Jesse bit back a chuckle at the five-year-old's sigh. Then when the boy snuggled close and almost instantly relaxed in sleep, his amusement changed to an unbelievable surge of joy.

Stroking the hair back from her son's face, Fantasy smiled. "He had a busy night. It's a wonder he isn't sick after all he ate."

"A boy can't go to the circus without having peanuts and caramel corn."

"Don't forget the candied apple and the sarsaparilla."

Fear clutched at Jesse's heart. "You don't really think he'll be sick, do you?"

Fantasy almost laughed at the panic she heard in his voice. "I don't think so. He's always been able to eat the most outrageous combinations and never get sick."

"I hope this is one of those times." He fell silent and continued walking. They'd only gone a few steps when Jesse blurted, "I didn't mean to let Robby eat too much. I just wanted him to have a good time."

Fantasy laid one hand on his arm. "I know that, Jesse. Don't fret about it. He's fine." She forced herself to remove her hand from the hard-muscled forearm. It wasn't proper to touch him like that, yet she couldn't deny the sensations skittering through her felt wonderful and very right.

Satisfied he'd done Robby no real harm, Jesse shifted the sleeping child more comfortably in his arms. In amiable silence, he and Fantasy walked the rest of the way to her boardinghouse.

An unusual quiet greeted them inside the front door. "Where is everyone?" Jesse asked in a low whisper.

Fantasy shrugged. "Mr. Lawson is working. The

rest are probably still at the circus or one of the saloons. Here, I'll take Robby now."

"That's okay. I'll help you get him into bed."

"He sleeps in my room. Come on, I'll show you."

The bedroom was as neat and clean as the sitting room he'd been in the first day he met her. A bright, patchwork quilt covered the bed to his left—Fantasy's bed he realized. He kept his eyes carefully averted from the tempting sight. On the opposite side of the room was Robby's smaller bed, also covered with a colorful quilt.

Without exchanging a word, Jesse helped Fantasy get Robby undressed and into bed. Strangely, those gratifying few minutes made Jesse feel closer to her than any conversation might have.

Not wanting to leave, but knowing Fantasy's exhaustion was nearly as complete as her son's, Jesse turned toward the door. "Well, I guess I'd better hit the hay myself."

Fantasy walked with him into the hallway. "I want to thank you for taking us to the circus. Robby and I had a wonderful time."

At the foot of the stairs, Jesse paused. "You're welcome." The softly spoken words sent a shiver of pleasure chasing up her spine.

Jesse abruptly turned and pulled her into his embrace. He held her tightly against his chest, then lowered his head towards hers. She knew he intended to kiss her, yet did nothing to stop him. Any protest she might have voiced ended with the warmth of his lips pressed to hers.

As Jesse's lips continued teasing hers, she could barely breathe, much less summon the strength to pull away. Against her will, Fantasy slipped deeper and deeper into the spell he cast over her. The magic of his kiss was something she couldn't get enough of. Tunneling her fingers through the thick hair brushing his collar, she pressed herself more fully against his solid body.

Groaning with a mixture of frustration and white-hot passion, Jesse knew he had to end the kiss. She had apparently forgiven him for their first kiss, but she might not do so a second time. Pulling her arms from around his neck, he took a step back. "Good night, Fantasy," he murmured in a raspy whisper.

One last brush of his mouth on hers and he disappeared up the stairs. Fantasy stood in stunned silence for several seconds, staring up the empty staircase. Touching her lips with shaking fingers, she moved trancelike back into her apartment.

Once she had changed into a nightgown, checked on Robby and slipped into her own bed, Fantasy found her exhaustion had fled. She tossed and turned, each new position more uncomfortable than the last. Every time she closed her eyes and thought sleep was about to overtake her, the kiss she'd shared with Jesse popped into her tired brain, the memory waking her with its intensity.

Along with her wakefulness, other emotions stirred as well: guilt for allowing the kiss in the first place and even more for enjoying it—no, not just enjoying it, but participating in it totally; doubt she should even be seeing Jesse socially; and, worst of all, frustration because Jesse had ended the kiss when he did, leaving her feeling . . . she wasn't sure what it left her feeling. She only knew she hadn't wanted him to pull away when he did. That last disconcerting thought brought back unwanted memories of her late husband.

Fantasy had never wanted Thomas to continue his kisses. The truth was she could have done without the rest of his physical advances as well. There'd been no pleasure for her in the marriage bed, although she'd never considered complaining. Biting off her tongue would have been preferable to speaking of such an intimate subject to her husband or anyone else for that matter. And besides, Thomas once told her she wasn't like the other women he'd known—they had responded to his lovemaking. His obvious disappointment left Fantasy with only one conclusion to draw. Something was wrong with her. There was no other explanation for why the tiny spark of desire Thomas had stirred early in their marriage always suffered a premature death—snuffed out like a pail of water dousing a fire.

Her inability to enjoy Thomas's lovemaking had given Fantasy only one option. Whenever he rolled toward her in bed, she forced her mind elsewhere—to a place where she didn't have to think about her lack of response, where she wouldn't be left feeling frustrated and dissatisfied.

After Thomas's death, Fantasy had vowed to steer clear of men—she wanted no part of another relationship as unsatisfactory as her marriage. Then Jesse McAllister marched into her life and stirred her blood like nothing she'd ever experienced. She couldn't help wondering if Jesse's caresses would be as wonderful as his kisses.

Rolling over, Fantasy gave her pillow a fierce punch to squash such thoughts. "This Arizona heat must have cooked my brain," she muttered, squirming in another attempt to find a comfortable position.

It was a long time before she found the sanctuary of sleep.

A few days after going to the circus, Jesse surprised himself by asking Fantasy and Robby to go on a picnic after church. Still uncomfortable with his unusual distraction from his assignment, he consoled his guilt by telling himself it wouldn't hurt to take one Sunday afternoon off.

He bought a basket lunch from the Melrose Restaurant, rented a buggy, then stopped at the boarding-house to pick up Fantasy and Robby. Slapping the reins across the horse's rump, Jesse directed the buggy up Fourth Street and out of Tombstone toward the Dragoon Mountains north of town.

Near the foot of the Dragoons was Granite Springs, a favorite picnic spot of the citizens of the area. Guiding the horse and buggy through the craggy cliffs and rocky spires of the mountain's foothills, Jesse halted the buggy beneath the spreading branches of a large cottonwood.

Jesse jumped to the ground, tied the reins to a tree branch, then went around to the other side of the buggy. He swung Robby to the ground, then turned back to Fantasy. Placing his hands around her waist, he lifted her from the buggy, then carefully set her on her feet. When he lifted his head to meet her gaze, he swallowed to ease the sudden tightness in his throat.

Her eyes were wide, her delicate nostrils flared. It took all his willpower to drop his hands from her waist and step back.

"Hey, Jesse, come here," Robby called from across the clearing.

Jesse looked over at where the boy stood looking up stream. Grasping Fantasy's elbow gently with one hand, he escorted her to the creek bank.

"What is it, Robby?"

"I hear something."

Jesse cocked his head to one side. "I hear it, too. Sounds like a waterfall."

Robby's face lit up. "Really? Can we go find out?"

Glancing at Fantasy for her approval, he turned back to the boy. Jesse smiled at the hopeful look on Robby's face. "Sure, Buckshot, let's go see."

On the opposite side of a large pile of boulders, a small waterfall dropped over a rocky outcropping into a widened stretch of the creek, forming an oval-shaped pond. The ground was sandy on the pond's edge and shaded by another large cottonwood.

"This looks like a good spot for our picnic. I'll go back and get the basket and a blanket."

As Jesse headed back to the buggy, he heard Robby ask Fantasy if he could take off his shoes. Smiling at memories of wading in the creek near his parents' ranch, he hooked a feed bag of oats over the horse's head, retrieved the basket and blanket, then headed back to the clearing.

"Robby, you be careful," Fantasy called. "The rocks in the water could be slippery."

The legs of his trousers rolled up to his knees, the boy stepped into the water. "I will, Momma." Giggling as the cool water lapped around his ankles, he turned to look over his shoulder. "You gonna wade with me, Jesse?"

"Not right now, Buckshot. I'll stay here and keep your mother company."

Robby nodded, then moved deeper into the water. Soon he was laughing and splashing along the edge of the pond.

Fantasy smiled at her son's antics. In spite of her reservations about following Mattie's advice, she was glad she had accepted Jesse's invitation. Robby needed to get away once in a while, and the truth be told, so did she.

Glancing at where Jesse sat next to her on the blanket, she felt the heat of a blush rush up her neck and onto her cheeks. Just looking at him filled her with a host of wonderful sensations—sensations that left her breathless, her body aching with reawakened physical need. Her hands clasped tightly in her lap, Fantasy pulled her gaze from him.

She tipped her face up to the sky and closed her eyes, willing her pulse to return to normal. "It's a beautiful day, isn't it?" she said at last.

Jesse turned toward her. A soft filtering of sunlight came through the cottonwood's leaves to dapple across her features. He longed to reach out and run his fingers across her cheek, but managed to keep them locked around his up-drawn knees.

"Yes, it is," he finally replied. After a moment's silence, he said, "Are you enjoying yourself?"

She opened her eyes and met his gaze. "Yes," she whispered, causing another, even more intense need to touch her to race through him. In spite of his longing to pull her into his arms, he realized just being in her company gave him immense pleasure—a kind of pleasure he had never experienced.

After eating their lunch, Fantasy let Robby play in the creek again while she and Jesse repacked the picnic basket.

Sitting back down on the blanket, Fantasy watched Jesse take off his shoes, then join her son. As the man and boy splashed in the water, she couldn't help laughing with joy. It was so good to see Robby enjoying himself. Once again, she thought of how good Jesse was for Robby, of how the boy needed a man in his life—even for the brief time Jesse would be in town. The thought of Jesse's leave-taking filled her with an inexplicable emptiness.

Though Jesse was loathe for the afternoon to end, the sun had begun to sink low in the western sky when he reluctantly announced it was time to head back to town.

He dropped Fantasy and Robby off at the boarding-house, returned the horse and buggy to the stable, then headed back to Fantasy's. As he walked along, his thoughts kept straying to the afternoon's activities.

Playing tag with Robby, even getting his trousers soaking wet in the process, had been great fun. But simply being near Fantasy, studying her lovely face when she wasn't aware of his scrutiny, feeling the warmth of her smile, had been the best part of the day—a memory he'd never forget.

Several days later, Jesse found Fantasy on her knees in the hallway of her boardinghouse, scrubbing the woodwork. He watched her for a moment, his eyebrows pulled together in a scowl. He had the urge to grasp her elbows and lift her off the floor. Instead, he said, "Fantasy, you shouldn't work so hard."

Her head snapped up. "You gave me quite a start."

"Sorry." His expression brightened. "Listen, would you like to go to the St. Patrick's Ball with me?"

Fantasy frowned. "The St. Patrick's Ball?"

Jesse felt a sudden tightness in his chest. "You aren't going with someone else, are you?" When she shook her head, the tightness eased. "So, will you go with me?"

She stared at him for a minute, then turned back to the pail of water next to her. She wanted to say yes, but she held her tongue. As she rinsed out her cleaning rag, Mattie's words came back to her again about spending time with Jesse, the reason she had agreed to accompany him on the picnic. Should she go to the ball with him for the same reason? Mattie would say she should.

Looking back up at him, she said, "Yes, I'd like to go with you." The beaming smile her answer brought to Jesse's face caused a warm glow deep inside her belly. She couldn't help smiling in reply. Yet, after he'd left her to her work, she wondered about why she'd really accepted his invitation.

Being completely honest with herself, she wasn't sure if she'd agreed to go to the ball with Jesse because of Mattie's advice, or because of how much she enjoyed being in his company and how her attraction to him continued to grow.

Later that evening, Fantasy sorted through the dresses in her armoire, discounting each one as a possibility for the St. Patrick's Ball. Pulling her mouth into a frown, she fleetingly wished she hadn't accepted Jesse's invitation. Except for her two best dresses which she reserved for church, everything she owned was painfully plain—serviceable, boardinghouse owner clothes. There had never been a reason for her to own a formal evening gown.

She heaved a sigh and closed the armoire door. As much as she hated to, she'd have to dip into her meager savings and buy an appropriate dress for the dance.

She hoped Mattie would have enough time before the ball to squeeze making one more dress into her busy schedule.

Sitting in the Oriental Saloon a week later, Jesse's conscience pricked him again. Several times after the first day he'd asked Robby what his mother liked, he had carefully pumped the boy for additional information.

The knowledge had been gained at a high price. He didn't like himself much for using the boy. Still, Jesse couldn't deny the information Robby so trustingly gave had begun to achieve the desired results. Or at least Jesse thought he was getting somewhere with Fantasy. He didn't think his imagination was playing tricks. She appeared to be less uncomfortable around him, not as wary as she'd been at first.

One of the qualities Jesse liked best about Fantasy was her gentle, loving nature, and it pleased him she could now relax enough in his presence to let him catch glimpses of that side of her.

Since their picnic, an intense need smoldered inside of him, growing hotter with each passing day. He forced himself to ignore his desire, steadfastly refusing to rush Fantasy into something she obviously wasn't ready for. Simply looking at her, the chance brushing of their fingers, the tinkling peal of her laughter and the occasional brief kiss he couldn't resist pressing on her sweet lips were enough.

"You're awfully quiet tonight." Nick's voice pulled Jesse from his ponderings.

"Yeah." Jesse shifted in his chair and glanced across the crowded saloon to where Jack Lawson stood behind the massive mahogany bar with its white and gilt trim. "I have a lot on my mind."

"I'll bet," Nick mumbled under his breath.

Jesse tried to avoid meeting Nick in public places with any frequency so their friendship prior to Jesse's arrival wouldn't be revealed. By chance, both he and Nick had come to the Oriental where Lawson was one of the three bartenders on duty.

"What was that?" Jesse's gaze swung back to Nick.

"Nothing. So what have you found out about our friend there?" Nick nodded towards the bar.

"Not much. He keeps pretty much to himself, like you said. He never eats breakfast with the rest of the boarders, and since he works 'til four in the morning, I can understand why. I met him a couple days after I moved into the boardinghouse. He was in the parlor reading a newspaper one afternoon when I came in, so I introduced myself."

"You're a pretty good judge of character. What do you think of him?"

Jesse shrugged. "He's a tough one to read. I got the impression he doesn't like anyone getting close to him. I tried to strike up a conversation, but he ignored me for the most part. When he did answer, his voice was cold and clipped. Not like when he . . ." He fell silent, reluctant to tell his friend what he'd been keeping to himself.

"When he what?" Nick prompted.

Jesse wished he could forget about the transaction he'd witnessed between Lawson and Fantasy. But it wouldn't go away. Shifting in his chair again, he replied, "I overheard part of a conversation between Lawson and our landlady. He was real friendly around her. I saw him give her some money—a lot of money. When he asked her to keep quiet about it, she didn't look surprised, like they'd played that little scene before."

"Hmm, that's real interesting." Nick removed a cigar from an elaborate case and carefully cut off the tip while mulling over Jesse's words. "So, do you think she's part of Lawson's gang?"

Jesse ran one hand over his face wearily. "I haven't found any evidence to prove she's involved. But it's something I can't ignore. These robberies have been going on too long. Wells, Fargo is beginning to look like a joke, so all possibilities have to be checked out."

Striking a match and holding it to the cigar clamped between his teeth, Nick nodded. "Yeah, our employer has really taken a lot of heat about this whole mess." He drew deeply on the cigar until the end glowed red, then exhaled a puff of smoke to extinguish the match. "But first we have to find out who else is in the gang. Though there's always four of them, we still only know the identity of one. Lawson."

"Well, sooner or later, he'll slip up and talk to someone or do something that will help us. I intend to watch his every move while he's at the St. Patrick's Ball tomorrow night."

"How can you keep an eye on Lawson when you're dancing with Fantasy Williams?"

"How'd you know I'm taking Fantasy to the dance?" Jesse demanded in a low voice.

Nick brought the cigar back to his mouth, a knowing smile hidden by his hand. *Jesse, old friend, you're as transparent as glass.* He blew a smoke ring, then said, "Just a lucky guess."

A nerve twitching in his friend's cheek prompted Nick to add, "Don't get your drawers tied in a knot, Jesse. Everyone's going to the ball. It's a big shindig for the folks around here. After what you just told me, I know you feel obligated to keep close tabs on Mrs. Williams in case she *is* involved in the robberies. And if you can have the pleasure of the lovely lady's company in the process, I can't say as I blame you for asking her to the dance. Only are you sure Lawson is going to be there?"

Jesse stared at Nick for several seconds, then moved his gaze back across the barroom. Lawson was pouring a drink for a man with a swarthy complexion and a thick black moustache. Rather than move away after serving the drink, Lawson remained across the counter from the man. The two appeared to be having a very serious conversation.

"He'll be there. I stood at the bar for a while when I first got here and overheard Lawson tell another man he won't be working tomorrow night 'cause he's going to the ball. Do you know the man Lawson's talking to?"

Through the blue haze of cigar smoke, Nick casually looked over his shoulder. "Yeah, that's Ramón García. He owns a grocery in the Mexican quarter. I've seen him around town some, but I don't recall ever seeing him in here."

As Nick and Jesse watched, García threw the last of his whiskey down his throat, nodded to Lawson, then headed for the door.

"I think I'll just follow him and see where he's headed," Jesse said, pushing his chair away from the table. "I'll see you later."

Nick watched Jesse slip out the bat-wing doors and turn in the direction García had taken. Swallowing the last of his beer, he rose and headed for the back of the saloon. Lou Rickabaugh, manager of the Oriental's gaming room, always had a poker game in progress, and Nick felt lucky tonight.

Fantasy lifted her arms and dropped the silk dress over her head. Pulling the skirt down to settle around her hips, the hem slid to the floor with a soft rustle. After adjusting the elbow-length ruffled sleeves, she fastened the hooks on the front of the bodice, then turned to look in the mirror.

Her eyes widened. The lace-trimmed square neckline was a bit more daring than she'd anticipated when she and Mattie had selected the pattern from a Butterick Catalogue. She'd never worn a dress where her entire neck and the upper swell of her breasts were revealed.

She studied the rest of the dress with a critical eye. The green silk was a good color for her, a nice contrast to her auburn hair as Mattie had pointed out.

Turning so she could look over her shoulder at the

back of the dress, Fantasy nodded. The overskirt, made from the same fabric and trimmed with lace, was gathered at the back of the waist and cascaded down the underskirt to form a floor-length train.

Though her fingers shook with both apprehension and a severe case of nerves, she managed to pull her hair up onto the top of her head and pin it in an arrangement of loose curls.

She studied her reflection one last time, noting her dilated eyes and flushed cheeks. Satisfied she'd done all she could, she gave herself a few moments to compose herself before leaving her apartment to join Jesse.

Waiting to escort Fantasy to the ball, Jesse paced the length of the boardinghouse parlor. He couldn't remember ever feeling so nervous, like a young boy calling on a girl for the first time. There'd been a number of women before Fantasy, but none had ever caused him such anticipation, such overwrought nerves.

He stopped in front of the parlor window to stare out into the darkened street. The opening of a door behind him pulled him from his musings. Drawing a deep breath, he exhaled slowly, then turned.

His heart leaped at the picture of Fantasy standing in the doorway to her apartment. Her beauty robbed him of his ability to speak. Snapping out of his momentary trance, he crossed the room. The silk of her gown, the color a perfect match for her eyes, hugged each soft curve of her slender body.

He had the sudden urge to run his fingers across the creamy flesh revealed above the lace-edged neckline, to press his lips to the hollow at the base of her throat.

Tamping down such urges, he smiled and offered Fantasy his arm.

* * *

The St. Patrick's Ball was well under way when Jesse stepped through the doors of the Schieffelin Hall ballroom with Fantasy at his side.

The appreciative glances the other men sent Fantasy filled Jesse with immense pride. But when he saw the spark of more than a passing interest in several pairs of male eyes, pride quickly gave way to jealousy. Schooling his features to betray none of his warring emotions, he ushered Fantasy across the room to join Mattie Moreland and Nash Sparks.

"Evenin', Miz Williams, Jesse." Nash smiled first at his landlady, then his fellow boarder, keeping one arm securely wrapped around Mattie's waist. "You look mighty fetchin' tonight, if you don't mind my sayin' so, Miz Williams. Don't you agree, Mattie?"

Mattie gave her escort an adoring glance before turning back to her friend. "Yes, I do, Nash. You look beautiful, Fantasy. I especially like your dress."

Her cheeks burning from the compliments, Fantasy laughed with delight. "Mattie, you're something, you know that? Like my dress, indeed! Well, you should, since you made it."

Mattie laughed too. "There's nothing wrong with likin' your own work, is there?"

" 'Course not. Everyone should take pride in what they do," Fantasy replied, giving her friend a quick hug.

Fantasy's last remark touched a sore spot in Jesse's conscience—the place at odds over his growing feelings for her and his dedication to his job. Dealing with constantly being pulled in two directions was becoming increasingly difficult. He promised himself to work harder on his assignment.

Needing to distance himself, even briefly from the source of his inner turbulence, Jesse said, "Would you ladies like some punch?"

After the men excused themselves and headed for the refreshment table, Mattie turned serious. "Fantasy, have you decided if Jesse's working for your mother-in-law?"

Fantasy shook her head, bouncing the carefully arranged cluster of curls. "I'm not sure. Sometimes I think he is nosing around, asking questions, and making a general nuisance of himself proves he's another of Mother Williams's lackeys. Then other times, I think maybe I'm imagining things. The other day he bought some property on the edge of town, and he says he's checking into buying a building on Toughnut Street. That sounds like he's really a land speculator."

"Well, if Jesse wasn't hired by Mrs. Williams, do you think she's sent someone else?"

"I don't know. She was so adamant about getting Robby back to St. Louis—all her letters, then hiring that no-account, fool investigator—I can't believe she'll just forget about it. I don't trust her, Mattie."

"I know ya don't, and well you shouldn't. The woman would make good buzzard bait, if the buzzard could stomach her," Mattie replied, her voice serious, but her eyes sparkling with mischief.

Fantasy's pensive mood evaporated instantly, laughter bubbling up in her throat again. "Oh, Mattie, you always cheer me up when I need it."

As she watched Jesse and Nash work their way through the crowd toward them, she turned pensive again.

"What is it, Fantasy?"

"There's something else bothering me. It's how Jesse always knows what I like, almost as if my mind is a book he can read at will." At Mattie's quizzical expression, she continued, "He took Robby and me for ice cream, on a picnic a week ago, then he asked me to this dance. How did he know I like all those things?"

"Maybe he's just real perceptive where you're concerned," Mattie offered. "Nash is that way with me sometimes."

"Maybe." The men were too close for Fantasy to

say any more, but Mattie's explanation didn't convince her.

As the dance progressed, Fantasy tried to put her disturbing conversation with Mattie from her thoughts. Yet the possibility of Jesse working for her mother-in-law refused to be subdued, coming back to haunt her at various times during the evening. Dancing with Jesse was the only time she managed to keep such fears from clouding her thoughts. Wrapped in his arms, her mind and senses overflowing with his masculine presence, left no room for anything other than the man holding her.

Jesse had trouble concentrating on anything other than his beautiful partner. Remembering the promise he'd made to himself, he knew he should be mixing with the crowd, searching for clues for his investigation. Yet, he couldn't make himself relinquish Fantasy to the eager young men who waited anxiously for their turn to squire her around the dance floor. Finally, he succeeded in forcing his investigation persona back into place. After leaving her with Mattie and Nash, he excused himself.

Before Jesse had moved six feet, a group of would-be dance partners surrounded Fantasy. He frowned. When he heard her tinkling laughter in response to something one of the young men said, a sharp pang of jealousy ripped through him. Grinding his teeth in frustration, Jesse headed for Nick and a group of men standing around the beer kegs on the opposite side of the ballroom.

"Let's go outside for some air," Jesse told Nick after getting a glass of beer.

Freshening his own glass, Nick nodded and followed Jesse through the front door. They walked in silence, waiting to speak until far enough away so they wouldn't risk being overheard.

"I thought Lawson was supposed to be here," Nick said.

"Maybe he likes to be fashionably late," Jesse joked, then turned serious. "Let's hope he shows up."

"What happened the other night when you followed García?"

"He went to the Western Union Office and sent a telegram."

"I don't suppose you found out who he sent it to."

" 'Fraid not. But I do know what the telegram said."

Nick looked at his friend sharply, unable to make out Jesse's features in the darkness. "Are you kidding?"

"No, I'm not kidding," Jesse replied with a laugh. "After García went into the telegraph office, I slipped around to the side of the building. The telegraph operator had already started sending the telegram by the time I found an opened window so I missed who the message was going to. But I got the rest of it."

"Damn, Jesse, it's a good thing you bothered to learn Morse code. It sure has come in handy. So what did García's telegram say?"

"The message was 'Sugar ready for pickup morning of the twenty-fourth.' "

Nick scowled up at the small sliver of moon. "Sugar?"

"Yeah. Could be a customer ordered sugar from García's grocery, and he's letting them know when they can pick it up." Jesse chuckled. "But if he's one of Lawson's gang, it's obviously a code they've devised."

"Reckon it is." Nick pulled his cigar case from his inside jacket pocket. "Have you learned any more about García?"

"No, not yet, but I'm still working on it." Jesse stared at Schieffelin Hall's hulking shape outlined against the deep purple of the night sky. Now that he was away from Fantasy, he felt the tug of wanting to be back at her side. He shook his head to clear his thoughts.

After discussing the case for a few more minutes, Jesse drained his glass, then said, "Come on, let's get back inside. Maybe Lawson has arrived by now."

Nick grinned at his friend's departing back, certain he knew the real reason for Jesse's sudden desire to return to the dance. "I'll be there in a few minutes. I'm gonna finish my cigar."

"Okay, see you later," Jesse called over his shoulder, heading toward the hall.

From the doorway Jesse spotted Fantasy talking with a group of women. Eager to hear her voice and smell the gardenia-scented perfume she favored, he started toward her. Halfway to his destination, someone called his name. He turned to find Jack Lawson walking toward him, a black-haired woman who looked vaguely familiar clutching his arm.

"Evening, Lawson," Jesse said, his mind working furiously to put a name to the woman's face.

"McAllister. I don't believe you've met Lola Blair." He turned to his companion. "This here's Jesse McAllister, Lola."

Extending her hand, Lola replied in a silky voice, "It's nice ta see ya again, Mr. McAllister."

Of course! Lola, from the brothel on Sixth Street. "Good evening, Lola. You're looking lovely tonight."

"Different than last time ya saw me, right?" Turning to Lawson, she added for his benefit, "Although I didn't learn his name, I met Mr. McAllister a few weeks ago when he was over by my place."

Lawson nodded absently, his attention focused on something across the room. Removing Lola's hand from his arm, he flashed her an apologetic smile. "Forgive me, Lola. There's someone I have to see. I'll be right back."

As Jesse watched Lawson slip through the crowd, he wondered how he could excuse himself without appearing rude. He needed to find out who Lawson was so eager to see, not entertain the man's companion.

"Mr. McAllister? Are ya all right?" Lola's sultry voice pulled him from his thoughts.

"What?" His brows drawn together in a frown, he brought his gaze back to the woman at his side.

"Yer acting mighty distracted. Is there anything I can do ta help?" She moved closer until one heavy breast pressed against his arm.

When Jesse looked down at where her bosom overflowed the neckline of her gown, he stifled a groan. He had to get free of this clinging vine before Fantasy saw them together.

"I told ya I know lots of ways ta please a man," Lola purred in a loud whisper. "Have ya been thinking 'bout my offer, Jesse? Have ya been thinking 'bout which way ya'd like ta try?"

A gasp of surprise from behind him brought Jesse's head up with a start. Pushing Lola away, he swung around and found Fantasy staring at them, her eyes wide with shock. Realizing she'd overheard Lola's less than discreet questions, the heat of a flush crept up his neck and cheeks.

"I'm . . . I'm sorry," Fantasy finally stammered. She'd only wanted to rejoin Jesse. She missed his company and had started looking for him. Finding him with a woman wasn't surprising, after all, Jesse was a very handsome man. But the identity of the woman falling all over him had been a total shock.

Fantasy remembered her from another of the town's social functions—Lola owned one of the houses on Sixth Street. Though there was an unwritten code the prostitutes of Tombstone were to keep to themselves in their part of town, the townsfolk grudgingly tolerated the *ladies* at events like the St. Patrick's Day Ball. From the snippet of conversation Fantasy had overheard, it was apparent Jesse had met Lola prior to tonight's dance.

Fantasy swallowed the lump of pain lodged in her throat. "I didn't mean to interrupt your conversation. Excuse me, I . . ." The rest of her sentence lost in the rustle of her silk dress, she turned on her heel and headed for the front door as fast as the crowd would allow.

Mumbling a hurried goodbye to a thoroughly amused Lola, Jesse followed. Unfortunately, the crowd shifted every time he tried to make his way to the door, so it took him much longer to reach the exit than he anticipated. By the time he stepped outside, Fantasy was nowhere to be seen. Hoping she would go straight home, he headed down Fourth Street.

Her heart pounding in her ears, Fantasy slipped inside the front door of her house. Jerking the pins from her hair, she ran her fingers through the jumble of curls and tried to smooth the heavy mass now trailing down her back. Sitting in the unlit parlor, she wondered at her reaction to hearing part of an obviously intimate conversation between Jesse and a painted woman.

How Jesse spent his time was none of her concern. So why did the discovery she'd made feel like a betrayal? Jesse didn't belong to her. And if he wanted to visit the red-light district, she had no say-so whatsoever concerning what he did. Although she knew all that to be true, Fantasy still couldn't justify her terrible agitation.

"Fantasy?"

She started at the soft voice coming from the doorway, a voice she would recognize anywhere. She'd been so engrossed in her thoughts she hadn't heard the front door open or the tread of Jesse's boots in the hallway.

"Fantasy?" Jesse said again. "I need to talk to you about what you overheard."

"You don't owe me an explanation, Mr. McAllister. What you do with your time is your business. I have no hold over you," she replied, trying valiantly to keep the tears at bay. She'd already been humiliated enough.

Entering the parlor and easing down next to her on

the settee, Jesse cupped her chin with one hand and turned her face toward his. Her eyes were luminous in the faint light coming through the front window, her hair cascaded in a wild tangle around her shoulders. His desire instantly stirring to life at the seductive picture she made, he fought down the urge to haul her off to his bed.

"Fantasy, you're so beautiful," he murmured before lowering his head to graze her mouth with his.

Her eyes drifted closed, the indifference she wanted to feel at the touch of his lips momentarily forgotten. When he pulled away, her senses returned. Ashamed she'd actually wanted him to deepen the kiss, she tried to turn away. His fingers tightened on her jaw, forcing her to meet his gaze.

"I have never been with Lola." At her dubious look, he added, "The first and only time I saw her was right after I came to town. She tried to get me to . . ." He cleared his throat, then said, "Anyway, I refused her then, and I haven't seen her since. Not until tonight at the ball."

She searched his face for several tense seconds before she replied. "I believe you, Jesse. But what I said is also the truth. I don't have any hold on you. So if you feel the . . . um . . . need to visit the houses on Sixth Street, it's none of my business."

Releasing her chin, he grasped her arms and gave her a gentle shake. "Listen to me, Fantasy Williams. The woman I want is not Lola or any other in that part of town." He paused to let his statement sink in. "Do you understand what I'm saying?"

The enormous welling of emotion in her throat prevented her from speaking. She could only nod her head. The look in his eyes and the husky timbre of his voice told Fantasy she hadn't misinterpreted his words—Jesse wanted her.

Heaven help her, she wanted him, too!

Chapter 5

"Fantasy, you didn't hear a word I said, did ya?"
Spud smiled with amusement in spite of his chiding.

Fantasy visibly started, pulling herself out of her
troubling thoughts. "Of course I—"

"Now don't be tellin' a fib, Fantasy me girl. You
were woolgatherin' to be sure."

She looked down at the pile of mending in her lap
and sighed. Spud was right. She lifted the sock she'd
been attempting to darn for nearly an hour; a shirt
missing a button came with it. "Drat."

From across the parlor, Spud snorted with laughter.
"Remind me to be doin' me own mendin' from now
on. Otherwise, all me socks will end up sewed to me
shirts."

"Oh hush, Spud." She flashed him an annoyed look,
making him laugh all the harder. Snatching up her
scissors, she attacked the straying stitches, grumbling
under her breath about cantankerous old men.

A week had passed since the night of the St. Patrick's Ball and the night Fantasy made the shocking
discovery she wanted more than Jesse's kisses—a
whole lot more. Although he hadn't tried to do more
than kiss her that night, she knew now if he had she
might have gladly offered herself—freely and completely. That she could have responded so wantonly,
that her self-control was nearly non-existent where
Jesse was concerned were completely foreign—not to

mention embarrassing—realizations to make about herself.

Once she'd accepted her desire for Jesse, she couldn't stop thinking about the taste of his mouth, the feel of his arms or the need burning inside her to experience more than his kisses. She tried to keep such thoughts at bay by throwing herself into her chores with renewed vigor. She even worked an extra afternoon at Doc McKee's office. Yet, her efforts failed. No matter what she attempted, her mind continued to dwell on Jesse. She didn't dare count how many times she'd had to do something over because her wandering thoughts caused her to make a stupid mistake.

After one last snip with the scissors, she pulled the sock free of the shirtsleeve. "There," she said with satisfaction, only to realize the sock now had a bigger hole than when she'd started. Her lips pressed firmly together, she pointedly ignored Spud's latest hoot of laughter. She cut another length of darning cotton, determined to concentrate harder this time.

For a few minutes Fantasy worked diligently on repairing the sock while Spud contentedly smoked his pipe. Then his voice broke their silence.

"When would ye be guessin' the posse might be gettin' back?"

Another stage had been robbed that morning and a quickly organized posse had been dispatched. Spud's question ruined Fantasy's chances of finishing her mending with any success, since thinking of the posse brought Jesse back into her thoughts.

When the sheriff had asked for volunteers to form a posse, Jesse offered his help immediately. The men left within hours of hearing about the holdup and still hadn't returned. Fantasy glanced out the window. "They can't track in the dark, so they'll have to come back soon. Dusk is only an hour or so away."

"If they found a trail to follow, they might be campin' out tonight." Spud's lips twitched around his pipe stem at Fantasy's reaction to his words. Obviously she hadn't considered the possibility of Jesse not returning that evening. Rising from his chair, he ambled toward the hall. "Guess I'll just be moseyin' on down to the sherrif's office to see what I can find out."

"You'll let me know if you hear anything, won't you?" Fantasy didn't give any thought to how her question must sound. Her only concern was Jesse's safety.

Assuring her he would, Spud left her sitting in the parlor staring at the sock still clutched in her hand. Although they had never discussed it, Spud knew Fantasy was tiptoeing around her attraction to Jesse. And a person would have to be blind not to see Jesse was smitten with Fantasy as well. "Durn fool younguns," he muttered, opening the front door and stepping onto the boardwalk.

"What was so all fired important that I had to meet you here at this ungodly hour?" Nick asked the question while leaning over the pool table to line up his shot. Jesse had left a message with Nick's landlady to meet him at Hatch's Billiard Hall. "Damn, I missed an easy shot. I didn't get to bed until almost five. I can't function at this time of the morning."

Jesse chuckled at his friend's grumbles. "Sorry you got only three hours of sleep, but I wanted to be sure we wouldn't be interrupted. This is one of the few places that empties out by daybreak." Rubbing chalk on the end of his cue, Jesse moved to the other side of the table.

Nick waited until Jesse took his shot before speaking. "Did you find something at the site of the stage holdup? Is that what this is about?"

"Yeah, I found something. Whether it'll be useful, I'm not sure. In all the reports from the previous robberies, I never saw mention of it. So I wanted to see what you thought. Near as I could tell, there were four horses again, and there were boot prints all around where the stagecoach was halted." Jesse paused to send another pool ball into a corner pocket.

"Come on, Jesse, I'm tired." Nick stifled a yawn. "Spit it out, will you?"

One eyebrow arching with amusement, Jesse turned to look at his friend. "You wouldn't happen to have a woman waiting in your room, now would you? You've never been this anxious to get to bed unless there was a piece of fluff waiting to keep you company."

Nick had the grace to flush beneath the dark stubble of his beard, but held any retort he might have made.

Grinning widely, Jesse gave him a slap on the back. "Well, it's good to see you haven't changed your ways. I'll make this quick so you can get back to—what'd you say her name was?"

"None of your damn business. Just get on with it, Jesse."

Jesse threw back his head and roared with laughter. Catching sight of the murderous look on Nick's face, he halted his mirth.

Holding up his hands in a truce, Jesse said, "Okay, okay, I'll tell you what I found." Leaning against the pool table, he crossed one ankle over the other. "One set of boot prints was real unusual. The right heel left an impression of a star."

Contemplating Jesse's words, Nick ran a hand through his hair. "You're right, I don't remember hearing about any boot print like that after the other robberies. So, is this a different gang or did one of them get a new pair of boots?"

"I'm fairly certain the same gang was responsible for this robbery. They did everything exactly like the others—waiting for the stage to slow down to cross the San Pedro River, then coming out of the brush firing their rifles into the air. All the passengers were told to get out and hand over their money and jewelry. One of the gang got off his horse to collect the strong box and the passengers' valuables while the others kept the stage driver and guard covered."

"So, if nothing unusual happened, why the new boot print?"

"Something unusual did happen, Nick. The Benson sheriff talked to the passengers after the stage arrived. One woman said she'd tried to keep the outlaws from taking her necklace—a rare jade pendant her father bought in the Orient. When she refused to remove the necklace, a second robber dismounted to make sure she handed it over."

"Ah, I see," Nick said. "The man with the star in his boot heel was in on the other robberies, he just never got off his horse."

"Exactly. Now I just have to find the man who wears boots with a star carved in the bottom of the right heel. I'll check around town, but I'll probably be wasting my time. These men are too smart to buy a pair of boots with such an easily traced heel here in Tombstone. My guess is they bought them a long ways from Arizona Territory."

That afternoon Jesse planned to head back out to the scene of the stage robbery. On the day of the holdup, the sheriff and his posse had tracked the gang into the mountains southeast of town, then lost the trail in the rocks. For the next several days, the sheriff or one of his deputies had taken turns riding out to try to pick up the trail. When each man came back with the same story—no luck—the sheriff called a halt to the search. Just like all the other robberies, the gang responsible had disappeared without a trace.

Jesse didn't give up so easily. One of his strongest attributes as an investigator had always been his persistence. Though two weeks had passed since the last robbery and the trail was definitely cold, he continued to spend part of each day scouring the area for clues the posse might have missed. After saddling the horse he'd rented from the Dexter Stable on Allen Street, he led the sorrel gelding around the corner to Fantasy's boardinghouse so he could change his clothes.

"Is that your horse, Jesse?" Robby's eyes widened with wonder as he watched Jesse loop the reins around the hitching rail.

"'Fraid not, Buckshot. I just rented him for the afternoon." Ruffling the boy's hair, he started to walk away then turned back. "Would you like to sit on him while I change my clothes?"

Robby's bright smile vanished. "I can't, Jesse."

"Sure you can," Jesse responded. "Come on, I'll lift you into the saddle."

"No!" Robby's shout halted Jesse's attempt to touch him.

"What is it? Don't you like horses?"

"Yeah, but I never been on one before."

Jesse's insides cramped at being reminded Robby didn't have a father to teach him to ride. Even at Robby's age, Jesse had been riding horses on his father's ranch in Texas for nearly two years.

Squatting down next to the boy, Jesse said, "It's okay, Robby, I understand. How about if I take you for a ride? You can sit in front of me and we'll just go around the block. Would you like that?"

Eyes shiny with unshed tears, Robby bobbed his head once and sniffed loudly. "Sure, Jesse."

"You wait here while I change into my riding duds."

When Jesse returned a few minutes later, Robby and the sorrel stood eyeing each other silently, bringing a smile to Jesse's lips.

"This here's Rusty, Buckshot. Why don't you pet him so he'll get to know you?"

At Jesse's nod of encouragement the boy tentatively reached out and touched Rusty's muzzle with one finger. "He's soft." Giggling with delight, Robby stroked the horse's nose with his hand.

"Yes, he is." Jesse's smile broadened at Robby's obvious enjoyment. "Ready for our ride?"

His plans for the afternoon temporarily forgotten,

Jesse swung up into the saddle then pulled Robby up in front of him. Keeping the gelding at a sedate walk, Jesse enjoyed their leisurely paced trip around the block as much as Robby did.

When Jesse pulled the horse to a halt in front of the boardinghouse an hour later, Fantasy stopped her frantic pacing. She'd gone outside to check on Robby and suffered a terrible fright when Spud announced he'd seen Robby on a horse. She had no fondness for horses, in fact they terrified her, and the thought of her son atop one of the beasts nearly scared the wits out of her. Now, seeing Robby had come to no harm, her panic began to recede.

"Momma, look at me. I'm ridin' a horse!" Robby's crow of delight brought a thin smile to Fantasy's trembling lips.

"So you are, sweetheart." Swallowing the lump of fear lodged in her throat, she reached up to catch her son as Jesse lifted him from the saddle.

She hugged the boy tightly before setting him on his feet. "Thank Jesse for the ride, then go wash up for dinner."

"Thanks, Jesse." Flashing a smile, Robby darted past them and charged into the house like a miniature whirlwind.

"You're welcome, Buckshot, any time," Jesse called after him, chuckling at the boy's energy. When he shifted his gaze to Fantasy, his smile faded. Her stiff shoulders, slightly puckered brow and pale face were a shock. Dismounting, he took one of her hands between his. Her fingers were ice-cold.

"Fantasy, what is it? Are you ill?"

Lifting her face, she met his gaze. "No, I'm fine. I was just . . ." Her voice trailed off, not certain she could tell him why she'd been so upset.

"You just what? Whatever it is, it can't be that bad. Now come on, tell me." He chafed her hand between his palms to warm her chilled fingers.

Her shoulders lost some of their stiffness, and her

face lost some of its tightness. "When Spud told me he saw Robby on a horse, I was frightened something would happen to him."

"You know I'd never let anything happen to Robby." The insinuation he'd let harm come to the boy stung.

The indignation in his voice brought a faint smile to her lips. "I know you wouldn't, Jesse. The fear I felt had nothing to do with you. I was afraid I might lose Robby the way I lost my father."

"What happened to your father?" Jesse asked softly when she fell silent.

"My father loved horses. His pride and joy was a black stallion he called Satan. The horse was well named; he had a mean streak a mile wide. But that's one of the reasons Father loved him so much. He said a horse should have spirit. Father dreamed of starting a prize-winning line of horses from Satan." Fantasy paused and released a shuddering breath.

"I was at the paddock, watching Father work with Satan, like I always did. Except that day the stallion was especially nasty. When Father tried to ride him, Satan went crazy, throwing Father to the ground. Before anyone could do anything to help, the horse trampled him to death."

"You saw your father get killed?" When she nodded, Jesse swallowed the bile rising in his throat.

"I was only four, but I remember that day as if it were yesterday." She looked up at Jesse, her tear-filled eyes imploring him to understand. "That's all I could think about when I heard Robby was on a horse."

Jesse longed to pull her into his arms and hold her close, but he made no move to do so. Instead, he said, "Fantasy, you can't keep dwelling on that day whenever you think about Robby riding a horse. If you're going to live in this part of the country where horses are a way of life, Robby should learn to ride."

Fantasy closed her eyes and sighed. "I know you're right, Jesse, but the thought terrifies me just the same."

"Not all horses are like Satan," Jesse said softly.
"Let me teach Robby to ride."

Her eyes flew open at Jesse's request, renewed panic
swirling in their depths. When her lips parted to voice
her objections, Jesse's finger stopped the words.

"Listen to me, Fantasy, before you tell me no. I was
raised on a horse farm in Texas. I learned to ride
almost as soon as I could walk, and I had my own
horse when I was about Robby's age. Who better to
teach him?"

"I don't know," she hedged, her uncertainty swaying at Jesse's speech.

"You agreed I'd never let anything happen to
Robby—I care about him too much. Please, Fantasy,
let me teach him so you can put your fears to rest."

Fantasy had no doubts Jesse would protect Robby
from harm. She trusted him with her son, although
that trust didn't extend to herself. Likely Jesse was
another unreliable man, and eventually—she halted
that line of thinking. Jesse was right about living in
Arizona Territory. If she planned on staying, Robby
should learn to ride. The only other man she trusted
with her son was Spud. As much as she and Robby
loved the old miner, she doubted his knowledge of
horses went beyond what he knew about his mule.

"Okay, if Robby agrees, you can teach him to ride."
After making the decision and saying the words aloud,
Fantasy found some of her earlier fear had retreated.

"Great." Jesse smiled his approval. "I could teach
you, too."

She returned his smile, but shook her head. "Don't
press your luck, Jesse. I've just agreed to something I
never thought I'd do, so be content with that."

As he lowered his face to hers, his smile faded. "I'm
content. For now," he murmured just before closing
the distance between them.

Realizing he meant to kiss her, Jesse's premonitory
words fled with the rest of her thoughts. It wasn't a
long kiss, only a brief, soft blending of their lips, yet

the reaction it fired in Fantasy's body staggered her. She found herself leaning toward him, her hands clutching his shirt front when he pulled away.

Holding her by the shoulders until she regained her balance, Jesse released her then stepped back. "Tonight, after supper I'll tell Robby we'll start his lessons tomorrow, okay?"

Her breathing shallow, Fantasy nodded mutely. Jesse stared into her flushed face for several seconds before turning away. He wanted desperately to kiss her again, but succeeded in tamping down the urge. Swinging up into the saddle, he touched his fingers to his hat brim. "See you later."

She shuddered again, not from fear this time, but from the pulsing desire coursing through her veins. Sagging against one of the wooden awning's posts, Fantasy watched Jesse ride down the street. At first, she ignored the women coming down the boardwalk toward her. But a comment by one of them jerked her out of her deep reverie.

"Did you see that? Why I never! Of all the nerve, putting on a display like that with one of her boarders, and right in broad daylight, too."

The voice was that of Myrtle Greene, one of the town's biggest busybodies, and unfortunately a member of Fantasy's church. Usually Fantasy shrugged off Myrtle's gossip. This time, she was brought up short by the woman's prattle.

"I certainly did, Myrtle. Humph! Makes a body wonder what else goes on in that house," Myrtle's companion replied.

Fantasy nearly groaned out loud. Myrtle never went anywhere without her twin sister, Maude, another town busybody and an expert at starting rumors she later claimed to know nothing about. The sisters, spinsters from a wealthy New York family, didn't have to work to support themselves so they filled their days with gossip and meddling. Rumor had it, Myrtle and Maude came to Tombstone to escape the wrath of a

powerful man in their home town because of a story
they circulated about his daughter. Guess they didn't
learn their lesson, Fantasy thought in a moment of
pique.

Holding her chin high, she turned around just as the
sisters reached her. Fantasy glanced at the small, spare
women in their matching dresses and pert little hats.
As usual, their mouse-colored hair was drawn back
into tight little knots, making their thin faces look even
more gaunt. Taking care to avoid meeting their
muddy-brown gazes and the censure sure to be there,
Fantasy said, "Good afternoon, ladies. Nice day for a
walk." Before they could respond, she rushed past
them and slipped inside the boardinghouse. Leaning
her forehead against the closed door, she prayed they
would leave without creating a scene. She'd had
enough excitement for one day, and she didn't need
any more—especially the kind those two could cause.

Robby's enthusiastic response to Jesse's offer to
teach him to ride temporarily put the Greene sisters'
earlier comments from Fantasy's mind. But after
Robby had eaten dinner and gone out to play, her
thoughts kept returning to their words. Although there
was no truth to their theory of other improprieties
going on beneath her roof, Fantasy couldn't deny they
had seen her kissing one of her boarders. That Jesse
was only the second man she'd ever willingly kissed in
her life would make no difference to them. They'd
already tried and convicted her of improper behavior.

Unfortunately, Fantasy realized the nosy spinsters
were right about one thing—she shouldn't be carrying
on with one of her boarders. Decent women don't do
those kinds of things—a convention she'd warned herself about but conveniently ignored. She'd allowed
Jesse to be her escort around town, and even let him
kiss her. Not just *let* him, she reminded herself, she'd
returned the kiss as well.

Oh God, what have I done? I've already agreed to let Jesse teach Robby to ride. I can't tell Robby I've changed my mind, it would break his heart. Heaving a sigh, Fantasy started washing the dinner dishes, her thoughts in a turmoil over what she should do. It shouldn't be such a hard decision, after all Jesse was a man—an untrustworthy man—and to continue seeing him meant running the risk of being abandoned again. Still, she liked Jesse, and heaven knew, she liked kissing him. But if their relationship became more intimate . . . she shuddered at the thought of Jesse learning the truth about her.

Over the next few days, Fantasy continued to ponder the situation. Jesse had taken Robby to the livery, found a small, gentle mare, and began the boy's lessons. Her son's excitement over his growing skill on a horse was a convenient excuse to put off making the decision hanging over her like an enormous thunderhead.

Oddly enough, the impetus to finally make that decision came from a source she hadn't anticipated. Fantasy had just returned from running an errand when she heard a commotion behind her boardinghouse.

"She is, too!" Willy's hands were planted on his hips, his jaw jutted forward in challenge.

"She is not," Robby retorted, face flushed, hands balled into fists at his sides.

"I heard my Ma say she is."

"You take that back, Willy Thompson, or I'll punch you in the nose."

Willy threw back his head and gave a hoot of laughter. "Betcha can't."

"Betcha I can."

"Oh, yeah?"

"Yeah!"

His body quivering with pent-up anger, Robby launched himself at Willy. Though the other boy was a year older and half a head taller, Robby didn't care. All he wanted to do was smash the smirk off Willy's face.

Fantasy rounded the corner of the house just in time to see Robby land a jab to Willy's nose, then see her son receive a retaliating fist to his right cheek.

Arms flailing wildly, each boy landed another punch, oblivious to Fantasy's shouts. "Robby! Willy! Stop it this instant." She had to shout a second time before the two reacted.

His arm cocked for yet another flurry of fisticuffs, Robby took a step back, his gaze riveted on his opponent. When Willy dropped his fists Robby followed suit.

"What's going on here, Robby?"

"Nothin'." He refused to meet his mother's piercing gaze.

"Nothing? A fist fight is a lot more than nothing." When her son remained silent Fantasy turned to his friend. Willy eyed her silently, his thin face flushed, his square jaw clenched. "What about you, Willy? What do you have to say about this?"

She saw a brief flare of emotion in his dark eyes, but it quickly died. Pushing a lock of black hair off his forehead, Willy shrugged.

Realizing neither boy was going to say anything within hearing of the other, Fantasy said, "You better go home and get cleaned up, Willy; your nose is bleeding."

Willy wiped his nose with his shirt sleeve, gave Robby a we'll-settle-this-later look, then stomped off.

Once they were in the kitchen and Fantasy had cleansed the small scratch on Robby's cheek and his scraped knuckles, she asked again what happened.

"Willy, he said somethin' about you," he mumbled in a pained voice.

Her brow furrowing, she asked, "What did he say?"

"He said he heard his ma say you and Jesse was doin' something bad."

"Something bad? Did he tell you what he meant?" Fantasy held her breath, her heart beating violently against her ribs.

Robby shook his head. "He just said cuz Jesse lives here, you and him was doin' something bad." He tipped his bruised face up to hers, his eyes bright with tears. "You and Jesse aren't doin' something bad, are ya, Momma?"

Fantasy's throat constricted, her mouth bone dry. Finally she managed to speak. "Most folks wouldn't think it's bad, sweetheart. But some people, well they don't always see things like the rest of us. Does that make any sense?"

Robby thought for a minute, then replied, "Ya mean like how Grandma was always sayin' I was doin' somethin' wrong when I wasn't?"

Fantasy smiled. "Yes, that's exactly right. Remember how I told you your grandmother wasn't used to having little boys around and got upset easily when you weren't behaving like she thought you should?"

Robby sniffed loudly, then nodded.

"Well, the same is true of Jesse and me. Some people don't think we're behaving like they think we should. So, in their eyes we're doing something bad. Do you understand?"

"Yeah, Momma." His russet eyebrows pulled together in a frown. "Does that mean you and Jesse can't do things together no more?"

"I don't know, sweetheart," Fantasy murmured, brushing an unruly lock of hair off his forehead. "I really don't know."

Robby's defense of her honor brought Myrtle and Maude's words to mind. They had chastised her for the exact same reason her son had fought with Willy— her keeping company with Jesse.

Fantasy knew what must be done. Yet finding the strength to voice her decision could be very difficult.

* * *

Jesse asked Fantasy to supper on several occasions after the day she'd decided on her course of action. Each time she politely refused, unable to find the words to explain. Thankfully, he'd accepted each excuse. Still, she wondered how long he'd go along with her obvious attempts to avoid his company before demanding an explanation. How long before she would be backed into a corner and forced to speak up?

Finally, her refusal of Jesse's invitation to a play at the Elite Theatre brought on the scene she dreaded.

"Dammit, Fantasy, you love the theatre. Why won't you go with me? And while we're at it, why did you turn down my other invitations?"

Fantasy winced. Jesse was angry—very angry—and he had every right to be. She shouldn't have strung him along for the last week. "I can't see you anymore." Her voice was a raspy whisper.

"What?" Jesse's heated glare bored into her.

She swallowed hard. "I owe you an explanation. I should have told you sooner, but I . . . I just couldn't make myself tell you. Now I have no choice."

Realizing whatever she was about to tell him was very difficult for her, Jesse's anger melted away. He crossed the parlor and knelt in front of her chair. "What is it, Fantasy?"

Jutting her chin forward, she tried to affect an air of cool reserve. "I've decided I can't see you anymore. No suppers, no ice cream, no picnics, no dances—" Her voice breaking, she bowed her head before he saw her tears.

"What brought this on? You didn't feel this way last week when I kissed you. You clung to me like a stickweed." Jesse knew he sounded spiteful, but he couldn't help it. Fantasy's announcement had taken him completely by surprise.

Being reminded of their last kiss and her shameful behavior made her face burn with a blush.

Jesse wanted to kick himself for embarrassing her.

"Fantasy," he murmured gently. "Tell me what happened to change your mind."

As she raised her face, the tears she could no longer hold in check ran freely down her cheeks. "The day you took Robby for a ride on your horse," she began in a quivering voice. "Someone . . . someone saw us kissing."

"So?"

"It was Myrtle and Maude Greene, the town's biggest gossips. The things they said made me realize I shouldn't be keeping company with you."

She couldn't find the courage to reveal the rest of how she'd come to make her decision—the real reason for the fight between Robby and Willy. There'd been no way to hide the boys' scrap from Jesse. Fantasy had passed it off as a simple disagreement between spirited boys. When he accepted the explanation, she convinced herself there was no need to upset him by telling him the truth. His voice jerked her back to the present.

"And you believe what two meddling biddies said?"

"You don't understand. They go to my church, and I couldn't face them and the rest of the congregation knowing they all think I'm carrying on with one of my boarders. I shouldn't have started seeing you in the first place."

Jesse studied her tear-stained face in silence for a moment, then squeezed her hands. "Would there be a problem seeing me if I wasn't one of your boarders?"

Her eyes widened. "What are you saying?"

"Answer my question. Would there be a problem if I didn't live here?"

"I don't think so."

"Good." Rising to his feet, he offered her his hand. "It's been nice staying here, Mrs. Williams, but as soon as I can find suitable lodging elsewhere, I'll be leaving your fine boardinghouse."

Dazed, Fantasy rose and shook his hand. This definitely wasn't what she'd expected. Jesse wanted to continue seeing her badly enough to find another place to live. Although she'd miss the income from his room until she could find another boarder, her heart felt lighter than it had in days. With a giggle of pure delight, she released his hand, stepped into his arms and pressed her lips to his.

Jesse started with surprise. She'd never initiated any intimacy between them and her behavior brought an instant arousal. Hearing his own moan of pleasure, he snapped out of his momentary lapse. *Not now,* he silently chanted. *Not now!*

He pulled her arms from around his neck and took a deep breath, then wished he hadn't. The intoxicating scent of gardenias filled his nostrils, making his head spin and rekindling his desire. Clearing his throat, Jesse managed to find his voice. "I'll start looking around town tomorrow. As soon as I find a place we'll go out and celebrate. Then Myrtle and Maude won't have anything to talk about, right?"

"Right," Fantasy echoed, then broke into peals of laughter. The rich sound brought a sweet pang of emotion to Jesse's heart. He realized he'd never grow tired of hearing her laugh.

The next morning Jesse came downstairs earlier than usual, eager to start looking for a new place to live. After he'd rashly told Fantasy he'd move out so they could continue seeing each other, he'd had second thoughts about his decision. His main reason for taking a room at Fantasy's in the first place had been to keep Jack Lawson under surveillance. If he moved out of the boardinghouse, his proximity to the suspected robber would end.

After mulling over the situation before going to bed the night before, Jesse concluded he'd already found out all he could about Lawson. The man had refused his overtures of friendship and maintained a solitary way of life, giving Jesse little hope of learning anything new.

Confident he'd made the right decision, Jesse had fallen asleep and dreamed about unleashing the passion he knew bubbled just beneath Fantasy's cool exterior.

Whistling merrily, Jesse found himself alone in the dining room. He would really miss the mornings around the breakfast table with the other boarders, Fantasy, and her son.

Robby. The thought of not being able to see the youngster each morning made Jesse regret his decision to move out. But he assured himself he'd still see Robby. After all, he hadn't finished the boy's riding lessons, and there'd be times when all three of them would do things as a family. His train of thought shocking him, Jesse stopped short. When had he begun thinking of Fantasy, Robby, and himself as a family?

Caught up in his musings, Jesse turned abruptly to leave the room, knocking over a wicker basket of laundry sitting on the table. He smiled at his own clumsiness, then crouched down to right the basket and stuff the laundry back inside. When he lifted one roll of clothes, a small leather pouch fell onto the floor with a soft thump.

"What the hell?" After staring at the pouch for several seconds, he reached down and picked it up. His curiosity piqued, he loosened the tie, opened the pouch, and shook the contents into his hand.

He sucked in a surprised breath. A man's pocket watch and several pieces of jewelry lay in his palm. One necklace in particular caught and held his attention—a jade pendant on a thin gold chain.

Closing his eyes, he took several deep breaths, warning himself to think rationally.

Back in control, he opened his eyes and studied the other pieces of jewelry in his hand. He made a quick mental inventory, then slipped everything back into the leather pouch, secured the tie and tucked it inside the roll of clothes. After replacing the rest of the laundry, Jesse got to his feet and set the basket back on the table.

He stared at the wicker basket with its hidden cache for several long seconds.

Dear God, Fantasy, what have you gotten yourself into?

Chapter 6

Jesse turned in the saddle, keeping a tight rein on the skittish horse beneath him. Having discovered the need to spend more of his time on horseback, he'd bought himself a horse—a young, spirited pinto he named for the banjo-shaped marking on the gelding's left hip. Banjo had promise, but being only green-broke, the horse gave Jesse a run for his money on who called the shots at every turn.

Murmuring softly to still Banjo's nervous prancing, Jesse smiled at his riding companion. He was amazed once again at how quickly Robby had taken to horseback riding. Although he'd like to take credit for the boy's skill, Jesse knew natural ability gave Robby his good seat in the saddle and soft hands on the reins. "How ya doing there, partner?"

Robby waved and shouted, "Great, partner." He pulled his mare, Maggie, to a halt next to Banjo. "How's Banjo doin'?"

Jesse chuckled and patted the gelding's neck. "He just wants to run so he can get rid of some of his piss and vinegar."

"His what?"

"Uh, never mind." Avoiding the boy's gaze, Jesse looked across the desert. "How about if we race to that clump of palo verde over there?"

Before Jesse could turn Banjo in the right direction,

Robby jabbed his heels to Maggie's sides, sending the mare into a wild run.

Jesse laughed, shaking his head with wonder at both the boy's enthusiasm and the amusing picture he made. Robby's small form bounced on the scaled-down saddle, the stirrups barely reaching halfway down the mare's sides. As the boy leaned forward to urge Maggie on, his hat blew off, dangling by the rawhide chin strap and slapping against his back.

Thoroughly enjoying the sight, Jesse let Robby get a sizable lead before adjusting his grip on Banjo's reins. "Okay, boy, let's see what you can do." Banjo's ears turned back at his new master's voice. The horse quivered with anticipation but held his ground until he received Jesse's command.

Jesse was confident Banjo would have handily defeated Robby's much smaller mare had they started at the same time. And although Banjo ran like the wind, Maggie had too large a head start for the gelding to catch her. Besides, seeing the look of triumph on Robby's face was more enjoyable than winning the race.

They rested their horses for a few minutes, then started back to town. As they walked along, Jesse realized for the first time in several days that he'd been able to think about something other than the leather pouch he'd found concealed in Fantasy's laundry basket.

After he'd gotten over his initial shock of finding the loot from the stagecoach robbery tucked inside a roll of dirty clothes, Jesse had decided to follow Fantasy when she left the house with the basket later that morning.

At a safe distance, he followed her to Hop Town, then waited in the shadows across the street when she entered Wing Fong's Laundry. She left a few minutes later and headed for the Mexican quarter.

Again Jesse followed at a discreet distance. His heart lurched painfully in his chest when she entered García's Grocery. "Damn," he muttered. *García again. He has to be mixed up in the robberies somehow.* Deciding to risk Fantasy seeing him, Jesse strode purposefully down the boardwalk toward the store.

As he passed the open door and turned to look inside, he saw Fantasy pull an envelope from her purse and hand it to Ramón García. Jesse couldn't hear their conversation, but the man looked extremely pleased.

Was Fantasy delivering part of the robbery loot to him, too? The thought didn't sit well with Jesse. Yet, it was a possibility he couldn't ignore. Hurrying past the store, he slipped into an alley before Fantasy left the grocery. Although out of the direct sun, the air in the alley was stifling. Jesse's nose twitched. A horrible stench wafted toward him. He checked his boots, relieved to find the noxious oder wasn't from something he'd stepped in. Trying to take shallow breaths, he loosened his collar and wished for a refreshing gust of wind to sweep down the narrow passageway.

When he heard the clicking of Fantasy's heels coming closer, he forgot about the heat and the smell surrounding him. Moving deeper into the shadows, he flattened himself against a building. After she'd passed the alley, Jesse remained in his hiding spot for a few minutes longer, pondering this latest information and how it fit into the puzzle of the stage robberies.

Jesse had decided taking Robby for a ride might keep the dilemma out of his mind. Until now, his idea had worked. The boy's voice pulled Jesse from his thoughts. "Sorry, Buckshot, guess I was daydreaming. What did you say?"

"I said, did you find a place to live?" From the expression on the boy's face, the prospect of Jesse moving out of the boardinghouse didn't meet with his approval.

"Well, actually, I have. I rented a house this morning, but I can't move in for a couple weeks." Finding a new place had been harder than Jesse had expected. But in retrospect, he was glad it had taken nearly a week. The time had given him a chance to think about Fantasy's possible involvement in the ring of thieves before continuing a relationship with her.

Now enough time had passed that Jesse had his thoughts in order—not that he liked some of them—but at least taking Fantasy out for an evening no longer threatened to be a double-edged ordeal. Confident he had control of the situation and would be able to hide his turmoil, he was anxious to spend some time with her. Although Fantasy's being part of Lawson's gang remained a possible explanation for what he'd uncovered in the last week, for now the important thing was seeing her again.

He was struck again by his unusual behavior. His career with Wells, Fargo had been a satisfying one—a career which had him moving up the ranks of the company with remarkable speed. Although he enjoyed his current position as special agent, he was ready to settle down in one place. He'd been given the Tombstone assignment with the promise of being promoted to Assistant General Superintendent at its conclusion.

Now instead of spending all his time investigating the stage robberies then heading back to San Francisco to claim his new position, he couldn't keep thoughts of Fantasy from his mind. He'd worked around beautiful women on previous cases and not once had one of them caused him to shirk his duty. So why did Fantasy Williams affect him so strongly? The answer came as a shock. He recognized his physical hunger for her as lust, but was he in love?

Thinking back over the past weeks since he'd first seen Fantasy, he was startled to realize he had fallen in love. The revelation made the one question constantly gnawing at him even more important. If he found out she was in fact an outlaw, what would he do? And now that he'd discovered his feelings for her, would duty or love win out? He wished he knew the answers.

Shaking himself out of his troubling thoughts, he glanced over at Robby. Seeing the boy's pout of displeasure, Jesse smiled. "Ya know, partner, if you don't pull in that lower lip, Maggie'll trip on it."

"Aw, Jesse, you're just teasin'."

"Yeah, I'm teasing. But listen to me, Buckshot. Even though I'll be moving from your mother's boardinghouse, nothing is going to stop me from seeing you. I'll still take you riding and to get ice cream, and anything else you want to do. Is that clear?"

A smile lighting up his entire face, Robby pulled Maggie to a halt. "I sure wish you could be my Dad."

Totally unprepared for the boy's declaration, an enormous lump formed in Jesse's throat. Swallowing hard, his voice broke when he replied, "I'd like that, too, Buckshot."

Staring into the beaming, dirt-smudged face of the five-year-old for several long seconds, another thought came to mind. Perhaps Robby knew something about his mother's activities that would prove useful to his investigation. Using the boy's love for him would put him on a level with snake dung, but Jesse had a job to do. Although he'd just discovered his feelings for Fantasy, he couldn't turn his back on the opportunity presented to him. He had to find out the exact extent of her entanglement with the robberies.

Jesse gulped down his self-loathing for what he was about to do, and prayed his voice sounded casual when he spoke. "So, how well does your mother know Mr. Lawson?"

Robby shrugged. "Don't know." After a moment, he added, "Momma does things for him."

"Things?" Jesse's heart pounded heavily in his temples.

"She takes his clothes to Wing Fong's when she takes ours. And she took a letter for him once. Stuff like that."

"Letter? Are you sure it was a letter?"

"I think so. He gave her an envelope and said take it to a friend of his."

Jesse wondered if Robby meant the envelope she delivered to García, or had there been others?

"Does she do those kinds of things for the other boarders?"

Robby looked puzzled for a second. "Don't think so."

They continued in silence for a mile or so when Robby suddenly said, "Mr. Lawson gives Momma money sometimes."

"All the boarders pay your mother rent," Jesse replied carefully.

"Yeah, I know. This is other money."

"How many times have you seen Mr. Lawson give your mother this other money?"

"Maybe three times."

Jesse squeezed his eyes closed, recalling the scene he'd witnessed on his first day in town. Robby must have seen similar incidents. Wishing he'd never started this conversation, Jesse opened his eyes and stared straight ahead. The boy's innocent comments were only adding credence to his own suspicions. "Let's talk about something else. How's your friend Willy? I haven't seen him around lately."

While Robby chattered away about his friend, Jesse's mind swirled with a hundred more questions. Questions he needed to find answers to, and soon.

Kuan Mei-Ling straightened from leaning over the washtub. Sweat beaded her brow and upper lip; the heat from the wash water was horrendous. Wiping her face on the sleeve of her dress, she looked at the pile of clothes to be washed, then sighed. How she hated working in her uncle's laundry. But she had no choice.

"Mei-Ling!"

Her back stiffened. *Speak of the odious dog.* "Yes,

Uncle, what is it?" As Wing Fong swept through the curtains separating their living quarters from the laundry she bowed respectfully.

"Mei-Ling, I need to talk to you."

"But I have laundry to finish."

Fong's lips curved into an evil smile, revealing yellowed teeth from the opium pipe he could not live without.

"You finish later, I need to talk to you now."

She bowed again, then followed him through the curtains. Sitting in his favorite chair, Fong made no move to offer Mei-Ling a chance to get off her feet. He knew she dared not sit without his approval. She remained standing, her head lowered. For several moments he said nothing, enjoying his niece's discomfort while he carefully chose his words. He had something important to tell her, but he must proceed with caution.

"I have good news, Niece. I have arranged an excellent marriage for you." In truth the arrangement was not a marriage at all. But to get Mei-Ling's cooperation Fong knew he must make the deal he had struck sound appealing.

Mei-Ling's head jerked up, her eyes wide with surprise. "Marriage, Uncle?"

"Aiee. Marriage to one of the most renowned members of the Tong."

"But, Uncle, I wish you had told me you were making such an agreement."

"Silence!" Fong bellowed. "Your mother, my sister, placed you in my care. You will do as I say."

Bowing her head, Mei-Ling swallowed her hatred of the man she'd been forced to live with after her mother's death five years ago. If only she could have stayed with her sister Ching-Ling in San Francisco. But their mother's other brother could take in only one of his nieces, so Mei-Ling had been given over to Wing Fong. "Yes, Uncle," she replied in a small voice.

Fong studied his niece for several long seconds, then smiled again. His chest puffed up with pride for making such a superb deal for Mei-Ling—a lucrative bargain to sell her as a concubine to one of the most powerful men in the Chinese community. Mei-Ling was young and very beautiful, so securing a large price for her had proven to be easier than he'd expected. That the man offering for Mei-Ling didn't want her as a wife was of no concern to Fong. He considered himself lucky to get someone to agree to take his niece. Mei-Ling had a defiant streak he had never been able to totally subdue. Chinese women were supposed to be subservient and obey without complaint—but not Mei-Ling. Born and raised in California, his niece had acquired many habits of the barbarian Americans. She always questioned his decisions, always wanted to know things she had no business knowing, always frustrated Fong with her disobedience. Then when she finally gave in and did as he bid, the look on her face told him he may have won another battle but their war of wills raged on.

Even now, standing before him with bowed head, the picture of respect and obedience, Fong could tell by the tenseness of her shoulders and the slight quiver of her clasped hands that Mei-Ling longed to question his authority. Fong shifted in his chair, forcing his irritation from his mind.

We'll see if your new master will put up with your wagging tongue. His lips twitched. *Perhaps he will not be so lenient. Perhaps he will beat you for your insolence.* Fong didn't care. All he cared about was the promised gold for his coffers. He stifled the urge to rub his hands together in glee. Mei-Ling's price would get him much closer to having enough money to fulfill his dream of returning to China and living out his days like royalty.

Staring at his niece through squinted eyes, Fong realized he'd have to placate her to gain her acceptance of the lie he'd told. He pushed himself out of his chair and moved to a black lacquered dresser. Opening the top drawer, he poked through its contents. After making his selection, he withdrew his hand and turned toward Mei-Ling.

"I have gift for you."

She lifted her head, her eyebrows pulled together. Her uncle had never given her anything. "A gift?"

Fong smiled, not at the pleasure he heard in her voice, but at his intelligence for knowing how to get her to do as he wanted.

"Your mother wanted me to give this to you on your wedding day, but I would like you to have it now." He placed a gold chain with a jade pendant in her work-reddened hands. "You must not tell anyone about this, Mei-Ling. I would lose face if it became known I betrayed your dying mother's wish." Having to fabricate another lie bothered Fong not in the least. That he had taken the necklace from the latest packet of jewelry Jack Lawson sent to him to be smuggled out of Tombstone and sold didn't cause even a twinge to his conscience.

"This was my mother's necklace? But I never saw her wear it."

Fong closed his eyes and drew in a deep breath. *Stupid, ungrateful woman! Why can't you accept gift and keep mouth shut?* Opening his eyes, he said, "She brought it with her when we left China, but she would never wear it. She kept it always to give to you." Grasping Mei-Ling's arms, he gave her a quick shake. "Promise me you will show no one this necklace and only wear it under your clothes."

"I promise, Uncle. And . . . and, thank you." Bowing, she backed out of the room.

Once she was alone in the laundry, Mei-Ling examined the necklace closely. The jade was Chinese, she was certain, but she didn't believe her mother had owned the necklace. One thing Mei-Ling knew for sure—her uncle was trying to buy her obedience by giving her the necklace.

Fastening the chain around her neck and tucking the pendant inside her dress, Mei-Ling smiled. There'd really been no need for the gift. She'd been raised with the expectation of having a marriage arranged for her, and would have accepted such plans. But she had no idea her uncle had been working on an arrangement. She figured he was in no hurry to lose her help in the laundry. That's why his announcement had been such a surprise.

Mei-Ling smiled again, thinking of her uncle giving up a valuable necklace in order to get her to agree. Picking up another bundle of laundry and throwing it into the washtub, she decided all the opium he smoked must have weakened his brain. *Even a fool could see I can't wait to get out of his house.*

Several days after his conversation with Robby about Fantasy and Jack Lawson, Jesse approached a house on Allen Street, just west of Third. The house was located in Hop Town and owned by a woman known as China Mary and her husband Ah Lum.

Since renting a house for himself, Jesse had realized he would need a housekeeper. He began asking around, and soon learned all cooking, cleaning, and yard work done in Tombstone was done by the Chinese. And all Chinese labor, without exception, was hired through China Mary. The rest of the Chinese population refused to talk to the round eyes, so the responsibility fell to China Mary.

Jesse had also learned China Mary was the absolute ruler of Hop Town and handled all narcotics and Chinese red-light girls as well. While he didn't hold with smoking opium or the selling of women as either prostitutes or slaves, he wasn't in Tombstone to close down the opium dens or halt the peddling of human flesh. He would overlook China Mary's other business ventures, if she could find him a housekeeper.

When Jesse was ushered into the room where China

Mary sat, he found an unusually buxom Chinese woman wearing a heavily brocaded silk dress and a great deal of jewelry. Two Chinese men, obviously bodyguards from their deadly weapons and fierce demeanor, stood unobtrusively behind and to either side of their employer. Bowing respectfully, Jesse remained standing until his hostess motioned him to a chair.

Once he was seated, she spoke. "China Mary hear you want housekeeper."

Jesse had heard China Mary knew everything that went on, not only in Hop Town, but in all of Tombstone. Nevertheless, he hadn't expected her to know about his inquiries around town. "Yes, I'll be moving into a house on Fifth Street in a few days, and I need someone to keep house and cook for me. I understand you might know of such a person." She remained silent, studying him with intelligent, black eyes.

"China Mary can help," she said at last. "I send word when me find Chinese girl to work for you."

Hearing the dismissal in her voice, Jesse rose and bowed again. "Thank you, China Mary, I will be waiting to hear from you." A servant suddenly appeared at Jesse's elbow to escort him to the door.

Mei-Ling gathered her meager wardrobe from her dresser and quickly wrapped them into a bundle. She took a deep breath and swallowed the tears filling her throat. She should have known her uncle hadn't told the truth. He'd never done anything for her in the past that could be considered a kindness—everything always had profit in it for him. Although she'd been astounded by the wedding arrangement he'd told her about ten days earlier, she'd allowed herself to believe him—allowed herself to look forward to the day she would leave Wing Fong's house forever as a new bride.

Then this morning she'd learned the truth.

She'd been doing the daily grocery shopping. Although she was treated no better than a servant in her uncle's home, at least this daily outing gave her a chance to talk to others. Fong didn't let her talk to the customers at his laundry nor socialize with the Chinese in Hop Town. Had he known how much she enjoyed getting out each morning to visit the local Chinese grocery, he surely would have taken that small privilege away as well.

As soon as she entered Quong's store, Kee, son of the owner and one of Mei-Ling's few friends, rushed over to her. "Mei-Ling, I so sorry to hear about agreement your uncle make," he whispered, his dark eyes filled with sadness.

A shiver of dread wracked her body. "What about the agreement?" Her grip tightened on the shopping basket clutched in her hands.

"Hing Fat does not deserve you. I wish I was older so I could have pleasure of ripping out your uncle's throat."

"Kee, I don't understand what you're trying to say. Hing Fat is married. Why would he make an agreement with my uncle?" Meeting Kee's concerned gaze, Mei-Ling's eyes widened.

"Oh no! My uncle arranged for me to be Hing Fat's concubine. Is that what you're trying to tell me, Kee?"

"Aiee, Mei-Ling. Your uncle will have money for all the opium he could ever want when Hing Fat pays for you. I thought you knew what your uncle planned." Kee wished he could reach out and soothe the hurt he saw in Mei-Ling's eyes, but such behavior was strictly forbidden.

"My uncle told me I was to be married. He never told me the man's name."

"Now that you know about Hing Fat, what will you do?"

Mei-Ling shook her head, her shoulders shivering with revulsion at the thought of Hing Fat's touch. Her uncle had been truthful about one thing—Hing Fat was a powerful member of the Tong. But that wasn't what frightened her most—the man also had a reputation for being excessively cruel to women. His wife was often indisposed for lengthy periods of time, and talk among the Chinese servants said she stayed inside to hide the bruises Hing Fat gave her. Rumor even had it a previous concubine had died from his brutal treatment. Since the Chinese culture allowed women to be sold and used as their masters saw fit, no one in Hop Town outwardly condemned Hing Fat.

"I don't know, Kee. I . . . I have to think." Forgetting her purchases, Mei-Ling had turned and fled from the store.

Hugging the bundle of clothes to her chest, Mei-Ling remembered her conversation with Quong Kee and walked silently through her uncle's house. Thankfully Wing Fong was still asleep. He'd been out late again, undoubtedly visiting one of the many opium dens in the tunnels beneath Hop Town. She carefully eased the front door open and stepped outside. Once she was a few yards from the house, Mei-Ling ran toward the one person she prayed would help her.

At China Mary's front porch, Mei-Ling stopped to catch her breath before climbing the steps. When she finally worked up her courage, she approached the front door and lifted one shaking hand. Her heart pounding in her throat, she waited for someone to answer her knock.

After being led into China Mary's opulent parlor, Mei-Ling threw herself at the woman's feet.

Mary's forehead puckered at the young girl's behavior. "Rise, Mei-Ling, and tell me what brings you to China Mary."

"I need your help, China Mary. My uncle plans to sell me to a terrible man." Quickly Mei-Ling told Mary of her uncle's duplicity and how she'd learned the truth.

"Sometimes we must do things we not like. Your uncle make honorable Chinese arrangement for your future."

"I know. But Hing Fat is old enough to be my grandfather," Mei-Ling cried.

Mary nodded. "Aiee, Fat many year. So can you blame him for wanting young girl in his bed? Maybe he need you to bring back strength for pillowing."

Mei-Ling's face burned at China Mary's frank words. "I've heard he takes pleasure from inflicting pain on women."

"I hear stories, too, of how Fat treat women. Perhaps they deserve his punishment. You not know whole truth."

Mei-Ling lowered her head, afraid she'd made a mistake in coming to China Mary for help.

Mary studied Mei-Ling's bowed head for several seconds, knowing the girl had reason to be frightened. In spite of her earlier words, Hing Fat was known for his cruelty, a true locust on the Chinese community. Yet, Mary knew he had every right to do with his wife and concubines as he wished.

"What you want China Mary to do?"

Lifting her head, Mei-Ling met Mary's gaze. "I want protection from my uncle, so he cannot force me to carry out his plans." With a determined thrust of her chin, she added, "I will not become another of Hing Fat's playthings."

Mary stared at the beautiful young woman before her, thinking about Mei-Ling's offended sensibilities. Not so many years ago, a woman would have been killed for even hinting at refusing an order from the head of her family. Seeing a lot of herself as a girl in Mei-Ling, Mary smiled.

"You stay here until me talk to Wing Fong." Watching the relief wash over Mei-Ling's face, Mary quickly added, "I not promise anything. Your uncle may refuse to cancel agreement with Hing Fat. Or Hing Fat may not want to give you up. I will see what can be done."

China Mary made good her word and took Mei-

Ling in until the girl's future could be decided. As promised, she went to see Wing Fong.

Furious with his niece for seeking refuge with the one person in town he could do nothing against, Fong also knew China Mary's word was law. So when Mary came to him and asked him to stall Hing Fat, he readily agreed. Not happy about having to humble himself in front of Hing Fat, Fong was even angrier about having to wait for the money Fat promised him. But as long as Mei-Ling was under the protection of Hop Town's honorable leader, Fong had no other choice.

"Well, that's everything." Jesse lowered his carpetbags to the dining room floor and turned to face Fantasy. Dawn still an hour away, the single lamp burning at one end of the table cast the room in a soft yellow glow. Jesse had purposely planned his leave-taking of the boardinghouse for this early to give him a few minutes alone with his soon-to-be-former landlady.

He moved closer, then withdrew something from his jacket pocket and held it out to her. "Here's my key."

As he pressed the cold metal into her hand, Fantasy resisted the urge to shiver with pleasure. His husky voice and warm fingers were doing wonderfully wicked things to her insides. Flustered by her reaction, she couldn't bring herself to meet his gaze.

"I'm going to miss living here."

A strange welling of emotion clogging her throat, she hoped she could force the words past the tightness. "I'll miss you, too."

Jesse smiled. "I sure hope so." Placing the knuckles of one hand under her chin, he tilted her face up. "I sure hope so," he whispered again, his mouth mere inches from hers.

When he halted his advance, Fantasy groaned with frustration and rose up on her toes to close the distance between them. Jesse swallowed a chuckle at her impatience, meeting her eager mouth with his own hungry lips. He pulled her fully against him, feeling her arms slip around his neck. Clasping the back of her head with one hand and bending her backwards over his other arm, his lips sought the secrets of her mouth.

Two long weeks had passed since their last kiss, and slowly he reacquainted himself with the taste and texture of her mouth. Jesse traced the outline of her lips with the tip of his tongue, then drew her lower lip into his mouth to suckle it gently.

The tugging sensation sent a staggering flash of desire through Fantasy's body. Her breasts tingled, their tips hardened pebbles pressing into Jesse's chest. There was a strange throbbing, a heavy fullness, low in her belly. Mostly there was heat, an intense inferno, racing through her veins, until she thought she'd surely burst into flames. Just when she believed a fiery explosion was imminent, Jesse ended the kiss.

His breath coming in short, harsh pants, Jesse straightened. Releasing Fantasy, he stepped back. In a raspy whisper, he said, "See you tomorrow night."

"Yes, tomorrow night," she managed to reply, her voice slightly breathless. Through glazed eyes, Fantasy watched him pick up his luggage then head for the door. As he disappeared from her boardinghouse, she wondered how she could get through the hours until Jesse came to fetch her the following evening.

In the pre-dawn darkness, Jesse headed toward his new home for the duration of his stay in Tombstone. Tomorrow night was the celebration he'd promised Fantasy when he found new lodging.

He planned to take Fantasy and Robby to the Can Can Restaurant for supper, but if she kissed him again like she just did . . . he didn't dare think about what might happen if she did. He already had difficulty concentrating on anything save Fantasy. Though he now knew the reason, his newly discovered love made it even more difficult to stop thoughts of doing more than kissing her. One more taste of her sweet mouth, or another of her soft moans of pleasure could easily send him over the edge. His body ached with the need to make her his completely, to show her how much he loved her. Yet, he was still determined to wait until the time was right.

Approaching the adobe house on the north end of Fifth Street, Jesse was thankful he'd included Robby in his invitation for supper at the Can Can. Otherwise, if he and Fantasy were alone for the entire evening, his plan to remain celibate until she was ready to take that step would more than likely get blown to smithereens.

Chapter 7

China Mary drank her tea in silence, watching Mei-Ling and wondering how to tell the girl about her visit to Hing Fat. Normally she did not interfere in agreements made between her people, but simply let them take place as it was done in China. Nevertheless, after Fat refused Wing Fong's request to extend the deadline for delivering Mei-Ling to him, Mary decided to step in and accomplish what that miserable slug, Fong, had failed to do.

Mary paid a visit to the honorable Hing Fat to convince him to wait—the girl he wanted so badly must have time to become accustomed to her fate. The mere presence of Hop Town's indisputable ruler in his home gained China Mary Fat's instant approval. Knowing how Hing Fat's impatience to have the young girl—in spite of his agreeing to a delay—would affect Mei-Ling, Mary decided to keep that fact to herself.

Setting her cup down, Mary spoke to her young house guest in English so her bodyguards wouldn't learn of her interference. "I visit Hing Fat three day ago."

Her heart pounding, Mei-Ling's gaze sought Mary's round face. "What did he say?"

"Fat not important now. I decide you work as housekeeper for round eyes. Keep your mind off uncle's agreement."

Mei-Ling's brow furrowed. "I do not understand. I will work for an American if you want me to, but what about Hing Fat?"

"Work as housekeeper for now, Hing Fat agree to wait. I send word to Mr. McAllister."

Mei-Ling heard the finality in China Mary's voice and nodded. Thankful to have won a reprieve, she pushed her fear of eventually having to submit to the lecherous Hing Fat to the back of her mind.

Jesse had been in his house several days when word came from China Mary. On his second visit, Mary told him a young Chinese woman had been selected to become his housekeeper.

"Who is she?"

"Her name Kuan Mei-Ling. She young, seventeen year, but strong. You not be disappointed."

"I'm sure I won't. If you recommend her, I'm sure she'll do just fine," Jesse replied.

"Guarantee all Chinese me recommend do good. They all honest and good worker. Them steal, me pay!" she stated proudly.

Mary clapped her hands sharply. Jesse's new housekeeper was ushered into the room. "This Kuan Mei-Ling, she work hard for you." Pushing Mei-Ling forward, China Mary lifted the girl's lowered face with a pudgy finger. "This new boss-man, Jesse McAllister. You do what he say."

Mei-Ling's frightened gaze tentatively moved from the woman who had taken her in a week ago to the man she would be working for. China Mary had talked with her at great length the previous night about going to work for Mr. McAllister. Although uneasy about working for a round eyes, Mei-Ling agreed to do as Mary asked, promising not to give her reason to regret her decision.

With the moment upon her, Mei-Ling's apprehension about leaving the safety of her protector's home

returned. As China Mary and Mr. McAllister discussed the usual arrangement for her wages to be paid
directly to China Mary, Mei-Ling surreptitiously studied her new employer.

He was tall and well-built, fashionably dressed and
clean shaven. More importantly, he had kind eyes.
Mei-Ling heaved a silent sigh of relief. After China
Mary had told her about visiting Hing Fat and her
decision to put her to work, Mei-Ling had transferred
her fears about her future to the man she would be
working for. Now those fears eased. She trusted a
person's eyes to reveal his true nature. Mr. McAllister
was a kind man.

After Mei-Ling retrieved her belongings, she bid
China Mary goodbye then followed her new employer
down the street.

Ten days had passed since Jesse brought Mei-Ling
to the house he'd rented on the northern edge of town.
She was a capable housekeeper and a good cook, although Jesse seldom ate at home. Today he planned to
take Robby for a ride. The boy really didn't need any
more riding lessons, but Jesse enjoyed his company.

"Don't plan on me for dinner or supper, Mei-Ling.
If there's something you'd like to do today, go ahead
and go." Jesse had suggested several times that Mei-
Ling go out for an afternoon—with only him living in
the house there really wasn't enough to keep her busy
all day—but she always refused. Although the initial
fearfulness he sensed she felt toward him had faded,
Jesse was certain Mei-Ling was still frightened of
something, or someone. So far his attempts at conversation with her were entirely one-sided. She said very
little, only speaking to ask him a question about the
house, what he wanted to eat or when to expect him.
Whatever frightened her, she kept to herself. And since
it didn't affect the fine way she ran his house, Jesse

didn't dwell on it. He had enough on his mind without trying to unravel another mystery.

"What's down there, Jesse?"

"I'm not sure." Touching his heels lightly to Banjo's sides, Jesse urged the gelding forward. "Come on, Buckshot, let's go see."

Together Robby and Jesse let their horses carefully pick their way down the rocky hillside. They were in the Huachuca Mountains, southwest of Tombstone, and had come upon a small, hidden canyon.

At the canyon bottom Jesse found a campsite. A circle of rocks formed a fire pit, several logs pulled up on either side.

"Who do ya think stayed here?" Robby asked.

Jesse studied the ground around the crude campsite. "I don't know. Drifters maybe, or miners." Easing off Banjo's back, he approached the remains of the campfire. Although long-dead, Jesse was certain only a few weeks had passed since someone had used the fire pit. Any tracks left in the soft dirt had been erased by wind sweeping down the narrow canyon.

"Damn," he muttered, poking a stick into the charred wood of the campfire. Something told him this place was important to his investigation, yet he couldn't find any clues to confirm his intuition. He rose and tossed the stick into the ashes. Looking at the small stream cutting through the floor of the canyon and the pine trees tenaciously hugging the canyon's rocky sides, Jesse saw no other signs of human habitation.

He stepped into the stirrup and swung onto Banjo's back. "We'll let the horses get a drink, then we'd best head back."

Jesse forgot about the abandoned campsite until another ten days had passed and the gang of *cow-boys* struck again. This time the Bisbee stage carrying the Tombstone Mill and Mining Company payroll was the target. Like all previous holdups, a posse was immediately organized. And, like all previous posses, this one came back emptyhanded.

Exhausted after returning home from his third day spent in the saddle in the strength-sapping heat of the Arizona desert, Jesse fell into bed with a groan. He hadn't even eaten the supper Mei-Ling had kept warm. Mumbling something about being too tired to eat, he had headed for his bedroom. Just as he started to fall asleep, the memory of the campsite in the hidden canyon jolted him awake. *I should've thought of it sooner.* After forming plans to follow up on his hunch the next day, he allowed his tired body to relax in sleep.

The following morning Jesse left Tombstone at first light. Banjo's long strides quickly ate up the miles to the Huachuca Mountains, the sun just easing up over the horizon when Jesse headed down into the canyon.

"God dammit to hell." His shout rang off the surrounding rock, echoing down the canyon. *Why didn't I think of this place three days ago?* Sliding off Banjo's back, Jesse stalked to the still-warm campfire. After checking the fire, he decided whoever camped here had been gone for no more than several hours.

Standing and brushing off his hands, Jesse's gaze scoured the ground around him. He slowly walked around the camp, careful to avoid the many boot and hoof prints. At last he found what he was looking for. He crouched down to get a better look at the impression, then smiled. *I knew it. Damned if I didn't.* There in the dirt was the outline of a star clearly visible in the right heel of one set of boot prints.

Jesse continued checking the area, working outward in an ever-widening circle until he found something he hadn't noticed when he'd first ridden into camp. In some brush off to the right of the campfire, lay a Wells, Fargo strongbox. The padlock had been shot off, and the lid gaped open, revealing its empty interior.

Certain the recent occupants of the camp were the same men who'd robbed the Bisbee Stage, Jesse grabbed for Banjo's reins, intent on seeing if he could pick up a trail.

Swinging into the saddle, Jesse nudged the pinto forward. He kept the gelding at a slow walk while he watched the ground ahead of them. They'd just come out of the mountains when the trail left by the four horses he'd been following divided. Jesse pulled up, studying his choices. Two sets of tracks angled north; the other two veered to the northeast.

Jesse decided to head north and urged Banjo forward. A half hour later, he entered the town of Charleston and lost the tracks he'd been following in the well-trod street. Disappointed to have his search aborted, Jesse looked around the small town. He'd heard of Charleston, one of the half-dozen or so communities along the San Pedro River, springing up after the silver strike in Tombstone, but he'd never made the nine-mile trip to visit the place. He could hear the incessant pounding of the town's two stamp mills as the quartz rock-breakers crushed the ore brought in from the mines. As he moved down Main Street, Jesse wondered how the workers in the mills could stand the noise.

Since he had no idea what the men he'd followed to Charleston looked like, Jesse knew it was useless to stick around. He turned Banjo toward the river and the road heading back to Tombstone, letting the gelding set his own pace. Since the day promised to be another scorcher, Banjo seemed content to stay at an easy lope.

The bright green bark of the palo verde, the scraggly, stiff branches of the greasewood, and the thorn-covered stems of an occasional ocotillo cactus faded from Jesse's sight. Instead he saw Fantasy rather than the passing desert terrain. Fantasy serving breakfast while exchanging light banter with her male boarders. Fantasy bending down to examine something Robby brought home to show her. Fantasy lying on a bed, her glorious auburn hair spread around her like a silken cape.

Banjo pulled up sharply, jerking Jesse from his wayward thoughts. His unconscious reaction to the tantalizing images running through his mind had apparently been pulling back on the reins. "Sorry 'bout that, boy," Jesse crooned, feeling like a fool for allowing himself to become so distracted.

Looking around, Jesse didn't recognize his surroundings. Banjo must have left the road to Tombstone some time back while Jesse's thoughts had taken a detour. They were north of town by his estimation. *Guess I'd better pay attention.* He turned the gelding back toward Tombstone. *Otherwise, there's no telling where we'll end up.*

Jesse tried to keep his mind on simply getting back to Tombstone without any other side trips, but visions of Fantasy continued to intrude on his good intentions. Many questions still needed answers—highest on the list was whether she was a member of Lawson's gang, and if so how much she knew about their plans and activities.

Yet, regardless of the outcome of his investigation, Jesse couldn't stop his body from wanting her or his heart from needing her. In spite of the possible ramifications of Fantasy being a criminal, Jesse knew his love for her would never change.

The loud clanging of the fire bell and the rumble of a fire wagon woke Spud with a jolt. He absently scratched his belly, then stretched his arms over his head, wondering what had caused all the commotion. Yawning loudly, he glanced down the street, then rose from the chair where he'd been dozing on the boardwalk in front of Fantasy's boardinghouse.

"What the devil?" He shook his head to clear the last cobwebs of sleep. Surely his eyes must be playing tricks. Spud stepped off the boardwalk and moved to the center of the street.

It was no trick. Huge black clouds of smoke billowed from the corner of Allen and Fourth Streets, just half a block away. The roar of the fire grew louder, drowning out the mingled shouts of the townsfolk running to escape the blaze and the firemen fighting to put it out.

For several minutes Spud stood transfixed, shocked yet strangely attracted to the horrible sight before him. As he watched, the fire moved closer, devouring everything in its path, turning the afternoon sky black with soot and smoke.

"Oh me God, Robby!" Remembering the boy left in his care, Spud bolted for the alley next to the boarding-house.

Before he'd taken a half-dozen steps someone grabbed his arm. "Hey, old timer, you can't go back there. The fire started behind the Tivoli Saloon and is spreading so fast we may not be able to stop her."

"Ye don't understand." Spud tried to pull free of the fireman's grip, pointing down the smoke-filled alley with a shaking hand. "Fantasy left me in charge of her son. He was playin' out back a few minutes ago, and I have to be finding him."

The other man just shook his head, then nodded toward the building on the other side of the alley. "I'm sorry, mister, but the fire has already spread to Spangenberg's Gun Shop. With the gun powder and cartridges stored in there, we have to evacuate the area." He pointed to the flames licking from the roof of Fantasy's house. " 'Sides, it's too late. This here house is already on fire. It's a goner for sure."

Escorting Spud up the street where he'd be safe and out of the way, the fireman added, "Maybe the boy got out in time."

As the house Spud called home became totally engulfed in flames, he stood in the crowd gathered on the

corner of Fremont and Fourth Streets. Fear for
Robby's safety squeezed his heart.

Several miles from Tombstone, Jesse pulled Banjo
to a halt and stood up in his stirrups. Squinting against
the blinding glare of the sun, he could see a strange,
dark cloud hanging over the town. Dropping back into
the saddle, he jabbed his heels to Banjo's sides and
urged the horse into a gallop. The campsite in the
mountains, Charleston and his questions about Fantasy were quickly forgotten. Banjo raced into town,
crested the hill at the north end of Fifth Street, then
snorted and slid to a stop.

The gelding danced nervously, his eyes rolling
wildly. As Jesse tried to calm the horse, the reason for
Banjo's behavior drifted toward him. Smoke, just as
he'd feared. Glancing toward the main section of
Tombstone, Jesse froze. The cloud of pitch-black
smoke he'd spotted just minutes before had grown in
size and now covered the center of town. The slight
breeze sent smoke and ash drifting slowly to the northwest. Even from the several blocks separating him
from the heart of the fire the roar of the blaze was
deafening as the flames advanced hungrily on the
bone-dry wooden buildings in its path—straight toward Fantasy's boardinghouse.

Jesse jumped off Banjo's back, secured the reins to
a hitching post then raced toward Fourth Street. With
each stride, he prayed Fantasy and Robby had escaped
the fire's wrath.

Pushing his way through the throng of people filling
the streets, Jesse cut kittycorner through the back lots
between Fifth and Fourth Streets. The heavy smoke
made breathing difficult. The intense heat caused an
instant film of sweat on his skin. He stopped to wet his
handkerchief in a water barrel and tie it over the lower
half of his face.

By the time he reached the back of Fantasy's boardinghouse, the gun shop next door was ablaze. Seeing flames leaping from the roof, Jesse knew he had very little time before the gunpowder inside the building exploded.

Calling for Fantasy and Robby over and over, his throat parched and raw from the smoke, Jesse finally saw movement to his right—a brief flash of blue. His eyes squinted against the acrid smoke, he scanned the area. At last he spotted something.

Jesse found Robby crouched in a corner between the boardinghouse and a small lean-to built against the back wall. Though paralyzed with fear, the boy appeared to be unhurt, his only movement the occasional wiping of his eyes with the sleeve of his blue shirt—the movement Jesse had seen.

Thankful he'd found Robby in the dense, suffocating smoke, Jesse hunkered down in front of the boy. "I'm here, Robby. Everything's gonna be okay."

The roar of the fire absorbed his words.

Robby seemed unaware he was no longer alone until Jesse grasped his arm. "Lean forward, Buckshot." As Jesse reached behind Robby to tie the handkerchief he'd removed from his own face over the boy's mouth and nose, Robby's gaze finally shifted from the mesmerizing flames.

Jesse tried to keep the panic out of his voice when he asked, "Where's your mother?"

The boy merely stared at him, recognition slowly replacing the stupefied horror in his eyes.

Giving him a gentle shake, Jesse repeated the question. This time Robby responded by shaking his head.

Jesse pulled the boy against his chest, squeezing his eyes closed. He silently repeated his prayer for Fantasy's safety, then relaxed his hold on Robby. He had to get the boy to safety or they'd become victims of the encroaching inferno.

Hoping to stay beneath the choking smoke, Jesse remained crouched on the ground, his arms around Robby. "We have to get out of here. Fast!" The smoke grew heavier, thicker. The heat from the rapidly advancing flames continued to increase. Each way Jesse looked, a wall of flame blocked their exit.

Shocked the fire had spread so quickly, he knew time was running out. A sudden burst of rapid explosions signalled the fire had reached the ammunition in Spangenberg's Gun Shop and spurred him into action. Trying to see through the smoke, he said, "I've got to find a way out of here."

"I know a way, Jesse." Robby's voice was hoarse from the smoke and muffled by the handkerchief. At Jesse's surprised look, Robby pointed to the lean-to behind them.

When Jesse looked skeptical, Robby added, "We can get to the tunnel from in there."

"Tunnel? Are you sure, Buckshot?"

At Robby's nod, Jesse shrugged. "Well, we don't have much choice."

Grabbing the boy's hand, Jesse headed toward the lean-to. Inside, Robby showed him a small trap door in the floor, the door's placement so cleverly concealed it would never be discovered unless a person knew of its existence.

When Jesse lifted the heavy wooden door, a cool breeze hit him in the face. He inhaled, filling his lungs with smoke-free air only to trigger a fit of coughing. Tears coming to his already smarting eyes, he doubled over, his body struggling to expel the burning smoke from his lungs. Each painful cough wasted precious time, allowing the fire to creep closer.

When his coughing finally stopped and he'd caught his breath, he looked around the lean-to. If they were going down into a dark tunnel, they'd need some sort of light. He spotted a small lantern and a box of matches on a shelf in a corner. Lighting the wick and adjusting the flame, Jesse turned back to Robby. "Come on," he managed to croak. "Let's get the hell out of here."

Jesse lifted the boy into his arms, then picked up the

lantern and stepped down into the yawning hole. When he reached the floor of the tunnel, he lowered Robby to his feet. "Are you okay?"

His eyes still wide with fright, Robby nodded.

"I have to go back up and close the door. Don't move, okay?"

At Robby's second nod, Jesse smiled at the boy's bravery. "Thata boy. I'll be right back."

After securely closing the door so smoke wouldn't be sucked into the tunnel, Jesse rejoined Robby. The temperature underground was considerably cooler, the chilly air a blessed relief after the intense heat of the fire. In the damp, stone passageway, memories of the fire faded until it was like a bad dream.

The fire was out. Although hampered by lack of pressure in the water mains, the firemen had successfully broken the fire's stranglehold on their town and halted its progress. Yet the blaze had taken only fifteen minutes to turn nearly the entire square block bounded by Fremont, Fifth, Allen, and Fourth Streets into a charred ruin.

Spud sat on the boardwalk that had miraculously escaped the fire across the street from what used to be Fantasy's boardinghouse. There was nothing left; only a pile of smoldering wood remained where the building had once stood.

"Was that your house?" A man's voice pulled Spud from his tormenting thoughts.

"What?" Spud looked up to see a man scribbling in a notebook.

"I said, was that your house?" The man pointed to the rubble across the street.

"No. The house belonged to me landlady, Fantasy Williams. Who might you be?"

"Name's Samuel Purdy. I bought the *Epitaph* a few weeks ago. Was your landlady here when the fire started?"

Spud shook his head at the newspaper man. "She went with some ladies from her church to Watervale. A miner got hisself hurt, and Fantasy and the others were gonna take his wife the money they collected."

"It's a good thing. That place went like that." Purdy snapped his fingers. "If your landlady had been inside, I don't think the firemen could've gotten her out safely."

Spud nodded glumly.

"That was one hell of a blaze," the man mused more to himself than to Spud. "Worse than the one last year, I hear. Good thing the wind didn't pick up or the whole town could've been wiped out." Mumbling about the need to do something about the town's water supply, Purdy ambled off to dig up more tidbits for his story.

Spud shifted his gaze back to what was left of the boardinghouse. In a ragged voice, he whispered, "Aye, Fantasy is safe. But what about Robby?"

Ignoring the tears streaming unchecked down his cheeks, Spud continued to stare at the devastation the fire had caused. He heard someone running on the boardwalk but didn't look up. The person's horrified gasp finally pulled him from his stupor.

"Spud? My God, Spud, what happened?"

He swallowed a sob, then lifted his face. "Oh, Fantasy, lass, the fire. It were mighty terrible. The whole block was one ball of flame in no time a'tall. I tried to get down the alley, but they wouldn't let me. They made me move down the block cuz Spangenberg's Gun Shop was already on fire. I wanted to die when I saw yer house go up like a matchstick. Oh, Fantasy, lass, I tried. Believe me I tried. Please don't be hatin' me."

Fantasy stared at the haggard face of the old miner, her eyes still wide with shock over what she'd seen after returning to town. Looking around and not seeing her son, Spud's disjointed explanation became painfully clear. If Robby wasn't with Spud . . .

Tears running down her own face, she sank to her knees in front of the now sobbing Spud. She reached out and touched his quaking shoulder and asked the question she had to ask. "Where's Robby?"

Spud sniffed loudly. "I left him playin' behind yer house. I sat out front, and I guess I musta fell asleep, cuz the next thing I knowed, the fire bell is a clangin' and the fire wagons are a comin' down the street." He sniffed again. "I couldn't believe my eyes. I just stared as the flames came this way. That's when I be rememberin' Robby and I started down the alley." He pulled a handkerchief from his pocket, dabbed at his eyes, then blew his nose with a loud honk.

"Did you find him?"

Spud shook his head wearily, a fresh gush of tears spurting from his eyes. "A fireman stopped me, said I couldn't be goin' into the alley and made me move up the street. I watched the men fighting the fire, but it weren't no use. Yer house was gone in no time."

"Could Robby have gotten out another way?"

Spud blew his nose again and scrubbed at his reddened eyes. "I thought a that, too. But the fire spread so fast I ain't sure he had time. And even if he did, I been a waiting here every minute since the fire got put out and he ain't come home." He drew a deep shaky breath. "I don't think he made it, lass."

The tenuous thread holding her pain at bay while Spud told his story snapped. Falling into his arms, a strangled cry escaped her lips. "Nooooo."

As they walked through the network of tunnels beneath Tombstone, Jesse wondered how Robby knew about the entrance they'd used. He'd heard about the tunnels from Nick. Once part of the Goodenough Mine, they honeycombed the area beneath Hop Town and were used by the Chinese for gambling and opium dens. Seeing his young, smoke-covered companion had evidently gotten over his initial shock, Jesse's thoughts turned back to the boy's mother and whether she had escaped the fire. At the moment there was nothing he could do to find out, so he asked the question nagging at him. "How did you know about this tunnel, Robby?"

"I saw Mr. Lawson go into the lean-to one time, but he never came out. I went inside, but he wasn't in there. Next time I watched him through a crack in the wall, and I saw him go through the door in the floor."

So that's how Lawson got out of town without anyone seeing him! "Does anybody else know about the trap door or the tunnels?"

Robby's shoulders lifted. "Don't know."

Jesse thought about Robby's words while they worked their way through the underground passageway. Did Fantasy also know about the tunnels? Maybe she was the one who showed Lawson the trap door, after all it was on her property. His ruminating halted when the angle of the tunnel changed to an incline. They picked up their pace and soon came out at ground level near the center of Hop Town.

"Can we go find Momma?"

"Do you know where she is?"

"She went with Aunt Mattie to see some lady. Her husband got hurt and Momma was gonna take her some money."

Robby's answer eased Jesse's fears about Fantasy's safety. Then something else the boy said registered. "She took money to a lady whose husband was hurt?"

Robby nodded.

"Where did she get the money?" He waited for the boy's answer, his heart thundering in his ears.

"She helped the other ladies in our church collect it."

The hammering of his heart had begun to ease when Robby's next statement sent it back into double time.

"Mr. Lawson gave her some money."

Jesse forced himself to exhale slowly. Was Fantasy collecting for some charity the other times Robby saw

her take money from Jack Lawson? And was that also
an explanation for the scene Jesse witnessed between
Fantasy and Lawson? Don't read more into this than
there is, he cautioned himself. The first time he'd discussed Fantasy with Nick, his friend said she worked
with the Ladies Aid Society from her church. That still
didn't rule out the possibility the money he'd seen
change hands was a pay off. Nor did it prove Fantasy
wasn't part of Lawson's gang.

"Can we go find my Momma now?"

Though uncertain what this latest bit of information
meant to his investigation, Jesse smiled. "You bet,
Buckshot. Let's go find your Momma."

Her heart-wracking sobs reduced to an occasional
sniffle, it took several seconds for Fantasy to realize
she and Spud were no longer alone.

"Momma? Why're you crying, Momma?"

Turning toward the sound, Fantasy pulled her rumpled skirts from beneath her knees and struggled to her
feet.

"Robby? Oh, thank God!" As she stooped to gather
her son into her arms, a fresh rush of tears streamed
down her face, tears of joy. "Are you okay, sweetheart? Momma's so glad to see you," she murmured
into his smoke-scented hair.

"I'm fine, Momma. Jesse saved me."

Fantasy glanced up to find Jesse standing unobtrusively nearby. For a brief instant, their gazes met and
held. As her gaze traveled over Jesse's soot-covered
face and his torn and scorched clothing, Robby's explanation drifted in and out, mixing with her thoughts.
". . . playin' in the back yard . . ." *Jesse looks tired.* "I
heard the fire bell and . . ." *I hope Jesse's not hurt.*
"Then Jesse found me and we went into the tunnel,
and . . ."

Her son's last words caught her attention. "Tunnel?"

"Yeah, Momma, the—"

"The tunnel running from behind your house to Hop Town," Jesse interrupted, watching her face carefully.

Fantasy's brow puckered at his statement, but she didn't comment. Her brain probably hadn't even registered what he said, Jesse realized with a pang of disappointment.

"I . . . I can't thank you enough, Jesse. You saved Robby and I'll be eternally grateful. I wish there was some way I could repay you."

Jesse shook his head. "That's not important, Fantasy."

"Yes, it is important. My son means the world to me, and I owe you for rescuing him."

Seeing the stubborn angle of her chin, Jesse replied, "We'll talk about this later. Right now there are more pressing things to take care of."

Fantasy winced when she glanced at Robby's filthy clothes and her own wrinkled dress. Looking across the street, she sighed. "Yes, we have only the clothes we're wearing, and—" Her eyes widened. "We don't have a place to stay tonight."

Taking Fantasy's elbow, Jesse said. "Yes, you do. You're going home with me. I have an extra bedroom where the two of you can stay."

"Can we, Momma? Can we stay with Jesse?"

Lowering Robby to his feet, Fantasy brushed his hair back from his face. "I don't know, sweetheart. That's an awful imposition on Jesse."

Robby turned his hope-filled face up to Jesse's. "I won't be an impo . . . impo . . . whatever that word is, Jesse. I promise."

Jesse chuckled and ruffled the boy's hair playfully. "I know you won't, Buckshot." Shifting his gaze to Fantasy, he added, "And your mother won't be an imposition either. I have a housekeeper with time on her hands, and I'm sure she'll have no objections to my bringing home guests."

Seeing Fantasy still didn't look convinced, Jesse decided on another tact. "Think of the boy," he whispered. "Do you have another place you can take him?" Before she could answer, he continued. "He's exhausted, he needs a bath and he's probably hungry."

Fantasy saw the concern on Jesse's face and knew he spoke the truth. Mattie's place was too small for two more people, and the hotels and boardinghouses left unscathed by the fire would be crowded with others in the same circumstance. Looking down at her son, his pitiful appearance brought fresh tears to her eyes. She looked back at Jesse and nodded her agreement.

Jesse grasped her elbow more firmly and pulled her gently down the boardwalk. "You'll be okay, won't you, Spud?" he called over his shoulder.

"Aye, I'll just be bunking in with Con at the livery. Don't be worrying none about the likes a me, I'll be a heading back to me mine in a few days."

Skirting the slow-to-disburse crowd and the men standing guard to make sure the fire didn't rekindle, Jesse escorted his guests toward his house. Glad he'd been able to convince Fantasy to stay with him, he tried to convince himself he'd extended the invitation in order to keep an eye on her. While that was true enough, he also knew it wasn't the only reason.

As Fantasy walked beside Jesse and her son, her head spun with conflicting emotions over the events of the last few minutes: shock at losing her house and everything she owned; gratitude to Jesse for saving her son and for offering them a place to stay; and panic at the idea of living in such proximity to Jesse. Although he'd lived in her boardinghouse, at least she'd had the buffer of their rooms being on separate floors. That would no longer be the case in the single-story house she'd heard Jesse describe to Robby.

Well, there was no hope for it now. Circumstances being what they were, she and Robby had no choice except move in with Jesse.

* * *

Once Robby had been bathed, fed, and tucked into bed wearing one of Jesse's old shirts, Fantasy waited nervously for her host to return. She sat in the parlor of Jesse's house, idly twisting a strand of hair. Freshly washed and brushed nearly dry, she'd left the heavy tresses down after her bath. Jesse had gone to one of the bath houses in town to give her and Robby some privacy. She wished he'd hurry. She had something to talk to him about and wanted to get it over with. Just then she heard the clomp of his boots on the porch followed by the squawking of the front door. Rising from the settee, she turned to face the hall, her heart pounding in her ears.

Jesse started when he saw Fantasy standing in his parlor. She looked more beautiful than he thought possible. She wore the silk dressing gown he'd retrieved, along with a few other things, from Mattie as soon as he'd deposited Fantasy and Robby in his house.

Fantasy's face glowed pink and shiny from her bath, her green eyes sparkled in the lamp light, and her hair—it was her loose hair that sent desire rushing to his groin with blinding speed. His hands clenched into fists at his sides to keep himself from touching those lustrous auburn locks, he stepped farther into the room. "I thought you'd be in bed."

The look in his eyes and his husky voice nearly sent Fantasy running from the room. But she held her ground. "I'm not really tired, and besides I wanted to speak to you."

"Oh, about what?"

Standing next to her, his overpowering masculine presence nearly made her swoon. Dropping back onto the settee, she took a deep breath. "It's about our conversation this afternoon. I meant what I said about wanting to pay you for saving Robby's life."

"Fantasy, I told you. That's not—"

"Yes, it is, Jesse. You deserve a reward for your bravery." She sighed. "I lost everything in the fire so I don't know how I can pay you, but I still intend to, somehow."

One eyebrow quirked with amusement, Jesse sat down next to her and studied her upturned face. No longer able to curb his overwhelming need to touch her, he lightly stroked her cheek with the tip of one finger. "Is that right?"

Resisting the urge to shiver at his touch, Fantasy realized she'd left herself open. Obviously, Jesse could think of a way. *Well, you've gone this far, you might as well go the whole hog.* She squared her shoulders, met his gaze steadily and nodded. "Do you have a suggestion?"

Jesse blinked with surprise. *My God, I was only teasing, but she's serious! She actually plans to repay a debt she thinks she owes.* He wouldn't be so callous as to accept payment for saving a boy he'd come to love. Yet, for a brief moment he allowed himself to picture what he could ask for. Another rush of white-hot need surged through him. Tamping down his desire, he exhaled slowly. "Listen, Fantasy, this has been one hellish day, and I think we both need some rest." With that he rose from the settee.

"But—"

"Look, I'll think about it, and we'll discuss it again in a few days. Okay?"

She murmured her acceptance, then watched him leave the room. She closed her eyes and sighed. *Well, now you've done it.* She hadn't missed the unmistakable desire flash in Jesse's eyes, and for a moment she wished she could take back her words. But she owed Jesse for saving her son, and she'd do whatever he asked in payment. Unlike a man, she intended to keep her word. Only, what if he asks me to—her eyes flying open, she leaped to her feet.

Marching to the bedroom where Robby slept, she told herself not to think about it. Unfortunately, her mind didn't listen.

Chapter 8

The first five days after the fire were the longest Fantasy had ever known. What Jesse might ask of her continually occupied her thoughts. Even the escape of sleep didn't free her from imagining his possible response, her dreams filled with the various consequences of her trauma-induced rash words.

In the first dream, Jesse asked for nothing more than a kiss, then in the next his kisses advanced to touching her, the next to full-fledged caresses. After that, each dream became progressively more erotic until the one the previous night. She'd woken breathless, bathed in sweat, her entire body throbbing for some unknown relief.

Now as she helped Mei-Ling clear the dinner dishes from the table, the dream replayed in her mind's eye. Short vignettes appeared in her head like view cards played one after another through a stereoscope.

The dream began as she and Jesse entered an elegantly furnished hotel suite with an equally sumptuous private bathroom. As soon as the porter deposited their luggage in the suite and left, Jesse began stripping off his clothes. Then the scene changed. Fantasy saw herself naked and kneeling on the bathroom floor next to where Jesse sat in the filled bathtub. His head resting against the back of the tub, she leaned over to run a sponge across his furred chest.

Recalling her dream made Fantasy's pulse pound

loudly in her ears. The tips of her fingers tingled as if she could feel the silky hair covering Jesse's muscular chest. She had to bite her lip to stifle a moan of pleasure. Hoping she hadn't let the sound slip out, she glanced at Mei-Ling. Relieved to see the young woman busy at her task, Fantasy heaved a thankful sigh.

"What Missy Fantasy doing today?" Mei-Ling asked as she finished clearing the table.

Fantasy stared at the lovely Chinese girl for several seconds. Although the two women had shared the same house for five days, they'd never had a private conversation. When Jesse introduced them, Mei-Ling merely bowed her greeting, then slipped from the room. That's how it had been since, Mei-Ling keeping to herself, quickly appearing and disappearing throughout the house. Though Fantasy had never spoken directly to the girl, she had overheard several conversations between Mei-Ling and Jesse.

"Mei-Ling, it isn't necessary to talk to me in Pidgin English. I know you speak English as well as I do."

Mei-Ling flushed and dropped her gaze to the dishes piled on the table. "I'm sorry, and you're right. My mother insisted I learn to speak English and Chinese equally well. But my uncle says barbarian Americans—" Her flushed deepened. "—expect us to speak like stupid Chinks."

Fantasy's outrage at Mei-Ling's words flared. She hated to see anyone mistreated the way the Chinese were. Just because their skin was a different color and they dressed differently didn't give Americans the right to call them such horrible names. Yet, she'd heard the Chinese of Tombstone called Pigtails, Chinks, or worse. She pushed her fury at the prejudice against Orientals aside. "You don't speak to Jesse like that. Do you?"

Mei-Ling shook her bowed head. Her long, black braid danced on her back with the movement.

"Then, I don't want you speaking to me, or my son, that way either. You're an intelligent, educated young woman, and I won't have you talking like the fools in this town think you should." Touching the girl's arm, she added in a soft voice, "Do we have an agreement, Mei-Ling?"

The girl bobbed her head once, then lifted dark tear-filled eyes to meet Fantasy's gaze. "You are very kind to me, Fantasy, and I won't forget."

Grabbing a stack of dishes, Fantasy headed for the kitchen. "Come on, let's get these washed. I have some shopping to do this afternoon; Robby and I still need a few things. Would you like to come with me?"

Mei-Ling's face drained of color. "No, I . . . I can't, I have work to do."

"Yes, you can. I'm sure Jesse would give you a few hours off to go shopping. Shall I ask him for you?"

"No! Really, I can't go." Mei-Ling lived with the constant fear China Mary would somehow be unable to protect her if she left the security of Jesse's house. She refused to go anywhere near Hop Town, afraid her uncle or Hing Fat might abduct her right off the street.

Fantasy saw the look of terror on Mei-Ling's face before the girl turned away, and realized she was terrified of leaving the house. Not pressing for an explanation, Fantasy set the stack of dishes in the wash basin, then moved to the stove and picked up the teakettle of hot water. "Well, maybe some other time."

Mei-Ling squeezed her eyes tightly closed, grateful Fantasy hadn't pressed her further. "I'd like that," she finally replied honestly, hoping her future would allow the opportunity.

After Fantasy finished the last of her shopping at Cohen's Clothing Store on Allen Street, she stopped by the Clapp and Murray Insurance Agency. Assured the claim for her boardinghouse would be paid within a month, she left a few minutes later. She headed back to Jesse's house, relieved she'd spent part of the cash Thomas left her to buy insurance—most of the businesses lost in the fire weren't insured. Still, she was disappointed the rebuilding of her home wouldn't begin sooner.

She didn't like being beholden to Jesse for the roof over her head, but until she got her insurance money she couldn't afford to live elsewhere. At least she'd had enough money in the bank to buy herself and Robby new clothes and had been able to refuse Jesse's offer to clothe them. She certainly didn't want to be indebted to him for anything else.

Her activities that afternoon had thankfully kept the dream she'd had the previous night from entering her mind. But walking into Jesse's house and catching a whiff of his sandalwood shaving soap, the titillating yet disturbing dream returned—this time several vignettes later into the scene in the hotel bathroom.

After she'd washed Jesse's chest and arms, he pulled her into the tub with him, sloshing water over the sides and onto the tile floor. He nipped her neck in mock ferocity, growling deep in his chest, while his hands explored her curves. Retrieving the sponge, he carefully and thoroughly bathed her until she quivered with desire and anticipation. Satisfied he'd aroused her senses to a fever pitch, Jesse tossed the sponge across the room. It hit the wall with a loud smack, sliding to the floor and leaving a soapy trail down the flowered wallpaper.

His hands around her waist, Jesse lifted and turned her until she sat astraddle his thighs. Murmuring her name, he moved his hands upward to cup her breasts, his thumbs gently rubbing her nipples in circular motions.

Eyes closed, her head thrown back, an animal-like moan vibrated in her throat. "Jesse."

"What?"

Fantasy came crashing out of her dream with a gasp of shock. Whirling around, her packages flew out of her arms. One hand pressed over her pounding heart, her wide-eyed stare found Jesse standing in the parlor doorway. She inhaled deeply, then said, "You scared the daylights out of me."

"Sorry." Jesse cocked his head at her questioningly, then stepped into the room. "Here, let me help you." He bent to gather up the packages scattered at Fantasy's feet. "Did you want something?"

"Want something?" For an instant the dream came flooding back. Yes, she did indeed want something, but she couldn't tell him that! "No, I didn't want anything."

"Hmm, I could have sworn I heard you call me," he murmured as he straightened. Looking down at her, he noted her dilated eyes and deep blush. A cold chill darted up his spine. "You look flushed. Are you ill?"

"No, I . . . I, um . . ." Fantasy cleared her throat, unable to meet his gaze. "I'm just a little warm. I spent all afternoon shopping. Both Robby and I still needed some things. I had to go to nearly every store in town. You'd think I would be used to the heat by now, but I guess it must have gotten to me today." Realizing she was rattling on foolishly, she clamped her mouth shut.

Jesse studied her face during her rambling discourse and decided she didn't look feverish in spite of her bright color. Yet her odd behavior concerned him. "Are you sure you're okay?"

"Yes, I'm fine."

"Good, I don't want you taking sick, 'cause I've finally decided what I want as my boon."

Accepting the packages from his outstretched hands, Fantasy looked up at him sharply. "You have?" She hoped her quaking insides didn't show when she added, "What do you want?" She took a deep, steadying breath, bracing herself for the worst.

Seeing the fear flash across her face, Jesse's brows drew together. "Have you changed your mind?" After the thought he'd put into his decision, he hoped not. He'd never intended to accept any kind of reward for

saving Robby from the fire. At the time, he only said
he'd think about it to placate a very distraught Fantasy. In truth, he'd hoped she would forget the whole
episode. Yet the more he thought about it, he finally
decided he could use the opportunity for his own selfish reasons. Though having just seen her reaction, his
plans could go for naught.

"No. I haven't changed my mind." Her voice was a
husky whisper.

"In that case, I want you to go with me to the
theatre, and then to a late supper at the Café François
tomorrow night."

"The theatre and dinner?" Her eyes widened.
"That's all?"

"Of course, what did you expect?"

"I don't know," she hedged, her mind swirling for a
plausible answer. "Money. Jewelry." She gave a feeble
laugh. "You know, something more valuable."

"Would you rather I ask for something else?"

"No," she answered quickly, then smiled, hoping
the relief hadn't been too evident in her voice. "The
theatre and dinner will be just fine."

"I'll be busy most of tomorrow, so if I don't see you
during the day, we should leave for the theatre at
seven-thirty. Do you want me to ask Spud to watch
Robby?"

"No. He left for his mine this morning. I'll see if
Mattie can keep Robby. She complained the other day
about how he hadn't stayed with her in a long time."

"Fine. Well, I have to be going." On sudden impulse, Jesse leaned down and planted a brief but firm
kiss on her mouth. "Bye," he murmured as he pulled
away.

Flashing a bright smile, he left her standing in the
parlor, packages still clutched in her hands, the scent
of sandalwood surrounding her. "Bye," she whispered
belatedly, then walked to her bedroom. As she methodically opened the packages and put away the
clothes she'd bought, she realized her growing ward-

robe didn't include anything appropriate for the theatre. What a shame she'd lost the green silk she'd worn to the St. Patrick's ball. Although all her clothes had been destroyed in the fire, she lamented the loss of that dress the most.

"I'll have to see if Mattie has something I can wear," she murmured aloud, folding the last of her purchases, a shirt for Robby, and tucking it into a dresser drawer. She gathered up the wrapping paper and string, making a mental list of what she needed to do the following day. *I'll see Mattie first thing. Then I need to stop by the church to see if the aid society needs me for anything. And I'll have to get back here in time to wash and dry my hair after my bath.*

Bath! There was that word again. Fantasy wasn't certain if she'd ever be able to say—or even think—the word without remembering her dream about bathing with Jesse. Not only bathing, she recalled with vivid clarity, they'd done a whole lot more than bathe. Was it really possible to make love in the cramped confines of a bathtub? She'd awakened before her dream had revealed the answer. Now she found herself pondering the question.

"Stop it," she nearly shouted, holding her hands over her ears, as if that would stop her thoughts from wandering down such a disquieting path. When her control returned, Fantasy left the bedroom, determined to put the dream and all the questions it spawned from her mind once and for all. She knew if she didn't, the alternative would easily be insanity.

"Oh, Mattie, I'm so happy for you." Fantasy gave her friend a tight hug. "So, when did Nash propose, and when's the big event?"

"Last night, and we haven't set a date yet. But within a month I think. Will you stand up with us, Fantasy?"

"Of course I will, I'd be honored. Will you be able to go on a honeymoon?"

"Yes, Nash is making arrangements for another teacher to take his place for a couple of months. He wants to take me to meet his family in Georgia, then we're going to visit my sister in Pennsylvania. Isn't Nash wonderful? I'm so lucky to have found him." Mattie sighed contentedly, tears of joy springing to her eyes.

Fantasy hugged her friend again. "Yes, you're very lucky, Mattie. And Nash is just as lucky to be marrying such a fine woman."

Mattie smiled, wiping her eyes with the corner of her apron. "So, how're Robby and Jesse?"

"They're fine. Robby is growing faster than a weed. I can barely keep that child in clothes. And Jesse is . . ." Her voice trailed off, a far-away look settling in her eyes.

"Jesse's what?"

Fantasy blinked, realizing she'd once again been caught in the snare of daydreaming about Jesse. "He's fine," she answered quickly, then changed the subject. "Listen, Mattie, I came to ask if you could keep Robby tonight, and if you have an evening dress I can wear."

"Of course, I'll keep Robby, and I probably have something that will fit you. What's the occasion?"

"Oh, nothing really," Fantasy replied, running her fingers over a length of pale pink faille. "Jesse asked me to the theatre, then to supper."

Mattie noticed her friend's high color and sparkling eyes, and knew the night was more than *nothing*. She still couldn't figure out why Fantasy fought the bit so hard where Jesse was concerned.

While Mattie pinned the necessary alterations on a stunning black silk evening gown, she quizzed Fantasy about the man she thought was perfect for her friend.

Preoccupied with the upcoming evening, Fantasy gave only monosyllable responses to Mattie's questions.

Frustrated with Fantasy's lack of cooperation, Mattie jabbed one pin into the dress with too much force, pricking Fantasy's skin.

"Ouch! Watch what you're doing, Mattie. I'm not a pincushion."

"Sorry. Guess my mind kinda drifted there for a minute. I understand Spud headed back to his mine."

"Yes, he left yesterday morning. I think he was tired of sleeping in the stable with Con." Fantasy chuckled. "Besides, this was the longest he's ever been in town. He always got the itch to get back to prospecting long before now." Her voice lost its light-hearted tone. "I wish he'd forget about looking for gold. He's too old to be digging in that mine of his. One of these days he could go in and not come out." Her shoulders rippled with a shudder.

"Stop being such a worrywart. Spud can take care of himself."

"I suppose you're right."

They spent the rest of Fantasy's visit talking about the upcoming wedding while Mattie put the finishing touches on the black silk dress. When Fantasy left with the gown later that morning, she felt a pang of envy at Mattie's good fortune.

Stop feeling sorry for yourself, Fantasy Williams. Mattie has Nash and you have Robby. Though she loved her son with all her heart, the comparison didn't help much. She still had an aching hollowness inside. An ache she feared no man—even Jesse—would be able to ease.

Forget-Me-Not, starring Miss Jeffrey-Lewis, was the premier performance for the acting troupe's first night in town. Traveling theatrical companies were very popular in Tombstone, and opening night was performed to another full house at Schieffelin Hall.

After the curtain came down for the last time and

the actors had taken their final bows, Jesse escorted
Fantasy through the departing crowd.

"Did you enjoy the play, Fantasy?"

Turning to look up at him, her face glowed with
excitement. "Oh, yes, it was wonderful. I love the
theatre."

Jesse looped her hand through his arm and turned
them toward Allen Street and the Café François.
"You'd like San Francisco. Some of the best theatres
are there, and the world's best acting companies take
turns performing."

"San Francisco? Is that where you live?" In the time
she'd known Jesse they'd never discussed his home.
She knew he'd been born and raised in Texas where his
parents still lived, but little else.

"Yes, I've lived there for the past four years." When
a drunken miner swaggered out of the Capitol Saloon,
nearly colliding with them, Jesse pulled Fantasy more
tightly against him. The scent of her gardenia perfume
wafted up to him in the still-warm evening air, sending
his senses reeling. He shook his head to clear the sudden dizziness.

"I thought you worked for a New York land company."

"I do. I work out of their California office." *Careful,
McAllister, you nearly muffed it that time.* He cursed
himself for once again not being able to concentrate on
his work when Fantasy was near and for having to lie
to the woman he loved.

"Are you hungry?" he asked, hoping to steer the
conversation in a safer direction.

"Starved." She turned a dazzling smile up at him,
making his heart pick up its rhythm.

Jesse ordered fresh fish, brought in from the Gulf of
California packed in ice, and a bottle of excellent
French wine.

In spite of saying she was starved, the evening had
been so exciting that Fantasy drank more than she ate,
making her feel wonderfully gay and carefree. Her

tongue loosened by the wine, she carried on an almost flirtatious dinner conversation with Jesse. She couldn't let the opportunity pass to tease him about playing marbles with her son.

He laughed at her slightly slurred speech. "I didn't mind getting dirty. Robby is a terrific boy, and I really enjoyed our game of marbles. You should try it sometime." He flashed her a devilish smile.

"Yes, maybe I should." Returning his smile, she lifted her gaze from her contemplation of his mouth to look into his amused blue eyes, their green flecks more pronounced.

Jesse had the feeling she referred to something other than playing marbles with a five-year-old boy. Deciding it must be the wine, he shoved the possible double entendre aside. "Are you ready to go?"

She nodded, then downed the last of her wine. "Lead on."

He assisted her from the table, then kept his hand pressed against her lower back as he escorted her across the restaurant. The intense heat of her skin burned through the black silk rustling beneath his fingers, sending an equally hot flame of desire searing through him. He clenched his teeth until he conquered the flare of need.

Content just to have Fantasy by his side, Jesse didn't speak during the several block walk to his house. Entering the parlor, he turned up the lamp Mei-Ling had left burning then turned to face Fantasy.

The sight of her in the low-cut gown, her exposed skin even creamier next to the black silk when bathed in the soft glow of lamplight, sent his pulse into another wild rhythm. His groin grew painfully full.

Never taking his eyes from her face, he approached her with slow, measured steps. Stopping directly in front of her, he cupped her chin with one hand. "You're so beautiful, Fancy. I want to kiss you. I've wanted to kiss you all evening, and now I'm going to."

As Jesse lowered his face to hers, her eyes fluttered

shut. Pulling her fully against him, he explored her mouth, nipping with his teeth, then soothing with his tongue. He sipped at her lower lip and teased the sensitive, velvety skin in the delicate groove of her upper lip.

Fantasy felt herself slipping away, completely powerless to do anything about it. She found herself transported to a world she knew little about—a world of sensual pleasures like nothing she had ever imagined, a world where Jesse reigned as undisputed master.

Acting totally on instinct, she pressed closer, grinding her hips against his muscular thighs. She heard his deep groan and felt the hard length of his arousal throbbing insistently between their bodies. Reveling in her apparent power over this man and her wine-softened inhibitions, she slipped her tongue into his mouth. She charted the sharp edges of his teeth, the silky underside of his lips, before concentrating on the rougher texture of his tongue.

Jesse grasped Fantasy's upper arms and wrenched away from her mind-boggling assault on his mouth. "Slow down, Fantasy. Much more of that and I might just carry you to my bedroom."

She stared up at him, chewing on her swollen bottom lip. What she wanted became crystal clear. Her voice was very low when she spoke. "I *want* you to carry me to your bedroom."

Jesse studied her through narrowed eyes for several long moments. "Do you know what you're saying?"

She nodded.

With a growl, Jesse swept her up into his arms. In his room, he set her on her feet next to the bed. After lighting a lamp on the bedside table and closing the door, he turned back to her. His gaze burned into hers, trying to read the thoughts behind her passion-darkened eyes.

"Are you absolutely certain?" He hoped his voice betrayed none of the apprehension he felt. As much as he wanted to make love with Fantasy, the prospect of competing with her dead husband terrified him. Fear of losing the competition made his voice unusually harsh when he added, "I don't want to get you into my bed, then have you change your mind."

"I won't change my mind, but . . ." Unable to finish, she dropped her gaze.

"But what?"

Twisting her hands in front of her, she finally said, "I'm afraid I'll disappoint you."

"Disappoint me?" Jesse nearly laughed. That's exactly what he'd been thinking, only he'd worried he would be the one doing the disappointing. He crossed the room, and ran the pads of his fingers across her right cheekbone. "Fantasy, I don't think you could ever disappoint me."

"You don't understand." She lifted her head and forced herself to meet his gaze. "I never—" Clearing her throat, she tried again. "I never enjoyed it when Thomas . . . I mean, he never hurt me, but I didn't. . . . That is . . . it had to be me. . . Thomas said I . . ." Seeing a muscle jump in Jesse's jaw, her words trailed off. She turned away, his apparent fury too painful to watch.

In spite of trying to be unaffected by Fantasy's revealing words, Jesse's anger sprang to life with surprising force. How could the bastard do that to her? It was bad enough Thomas Williams had never given her the pleasure she should have known. Letting her think she was at fault was far worse. Furious with the man, Jesse fleetingly wished Thomas were still alive so he could pound some sense into the man.

As Jesse strove to control his need to throttle Fantasy's deceased husband, compassion seeped into his mind, slowly replacing his anger. Realizing how difficult it must have been for her to make such a painful confession, the last of his anger melted away.

Pulling her into his arms, Jesse rocked her gently, one cheek pressed to the top of her head. "Forgive me for saying this, sweetheart, but Thomas was a fool. It wasn't your fault you didn't enjoy his attentions, and there's nothing wrong with you. The way you respond to my kisses is proof of that."

"Really?" she asked tentatively, her voice muffled against his chest.

"Yes, my innocent darling, really." Jesse smiled into her hair, then held her at arms' length. "Will you let me show you?"

She searched his face for some sort of trickery. Then, smiling timidly, she whispered, "Yes."

Jesse brushed her mouth with his, then carefully began undressing her. He worked slowly, lingering over each new patch of skin exposed to his hungry gaze.

At last she stood before him, completely naked. Quivering with a mixture of apprehension and excitement, Fantasy helped Jesse slip out of his clothes. Her eyes widened at her first view of a totally naked man. Thomas had always worn a nightshirt, even when he—she shoved that thought aside. Thomas wasn't the man in front of her. Jesse was here—tender, gentle, beautifully male, Jesse.

Her gaze feasted on his wide shoulders, hair-covered chest, and flat stomach. Forcing herself to look lower, his thick arousal brought a flash of intense heat to her cheeks. She quickly moved the focus of her attention to his heavily muscled thighs and calves, realizing her dreams hadn't done him justice.

Tossing back the covers, he slipped into bed, then pulled her down next to him. The cool sheets brought little relief to Jesse's burning skin.

Using more patience than he thought he possessed, he began the slow, gentle lesson of showing Fantasy how wonderful the act of loving could be. His fingers and mouth patiently played her like the finest of instruments. Like the maestro of an orchestra, he coaxed her body to produce a symphony more beautiful than any he'd ever heard. He touched her everywhere, her full breasts, satiny stomach, shapely legs, and the petals of her woman's flesh. All the while he teased and tasted her mouth in one heated kiss after another.

A flame of desire licked at each place Jesse touched, making Fantasy moan and writhe beside him. Unable to remain still, her hands explored his chest and back with increasingly bolder caresses. He groaned, shifting to allow her access to new territory. She was surprised to learn giving Jesse pleasure greatly increased her own. Her fingers tunneled through the hair on his chest, skimmed over his ribs, and gently kneaded the hard plane of his stomach.

When her fingers grazed his inner thigh, Jesse sucked in an agonized breath through gritted teeth. His hand grasped hers and pulled it away before she touched his throbbing manhood. "Not tonight, Fancy, I don't have enough control for that this time," he murmured before closing his mouth over hers.

Her lips opened for him. Her tongue parried with his in the duel of lovers, stoking the fire raging through him even hotter. At last he could hold back no longer.

He rose above her, settled between her opened thighs, and eased into her. Hot, moist, and unbelievably tight, she surrounded him, pulling him deeper and deeper. He partially withdrew, then sank back into her welcoming flesh. Repeating the motion, he felt his release begin.

It had been too long and Fantasy was so tight. "Oh God, Fancy, I can't wait," he groaned against her neck.

With two more quick, hard thrusts, he spilled himself deep in her depths.

Slowly the room righted itself as Jesse's senses returned. He rolled to his side, pulling Fantasy tightly against him. "Sorry, sweetheart. It wasn't very gentlemanly of me to leave you like that."

She drew a deep, shaky breath. "It's okay," she managed to say, hot tears of disappointment clogging her throat. She'd hoped it would be different with Jesse; he'd assured her it would be. He'd even called her Fancy, the nickname her mother had given her. Apparently they'd both been wrong—there *was* something wrong with her.

Sensing her sudden withdrawal, Jesse rose up on one elbow to study her face. "What is it, Fantasy? Did I hurt you?"

She shook her head, closing her eyes to his penetrating stare.

Understanding the look of defeat he'd glimpsed in her eyes, Jesse felt like a cad, disgusted with his behavior. *Helluva time to lose control. Fantasy thinks she can't experience pleasure because there's something wrong with her, and I add fuel to the notion by rutting like a green boy.*

"Look at me, Fantasy," he ordered softly.

She hesitated for a second, then thought better of it and slowly lifted her eyelids.

The pain he saw reflected in her eyes cramped his insides. "There's nothing wrong with you."

When she turned away, he grasped her chin and forced her to look at him. "I mean it, Fantasy. It was me this time; I was too quick for you. Do you understand what I'm saying? It was my fault, not yours, that you were left unsatisfied."

Removing his hand from her chin, he lowered it to the triangle of auburn curls between her thighs. He slipped two fingers through the downy nest until he touched the hard pearl of flesh nestled in the folds.

She jerked in reaction to his touch, her breath catching in her throat.

He smiled a lazy, I-told-you-so smile. "See, your body is still ready for pleasuring. I bet you ache there, don't you, sweetheart?"

She nodded, her eyes wide with wonder.

"Kiss me, Fancy. Kiss me, and I'll show you what you've been missing." He brought his mouth down on hers, his fingers beginning a slow, easy rhythm.

Her hips lifted and fell with each stroke of his hand. Her breathing became short, gasping pants. The pressure continued to build, a heavy fullness spreading outward from beneath Jesse's hand until her entire body throbbed with the need to find an end to the exquisite torment.

Just when she thought she couldn't stand a moment longer, a strangled cry erupted from her throat. As the convulsions of her release began, her body arched upward, her head rolled from side to side, one fist clutched a handful of sheet.

"That's it, love, that's it. Stay with it. Let it take you." Jesse's voice penetrated the fog of unbelievable sensations coursing through her.

His fingers still working their magic, his words of encouragement took her over the edge. Her hips bucked wildly against his hand. With a sob of joy she arched up one final time, then collapsed back on the bed.

Fantasy felt like she was floating, her body boneless and limp, on some unknown sea. When she finally opened her eyes, she met Jesse's amused gaze.

"Didn't I tell you?"

"Tell me what?" Her tongue felt thick, her mouth dry as cotton.

"I told you there was nothing wrong with you. Now do you believe me?"

She giggled. "Yes. It was wonderful, like nothing I've ever imagined."

He chuckled, then gave her a tender kiss. "You're wonderful, my beautiful Fancy. Next time it will be easier, now that you know what to expect."

She didn't reply, but snuggled next to him, sighing with contentment. Sleep claimed her as soon as her eyes drifted shut.

Jesse stayed awake a little longer, his thoughts on the beautiful woman nestled in his arms and snoring softly against his chest. *Fantasy, you truly are a marvel.* He smiled up at the ceiling. *I think I may have unleashed the wanton in you.*

When he remembered his reason for being in Tombstone, his smile faded. He closed his eyes, willing sleep to overtake him. Sleep came slowly, one disquieting question refusing to go away. *Am I willing to jeopardize my career because of my love for Fantasy?*

Chapter 9

"Fancy, love, wake up." Jesse accompanied his words with soft nibbles along the length of her neck. His lips lingered on the pulse point at the base of her throat. He smiled against her warm skin. Her heart hadn't been this calm a few hours ago.

Twice during the night, he'd pulled her from the depths of sated sleep to thoroughly explore the sensual pleasures created by the joining of their bodies. Just before he fell asleep the last time, he was certain it would be days before he recovered from such vigorous loving. Now, lifting his head to stare down at Fantasy's profile, the stirring of desire began anew. There isn't time, he reminded himself. Dawn was fast approaching.

"Fancy. Come on, love, it's time to get you back to your room." He pushed a lock of wavy hair off her face, then brushed his mouth across her temple. "Fancy."

"Hmm." Fantasy rolled toward the sound of his voice, a small smile curving her lips. "Jesse," she murmured in a silky whisper.

Jesse nearly lost control at the sound of his name on her lips. He took a deep breath, then exhaled slowly. Not now, he told his painfully throbbing body. Still, he couldn't resist tasting her kiss-swollen lips just once.

When he ended the kiss, Fantasy groaned in protest, her eyelids fluttering open. As her sleep-clouded gaze settled on Jesse, braced on one arm and leaning over her, a sultry smile played over her lips. He could tell the moment she remembered what had transpired during the night, the flare of desire unmistakable in the depths of her eyes. Then she looked around. Her body stiffened, the heat in her eyes cooled.

She jerked upright, one hand clutching the sheet to her chest, her cheeks burning with embarrassment. Unable to meet Jesse's gaze, she dropped her head, her hair forming a curtain around her face.

Lifting a strand of heavy, auburn hair and rubbing his fingers back and forth over its satiny texture, Jesse studied her bowed head. "You don't regret last night," he finally said in a quiet voice. "Do you?"

A twinge of pain gnawing at his heart, he watched her shoulders rise and fall on a sigh. As he waited for her answer his trepidation increased.

Fantasy's hand shook as she shoved her hair away from her face. Lifting her head, she looked up at him. Although still flushed, her eyes were clear and openly honest. "No, I don't regret it. I'll always be grateful to you for last night."

Grateful? Jesse's mouth fell open. The last thing he wanted was her gratitude. Snapping his jaw shut, he drew a deep breath then blew it out slowly. Apparently it would take more time before she returned his feelings.

Not commenting on her statement, he threw back the sheet and got out of bed.

Fantasy watched him, splendidly naked and positively, blatantly male, as he gathered her scattered clothes. When he moved around to her side of the bed, her heart began hammering a wild tattoo against her ribs. Dropping the bundle of clothes in her lap, he bent down and scooped her into his arms. "Jesse! What are you doing?"

"Returning you to your bed before Mei-Ling finds you in mine."

"But . . . but, we're naked." She sounded properly outraged, making Jesse laugh softly.

"Indeed, dear, sweet Fancy. We are very naked. But Mei-Ling hasn't stirred yet. So our state of dress, or rather undress, won't be noticed." Striding across the room, he flashed her a devilish smile. "Shall I fetch you a robe?"

She rather liked the feel of being naked in his arms, pressed to his equally naked chest, so she shook her head.

"Good, then will you open the door, love? My hands seem to be busy."

Chuckling merrily, Fantasy reached down to turn the knob.

He stepped through the door and moved silently down the hall. Jesse's concern about her reputation and wanting to return her to her room before their activities of the previous night were discovered deeply touched Fantasy. Her heart swelled in her chest, an emotion she wasn't able to name flooding in to fill its chambers.

He set her on her feet, then took the clothes clutched in her hands and tossed them onto a chair. After pulling back the covers, he leaned close. "Your bed, madame," he murmured next to her ear.

She giggled, then remembering Mei-Ling, clamped a hand over her mouth. Raising on tiptoe, she looped her hands around his neck and brought his head down to hers.

The sizzling kiss she planted on his lips would have knocked his socks off, had he been wearing any. Jesse would have smiled, but he was too busy returning her kiss. He wished he could toss her on the bed and show her again how wonderful making love could be. But the sky was already turning a soft shade of pink, and Mei-Ling would be up soon.

Pulling her hands from behind his neck, he held her at arms' length. "Take it easy, Fancy. More of that and you'll find yourself on your back, those long legs wrapped around my waist."

Embarrassment erased her momentary loss of control. She took a step back, belatedly wondering what he thought of her. Did he see her as another conquest, a plaything, or perhaps a harlot? " 'Night, Jesse."

One finger under her chin, he lifted her face until her gaze reluctantly met his. What was she thinking? He searched her eyes, hoping to find the answer. The room was too dark. Moving his hand to cup one cheek, he whispered, "Tonight?"

He felt rather than saw the confusion she experienced over his question. The slight stiffening of her body, the quick indrawn breath told him he'd hit a nerve. The problem was he didn't know which one. Would she refuse to return to his bed? Or would her newly awakened female passion crave another taste of the pleasure he could give her? He held his breath while he waited for her reply.

At first Fantasy didn't speak, she couldn't. Jesse's question had triggered a host of reactions. Primary among them was the need, the almost overwhelming need to seek out his bed and his body again. Although she feared she was condemning herself as a fallen woman, she couldn't stop herself from giving the truthful answer. "Yes."

The word was so softly spoken Jesse would have missed it had he not been so attuned to her every heartbeat, her every breath. He closed his eyes briefly, silently praying his thanks.

" 'Night, Fancy." He kissed the top of her head, then slipped from the room.

Fantasy got into her bed and pulled the sheet up under her chin. She'd never slept naked in her life. But since Robby was staying with Mattie, there was no need to get out of bed and don a nightgown. There was something sinfully delicious about the feel of the sheets on her bare skin. The only thing better was the feel of Jesse's skin against hers. The wickedness of that thought jolted her, bringing on another round of self-chastisement. *Fantasy Williams, what are you thinking? You've turned into a shameless hussy. Regardless of what you just told Jesse, this is the only bed you'll seek tonight!*

Although she told herself she had to follow her own command, she wasn't so sure she'd be able to resist the temptation just down the hall.

Four days after Fantasy shared his bed for the first time, Jesse turned his attention to his investigation. Now that the trauma of the fire had receded and the rebuilding of the burned-out section well underway, he knew it was time to get back to his reason for being in Tombstone. He made his first chore checking out the network of tunnels he and Robby had used to escape the fire. Since the tunnels had to be Lawson's avenue for the man's disappearing act, the catacombs deserved a thorough look-see.

After half an hour in the tunnel, Jesse's hunch proved to be a correct one. He was no longer alone. Dousing his lantern, he sidled into the shadows. From dead ahead voices bounced off the stone walls.

He stealthily inched forward until he could make out the outline of three men. A short, smallish man faced toward his hiding place. The other two, much taller, had their backs to him. As Jesse strained to hear their conversation, the sweet odor of opium assailed his nose, putting his location near an opium den beneath Hop Town.

"Okay, Fong, where's the money for the sugar our boss gave ya last time?" one of the taller men asked.

"Not be so impatient," Wing Fong replied. "I get lotsa dolla for jewelry boss-man have me sell." Pulling a cloth bag from the pocket of his loose-fitting jacket, Fong bounced it in his hand several times. "You have more for Fong to sell, Mista Buck?"

"Hush yer mouth, ya stupid Chinaman. I told ya before, never use our names."

"Take it easy, Buck. There ain't nobody in this here tunnel 'cept us," the third man said.

After a quick glance over his shoulder, Buck grunted. "Guess yer right. Just the durn fools in one of them opium dens, smokin' their pipes 'til they pass out." Turning back to Fong, he snatched the bag from the man's hands. "Yeah, Chinaman, we got more sugar." He chuckled, then immediately sobered. "But the boss will get it to ya."

"How he do that? That why we meet here. Fire destroy boardinghouse. Landlady no bring laundry to my place. How she bring . . ."

The crushing pain in Jesse's chest made the voices fade away, replaced by a loud buzzing in his ears. He pressed one fist against the cool stone wall, struggling to regain his composure. Finally his head cleared and the men's words filtered back to him.

". . . worry yer friggin' pigtail about it, Chinaman. The boss and his delivery woman will figure out a way to get the sugar inta yer yella hands."

Bowing toward the two men, Fong mumbled something Jesse couldn't make out, then backed away and disappeared in the shadows of the tunnel.

"Damn Chink," the one called Buck muttered.

"Yeah, but just get a gander at the money in that there bag," the other man replied.

Hefting the bag and hearing the jingle of coins, Buck's previous disgust evaporated. "We gotta get this here money to the boss. Come on little brother, let's get the hell outta this damn hole. It's givin' me the creeps."

Jesse waited until the sound of footsteps faded, then disappeared completely before moving. When he was within a few feet of where he estimated the three men had stood, he pulled a match from his pocket, scratched it against the stone wall and re-lit his lantern. After adjusting the wick, Jesse held the light out in front of him. Although the sides of the tunnel were solid rock, the floor varied from stone to a mixture of dirt and gravel. He peered carefully at the ground in front of him, relieved to see a large patch of soft dirt.

Searching the circle of light cast by the lantern, Jesse finally spotted what he'd hoped to find—the star-shaped design in one of the boot prints.

Buck and his brother, two of Lawson's cohorts, and since they'd mentioned sugar, likely the recipient of the telegram García had sent some time back. Jesse cursed his luck at not being able to get a look at the men's faces. At least he had one first name. Finding out their full identities shouldn't be difficult.

As he made his way out of the tunnel, Jesse replayed the conversation he'd overheard again and again in his head. Each time the words added up to the same conclusion. Fantasy had been working with Lawson. Getting the stolen loot—the *sugar*—to Wing Fong's Laundry had been her responsibility, just as he'd suspected. That was before the fire; now what were their plans? The fact he'd been right to suspect Fantasy's involvement in the robberies was not the least bit satisfying.

There had to be something he'd missed, something to prove he was wrong about Fantasy. Heading toward Allen Street, he vowed to double his efforts in digging up the truth. He'd start with the two men in the tunnel.

Although Jesse tried to concentrate on finding out the men's identities, his thoughts persisted in wandering. He kept recalling the questions he'd asked Fantasy the night before when she lay drowsy and sated in his arms. He'd casually asked her if she knew where the rest of her boarders were staying since the fire. She said she heard Nash Sparks had taken a room at the San José House, but wasn't sure about Gunderson or Baxter. When he asked about Jack Lawson, she didn't hesitate—he had a room at the San Francisco Lodging House on Allen Street.

Unable to bear finding out how she came to know where Lawson lived, Jesse had dropped the subject.

Ever since he'd found the hidden robbery loot in her laundry basket, he'd hoped she'd been ignorant of its existence. He'd also hoped she didn't know Lawson's whereabouts after the fire. The conversation he'd just overheard in the tunnel and her answers to his questions about her former boarders cast a heavy shroud of doubt over Jesse's hopes.

Three nights later, Jesse lay in his bed, contemplating the information Nick had dug up that afternoon. He now had names for the men he'd heard talking to Fong in the tunnel. Daryl and Clarence "Buck" Arnette. The brothers came to Arizona Territory from Kansas two years earlier and settled on a small ranch near Charleston. They supposedly raised cattle, but there was no record of either Arnette ever selling so much as one cow, yet according to Nick's source, they always had money to spend. Though pleased with what Nick had found out, the information wasn't nearly as gratifying as it should have been. Not when the extent of Fantasy's involvement still formed an enormous question mark in his mind.

Just then he heard the click of the latch on his bedroom door. Turning his head, he watched the door swing inward. The sight in the open doorway rocked him to the core, the same reaction he had every night when Fantasy came to his room. All thoughts of the possible consequences of her being an outlaw fled when she closed the door and moved toward the bed.

Then there were no thoughts at all as she slipped beneath the sheet next to him. There was only hot satiny skin, warm demanding lips and eager caressing hands. His mind dizzy with desire, his body throbbing with need, Jesse could only think of the woman in his arms. The woman firmly entrenched in his heart.

Much later, as they lay in the aftermath of their

near-frantic loving, Jesse stroked Fantasy's silky hair—the only movement his sapped strength allowed. Kissing her temple, he whispered softly, "I love you, Fantasy."

When she didn't respond, he sighed, telling himself her being asleep was just as well. She'd never given him any clue about her feelings for him. Oh, he knew she desired him. She'd become nearly insatiable under his tutelage. But beyond the physical, she was the only one who knew what she felt.

And besides the fact she might not return his love, there was still the mountain of her part in the robberies to scale. Sighing again, Jesse closed his eyes and willed thoughts of Fantasy going to prison from his mind. He wasn't sure he could survive if that came to pass.

Fantasy started and looked down at the plate she'd been washing. "Drat," she muttered, dismayed the dishwater had grown cold again. "I'll scrub the pattern right off these dishes at this rate."

Fetching more hot water, she tried to concentrate on finishing before Mei-Ling came into the kitchen and found her still doing the chore she'd volunteered to do an hour ago. Unfortunately, her hands sliding over the slippery suds-covered dishes made her think of Jesse's hands sliding over her body, then of returning the favor with equal thoroughness and growing skill.

Those memories stirred others—the faintly sweaty, musky smell of his body, the slightly salty, intoxicating taste of his skin, the rasping of his breathing, his husky voice whispering words of instruction and encouragement in her ear. Such erotic daydreams sent gooseflesh over her body, bringing her attempts at washing dishes to a halt again. How had she changed from such an innocent woman to a brazen, weak—yes, weak, she decided. Weak was exactly the word she sought to describe herself, even though it made her cringe. There wasn't anything in a person's makeup Fantasy hated more than weakness.

Thomas had turned out to be a weakling. Although looking back, it shouldn't have come as a surprise—considering the example his father had set.

Frank Williams, while an astute businessman and kind-hearted toward Fantasy, was the weakest man Fantasy had ever known. His wife led him around by the nose, always telling him where to go, what to do, when to do it. It was a wonder Henrietta didn't insist on accompanying him to the privy. Fantasy snorted with disgust.

Unfortunately, Thomas had turned out just like his father. Except Thomas's weakness was the promise of riches in first the gold fields, then the silver mines. The only time Thomas had displayed any backbone was when he married Fantasy over his mother's adamant objections. After their wedding Thomas quickly returned to his lap dog ways of doing as his mother bid. Until gold fever hit him—a weakness not even his mother could correct. A weakness that killed him in the end.

Grumbling to herself about dredging up her painful past, Fantasy knew the old memories accomplished one thing—they helped prove her point. She was as weak as Thomas and his father when it came to staying away from Jesse's room each night.

More than a week had passed since the first night in Jesse's bed when he'd awakened her slumbering passion. More than a week of days of commanding herself to stay in her own bed each night. And more than a week of ignoring her own commands and going to Jesse's room after Robby and Mei-Ling were asleep, where he took her to heaven on every one of those nights.

At least she'd been strong enough each morning to return to her own bed before dawn broke. Somehow that one small display of strength didn't make Fantasy feel much better. Even after Robby found her in Jesse's bed several nights earlier, she hadn't been able to stay away from her lover's room.

Robby had awakened in the night, found his mother's bed empty and started looking for her. Rubbing his sleep-filled eyes, he stumbled through the door to Jesse's bedroom, calling for his mother in a teary voice.

Dozing on Jesse's shoulder, her son's call awakened Fantasy instantly. "Robby, what is it?"

Jesse had also heard the boy's entrance and held his hand toward the door. "Come here, Buckshot."

Robby eagerly approached the bed where his mother was snuggled close to Jesse beneath the sheet.

"Are you okay, sweetheart?" Fantasy asked, reaching over Jesse to feel her son's forehead. "Are you sick?"

Sniffling loudly, the boy shook his head. "I had a dream. A man was chasin' me, but I couldn't run very fast." He drew a quivering breath, a shiver wracking his body.

"Shh, it's over now, Robby. You're safe with us." With a start, Fantasy realized where her son had found her, and worse she was naked beneath the sheet. Her cheeks warmed with a blush.

"Would you like to get in bed with us, Buckshot?" Jesse scooted closer to Fantasy to make room for the boy.

Robby nodded eagerly, then climbed up onto the mattress and settled on top of the covers next to Jesse.

Aware of Fantasy's concern about Robby finding out neither of them wore any bedclothes, Jesse carefully tucked the sheet securely around Fantasy's shoulders.

After squirming around to get comfortable, Robby suddenly asked, "How come you're in here, Momma?"

The prayers she'd been silently whispering to prevent that question died on Fantasy's lips. Wishing she could crawl under the covers and never come out, the words to answer her son's innocent question stuck in her throat.

Sensing Fantasy's uneasiness, Jesse said, "Your mother had a bad dream, too, Buckshot. And just like you, she came in here because she wanted to be near someone."

Fantasy held her breath while Robby thought about Jesse's explanation. She hoped it would satisfy his curiosity.

Robby reached over and gave her cheek a consoling pat. "You're not scared anymore, are ya, Momma?"

"No, sweetheart. I'm not scared anymore." She smiled at her son, her embarrassment forgotten.

Robby returned her smile, then yawned. Wiggling closer to Jesse, he closed his eyes and sighed with contentment.

In minutes, Robby slept peacefully on one side of Jesse while Fantasy slumbered on the other. Near dawn Jesse roused Fantasy, then carefully carried Robby to his own bed.

Robby hadn't mentioned that night again. Apparently Jesse's explanation had been sufficient, for which Fantasy would be forever grateful. Recalling Jesse's gentle handling of a very delicate situation made her heart flutter with pride and another emotion she refused to acknowledge. Thinking of Jesse's way with words brought to mind another of his speeches. This one from the previous night, and one which had pummeled her spirit with another staggering blow.

Last night Jesse had to go and say those words. She'd remained silent, feigning sleep because of her confusion about her own feelings. What she felt was different from anything she'd ever experienced. Yet she wasn't sure what name to tack on it.

She'd lain awake for a long time, Jesse's unexpected

declaration forcing her to examine her feelings again. After a great deal of soul-searching, she discovered something disturbing. What she'd felt for Thomas couldn't have been love; it wasn't even close to what she felt for Jesse. There was no comparison. She'd been infatuated with Thomas, after all he'd been the first man to show an interest in her, but in retrospect that's all it had been. The emotion unfurling inside her toward Jesse was definitely more intense, more consuming. But was it love?

The answer to that question had eluded her last night. Today it was obvious. Thinking back, she realized her love for Jesse could be traced back to the day they met. The tender seed had been planted that first day, and since then had sprouted and grown steadily, embedding its roots deeper and deeper in her heart.

A feeling of doom settled over her, making her shoulders slump in defeat. Every time she loved someone they were snatched from her life—first her father, then her mother, and finally Thomas.

"I can't love Jesse, I just can't," she declared, attacking the dishes with renewed vigor. "I don't want to lose him, too."

Knowing she couldn't bear the pain of losing another person she loved, she tried to convince herself what she felt for Jesse was lust—nothing more. That's what it had to be.

Two days later, Fantasy left Robby with Mei-Ling and headed down Fifth Street. Without the boarding-house to keep her busy, she had too much time on her hands to think. Wanting to keep her mind off her feelings for Jesse, she decided it was time to take charge of her life, having allowed Jesse too much control. She refused to let her lust for him lead to being completely under a man's control again, leaving her open to suffer the deeper humiliation of abandonment.

The first step in accomplishing her goal of independence was facing her fears head on and conquering them. Entering the livery stable, she forced her fright aside, determined to go through with this.

Spotting Gil Gunderson at the back of the stable, she dried her palms on her new split skirt then approached him.

"I appreciate you taking part of your day off to do this, Gil."

"Think nothin' of it, Mrs. Williams. I think y'all're right smart to learn to ride." He ran his hand down the neck of the gray horse standing quietly beside him. "I found this here little mare for you. Daisy is real docile, so y'all don't need to fear her none."

Wishing she could agree with Gil's assessment of the horse, she merely nodded, rubbing her hands on her skirt again.

"Okay, Gil, I'm ready for my first lesson."

He smiled, then led the mare into the corral behind the stable. "Give me your foot and I'll give y'all a boost into the saddle."

Fantasy swallowed, then moved to stand next to Daisy. She stared at the saddle for several seconds, thinking it had to be at least fifty feet off the ground. Squaring her shoulders, she placed her left foot in Gil's cupped hands and grasped the saddle horn. As Gil lifted her, she sucked in a deep breath and swung her right leg over the horse. Gingerly lowering herself onto the saddle, she slowly exhaled.

"It's okay, Mrs. Williams," Gil said in a low voice. "I won't let nothing happen to ya. We'll take it real slow." Wrapping the reins around one hand, he clucked his tongue at Daisy then led the mare and her rider around the corral.

Fantasy sat stiffly atop the horse, holding onto the saddle horn so tightly her hands turned white. When she finally became accustomed to Daisy's slow, rolling gait, Fantasy's fear began to recede. For a few minutes, she even enjoyed her vantage point on Daisy's back. And by the time Gil announced she'd had enough for one day and assisted her from the saddle, she found she no longer shivered with dread at the thought of her next lesson.

The next day, Fantasy watched Mattie put the finishing touches on the wedding dress she'd made for herself, then suddenly blurted, "I received another letter from Mother Williams yesterday."

Mattie looked over at where Fantasy sat sipping a glass of lemonade. Her brow furrowed with concern. "What did she say?"

"She knows about the fire. She knows my boarding-house was destroyed."

"How do ya suppose she found out?"

Fantasy shrugged. "I don't know. I'm sure the fire was reported in newspapers back East. But there's no way my boardinghouse would have been mentioned. Someone must be spying for her again."

Mattie digested that, then said, "So, what else did she have to say?"

"Mother Williams said she wants Robby sent to St. Louis on the first eastbound train. And if I don't—" she swallowed the lump of fear lodged in her throat. "If I don't send him, she'll take action to make sure he gets to St. Louis."

"Why that old battleaxe! If she was here right now, I'd smash her mealy-mouthed face in."

Fantasy smiled in spite of her worries about her mother-in-law. "Yes, I'm sure you would, Mattie. But that wouldn't help me any. It would just give Mother Williams another reason to want her grandson out of Tombstone."

Curbing her temper, Mattie sighed. "You're right. No need to make the woman any madder than she already is. We don't want to give her more ammunition to use against you." She turned back to the ivory satin dress, and continued sewing the tiny seed pearls on the bodice. "Have you given any thought to who might be supplyin' the Williamses with information?"

"Yes. But I haven't come up with anyone. I've thought about it so much I think I'm going crazy. If it weren't for—" She clamped her mouth shut, horrified she'd almost admitted how she spent her nights.

Mattie looked over her shoulder when Fantasy abruptly fell silent. "If it weren't for what?"

"Nothing," she answered quickly, then rose from her chair. "Listen, I have to go. I'll see you at church." With that she swept out the door, leaving Mattie to wonder what Fantasy had been about to reveal.

"Know what, Momma?"

"What's that, sweetheart?" Fantasy looked up from the shirt she was mending for Jesse to smile at her son.

"I like Jesse a whole bunch."

"Do you? Well, I'm sure Jesse feels the same way about you."

Robby was quiet for a minute, then said, "I think Jesse likes you a whole bunch, too, Momma."

"Oh?"

"Yeah. He's always askin' me questions 'bout ya. That means he likes ya, don't it?"

Fantasy heard a strange humming in her ears. "What questions?"

"What ya like to do. What ya did for the men in our boardinghouse. Stuff like that."

"What I did for—" she stopped abruptly, the humming louder. "When did Jesse start asking you questions about me?"

Robby shrugged his shoulders. "Don't know."

"Before the fire?" she prompted.

His brow puckered. "Yeah, it was before."

"Why don't you go see if Mei-Ling has a cookie you can have," she managed to say. Desperate to be alone, she was grateful when Robby skipped happily from the room.

Fantasy had never known such excruciating pain.

The shirt in her lap suddenly abhorrent, she wadded it up in a ball and threw it across the room.

How could you, Jesse? How could you do this to me? You even said you loved me. I thought all the things you did, all the places we went were because you truly cared. But all along you were just playing some sick game. You even dragged Robby, a little boy, into whatever despicable scheme you're part of.

Why, Jesse? Why? The question kept repeating in her head. The answer came to her in a sickening revelation. Jesse worked for her in-laws! It was the only explanation that made any sense. Remembering the letter she'd just received from Henrietta Williams, Fantasy now knew how she'd found out about the fire.

The letter had been bad enough, but learning Jesse's true motive for coming to Tombstone was an even harsher blow. Most painful of all was the realization he'd apparently decided his other tactics weren't enough—getting her into his bed would better serve his purpose. He'd been so clever. Asking Robby questions, then using the information her son had trustingly given to set the snare to seduce the Widow Williams and ruin her reputation. And how easily she had succumbed to his charm. A few pretty words, some ice cream, the theatre, and she was his to command—straight to his bed. God, how the truth hurt!

Now instead of looking forward to their lovemaking, Fantasy envisioned only empty nights looming ahead. Nights filled with the fear of Robby being taken from her and the horrible agony of Jesse's duplicity.

At least there was one thing to be thankful for. She'd learned Jesse's true colors before she'd stupidly blurted out her feelings for him. Although she'd tried to talk herself out of it, she knew it wasn't just lust she felt for Jesse. In spite of her misgivings about men and falling into the trap she wanted to avoid, she'd repeatedly ignored her own warnings. She loved Jesse. Though she'd kept the discovery to herself, she had made one concession. She no longer wore her wedding band, her

conscience not allowing her to wear one man's ring
when her heart belonged to another.

Certain Jesse would have found her confession
vastly amusing, Fantasy lifted her chin and straightened her spine. Well, he'd never have the satisfaction
of hearing those words now. Though she didn't want
to face him, let alone talk to him, she had to. She had
to confront him and hear of his double-dealing from
his own lips. The pain of listening to his admission of
guilt would be worse than anything she'd ever experienced, yet Fantasy knew she must force herself to do
so. She had no other choice.

Chapter 10

Fantasy's temper had reached full throttle by the time Jesse returned home later that afternoon. Thankful Mei-Ling was playing catch with Robby in the backyard, she looked up from nervously twisting her wedding ring to watch the focus of her anger walk into the parlor. Determined not to behave like a raving shrew, she took a deep, steadying breath.

Jesse's smile of welcome faded. Increasingly adept at reading her moods, the strange fire banked in her eyes scared the hell out of him. "What's wrong, Fantasy?"

She waved him to the chair opposite her and waited until he sat down before she spoke. "I want you to tell me the real reason you're in Tombstone." The calmness she affected pleased her.

"The real reason?" Jesse tried to hide his growing apprehension. The gold band on her left hand caused a cold fist of dread to squeeze his heart. Something had to be very wrong for her to start wearing her wedding ring again. Although they'd never discussed the subject, Jesse noticed she'd taken it off soon after their first night together. Perceptive enough to realize what the action symbolized, he had prayed he was correct—she had begun to care for him. Now the ring's return chilled him to the bone.

Fantasy took another deep breath, praying he wasn't going to make this more difficult than it already was. "I know you're not a land speculator."

"And how do you know that?" he asked carefully.

"Because I found out your true purpose for coming here, and it wasn't to buy land."

"It wasn't?"

Frustrated with his lack of cooperation, the temper she'd been holding in check flared. "Damn you, Jesse McAllister, stop playing dumb."

Jesse knew her swearing signalled something very serious. Fantasy wasn't one to curse. The knot of fear in his stomach tightened. "Okay, Fantasy, I think you'd better spit out whatever's eating at you."

"You must think I'm the biggest fool to ever walk the face of the earth—believing everything you said and did was because you really cared about me. All along you were really trying to get the evidence my mother-in-law hired you to find."

"Your mother-in-law? Why would I be working for your mother-in-law?"

Wrapped up in her fury, Fantasy dismissed the bewilderment on Jesse's face. "To get Robby away from me, of course."

"Robby?" Jesse reached out to grasp her tightly clasped hands, but she snatched them away before he could touch her. His eyebrows knitting together in confusion, he searched her pinched face for some clue to what was going on. "Fantasy, I don't know what you're talking about. And what's this about taking Robby away from you?"

Fantasy snorted with exasperation. "As if you didn't know. My mother-in-law, Henrietta Williams, wants Robby to live with her back in St. Louis. She's been trying for months to get her way. Before you came she hired another man to dig up dirt about me so she could force me to do her bidding." Lifting her chin, she pinned him with an icy glare. "But I sniffed him out, just like I did you."

"Wait a minute. Let me get this straight. Your mother-in-law wants Robby to live with her?" At Fantasy's curt nod he continued. "And she hired a man to snoop around for something she could use against you?"

"Not just one man, two. You're the second one she's hired."

"No, Fantasy. You've got it all wrong."

"I'd say I've finally got it all *right*. I told Mattie I suspected you when you first came to town. I should have taken my own advice and steered clear of you."

"Now look, Fantasy." Jesse's temper started to climb in spite of his efforts to remain calm. "You have the wrong man. I do not work for Henrietta Williams. I've never even heard of the woman until now."

"I think you have. And furthermore, I think when you couldn't find anything useful to use against me, you decided you'd personally have to see to my fall from grace. You asked Robby all those questions about me and used his answers to . . . to—" She couldn't bring herself to say it.

"To what?"

Swallowing the bitter tears clogging her throat, she said, "To seduce me. Then you could tell Mother Williams I'm a . . . a . . . loose woman. How could you try to take my son away? How could you live with yourself? How could you . . . ?" Her voice trailed off, her composure badly shaken.

"It isn't what you think, Fancy."

"Don't call me that," she snapped.

"Look, I did ask Robby questions about you. I won't deny that. But I swear it wasn't to lure you into my bed. That just happened." His voice turned hard. "Besides, you're the one who insisted I should have some kind of reward for saving Robby from the fire. If it hadn't been for—" He jabbed a finger at her. "—your insistence, we might not have made love that night."

Her face burning with shame, Fantasy couldn't refute his words. Perhaps it was partly her fault. But she rejected taking the entire blame for ending up in Jesse's bed. Summoning her strength, she refused to turn away from his scowling face. "Maybe so. That still doesn't excuse your behavior. Are you going to sit there and tell me you didn't use my son as part of your plan to paint me as a woman with no morals?"

Jesse wondered how he could answer her accusations without revealing the whole truth. "That's exactly what I'm telling you." The volume of his voice rose sharply, making Fantasy flinch. "I love that boy, you should know that by now. How can you think I'd be party to a scheme to take him away from you?"

When she remained silent, he added more gently, "Fantasy, I already admitted I asked Robby about you. But it wasn't because I was trying to seduce you. Although I won't lie and say I'm sorry it happened, or that I haven't enjoyed each night we've spent together."

Her cheeks burned even more at the reminder of their nightly trysts. But she refused to be cowed by his remark. Instead she kept her chin at a defiant angle. "All right, I'll concede that maybe you didn't intend for us to become lov—" She cleared her throat hastily. "That still doesn't prove anything. Perhaps you didn't know Mother Williams's true reason for hiring you."

"I'm telling you, Fantasy, I don't work for the woman." Realizing she apparently wasn't going to let this rest, his jaw worked spasmodically with his returning fury.

Fantasy stared at Jesse for several long seconds, mulling over his words. "So, if you don't work for Mother Williams, who do you work for?"

"I told you, I work for a land—"

"Stop it! I know what you told me, but I think it was all a pack of lies."

Jesse's temper finally leaped over the barrier he'd been struggling to keep it behind. "All right, dammit, I'm not a land speculator."

Even his anger didn't stop Fantasy's rush of joy. "And if you aren't working for my mother-in-law as you claim, then why are you in Tombstone?" The guilty flush creeping up his neck snuffed the life from her newborn hope.

Jesse eased back in his chair, his fury slowly changing to resignation. "I can't tell you." Seeing the immediate stiffening of her shoulders, Jesse quickly added, "But as God is my witness, I don't work for your mother-in-law."

Fantasy couldn't bear to hear any more. In addition to her earlier feelings of betrayal and anger, she felt a crushing sorrow over Jesse's refusal to be honest with her.

Overwhelmed with what had happened in just one afternoon, she was sure of only one thing—she absolutely refused to make the trip to Jesse's room that night—or any other night. There was no way she would seek his bed, not when she didn't know where the truth left off and the lies began. He claimed he wasn't working for Mother Williams; he'd even used the Lord's name in his decree. Yet if that was true, why had he come to town? His refusal to tell her rankled and renewed her suspicions.

Jesse watched with trepidation as the emotions flickered across Fantasy's face. The last one to settle there cut him to the quick. He wished he could erase the defeat he saw in her eyes, but he couldn't say the words she longed to hear. He'd already said more than he should have—he'd even lost his temper and admitted he wasn't what he'd presented himself to be. But he couldn't do what Fantasy wanted and reveal his real reason for being in town. When she rose from the settee and moved with stiff strides to the hallway his heart cramped with misery. Dropping his head back against the chair, he closed his eyes. *You've done it now, McAllister. You've gotten yourself into one helluva jam.*

Jesse's initial concern over the mess he'd made for himself increased over the next several days. While

Fantasy continued to live in his house—only because she still had nowhere else to go, he was sure—her manner toward him turned decidedly cool, almost frigid in its formality.

Watching her move around the house, or down the street, as if she were in a trance made Jesse heartsick. How he longed to feel the warmth of her smile and the passion of her lovemaking. But she barely gave him the time of day, let alone show any inkling she missed spending their nights together.

Though he knew he loved Fantasy, the last few days brought the magnitude of his love sharply in focus. All his adult life he'd always thought he had everything he wanted. It took meeting and falling in love with Fantasy for him to realize there had been something missing. Now that he'd found her, the possibility of losing her filled him with a bone-deep fear.

Jesse refused to just ignore Fantasy's withdrawal and let her slip further and further away. He had to gain her trust—and more importantly win her love. And since their future depended on her involvement in the robberies, he was also determined to learn the truth.

A visit to Mattie Moreland was first on his agenda. Perhaps Fantasy's friend could enlighten him with something to help his cause. After entering her dress shop, he said, "I've come to ask for your help, Mrs. Moreland."

"Call me Mattie. And what can I help you with?"

Uncertain where to begin, Jesse paced the short length of Mattie's shop while trying to put his thoughts into some semblance of order. "Have you seen Fantasy lately?"

"Yes. I saw her yesterday, as a matter of fact. Why?"

"Did she . . . um . . . did she seem like herself?"

Mattie tipped her head to one side, studying Jesse carefully as he nervously moved back and forth in front of her. "She hasn't been herself lately, that's been obvious. But she said it's the strain of waiting for her boardinghouse to be rebuilt."

"And, do you think that's true?"

"What I think, Mr. McAllister, is that you should stop this pussyfootin' around and get to the point."

Running a hand impatiently through his hair, Jesse stopped and turned to face her. "You're right, Mattie, I'll get to the point. And please, call me Jesse." Idly fingering a piece of silk fabric laid out on the counter, he cleared his throat and dropped his gaze to the cloth in front of him. "The reason Fantasy hasn't been herself is because of a misunderstanding we had a few days ago."

"A misunderstanding?"

"Yes, she accused me of working for her mother-in-law."

"And do you?"

The frankness of Mattie's question brought his head up with a snap. There was no censure in her eyes, only genuine concern. He managed a thin smile. "No, Mattie, I am not working for Henrietta Williams."

After a few silent moments while she searched Jesse's face, Mattie spoke. "I take it Fantasy didn't believe you."

Jesse sighed, his shoulders losing some of their tenseness. "No, she didn't. When I told her she was wrong she demanded to know why I'm in Tombstone. And when I said I couldn't tell her, the look on her face was plain as day. My refusal to answer only confirmed her guilty verdict against me."

Mattie clucked her tongue knowingly. "That sounds like Fantasy. Once she forms an opinion about someone, she's as stubborn as that old mule of Spud's about changin' it."

Moving to the opposite side of the counter, she looked him squarely in the eye. "Listen, Jesse, that boy of hers is the only thing she's got in this world. And she'll fight to her last breath to keep him from being taken from her. So you have to understand how upset she was when she found out about the first man Henrietta Williams hired to do her dirty work. Then when she thought you were here for the same reason, after she'd begun to—well, never mind about that. Just try to understand her side of it."

Jesse nodded, then said, "Tell me about this Henrietta Williams, and why she would try to get Robby away from Fantasy."

Mattie thought about his request for several seconds. "I won't tell you the whole story, 'cause it's not my place to be sayin' anything. But I will tell you this much. Fantasy's lost everyone who was important to her—both her parents and her husband, even though he was a no-account dreamer. Then after she decided to stay in Arizona, her mother-in-law had a hissy-fit. Henrietta didn't want her grandson raised in a town she thinks is one step above Hell."

Mattie made a sound of disgust, then cleared her throat. "Anyway, Fantasy didn't take Henrietta's letters asking her to move back to St. Louis seriously at first. Then a private investigator showed up, poking his nose where it had no business being, and Henrietta's cussed stubbornness hit home. Now Fantasy fears the woman is so obsessed with getting Robby out of Tombstone that she'd stoop so low as to have the boy taken from his mother.

"The letter Fantasy received last week scared her to death. Henrietta knows about the fire destroying the boardinghouse, and Fantasy is afraid another man has been hired to spy on her."

"The fire in Tombstone would make the papers back East, but likely wouldn't mention the names of any of the businesses that were lost," Jesse theorized aloud. "Is that why Fantasy suspects her mother-in-law has someone working for her?"

Mattie nodded. "Yes. To Fantasy's way of thinkin', the only way Henrietta could've learned about the boardinghouse is by having another man in her employ here in town. Now I hope you can see why Fantasy's been so upset about all of this. And don't be too hard on the poor thing for the way she's been treatin' you."

Mattie placed a hand on Jesse's forearm. "If you care for Fantasy like I think you do, give her time. She'll come to see the truth."

"I do care for her, Mattie. I care a helluva lot, and I hate seeing her suffer. But I'll take your advice." He paused, then flashed her a grin. "That doesn't mean I can't court her at the same time, does it?"

Mattie couldn't help returning his grin, then squeezed his arm before withdrawing her hand. "I think courtin' is just the thing Fantasy needs right now. Good luck to you, Jesse."

After he left Mattie's dress shop, Jesse began forming plans to resume his courtship of Fantasy. He refused to consider the possibility she might not take kindly to his attention. There had to be a way to successfully woo her, and he was determined to find it. He knew what she liked. How he'd come to possess such knowledge gave him a momentary twinge of guilt, but he shoved it aside. That didn't matter now. What did matter was finding ways to put the information to good use and win back the woman he loved.

The following Sunday Jesse asked Fantasy if he could take her and Robby to church. She had her misgivings about accepting Jesse's invitation, but since church seemed safe enough she saw no reason to refuse. And even when he asked them to go to the baseball game afterwards, she couldn't bring herself to deny Robby the outing. Just because she didn't want to be around Jesse McAllister didn't mean she had to keep her son from seeing the man he adored. Still uncertain what business Jesse had in Tombstone, and determined her son wouldn't be a pawn again, she vowed to keep her eyes on Jesse's every move.

Dropping Fantasy and Robby at his house, Jesse

turned to leave. "I'll be back in an hour and we'll head for the ball field, okay?"

"Sure, Jesse," Robby crowed. Fantasy remained silent, content to let her son speak for both of them.

Jesse returned in a rented buggy, Robby's horse, Maggie, tied to the back. Jesse hurried inside to change, then called to Robby and Fantasy to meet him outside.

Robby bolted through the front door, then skidded to a halt next to the buggy. "Why'd ya bring Maggie?"

"I thought maybe you'd like to ride her, instead of in this stuffy, old buggy," Jesse whispered, casting a glance at Fantasy as she stepped through the door. "How's that sound, Buckshot?"

"Great!" Turning to face his mother, Robby shouted, "I'm gonna ride Maggie, Momma!"

Realizing she wouldn't have the buffer of Robby's company for the ride to the ball field, her smile at his enthusiasm faltered. She refused to let that small problem detract from the day's plans. Lifting her chin, she stepped into the street and allowed Jesse to help her into the buggy. That her skin became uncomfortably warm at his touch momentarily flustered her. But as soon as Jesse removed his hand and she was settled on the seat, the cool wall of indifference she tried so hard to maintain was back in place.

In spite of the fact that most recreation in town took place indoors—the saloons, bawdy houses, and casinos stayed open the clock around, seven days a week—a large crowd had gathered in the field at the edge of town. For some of the men who had their Sundays free, either playing on or watching Tombstone's new baseball team was a welcome diversion from swilling whiskey and lingering at the gambling tables.

Reverend Endicott Peabody, pastor of Fantasy's church, had organized the team after arriving from Boston to begin his ministry five months earlier. He'd agreed to games on Sunday only if the team attended church first. Since Cotty—as his friends called him—was a big, strapping man and a first class boxer, no one objected to his request. Today, Cotty was serving in his usual capacity as referee for the game against the team from Fort Huachuca.

After spreading a blanket for Robby and Fantasy in the area reserved for spectators, Jesse placed a picnic basket in the center. Rolling up his shirtsleeves, he said, "I've been asked to play in the game, so go ahead and dig into the food whenever you're hungry. I'll eat later."

For the first time, Fantasy noticed the way Jesse was dressed. She'd been so determined not to let his proximity in the buggy affect her that she hadn't realized he no longer wore the formal suit he'd worn to church. He now sported a loose-fitting shirt and a pair of not-so-loose denim pants. He looked wonderfully handsome, blatantly male. Her pulse quickened from just looking at him.

"You changed your clothes," she blurted before she could stop the words.

Feeling her face warm with a blush from both her perusal of Jesse's attire and her foolish remark, Fantasy jerked her gaze away from where it had strayed only to collide with his piercing blue stare. He tipped his head in acknowledgment, a lazy smile curving his lips. She resisted the urge to squirm under his scrutiny, then sighed with relief when he was the first to look away.

As he turned toward the ball field, Jesse tried to forget the look on Fantasy's face, the unmistakable flare of desire in her eyes. His voice was raspy when he turned back to Robby. "I've gotta go warm up with the team. Take care of your mother, okay, Buckshot?"

"Sure, Jesse." Robby watched Jesse trot over to where the rest of the men were tossing baseballs back and forth and doing exercises to stretch their arm and leg muscles, then turned back to his mother. "I betcha Jesse plays baseball real good, don't you, Momma?"

Glancing over to the Tombstone side of the field, Fantasy picked out Jesse immediately. His height and breadth made him easily recognizable among the other ball players. "Yes, sweetheart, I'm sure he does." It seemed there wasn't anything Jesse didn't do well. That thought filled her with a mixture of pride and chagrin. When he turned to look in her direction she swiftly forced her gaze to the other members of the team. Unconsciously making mental comparisons between them and Jesse, she found the other men all lacking in one way or another. Jesse was definitely the best in all categories. She sighed. *Except for being truthful with me.*

Never having seen a baseball game, Fantasy wasn't sure if she'd like the sport. But she quickly picked up the rules, and was soon yelling and cheering as loudly as the rest of the crowd.

Robby had been absolutely right in his child's boast about Jesse's ability as a baseball player. It was obvious the man had played the game before coming to Tombstone, and with a great deal of skill.

Each time it was Jesse's turn to bat, Fantasy couldn't stop looking at him. It was as if he'd been made for her eyes alone. She watched the muscles of his back flex and his arms bulge with each swing of the bat, reminding her of how his back flexed and his arms bulged when he'd braced himself above her in his bed. She watched his solid, muscular thighs bunch and stretch as he raced around the bases or ran after a fly ball, reminding her of how his thighs bunched and stretched as he moved over her before claiming her body with his. She watched the sweat form on his brow and bead his upper lip, reminding her of his sweat-slicked body after their heated lovemaking.

Dismayed her vow to watch Jesse's every move hadn't been such a good idea, Fantasy swore she wouldn't look at him. Yet her gaze continued to seek him out, clinging like burrs to a horse's tail. Even the repeated mental scolding she gave herself didn't help.

The only thing she could be thankful for was Jesse's apparent oblivion to her watchful eyes.

Jesse was fully cognizant of Fantasy's line of vision. He'd have to be dead not to feel the scorching looks she cast his way. Each time her gaze touched him it was as if she had reached out and slid her hand over his body. His shoulders rippled with the warmth of her visual caress, and his heart picked up its cadence. He had to use every bit of his concentration to keep his mind on the baseball game, and not on what he'd like to be doing to Fantasy Williams.

When the game ended, Jesse joined Fantasy and Robby, sinking down on the blanket with a grateful sigh. "This heat's worn me to a frazzle."

Feeling her own exhaustion, though from mental not physical exertion, Fantasy nodded and handed him a plate of food.

Robby's excited chatter while Jesse ate kept Fantasy from having to speak. Her son's enthusiasm was a godsend. She wasn't sure she could make her vocal cords work to save her life.

As he bit into a piece of chicken, Jesse stole a glance at Fantasy. Although her eyes still held remnants of pain, he also saw something more in her luminous stare. She wasn't as indifferent to him as she wanted him to believe. He longed to gather her in his arms, but he resisted the urge. Although he recognized the signs of desire, he couldn't be certain if she was also aware of how she'd reacted to him.

Regardless of the answer, he knew he would make no attempt to resume their physical relationship until she gave some sign of her willingness. Until then, he'd just have to be patient.

The ride home was pure torture. With every passing mile, Jesse cursed himself for deciding to bring Robby's horse. He'd thought his idea had been exceptionally clever, using the boy's love of riding to his own advantage.

He didn't feel so smug now. It was pure hell sitting

next to Fantasy and not being able to touch her. He shifted on the seat, trying to ease the aching fullness of his groin. Casting a sidelong glance at the cause of his discomfort, Fantasy's placid face disheartened him. She seemed completely unmindful of his presence, making him ache all the more.

Ever since the baseball game ended and Jesse dropped down on the blanket next to her, Fantasy's brain had nearly ceased functioning, her breathing becoming seriously impaired. Much to her annoyance, she still had trouble keeping her eyes off him. If possible, the energetic baseball game had served to increase his good looks. His disheveled state—dirt-covered clothes, rumpled hair, and sweat-dampened skin—only added to his masculine appeal.

Now on the ride back to town, their closeness in the buggy was even more disconcerting. Fantasy tried to keep her mind on something other than the man next to her. She turned her thoughts to her next riding lesson with Gil. He'd told her she was doing real well, and would be riding like she'd been born in the saddle in no time. While she didn't share his optimism, she was happy with the progress she'd made in just a couple of lessons. She no longer felt the almost paralyzing fear she'd always suffered when around horses.

If only she could make some progress in her efforts to get over her discomfort when Jesse was near. The wind kicked up just then, buffeting the side of the buggy and carrying Jesse's wonderful male scent to her nose. The tang of his sweat keenly reminded her of the smell of his skin while they made love. Her fingers itched to reach out and touch the muscled hardness of his hair-dusted forearm. Not trusting herself to keep her thoughts from becoming reality, she clenched her hands tightly in her lap.

Jesse shifted again, his thigh accidently brushing hers. A current of need raced through her, settling low in her belly.

When they pulled up in front of his house, she didn't

wait for Jesse to assist her from the buggy. She hiked up her skirts and jumped down, unconcerned about the good deal of leg she revealed in the process.

Murmuring something Jesse couldn't make out, she ran into the house before he could open his mouth. For several seconds he stared in stunned silence at the door. The tenseness he'd felt sitting next to a rigid-backed Fantasy melted away, a knowing smile touching his lips.

He chuckled, certain he'd just witnessed another indication of her lack of immunity to him. Feeling carefree for the first time in days, he wrapped the reins around the brake handle and leaped from the buggy. When his feet hit the ground, he sucked in a surprised breath. Every muscle in his body screamed in protest at the bone-jarring landing.

Gritting his teeth against the ache in his back and the stab of pain in his legs, he limped over to help Robby off his mare.

"Are ya okay, Jesse?"

Jesse managed to smile at the look of concern on the boy's face. Although he'd overdone it, his muscles tightening up fast, his elation at Fantasy's telling behavior overrode the pain. His smile widened. "Couldn't be better, Buckshot. Couldn't be better."

Chapter 11

Tombstone's celebration of the United States's one hundred and sixth Independence Day was a gala affair. But as the parade moved past Fantasy's vantage point on Allen Street, she just couldn't summon up enthusiasm to match the rest of the townsfolk.

She glanced at her son, secure in Jesse's arms, and smiled. Robby's obvious excitement raised her flagging spirits, if only for a little while. Turning her attention back to the street, she watched the cavalry band from Fort Huachuca file past.

Next came a procession of the town's fire companies, members of the Daughters of Rebecca, Knights of Pythias, and the local post of the G.A.R. The latter, veterans of the Union forces in the War between the States, shouted and waved as they passed, bringing a round of equally loud yells from the crowd gathered on the boardwalks. At the end of the parade came the Tombstone Band, the mayor and city council, and finally citizens on horseback, in carriages or afoot.

When the music faded away and the dust settled, Fantasy sighed wearily. She'd barely paid attention to the last of the marchers. Her thoughts kept returning to Mattie's wedding four days earlier.

Mattie and Nash had been married on the last day of June in a filled St. Paul's Episcopal Church. Recalling Mattie's glowing face and Nash's beaming smile as they were presented to the congregation as Mr. and

Mrs. Sparks, Fantasy experienced another stab of envy. She wished again she had been the one getting married that day. *Stop it! It's a sin to covet what another has. Mattie deserves your best wishes, not your jealousy.*

Fantasy wondered where Mattie and Nash were on their wedding trip. They'd be gone for two entire months. Before their departure, the length of her friends' absence from town hadn't sunk in. Now the prospect of two months without seeing Mattie was truly a dismal one. If only Jesse hadn't—

"Fantasy?"

"Hmm?" She turned to look at the object of her thoughts, surprised to see his face creased with concern. "What is it?"

"Are you all right? I've been calling you, but you were a million miles away."

"Not so far as that." She gave him a wan smile. "I was just wondering what Mattie and Nash were doing."

Jesse lowered Robby to the boardwalk. As he straightened he murmured next to her ear, "Being newlyweds, I'm sure they can think of something to keep them busy."

A picture of Jesse's naked body entwined with hers flashed through her mind, causing a blush to warm her cheeks.

If Jesse was aware of her discomfort, he gave no sign of it. "So what would you like to do now?"

She lifted one shoulder in a shrug. "It doesn't matter."

Jesse's throat closed with pain at her obvious indifference. He'd done everything he could since visiting Mattie to prove to Fantasy his feelings for her were sincere. Though he'd spent every available minute with her, she kept her thoughts and feelings guarded at all times. He'd never felt so helpless. Carefully hiding his pain, he shifted his gaze to Robby. "How about you, Buckshot. What would you like to do?"

"Can we get some ice cream?"

Smiling at the hopeful look on the boy's face, Jesse turned back to Fantasy. "That okay with you?"

"Fine," she replied absently, and Jesse was sure her thoughts had already drifted to something else. Wrapping her arm through his, Jesse wondered what was keeping Fantasy so preoccupied. Was it Mattie and Nash again? He didn't dare hope her thoughts were about him. She'd given him no indication she still believed he worked for her in-laws. Then again, she'd given him no indication she believed he didn't. He knew she still responded to him physically. He'd seen her eyes darken with desire as she watched him. He'd noticed her pulse throbbing wildly at the base of her neck whenever he was near. He'd felt her skin quiver beneath his touch, just as it did now. Yet he'd done nothing about such knowledge; he wanted more than her physical reaction. He wanted her trust and her love.

It was very late when Jesse and Fantasy finally returned to his house. After an afternoon filled with a baseball game, shooting contests, sack races, and more food, the Fourth of July festivities had concluded with a dance hosted by the town's fire fighters and a spectacular display of fireworks exploding over the desert.

Carrying a sleeping Robby cradled in his arms, Jesse allowed Fantasy to open the front door, then followed her into the house. The lamp Mei-Ling left burning in the parlor gave off enough light for them to see down the hall to Fantasy's room.

As she and Jesse worked together to undress her son, Fantasy was reminded of the first time they'd shared this chore. She watched Jesse's hands gently remove Robby's shoes and socks, tears suddenly blurring her vision. Nearly overcome with the need to feel those strong hands caressing her body, she forced herself to look elsewhere.

When Robby was tucked into his bed, Jesse stood staring at the young face for several long seconds. His heart was so full of love for the boy he thought it would burst. Drawing a ragged breath, he turned to leave. Fantasy's hand on his arm stopped him. Standing beside her, he kept his eyes lowered. He couldn't meet her gaze for fear she'd be able to read his innermost thoughts.

"Thank you for a wonderful day."

"No need to thank me." He exhaled heavily. "Besides, I'm not sure . . ."

"You're not sure what?"

He cleared his throat, then lifted his head to look at her. "I'm not sure you had such a good time today."

Her quick indrawn breath told him he'd hit his mark.

Fantasy's shock at his comment quickly turned to shame. He was right. She had acted like she hadn't enjoyed the day or his company. "I'm sorry if I gave you that impression. I assure you, I didn't mean to. It's just that I've had a lot on my mind lately, and . . ."

Before she could find the words to go on, Jesse touched his fingertips to her lips. "I know," he whispered, then turned and walked from the room.

Sleep came very slowly for Fantasy. Although exhausted from the long day, her mind refused to let her body find its much needed rest. Instead, she relived every day since Jesse had entered her life. By the time her memory finished replaying every night of their lovemaking, her body was no longer tired, but agitated and as tight as a bowstring. She squirmed restlessly in her bed, longing for Jesse's touch to take away the ache.

As the minutes crawled by, her thoughts moved on to Jesse's behavior since she'd confronted him with her suspicions. She had to admit he'd done nothing to indicate he was working for Mother Williams. Even so she wasn't sure she was ready to trust him again. Slipping into a fitful sleep, Fantasy's last thought was regardless of all that had transpired, one thing hadn't changed. She still loved Jesse.

Jesse spent time the next day seeking more information about Ramón García. In a vacant lot behind Walsh's Saloon on Allen Street, he ran into Nick at one of the favorite pastimes of the local men.

Jesse turned away, bile rising to his throat. The shouting of the men gathered to watch pair after pair of roosters ruffle their plumage, prance around in little jumps, then leap in the air with spurs flashing toward a vital spot on their opponents, continued behind him. How anyone could enjoy cock fights completely alluded him.

"No stomach for this so-called sport, huh?"

Jesse frowned at Nick's amused smile. "No. Does your presence mean you like it?"

Nick's smile faded. In a low voice said, "Definitely not. This business of betting on the outcome of roosters having at each other in a death fight sickens me, too. As barbaric as cock fighting is, the violence isn't always confined to the cockpit. Not long ago, two men got into such a heated argument after a match was declared a draw, one of them pulled a gun and killed the other."

"So, if you don't like this kind of entertainment," Jesse said, "what are you doing here?"

"The men I'm keeping an eye on like cock fights, so I have to pretend to enjoy them."

"Who's that?"

"The men you were asking about a few weeks ago."

"The Arnettes? I followed García here, but didn't know the Arnettes liked this kind of thing." Jesse scanned the crowd of men clustered around the roped-off area. "Where are they?" Since learning their names he hadn't had the opportunity to see their faces.

"Over there." Nick nodded toward the right side of

the cockpit. "You can't miss them. They're the ones yelling the loudest. Buck's the taller one."

Jesse scrutinized the two men. They were about average height, though as Nick had pointed out, Buck topped Daryl by a couple of inches. Besides being clean-shaven and having long, brownish-blonde hair, Jesse couldn't make out anything more about their features because of the distance separating them.

His disgust growing, Jesse watched the Arnettes hoot and holler their approval for a Black Minorca Rooster who'd slashed his opponent so many times the loss of blood left the bird near death. Pressing his lips into a flat line, he turned to Nick. "Let's get the hell out of here."

Slapping Jesse on the back, Nick said, "Come on, I'll buy you a beer."

"I think I need something stronger to wash the vile taste from my mouth," Jesse grumbled.

Once they had each tossed down a shot of whiskey and settled at a table to sip their second drink, Nick said, "So, how're things going? I haven't talked to you in a while."

" 'Bout the same. I'm pretty sure I now know the names of all the members of Lawson's gang, and I know Wing Fong, the owner of a laundry in Hop Town, is their fence for the jewelry they take from the stage passengers."

"You don't sound very happy."

"I'm not sure John will think I have enough to issue warrants. I need some physical evidence to strengthen our case. But if I don't come up with something soon, I'll contact John anyway and see what he wants to do."

Nick pulled his cigar case from his jacket pocket. Withdrawing and lighting a cheroot, he studied his friend with eyes squinted against the smoke curling upward. He eased back in his chair and exhaled the blue-gray smoke, noting the slump of Jesse's shoulders and the almost bleak look haunting his eyes.

"Something else bothering you, Jesse?"

For a minute Nick didn't think he was going to answer. Then finally Jesse said, "Yeah. Remember I told you Fantasy's mother-in-law is bent on having Robby live with her in St. Louis?" Nick nodded. "Well, the other day I ran into Garland Baxter. He asked about Fantasy and if she was planning on moving back East. When I asked him why he would think such a thing, he got real antsy, like he'd said too much and couldn't wait to get out of my sight."

"So what'd he say?"

Jesse took a sip of his whiskey. "He mumbled something about since her boardinghouse was gone he figured she'd probably want to move back to St. Louis. Then he made some lame excuse and hot-footed it outta there before I could ask him any more questions."

"Do you think he's the one who tipped off the Williamses about the fire?"

"I don't know. Could be. I noticed something I never caught before. He looked pretty shabby. The collar and cuffs of his shirt were worn thin, his suit nearly threadbare. Must be his job doesn't pay well, or else he spends every cent he makes."

"He gambles a great deal. I've seen him shoot craps a few times. He always lost more than he won."

"If he has big gambling debts, that would explain why he might be willing to work for Henrietta Williams."

"Are you going to tell Fantasy?"

Jesse's mouth curved into a bittersweet smile. "No. I'm afraid she'd accuse me of trying to shift the blame to someone else for what she thinks I did. Besides, it's only a feeling I've got. I don't know for a fact it was Baxter."

Nick smoked his cigar in silence, mulling over Jesse's predicament. Although his friend had never admitted it, Jesse was obviously in love with Fantasy Williams, and her cold shoulder was taking its toll.

Softly, Nick said, "What're you gonna do about Fantasy?"

Jesse blew out an exasperated breath. "I wish I knew, Nick. I'd try anything, even sit on a damn cactus, to get her back."

Nick's laughter broke the somber mood. "Don't wish for that too hard, ol' friend, or you just may get it."

Jesse chuckled. "Oh, come on, Nick, you don't believe that old saying, do you?"

"I don't know. My mother always swore it was true."

"I think your mother was just superstitious."

"You're probably right," Nick said, smiling around the cigar clamped between his teeth.

The next day, Jesse and Robby headed out into the desert of the San Pedro Valley on horseback. The sun was a bright glow in a deep azure sky. There wasn't a cloud in sight. A stiff breeze kept the afternoon from being unbearably hot.

They had only gone about a mile southwest of town when the wind picked up. The dust swirled around the horses' legs, making Banjo toss his head and sidestep nervously each time a gust of wind buffeted him. Normally on the lookout for his horse's antics, Jesse paid little attention to the gelding's highly agitated behavior. His concentration dulled by jumbled thoughts of Fantasy and his job, he acted strictly by rote to keep the horse in line.

From behind a clump of ocotillo, a quail darted in front of Banjo. The horse shied sideways, his eyes rolling wildly, his ears flattened against his head. Before Jesse could react and calm the gelding, a second quail scampered after the first. The sudden movement near his hooves sent Banjo into a panic. Rearing, the pinto flipped a totally unprepared Jesse from his back.

Frightened and confused, Banjo turned toward town and took off at a gallop.

"Jesse? Are ya all right, Jesse?"

Robby's voice came to Jesse as if from a great distance. His chest hurt from having the wind knocked out of him, making it impossible to talk.

"Jesse!"

Hearing the panic in the boy's voice, he wished he could do something to ease it. But it took all his concentration just to breathe. Finally the ache eased and he managed to draw a deep breath. He opened his eyes, squinting against the intense glare of the sun. When his surroundings came into focus, he saw Robby standing a few feet away. Attempting to get up, he shifted from his sitting position on the ground. "Owww. What the—" He dropped his gaze to the ground next to him and bit back a particularly nasty curse word.

He blinked several times before his abnormally slow-to-function brain finally accepted what his eyes saw. He was sitting smack-dab in the center of a patch of prickly pear. He shifted again and immediately wished he hadn't. He felt another sharp jab in his rear end, and knew that particular part of him had been turned into a pincushion, filled with cactus spine pins.

"Robby, can you come here? Looks like I'm gonna need your help."

"Whatcha want me to do, Jesse?"

"Bring Maggie as close as you can, then hand me her reins. I'm gonna use her to pull me up."

Doing as Jesse asked, Robby got Maggie into position, then gave her the command to back up. The mare's reins wrapped around his hands, Jesse gritted his teeth as Maggie pulled him from his thorny seat. But not before his bottom bounced several times on the cactus as he struggled to find his footing.

Jesse straightened carefully, uncertain if the extent of his injuries went beyond a prickly behind. He winced when the movement made the cactus spines

poke deeper. With Robby's help he pulled out as many
of the needle-sharp spines as he could, but there were
others he couldn't get at. They'd gone clean through
his jeans, embedding themselves in his flesh.

"Jesse, ya wanna ride double?"

"I wish I could, Buckshot. But I don't think I'd
better chance sitting down. I already got me a seat full
of that old prickly pear's spines and I don't want to
push them in any deeper. You go ahead and mount up.
I'll just walk back to town."

Robby looked at him dubiously, then finally hoisted
himself into the saddle. He tried to keep a conversation
going on the long, hot walk to Tombstone, but finally
fell silent when Jesse responded with only a grunt, if at
all.

At the edge of town Jesse said, "Go on home,
Robby. I'm heading for Doc McKee's office." Not
giving the boy time to answer, Jesse strode gingerly
down Allen Street and turned south on Fifth.

Grimacing with each painful jolt of his body, Jesse
called Banjo every foul name he could think of. As he
entered the small office of Dr. McKee in an adobe
building on the west side of Fifth Street, Nick's words
came back to him about making brash wishes.

"Naw, it couldn't be," he grumbled aloud. A grim
smile twisted his mouth. Then again, that *was* the only
prickly pear he'd seen for miles.

Glancing around the outer office, Jesse sighed with
relief. Thank God no one would witness his humiliation. He'd never hear the end of it if word ever got out
about this.

"Momma, Momma!"

Robby bolted through the front door and raced into
the parlor where Fantasy sat crocheting a lace edge on
a pillow slip she'd embroidered. "What is it, sweetheart? Calm down and tell me what's so important."

"Jesse," he wheezed. "It's Jesse."

Fantasy's heart leaped to her throat. "What about Jesse?"

"He got throwed from Banjo, and—"

"Thrown? Oh my God, what happened? Is he hurt? Where is he?"

Uncertain which question to answer first, Robby finally decided on the last one. "He went to Doc McKee's office."

Jamming her crocheting into her new sewing basket, Fantasy was off the settee and opening the front door before her son had time to blink. "You stay here with Mei-Ling. I'm going to . . ." The rest of her words were lost as she sailed out the door and pulled it closed behind her with a loud bang.

Her heart hammering against her ribs, Fantasy tried to keep her wits about her as she nearly ran the two and a half blocks down Fifth Street to Dr. McKee's. But her wits weren't listening. They continued to conjure up all kinds of possible injuries that Jesse might have suffered, each one more horrible than the last.

Breathless, she arrived at the doctor's office and burst inside. Her gaze fixed on the closed examination room door, she marched across the reception area, and grabbed the door knob.

When the door swung open, the sight meeting her eyes wasn't at all what she'd expected.

Jesse was lying on his stomach on the table, arms folded in front of him, chin resting on his crossed hands. Moving her gaze down the length of his body, her eyes widened. He was naked from his hiked-up shirt at his waist to where his pants bunched around his knees.

Her gasp of shock caused Jesse and Dr. McKee to look in her direction.

"Fantasy!" the two men said in unison.

The doctor chuckled. "I take it, Mr. McAllister, you know my assistant. Though I wasn't expecting her today."

"Yeah, Doc, I know her."

In a low voice, the doctor said, "Should I ask her to leave?"

Jesse studied Fantasy's face for several seconds. A lazy smile playing about his lips, he said, "She can stay if she wants."

Doc McKee nodded, then went back to his task. "As long as you're here, Fantasy, will you bring me the bottle of antiseptic?"

Fantasy stood transfixed just inside the doorway, her gaze alternating between Jesse's face and his buttocks. Relief he wasn't hurt as badly as she'd envisioned rushed over her.

"Fantasy, I asked for the antiseptic."

Doc McKee's voice jerked her back to the present. She glanced at the man she worked with several afternoons a week. Piercing blue eyes beneath drawn-together graying eyebrows peered at her over the top of his glasses. *Oh no, what have I done?* She wondered how a person got out of such an embarrassing situation.

She cleared her throat, trying her best to sound unaffected by Jesse's near-nakedness and the hot flush burning her face. "I can't stay. Doc. Robby said Jesse had been thrown from his horse, and I was concerned—I mean Robby was concerned about him. Jesse's one of my boarders, and . . . anyway, now that I know he wasn't seriously hurt, I'll just . . . um . . . leave."

"Fantasy, you don't have—" The slamming of the door cut off Jesse's words.

The pain from Doc McKee's jabbing and poking at his tender flesh faded as Jesse remembered Fantasy's sudden entrance and equally fast exit. He smiled again, recalling the look on her face when she'd barged into the examination room. There was no mistaking that look. She cared. And if he had read her eyes correctly, she cared one hell of a lot.

His mood lighter than it had been in several weeks, Jesse accepted the jar of salve Doc McKee handed him, paid his bill, and headed for home. Although his pants chafed against the places where Doc had dug out the cactus spines, the pain wasn't unbearable. And thinking about the discovery he'd made about Fantasy, he barely noticed the discomfort.

Fantasy paced the floor of her bedroom restlessly. Robby had been asleep for several hours and still she didn't feel the least bit sleepy. She was wide awake, her nerves on edge, and she knew why.

Jesse.

She kept seeing him stretched out on the table in the doctor's office, pants around his knees, his muscular buttocks drawing her gaze time and again. There was a strange tightness throughout her body. A tautness that didn't ease with her pacing, but continued to pull tighter.

Stopping abruptly, she knew what she must do. What she wanted to do. She'd been a fool to deny what she wanted for so long. Before she changed her mind, she slipped from the room. Moving quietly down the hall, she stopped in front of Jesse's room and took a deep breath.

She wiped her palms nervously on her skirt, then reached out and touched the door. It wasn't latched and swung inward easily. Through the partially opened doorway, Fantasy could see into the bedroom.

A single lamp on the bedside table illuminated the room with bright, golden light. Her quick visual search found Jesse standing in front of the full-length mirror in one corner. Pressing a hand against her mouth to stifle a gasp, her eyes widened. A curl of heat formed low in her belly, sending fingers of fire surging through her body. Jesse was naked!

Although facing her, his torso was twisted sideways so he could look in the mirror while he tried to apply some kind of cream to the angry red spots on his bottom.

Wish You Were Here?

You can be, every month, with Zebra Historical Romance Novels.

AND TO GET YOU STARTED, ALLOW US TO SEND YOU

4 Historical Romances Free

AN $18.00 VALUE!

With absolutely no obligation to buy anything.

YOU ARE CORDIALLY INVITED TO GET SWEPT AWAY INTO NEW WORLDS OF PASSION AND ADVENTURE.

AND IT WON'T COST YOU A PENNY!

Receive 4 Zebra Historical Romances, Absolutely *Free!*

(An $18.00 value)

Now you can have your pick of handsome, noble adventurers with romance in their hearts and you on their minds. Zebra publishes Historical Romances That Burn With The Fire Of History by the world's finest romance authors.

This very special FREE offer entitles you to 4 Zebra novels at absolutely no cost, with no obligation to buy anything, ever. It's an offer designed to excite your most vivid dreams and desires...and save you $18!

And that's not all you get...

Your Home Subscription Saves You Money Every Month.

After you've enjoyed your initial FREE package of 4 books, you'll begin to receive monthly shipments of new Zebra titles. These novels are delivered direct to your home as soon as they are published...sometimes even before the bookstores get them! Each monthly shipment of 4 books will be yours to examine for 10 days. Then if you decide to keep the books, you'll pay the preferred subscriber's price of just $3.75 per title. That's $15 for all 4 books...a savings of $3 off the publisher's price! (A nominal shipping and handling charge of $1.50 per shipment will be added.)

There Is No Minimum Purchase. And Your Continued Satisfaction Is Guaranteed.

We're so sure that you'll appreciate the money-saving convenience of home delivery that we guarantee your complete satisfaction. You may return any shipment...for any reason...within 10 days and pay nothing that month. And if you want us to stop sending books, just say the word. There is no minimum number of books you must buy.

It's a no-lose proposition, so send for your 4 FREE books today!

YOU'RE GOING TO LOVE GETTING
4 FREE BOOKS

These books worth $18, are yours without cost or obligation
when you fill out and mail this certificate.
*(If the certificate is missing below, write to: Zebra Home Subscription Service, Inc.,
120 Brighton Road, P.O. Box 5214, Clifton, New Jersey 07015-5214*

Complete and mail this card to receive 4 Free books!

Yes! Please send me 4 Zebra Historical Romances without cost or obligation. I understand that each month thereafter I will be able to preview 4 new Zebra Historical Romances FREE for 10 days. Then, if I should decide to keep them, I will pay the money-saving preferred publisher's price of just $3.75 each...a total of $15. That's $3 less than the publisher's price. (A nominal shipping and handling charge of $1.50 per shipment will be added.) I may return any shipment within 10 days and owe nothing, and I may cancel this subscription at any time. The 4 FREE books will be mine to keep in any case.

Name _____

Address _____ Apt. _____

City _____ State _____ Zip _____

Telephone ( ) _____

Signature _____ LP1194
(If under 18, parent or guardian must sign.)

Terms, offer and prices subject to change without notice. Subscription subject to acceptance by Zebra Books. Zebra Books reserves the right to reject any order or cancel any subscription.

Sensing someone's presence, Jesse's head snapped up. His intense, piercing gaze met and held Fantasy's wide-eyed stare in the mirror. The jar in his hand forgotten, as well as the stinging of his wounds, he turned toward the door. He exhaled a breath of relief. He hadn't imagined her there.

For several long seconds neither of them moved, then finally Fantasy shook herself out of her trance. Stepping into the room and closing the door behind her, she kept her gaze carefully on Jesse's face as she approached him. When she stood in front of him, she gently removed the jar from his hand. After glancing at the label, she allowed her gaze to roam hungrily over his heavily muscled, hair-covered chest before returning to his face.

"May I?" she asked in a husky whisper.

Swallowing hard, Jesse nodded. When she lowered herself onto her knees behind him, his breath stuck in his throat.

Her fingers dipped into the jar of salve, then reached toward one of the red marks marring his otherwise perfect male beauty. Abruptly her hand stilled.

Jesse nearly swallowed his tongue when her lips touched his right buttock. Unable to stop himself, he turned his head to look in the mirror. *Sweet Mother of God.* He clenched his fists at his sides, wanting to tear his gaze away from the picture of her kneeling behind him, her lips brushing his flesh. But he couldn't. The touch of her soft mouth had aroused his body, but watching her erotic ministrations proved even more stimulating. Although on the verge of losing control, he couldn't look away from the reflection in the mirror.

After Fantasy kissed each place a cactus spine had pierced his flesh she applied the salve in gentle, kneading, circular motions. The curl of heat between her thighs had increased to a raging inferno and continued to intensify with each touch of her fingers on his skin. When the last of his wounds had received her full attention, she wiped her hands on a towel draped over a nearby chair and started to get to her feet.

Jesse turned around, grasped her elbows, then hauled her up. Holding her at arms' length, he studied her face silently. Finally satisfied with what he found, he pulled her slowly toward him. In a low whisper, he said, "If you want to leave, go now."

She shook her head, never taking her gaze from his. A moan rumbling in his chest, Jesse lowered his head and captured her mouth in a burning kiss.

One kiss led to another, kisses led to caresses, until she found herself lying across his bed as naked as Jesse.

Although he wanted nothing more than to take her quickly, almost violently, he forced himself to draw out their mutual pleasure. He wanted to savor every kiss, every touch until they were both drunk with need. He began with tiny, fluttery kisses on her nose, cheeks, and chin, then moved lower to whisk across her collarbone, the pert peak of one breast and the downy skin of her belly.

Her stomach muscles contracted when he didn't stop his explorations but continued his descent. Jesse nuzzled the auburn nest guarding her femininity and inhaled her scent. His tongue pushed through the tight curls until he touched the pink folds of skin hiding beneath. Her body's stiffening with shock didn't go unnoticed. He kissed the triangle of silky hair and reluctantly lifted his head, promising himself some day soon he would show her the pleasure he could give her with his mouth.

Stretching out on his left side next to her, Jesse braced himself on one elbow and lowered his lips to hers. He drank deeply from the well of her mouth, quenching his thirst and at the same time making him thirst for more.

"Fancy. Fancy," he whispered against her neck. "I want you so much."

She turned her head to give him better access to her throat. "Jesse, please. I can't . . ."

Lifting his head and staring down into her passion-clouded eyes, he lazily ran one finger around the tip of one distended nipple. Her eyes fluttered closed, and she moved restlessly beneath his touch.

"You can't what?"

Her eyelids opened slowly. "I can't wait . . ."

"Tell me, Fancy. Tell me what you can't wait for."

A moment of panic flashed in the depths of her eyes, but quickly fled when his hand squeezed her breast. "I can't wait to have you inside me," she finally said in a faint whisper. But Jesse heard, and his heart began an even wilder, more savage rhythm against his ribs.

A growl of pleasure escaped his lips. As he melded his mouth to hers, he rolled her so she was lying on her right side facing him. He taunted and teased her lips, and then her tongue until she whimpered in protest. Lifting her left leg, he draped it over his right hip, then thrust his pelvis forward.

The feel of his fully aroused manhood pressing against her belly caused her to moan and strain to get closer to his hardened flesh. When she tried to roll onto her back, he stopped her. "No, love, stay on your side. We'll make love like this."

Not sure what she was supposed to do, she let him take the lead. But when he grasped her hand and lowered it to his throbbing arousal, she knew what he wanted. He was hot and hard and pulsed against her hand as she guided him to the sanctuary of her moist center.

He pushed into her slowly, gently, though he wanted to drive forward with one mighty plunge. When he was at last fully encased in her warmth, Jesse heaved a long sigh of pleasure. He heard her answering sigh and smiled into her flushed face. "I never knew anything could feel this good," he admitted as he began rocking his hips in a slow, easy motion.

"Neither did I," was her whispered reply.

Grasping her bottom, he pulled her closer and felt himself sink even deeper into her tight sheath. He clenched his teeth to stop his fast-approaching climax, but he had little success. "Damn, not yet," he groaned, as the milking action of her muscles stripped him of control.

Sensing his release was near, Fantasy increased the tempo of her thrusts against him and kissed him wildly.

Somehow through the fog of his passion, Jesse realized Fantasy wasn't going to join him in reaching the ultimate satisfaction. Determined she wouldn't be denied, he lowered one hand and quickly found the nubbin of flesh just above where their bodies were joined. Concentrating on guiding her to her pleasure momentarily took his mind off his own release. But as soon as she started bucking against him and tossing her head from side to side, the pressure returned full force.

Their hips thrusting in unison, his hand rubbing her sensitive flesh, they shouted their joy just moments apart.

His arms and legs heavy with the aftermath of incredible, heart-stopping pleasure, Jesse shifted onto his back as he carefully pushed Fantasy's leg from his hip. He slipped one arm under her shoulders and rolled her against his chest. Wrapping his arms around her, he held her tight, brushing his lips across her forehead.

Fantasy snuggled close, pressing her face against his chest. The frenzied thumping of his heart beneath her cheek matched her own racing pulse. She turned to kiss the ridge of muscle and smiled when the thick patch of hair tickled her nose.

As Jesse smoothed the long, silky length of her hair over her shoulders and down her back, she let her body relax and her mind wander. Basking in the afterglow of spent passion, Fantasy sighed with contentment. She had never been happier.

Chapter 12

A week later, Fantasy's newfound happiness was shattered.

Swallowing hard, Fantasy managed to clear only part of the enormous lump stuck in her throat. Tears stung her eyes as she stared out the parlor window. *Why won't they leave me alone? Why won't Mother Williams let me live my life in peace?*

Wiping her eyes, she picked up the telegram and reread Henrietta Williams's straightforward message. Will arrive in Tombstone on twenty-fourth. Expect Robby to return with us. There was no mention of Fantasy, but then that was no surprise. Mother Williams had always had difficulty accepting her as family, and the woman had never made any bones about it.

Fantasy folded the telegram carefully, holding back the urge to rip it to shreds, then rose from her chair. In her bedroom, she slipped the telegram into the top drawer of her dresser, wishing she could forget about it as easily as it disappeared beneath her clothes.

What a fool I've been. Sinking onto her bed, she sighed. *Just a silly, naive fool to think my happiness with Jesse these last few days could erase the problem of Henrietta.*

Stretching out on top of the quilt, she rolled over to face the wall. *Oh, Mattie, I wish you or Spud were here. I need to talk to someone.* For a fleeting second she considered talking to Jesse. But her determination to be independent and to take charge of her own life squashed the idea. Maintaining her independence meant dealing with whatever cropped up. She'd have to take care of this latest setback on her own.

Fantasy had always been able to handle Mother Williams's demands when they lived over a thousand miles apart. Now the woman was coming to the Arizona Territory, and Fantasy was terrified the woman would find some way to get what she wanted. A sob welled up in Fantasy's throat and escaped before she could stop it. What would she do if Henrietta managed to take Robby away from her? She bit her lip to stop the tears, but they overflowed and streamed down her cheeks.

Unable to come up with a plan for the showdown with her in-laws, Fantasy went through the next several days in a stupor of confusion. Only one thing kept her from losing her mind completely—the haven of Jesse's arms. At night when she sought his bed and the comfort of his touch, the fear of Mother Williams's impending arrival faded from her conscious thoughts.

Jesse sensed a change in Fantasy, but was unable to discern the cause. She said very little; in fact, she was extremely quiet—until she came to his room each night. Then it was as if a spigot had been opened and all her pent-up energy rushed out in a deluge. Though she'd never been passive in bed, she became more aggressive. Within the privacy of his bedroom, she shed her daytime reserve and turned fierce and demanding.

While he found no fault with her bold forwardness, he knew it hadn't come about as the natural progression of their physical relationship. Something else had driven her to this new behavior. But what?

The solution to the puzzle haunted Jesse constantly. His attempts to get her to talk gained him nothing. She said only that she could deal with it. Whatever *it* was, Jesse didn't agree with her. He'd studied her carefully and observed her nervous pacing when she thought no one was watching. He'd seen the faint smudges of color under her eyes. Apparently even their vigorous lovemaking wasn't tiring her enough to allow her to get the rest she needed. Finally Jesse could stand being a witness to her suffering no longer.

"Jesse, where are you taking me?" Fantasy said, trying to halt their progress across the parlor of his house.

Jesse smiled but didn't stop. He kept on walking toward the front door, pulling a still resisting Fantasy behind him. "We're going for a ride," he said over his shoulder.

"Ride?" Fantasy managed to jerk her arm free. Her heart pounded heavily against her ribs. Had he found out about her riding lessons? She had taken great pains to make sure no one knew about the time she'd spent with Gil, planning to keep it secret until she'd conquered her fear of horses.

Jesse turned to look at her, his brows pulling together at the panic reflected on her face. Grabbing her shoulders, he held her gently at arms' length. "I thought we'd go for a buggy ride out to Granite Springs. You seemed to like the mountains last time we were there. Wouldn't you like to go back?"

She closed her eyes for a second. *Thank goodness, he doesn't know.* Meeting his gaze, she attempted a smile. "I suppose. I do like the mountains."

He bussed her nose with a quick kiss, then released her arms. "Good, come on then." He opened the door, then allowed her to step outside first. "It'll do you good to get away and get your mind off whatever's bothering you."

Her expression changed immediately, fear flashing across her features again before a shutter dropped down to hide it from his view. Jesse wanted to shake her and make her tell him what had her so upset. Instead he turned towards the horse and buggy waiting in front of the house.

Once Fantasy settled on the buggy seat next to him,
she relaxed, the tense moments between them forgotten. As Jesse directed them across the desert toward
the Dragoon Mountains, she forgot about Henrietta's
arrival and concentrated on the man sitting next to
her.

Convinced he'd succeeded in taking Fantasy's mind
off whatever was bothering her for a little while that
afternoon, Jesse smiled. Recalling the look on her face
while she dangled her toes in the cool mountain stream
beneath the stand of cottonwood trees, his smile
broadened. She looked so carefree, so content during
their time at the spring. Unfortunately, it was a short
reprieve. As soon as they reached the outskirts of town
on the return ride, he'd felt her stiffen next to him. Her
light mood vanished, replaced by somber silence. Yet
when he asked, she insisted nothing was wrong.

As he prepared for bed, Jesse decided to make sure
he found other diversions to keep her occupied. He
had to find a way to break down her resistance. He
wanted desperately to help, but first she had to talk to
him. The woman he loved was proving to be extremely
stubborn. He smiled again as he pulled off his boots,
then stripped out of his clothes.

He had just thrown back the covers and stretched
out on the bed when the door opened and Fantasy
stepped over the threshold. As always, the sight of her
standing in his room, her hair loose around her shoulders, sent his pulse to a faster pace. When she reached
for the buttons of her shirtwaist, his heart rate increased even more.

Shinnying out of her dress and petticoat, Fantasy
kicked them aside and reached for the hem of her
chemise. Her arms moving in provocative slow motion, she lifted the lace-trimmed undergarment upward. Her ribs, the creamy undersides of her breasts,
the rosy nipples and finally her entire tantalizing

bosom appeared to Jesse's hungry gaze. Without breaking eye contact, she tossed the garment to the floor, then lowered her hands to the waistband of her drawers. One pull and the bow came free. Wiggling her hips, the white muslin slithered down her legs. She tipped her head back and gave her hair a shake, sending the heavy, auburn cascade swaying around her shoulders. Stepping out of the soft pile of muslin encircling her feet, she slowly moved toward him.

Jesse growled with pleasure. "What a temptress you are." Reaching up to grasp a handful of her hair, he wrapped it around his fist as he gently pulled her down next to him.

Their lips came together with a need that surprised him. Her teasing game of undressing had excited him beyond anything he'd expected, setting his body ablaze with desire.

Beginning with his mouth Fantasy began a kiss caravan over his face, kissing his chin, his cheeks, then finally back to his mouth. Wild with the need to please Jesse as much as she wanted to be pleased, her hands were as busy as her mouth. She caressed the bulging muscles of his arms, his hair-covered chest, then the flat, tautness of his belly until he groaned and shifted restlessly next to her.

In one fluid motion, she pushed him onto his back and rolled atop him, her mouth absorbing his grunt of surprise. Thrilled with her new position of dominance, Fantasy savored the heady feeling of being in command. Her lips clinging to his, she touched every place her hands could reach, twisting and wiggling her body to allow her fingers better access.

"Fancy, slow down, for heaven's sake," Jesse said when she finally broke the kiss.

"Don't you like what I'm doing?" she responded in a husky whisper, before nipping his earlobe with her teeth.

"Jesus!" The breath rushed from Jesse's lungs. "Yes, oh God, yes," he gasped, his already engorged sex growing fuller as the tip of her tongue teased the inside of his ear.

Feeling the insistent throbbing of his arousal against her belly, Fantasy rotated her hips suggestively and was rewarded by a groan from deep in his chest. She shifted her position again, bringing her knees up until she sat straddling his thighs. Watching his face carefully, she lowered her hand to between their bodies and firmly grasped his manhood.

Jesse groaned again, squeezing his eyes closed. Reveling in this unfamiliar feeling of control, Fantasy tightened her fingers. His pulsing response within the circle of her grip and the lifting of his hips encouraged her to continue. In a slow, easy tempo she stroked up and down the length of his shaft until he jerked her hand away.

"No more," he said in an agonized whisper.

Grasping her around the waist, he lifted her off him. Suddenly their positions reversed, she flat on her back and he on his knees between her thighs. He lazily ran his hand up the inside of her right leg from her calf to just below the nest of auburn curls. She mumbled a protest when he didn't touch her heated flesh but began a downward journey on her left leg.

"You teased me, now it's my turn," he said just before lowering his head and running his tongue around her navel.

"But, I wasn't teasing," she replied, sounding breathless.

"No? Then I shan't tease you." He smiled, his lips just inches above his next target. Dropping his face, he nuzzled the silky hair and felt her instant stiffening. He persisted, kissing the soft triangle while his fingers sought her woman's center. When he kissed the exposed pink flesh, she bucked beneath him, her hands pushing frantically at his shoulders. He raised his head to look into her face. Her eyes were dilated and wide with a combination of shock and desire.

"Your husband never loved you like this, did he?"

Although mortified to the core at Jesse's question, Fantasy found she couldn't look away from his intense stare. She shook her head.

Though he'd been sure what her answer would be, her negative response still sent relief rushing through him. He wanted to be the first to love her this way. "He was a fool, Fancy. Let me love you, sweetheart, let me love you like you were meant to be loved."

She said nothing, yet Jesse felt her consent in the slight easing of her tense muscles. Lowering his head once more, he touched her gently with his tongue.

She nearly came off the bed from the bolt of lightning ripping through her. "Jesse?"

"It's okay, love," he murmured against her, then began flicking his tongue against the hardened kernel of her femininity.

With the wildfire his mouth fostered surging through her veins, Fantasy's inhibitions fell away. She gave herself over to her fast growing need to find relief from the pleasure-torture of his loving. As the pressure continued to build she rhythmically lifted her hips from the bed to push against him. Her breathing became short, harsh pants until she sucked in one great gasping breath. "Jesse, I'm . . . Jesse, please!" Arching up one last time, her release overtook her in one shattering spasm after another. As the last of her tremors rippled through her body, Jesse rose above her. Pulling her legs up around his waist, he pushed into her with one swift thrust. Coming very close to climaxing himself when she'd reached her peak, just a few quick strokes returned him to that same level of excitement. As he increased the tempo of his thrusts, he was surprised to feel Fantasy responding again. Rocking forward, he changed his movements to rub more fully against her still aroused flesh.

She bucked wildly beneath him, her nails biting into his back. Feeling the contractions of her inner muscles tightening around him with her second release, Jesse finally let himself find his own pleasure. With a loud groan, he thrust one last time, then collapsed on top of her.

As the wild thrumming of his heart calmed, the tension slowly seeped from his body. When his senses returned enough to realize he still lay sprawled atop Fantasy, he gathered the last of his strength and rolled off her. Pulling her into his arms, he settled her head on his shoulder and ran his fingers through her hair, trying to smooth the tangled curls.

"Are you okay?" he finally asked.

"Hmm, yes," she answered, her voice drowsy.

He smiled against the top of her head. "You aren't upset with me for what I said about your husband, are you?"

Fantasy rubbed her cheek against his shoulder. "About being a fool? No. Thomas was a fool. I mean . . . I never knew a man could . . . anyway, Thomas was a fool about a lot of things."

Jesse hugged her tight. "Don't be embarrassed, Fancy. What I did is perfectly natural. I want you to know that, though some people may not share my opinion."

"They're fools, too," she said, her cheeks burning.

Jesse chuckled and hugged her again. "You're absolutely right. They are fools."

They were silent for a long time, content to share the aftermath of their passion without speaking. At last Jesse said, "Fancy, tell me what's been bothering you." He felt the tension creep back into her body and feared she wouldn't answer. "I want to help if I can, Fancy. Please believe me."

She sighed heavily, then placed a kiss on his chest. "I know that, Jesse. I just don't think there's anything anyone can do."

"Why don't you tell me, and let me decide?"

Shoving away from him, she flopped onto her back and draped one arm over her eyes. She'd tried so hard to come up with something on her own, some way to stall Henrietta's arrival and more importantly find a way to thwart the woman's plans. So far her efforts to be independent and handle this by herself had gained her nothing. She'd worked so hard to make it on her own, to not need anyone before the fire. One telegram had changed everything.

Though the realization she couldn't handle this herself was a harsh blow to her ego, the idea of allowing someone else to help carry the burden she'd been carrying was a welcome one. "I heard from Mother Williams again. She and her husband will be here in a little over a week."

"Here! They're coming to Tombstone?"

She dropped her arm to her side, then sat up. Tossing her hair over her shoulder, she said, "Yes, they're supposed to arrive on the twenty-fourth."

Jesse sat up, too, then scooted up against the headboard. "Why don't you tell me about this from the beginning?"

He watched Fantasy as she considered his request. She appeared to be fighting some inner battle. At last she took a deep breath and nodded. He patted the bed beside him in invitation.

After moving up and settling next to him, she entwined the fingers of her left hand with his right.

Staring at their clasped hands, she began speaking in a low voice. "I was in an orphanage in St. Louis when I first met Henrietta Williams."

Jesse blinked. "You were in an orphanage?"

"Yes. I told you about my father being killed." She looked up long enough to see his nod, then returned her gaze to their hands.

"I was a late-in-life baby, and my mother never fully recovered from the birth. My earliest memories are of her spending a good deal of each day in bed fighting the continual illnesses. When I was six another of the fevers she suffered proved too much for her weakened body." She paused to draw a deep, shuddering breath.

Jesse waited in agonized silence, his heart aching with Fantasy's remembered pain.

Gathering her strength, she picked up her story. "Since neither of my parents had any family, I was sent to the local orphanage. I'd been there five years and given up hope of ever being adopted when Henrietta marched in one day. She announced her plans to offer a good home to some poor, deprived orphan.

When Henrietta picked me, an eleven-year-old, over the younger children, I was thrilled. What she didn't say was that she wanted someone to do her housework more than she wanted a daughter."

Jesse gave her hand a squeeze, but kept his sudden anger to himself. Now that Fantasy was talking, he didn't want to do or say something to halt her narrative.

"Thomas was sixteen the first time I met him. He didn't pay much attention to me at first, and I was too busy doing whatever Henrietta wanted to worry about getting to know him. Thomas went away to school a few months after I moved into their house, and I didn't see him again until he came back several years later.

"By then I had . . . uh . . . filled out, and I guess I caught his eye because he started spending time with me. He even helped me with some of my endless housework. No one had shown me any kindness since I left the orphanage, so I guess I just naturally blossomed from Thomas's attention."

"Henrietta didn't object to her son spending time with you?"

"Oh, I'm sure she never knew. Thomas was always careful to spend time with me when his mother was out of the house. He knew how she could be, and he didn't want to cross her. When I turned sixteen Thomas asked me to marry him. I was flattered, and I even believed I was in love with him. But I also knew his mother would never allow it, and I told him so. He made me promise to marry him if he could get his mother to agree. You can imagine my shock when he told me his parents had agreed to the marriage when I turned seventeen."

"How do you think he convinced them?" Jesse asked, absently running his fingers over her knuckles.

"I found out later he threatened to run away with me and never return if they didn't allow us to get married. Henrietta loved her son above all else, so a month after my seventeenth birthday, Thomas and I were married."

"I hope you moved out of her house," Jesse said, his fingers tightening on hers.

Fantasy smiled wryly. "No. Thomas may have defied his parents to marry a nobody like me, but he wouldn't listen to my pleas to leave. He said his parents insisted we stay. Of course I didn't tell Thomas I was sure his mother had undoubtedly made the loudest noises about wanting him to stay, or about my suspicions on the real reason for her insisting she wanted us under their roof." Fantasy sighed heavily. "I was right. Henrietta wanted me to continue keeping her house while she spent her days lolling around or visiting her snooty friends. Every morning she rattled off a list of what she and I were to do that day. Of course, she never lifted a finger, so all the work fell to me. Within a month I was with child, but that didn't lessen my duties."

"Surely Thomas intervened for you."

"By then, I think Thomas had decided marriage wasn't to his liking." At Jesse's indrawn breath, she went on quickly. "Oh, he probably did love me in his own way, and I believed him when he said he was thrilled about the child. But a month later none of that mattered. He was struck with gold fever.

"He left for Nevada, promising to make us rich and swearing he'd be back before the birth of our child." She swallowed hard. "He arrived in St. Louis when Robby was three weeks old. But the lure of the mine fields was just too strong for him to resist. Even his family couldn't cool his gold fever. He left a week later."

"How long was he gone that time?"

"I never saw him again. He wrote whenever the mood hit. Or his conscience bothered him," she added, bitterness creeping into her voice. "At any rate, he didn't write very often, and he moved around a lot. When one strike petered out he'd pack up and head for the next promising find. That's how he ended up in Tombstone. When word of finding silver spread, he headed here immediately. That was two years ago.

"Then last summer he wrote and said he'd saved enough money for me to join him. Mother Williams wasn't too happy about my leaving and taking her grandson, but she wanted her son to be happy and having his family with him seemed to be what Thomas wanted." Fantasy fell silent, reliving those days in her mind and experiencing the pain again. When Jesse asked her what happened she told him about arriving in Tombstone with the son Thomas had only seen as a baby, but her husband didn't meet her stage.

"I started asking around to see if anyone knew where he was. Someone finally directed me to the sheriff. That's when I learned Thomas had been killed two weeks before I arrived."

"Why didn't you go back East, instead of staying in a strange town where you didn't know a soul?"

"Like I said, I had no family of my own to turn to, and I refused to go back to St. Louis and become Mother Williams's slave again. When the sheriff said Thomas had left some money in the bank I decided Tombstone was as good a place as any to begin my new life. So I took the money and opened the boardinghouse. I was happy here until Mother Williams started writing."

"She wanted Robby?"

"At first she didn't say that directly. She said she wanted both of us to move back to St. Louis, and she probably would have tolerated me in order to have the only thing left of her son, Robby. But I'm sure she would have been even happier if I'd remained here as long as I sent Robby to her.

Though hesitant to bring up the cause of the rift they'd had weeks before, Jesse finally said, "You mentioned Henrietta had sent someone to spy on you."

"Yes. She hired a private investigator. In some ways, I don't blame her for that. I mean, Tombstone does have a well-deserved reputation as a rough place. And I guess if I'd been in her shoes, I'd be concerned about the kind of town my grandson was living in."

"But that wasn't really why the man came here, was it?"

"No. After Mattie told me some man was asking around town about me, I went to see him. I must've been his first assignment, or else he'd never had the person he was investigating confront him directly, because my badgering for the truth paid off.

"He admitted Henrietta had hired him to learn everything he could about my life here. And if there was even one crumb of evidence that hinted at a scandal, she wanted to hear about it immediately. Although the man couldn't prove it, he said he was certain Henrietta intended to use the information to bribe me into going back to Missouri."

"But he didn't find anything, did he?" Confident he knew the answer, Jesse still wanted to hear her say the words.

Fantasy shook her head. "If he'd found anything he thought Henrietta could use, I doubt he would have allowed me to get near him. After talking to me, he decided he didn't want to get mixed up in a family squabble. He sat down right then and wrote a telegram to Henrietta telling her he'd found nothing and severing their relationship. To prove his sincerity, he asked me to take the message to the telegraph office."

"That didn't deter Henrietta though, huh?"

"No. In fact, it probably made her more determined. She never could stand being bested. She continued writing letters, each one more insistent that Robby should be raised in St. Louis. It wasn't until I received the telegram that I began to think she might—" her voice cracked pitifully, "—actually take Robby from me against my wishes."

"What do you mean?"

Fantasy turned to look into Jesse's face, her eyes shiny with tears. "The telegram I received a few days ago, the one announcing their visit, also said—" she swallowed the tears clogging her throat. "Henrietta expects Robby to return with them."

Jesse cursed beneath his breath, then aloud he said, "No wonder you've been so upset. I wish you'd told me sooner. I hate the idea of you suffering through this alone."

A lone tear rolled down Fantasy's cheek, making Jesse's heart cramp painfully. Brushing the wetness away with the pad of his thumb, he pulled her into his arms and held her close.

"I didn't know what to do," she said, her voice muffled against his chest. "I'm so afraid of what will happen when they get here. When they find out I'm living in the same house with a man I'm not married to Mother Williams will hit the ceiling—not with anger, but with triumph. This is exactly the type of situation she'd hoped for earlier, catching me in some sort of shameful behavior. Believe me, she'll waste no time in throwing the scandal in my face. I have to find another place to live, Jesse. I don't see any other choice."

Jesse stroked her back, working his fingers to ease the tension in her muscles. After a long silence, he said, "There is another choice, Fancy."

She tipped her face up to look at him. "What choice?"

Meeting her expectant gaze, he stared long and hard, then said, "Marry me."

Chapter 13

"Marry you?" Fantasy repeated. Bracing her hands on his chest, she pushed away from him so she could study his face. "Did I hear you right?"

"Yes, marry me, Fancy. Be my wife, my partner, my . . ." He brushed his knuckles down one cheek. ". . . lover," he finished softly.

Heat again flooding her face from both his touch and his words, Fantasy could only stare at Jesse in wide-eyed shock. Marriage was not a solution she'd considered. "I hope you don't think I was fishing for a proposal when I told you about Henrietta and Frank coming here."

"Of course not. I know you better than that."

Cocking her head to one side, she studied him silently. Only open honesty shone in his eyes. At last she said, "You're serious, aren't you?"

"Absolutely. I've never been more serious in my life. I want to marry you." With a start he realized his words about how well he knew her were more prophetic than he'd thought. He did know Fantasy better than anyone—well enough to know she couldn't be involved in the robberies, and he intended to prove it.

"Are you offering marriage just so Henrietta can't accuse me of being a woman of loose morals?"

"Your concern about what she'll think prompted my proposal, I admit. But the real reason is because I love you, Fantasy. And you know I love Robby; I'd be a good father." When she didn't respond, he continued, "You said yourself Henrietta would hit the ceiling if she found us living in the same house. So why not present a picture of a perfectly legal, respectable family? That would certainly deflate her sails and help your cause. Wouldn't it?"

Worrying her bottom lip with her teeth, Fantasy mulled over Jesse's words. She knew he spoke the truth about loving Robby, feelings she also knew her son returned, and she had no doubts Jesse would be a good father. Robby would certainly benefit from having the man as a permanent fixture in his life.

But what of Jesse's declaration of his love for her? Thomas had professed his love, too, but that hadn't stopped him from leaving her high and dry. *Stop it, Fantasy, this isn't Thomas!* But marry Jesse? Thomas had found the thrill of the chase in pursuing her more enjoyable than being married. Would Jesse feel the same way? She swore after learning of Thomas's death she'd never allow herself to be used a second time. She didn't want to belong to another man, especially through the bonds of marriage.

Still, Jesse had a point when he said the appearance of a happily married couple would do a lot in ridding her of the pesky Williamses. She sighed heavily, the burden of the decision she must make pressing down on her.

Jesse remained silent, giving her time to work through everything. He watched her struggle with her thoughts, a bevy of emotions flitting across her face. He wished he could read her mind.

Fantasy glanced at the man sitting next to her, his fingers still tightly clasping hers, her thoughts moving to another issue, one she knew must be considered before she gave her answer. What about her feelings for Jesse?

She realized now it had been ridiculous to ever question what she felt for him. If she hadn't loved Jesse, she would never have surrendered to his touch, and there was no denying she enjoyed the intimate side of their relationship. Thinking about how she responded to Jesse made her body throb with a hunger that was never completely satisfied. Her face burning with another blush, she forced her mind back to the real crux of the matter—her son and the possibility of losing him. Robby had to be her primary concern! Telling herself it was solely for her son and her willingness to do anything to keep him, rather than for her own personal feelings, she turned to meet Jesse's expectant gaze. "I accept."

Wishing again he could read her mind, Jesse couldn't squash the suspicion her heart hadn't played a major part in her answer. Yet he refused to let that dampen his excitement. "Since the Williamses will be here in ten days, we don't have time to plan a big wedding. Does that bother you?"

Fantasy shook her head.

"I understand Cotty will be leaving soon."

"Yes," she replied. "He's finished his six-month ministry, so he's going back to Boston at the end of the week."

"Shall I ask him to marry us before he leaves?"

"I'd like that. I just wish . . ." Her voice trailed off into another sigh.

"You wish what?"

Her eyes revealed a trace of sadness. "I wish Mattie could be here to me my bridesmaid."

"I wish she could, too, love," Jesse said, brushing a wisp of hair away from her face. "I'm sorry she won't be here. But you know we can't wait until she and Nash return."

"I know. I think I'll ask Mei-Ling. We've grown close over the past few weeks."

Jesse nodded, then said, "Fantasy, are you sure you want to go through with this?" His heart hammered painfully while he waited for her answer.

"Yes, I'm sure," she replied. Her voice never wavered in spite of the uncertainty Jesse sensed she felt.

He studied her silently for several long seconds, but found no reason to doubt her words. "You won't be sorry," he murmured, his breath fanning her cheek as he closed the distance between their mouths. "I love you, and I swear I'll make you happy."

As his lips captured hers, Fantasy prayed she wasn't making another mistake. She'd suffered through one disaster of a marriage and she certainly didn't want another. One ray of hope boosted her spirits. Jesse wasn't weak like Thomas. Jesse was a man of honor. He would never forget his promise to take care of her. He would never abandon her.

When the kiss ended, Jesse asked if she wanted Mei-Ling to stay on as their housekeeper.

"I can certainly take care of this house, Jesse," Fantasy said with a lazy smile. "Remember, I ran a boardinghouse. You and Robby could never create as much work as the five boarders I rented rooms to."

Jesse kissed the top of her head. "I know that, love. It's just that I think maybe we should keep Mei-Ling on a little longer."

"What are you trying to tell me?" She rose up on one elbow to look down into Jesse's relaxed face. A slight frown turned her kiss-swollen lips downward.

Jesse smiled. "Don't look so worried, Fancy. I don't want another woman in this house for any of the sordid reasons spinning around in that lovely head of yours."

Receiving a playful punch in the stomach for his taunting words, his breath whooshed out in a rush of mock pain. "Hey, don't get your dander up, wife-to-be. I can't explain it exactly, but ever since I first met Mei-Ling, she's acted like she's afraid of something or someone. I'd hate to send her packing if there's a valid reason for her fear."

Fantasy's forehead furrowed. "I know what you mean. I tried several times to get her to go shopping with me, but she always refused. I thought it strange at the time, but I guess I just forgot about it. Mei-Ling and I have become friends, but now that I think about it, I don't know anything about her. Do you have any idea what she's afraid of?"

"No. I tried to get her to talk about herself once, but all she told me was that she was born in California and has a sister still living there." Jesse sighed. "She refused to tell me how she ended up in Tombstone, or what she did before China Mary arranged for her to work for me."

Fantasy pondered his words for a few seconds, then said, "I think she should stay here."

"You really wouldn't mind if she stayed on?"

"I have to admit, it has been nice having someone else do most of the work since Robby and I moved in with you. So," her eyes twinkled with mischief, "I suppose I could get used to having Mei-Ling around a little longer. And besides," she kissed his nose playfully, "that will give me more time to take care of my husband." She ran one finger down his chest, delved briefly into his navel, then followed the line of dark hair steadily lower to its source. "What do you think about that?" she asked in a silky whisper.

"What I think," Jesse replied in a strangled croak, "is that you're playing with fire, my beautiful Fancy."

"Oh? I thought I was playing with your—"

Her words were cut off as Jesse grasped the back of her head and brought her mouth down to his in one swift motion. The intensity of his kiss left no doubt in Fantasy's mind. He completely agreed with her boastful words, and spent the next hour showing her exactly how he wanted to be cared for.

"Married?" Nick said in response to Jesse's announcement. "Have you taken leave of your senses? You've only known Fantasy a few months." He paused, his eyes squinting to probing slits. "Besides, there's no reason for you to marry her; you're already getting the benefits of the marriage bed, aren't you?"

Jesse's hands balled into fists, and only through an extreme effort of will did he keep himself from punching his friend. "Don't ever talk like that again, or I swear I'll beat you so bad not even an ugly old crone will give you a second glance."

Nick raised his hands to signal a truce. He regretted his crude remark, but it had served its purpose.

"Take it easy, Jesse. I meant no disrespect. I just had to find out which way the wind was blowing."

Jesse's tense muscles relaxed slowly as his fury ebbed, then disappeared altogether. "That's a helluva good way to get that pretty face of yours messed up," he said, still not happy about Nick's taunting words.

"I know. But I was counting on you thinking twice before you hit an old friend, and that gave me the time I needed to find out your intentions. You aren't gonna hold a grudge, are you?" Nick's teeth flashed in one of his most charming smiles, one usually reserved for the ladies.

"No, I guess not," Jesse allowed, no longer angry but not condoning Nick's tactics either.

Nick slapped Jesse on the back. "Now, are you gonna ask me to stand up with you? Hooking his thumbs in the pockets of his trousers, he puffed up his chest and rocked back on his heels. "There's no doubt I'm the best man around these parts."

For the first time since finding Nick at his favorite haunt, the newly rebuilt Alhambra Saloon, Jesse smiled. "Well, Nick, it can never be said you have a low opinion of yourself." Jesse's smile broadened. "Best man, my ass. More like best braggart."

Nick tipped his head to one side, giving his friend an innocent look. "Hey, if you don't sing your own praises, you might never hear the song being played."

Jesse chuckled. "Yeah, I guess you're right. And to answer your original question, that's why I tracked you down tonight, to ask you to stand up with me."

" 'Course I will, I thought you'd never ask." Then in a softer voice, Nick said, "You really love her?"

"Yes," Jesse responded in an equally low tone.

The two stood at the bar in silence for several seconds, then Nick broached a subject he couldn't ignore. "So, what about Fantasy's involvement in Lawson's gang? Have you considered what could happen if she's really one of his partners?"

A bleak look passed over Jesse's face. "Yes, I've considered that possibility. Though my gut instinct tells me she isn't involved in the gang, so far everything I've turned up says she is. For right now all that matters is I love Fantasy and I'm going to marry her. If I'm wrong and she proves to be a thief, well, I'll just have to deal with it then."

"You may kiss your bride, Mr. McAllister." Reverend Peabody's loud whisper brought Jesse out of the trance he'd been in since hearing Fantasy repeat her vows. She had pledged herself to him in a low but firm voice, and now the reverend had just pronounced them man and wife. His wife. Though he loved Fantasy more than he'd ever thought possible, he was still amazed at how good those two words sounded.

Pulling her into his arms, Jesse gave her a quick but thorough kiss before relinquishing his hold. He gazed into her flushed face, wishing they could be alone. Unfortunately, his desire to have his wife all to himself would have to wait a little while longer. Endicott Peabody was leaving Tombstone in the morning. The church congregation had arranged a going-away party in his honor that evening, and of course Fantasy and Jesse would have to put in an appearance.

As he followed Mei-Ling, Nick, Robby, and his new bride out of the church, Jesse silently promised himself their appearance at Cotty's party would be damn short.

"Well now, I think this occasion deserves a celebration," Nick said. "How about if we go some place for a drink? I'll buy the champagne."

Jesse turned to Fantasy. "Would you like a glass of wine?" He gave her an almost imperceptible, helpless shrug of his shoulders.

The heat in Fantasy's gaze nearly singed his eyebrows. Though she nodded her agreement to delay consummating their marriage, the eagerness in her eyes pleased him. Jesse longed to check his watch to see how many hours he had to endure before they truly became man and wife, but he stifled the urge. If Nick saw his actions, he'd never hear the end of it.

Jesse turned back to Nick. "I promised Fantasy we'd have Camillus Fly take our wedding picture. But afterwards, as long as you're buying, we'd be pleased to join you for a drink."

Nick chuckled at his friend's gibe. "You don't think I'd make the groom pay for his own wedding toast, now do you?"

"Just wanted to make sure, Nick," Jesse answered, trying to quell his own laughter.

Nick shot him a dark look, then turned to where Mei-Ling stood off to one side with Robby. "How 'bout you, Mei-Ling, would you like some champagne?"

"No, thank you, Mr. Trask. I really should get back to the house."

Nick studied the young Chinese woman, thinking he'd never seen a more beautiful face. Her skin was unflawed, probably as soft as her silk dress, making his fingers itch to find out. Her shiny, black hair was piled in an elaborate arrangement atop her head, revealing a long, slim neck. Nick had the sudden urge to place his lips on that golden skin. Shaking himself out of such improper thoughts, he made a quick decision. "Say, Jesse, how about if I go get us a bottle of champagne and meet you at your house? That way Mei-Ling can join us."

Giving Fantasy a wan smile, Jesse said, "Sure, Nick. That'll be fine. We shouldn't be more than an hour. We'll see you then."

"Great. We'll celebrate with the finest champagne I can find." Although his words were directed at all of them, Nick kept his gaze on Mei-Ling. Suddenly aware of his rude behavior, he cleared his throat, then said to her, "You'll have a drink with us, won't you, Mei-Ling?"

Mei-Ling nodded her acceptance before she could stop herself. Then realizing her boldness, she quickly bowed her head, uncomfortable about her reaction to Nick Trask. An invisible pull existed between them that she'd never experienced before.

"See you in an hour." Wishing Mei-Ling would look at him one last time, Nick finally turned away and headed for the main section of town.

After Nick's departure, Jesse turned to Mei-Ling. "Robby's going to the photographic studio with us. You're welcome to come, too."

Mei-Ling glanced around where they stood on the corner of Safford and Third Streets. Jesse's house was only two blocks away, and while Camillus Fly's was no farther, the studio was right next to Hop Town. "Thank you, but I'll just go back to your house."

Before Jesse could reply, Mei-Ling started down Safford Street at a near run. His brows pulled together, he watched her retreating form. A tug on his sleeve pulled him from the puzzle of Mei-Ling's behavior. He looked down to see Robby, his turquoise eyes squinted against the late afternoon sun, staring up at him. "What is it, Buckshot?"

"Jesse, are you and Momma gonna get your picture took?"

"That's right. But it won't be just your Momma and me getting our picture taken. You're gonna be in one of the pictures, too."

"What?" Robby and Fantasy said in unison.

Jesse turned to meet Fantasy's surprised gaze. "We're a family now," he said softly. "And I want Mr. Fly to take at least one picture of the three of us. Is that okay with you?"

Fantasy struggled to hold back the tears stinging her eyes. Smiling at her new husband, she murmured her approval.

After having Camillus Fly take a variety of photographs to preserve their wedding day, Jesse ushered Fantasy and Robby from the studio and hurried to the house on Fifth Street. He expected to find Nick impatiently waiting, but Nick hadn't arrived. After another hour passed, the excitement that had kept Robby awake for most of the night before and the equally exciting day began to take their toll. Fighting sleep as long as he could, the boy finally gave in and curled up on the floor of the parlor.

Jesse grew more irritated by the minute. Half an hour later, Nick finally arrived, strolling into the house as if he had all the time in the world.

Pointedly ignoring the sexually charged air surrounding the newly married couple he'd come to toast, Nick said, "Sorry I took so long. But I had to look all over town before I found gen-u-ine French champagne."

By the time Jesse managed to wrest the bottle out of Nick's hands and pour each of them a glass, it was well past five o'clock. The party for Cotty was supposed to start at seven, which left very little time for anything of a conjugal nature.

Forty-five minutes later Jesse glanced over to where Nick sat next to Mei-Ling. *If he doesn't quit his yammering, that fool friend of mine will be here all night.* Jesse swallowed the last of his champagne in one gulp. He shifted restlessly in his chair, cleared his throat, then coughed loudly. Nothing succeeded in getting Nick's attention.

A sound suspiciously like a giggle drifted to Jesse, pulling him from his morose thoughts. Flashing his house guest an annoyed glance, he turned to find Fantasy with one palm clamped over her mouth. The green eyes above her hand danced with amusement.

His eyebrows lifted, then a slow smile erased his scowl. He rose from his chair and reached for Fantasy. Taking her hand, he pulled her to her feet.

"What—"

"Shh," he whispered, placing a finger on her lips. Pulling her behind him, he tiptoed around a still-sleeping Robby and left the room.

She remained silent until they were behind the locked door of their bedroom. "Jesse, what are you doing? We have guests."

"Guests who don't even know we exist, let alone if we're in the same room." Pushing her against the wall, he pinned her with his body then lowered his mouth to hers. After a slow, intoxicating kiss, he whispered, "Am I such a bad host to want some time alone with my wife, alone for the first time—" He glanced at the clock on the bedside table. "—since our wedding over four hours ago?"

"But Jesse, Cotty's party starts in less than an hour. We have to change, and I won't have time to redo my hair if we—"

"Hush, wife, I won't muss your hair," he murmured against her mouth. "I've wanted you all day, and I can't wait a minute longer." His lips ground against hers, demanding an equally heated response and getting it, plus a little more in return. When he finally lifted his head, her breasts heaved with her labored breathing, desire simmered in her eyes. Keeping her back pressed to the wall, Jesse lowered one hand and grasped her skirt. Before she could utter a word of protest, he had her skirt and petticoat bunched up around her waist and her drawers sliding to the floor.

Uncertain what to expect, yet experiencing a wild pounding in her veins, Fantasy eagerly opened her mouth to him when his head dipped down for another kiss. As Jesse's tongue sought the sweetness beyond her lips, his fingers sought the sweetness between her thighs.

She groaned when he touched her aching flesh, gasped when he slipped one finger inside her. Desperate for more, she pulled one foot out of the tangle of her drawers and locked her leg around his thigh, offering herself unashamedly.

Moaning her name, Jesse stroked her with his fingers until she sobbed and shook with need. His hands trembled as he struggled to unbutton his pants, finally managing to free himself. He lifted her off her feet, then slowly lowered her, using the downward movement to impale her on his turgid manhood.

When she had taken him fully, he held perfectly still. He wanted to savor this moment. The exact moment he claimed Fantasy as his wife.

As it turned out Fantasy and Jesse arrived late to Cotty's party. But no one seemed to notice, or if they did no one was rude enough to comment.

What Jesse had intended to be no more than a quick interlude had ended up lasting considerably longer. He should have known his new bride wouldn't settle for only a brief taste of passion. What he'd started against the bedroom wall Fantasy finished in their bed. Exhausted after their wild romp, they'd fallen asleep. When they woke three-quarters of an hour later, they hurriedly bathed and dressed. Their departure had been further delayed while Fantasy completely redid her hair.

Hoping she didn't look as flushed and disheveled as she felt, Fantasy tried to answer all the church women's questions about her hurried marriage. Although she knew most were just curious, a few just plain nosey, she hated being the center of attention and wished they would move on to another subject.

"Since Mattie is out of town, who stood up with you?" Myrtle Greene asked.

Fantasy cringed, praying Myrtle wouldn't make another of the indelicate comments she was noted for. "Nick Trask, a friend of Jesse's, and our housekeeper, Kuan Mei-Ling."

"Kuan—why that's a Chinese name! You don't mean to tell us you actually let one of those heathens in our church?" Two bright spots of color appeared on Myrtle's thin, pale cheeks.

Fantasy's eyes glittered with anger. "Mei-Ling is a fine young woman. In fact, she's a far-sight better than a lot of Occidentals I know." She gave Myrtle a pointed glare, then turned her back. Her spine stiff with indignation, Fantasy moved to another group of women a few feet away.

"Well, I never," Myrtle spouted, her entire face red with outrage.

"Guess she told you, huh, Myrtle?" Maude said in a whisper loud enough for anyone within ten feet to hear.

Myrtle gave her sister a withering glance. "She's got a lot of nerve. Doesn't she know everyone is tittering behind their hands that it's about time Mr. McAllister made an honest woman of her?" Squinting her eyes at the back of her adversary, she lowered her gaze to appraise Fantasy's waist. "Perhaps they have a more pressing reason for rushing to the altar."

"Myrtle! Keep your voice down." Her eyes glowing with the prospect of a new piece of gossip, Maude said, "Are you saying Fantasy's in the family way?"

Ignoring Maude's warning, she replied in the same piercing tone, "Well, of course that's what I'm saying. We both know it's the most common reason for such hasty weddings." Shifting her gaze back to her friend, a knowing smile curved her lips. "Don't we, Maude?"

Fantasy gave no sign she'd heard their cutting words, but inside her temper approached the boiling point at Myrtle's implication. Refusing to let the prattle of the spinster Greene sisters rile her into doing or saying something she'd regret, Fantasy nodded politely at the woman standing next to her, smiling until she felt certain her face would crack. After spending what she hoped passed for an acceptable amount of time chatting with the other guests, she excused herself and headed across the hall.

As Fantasy made her way to where Jesse, Endicott Peabody, and several men from the baseball team stood talking, Myrtle's question of their wedding attendants brought back a question of her own. How and when did Jesse and Nick meet?

When Jesse told her his best man would be Nick Trask, he explained the two of them had become friends after his arrival in town. Fantasy wasn't familiar with the name of Jesse's friend, no surprise when there were nearly ten thousand people living in Tombstone, so she hadn't questioned him further.

Yet when she'd first seen Nick and Jesse together, she got the impression they were a lot closer than a several-month-long friendship would make them. She'd asked Jesse how well he and Nick knew each other but received a noncommittal reply. Looking up and seeing the heated glance Jesse sent her way, thoughts of his evasive answers about Nick Trask vanished.

"Let's go home," Jesse murmured against her ear when Fantasy moved next to him and slipped her arm around his waist. Turning to the other men, he said, "Gentlemen, if you'll excuse us. My wife has had a very long day. We'll be taking our leave now."

After wishing Cotty Peabody a safe trip back to Boston, and good-naturedly taking the men's kidding about leaving so soon, Jesse took Fantasy's arm and escorted her from the party.

"Did I embarrass you by making our excuses so early?" Jesse asked on the walk back to his house.

"Yes, but I didn't mind. I planned on suggesting we leave, too. Only, I intended to say *you* were the one who'd had a long day."

Jesse chuckled, then quickly sobered. "You don't think Nick is still at the house, do you?"

"I hope not—" Fantasy was thankful the darkness hid the blush warming her cheeks. "I mean, I think it's wonderful Nick has taken a liking to Mei-Ling. She needs friends. But I want to be alone with my husband." Her face burned even hotter.

Jesse chuckled again. The huskier timbre didn't hide his fevered reaction to her confession. Instead of speaking, he picked up their pace, anxious to make her words reality.

The house was dark, save for the usual lamp left burning in the parlor. After checking on a sleeping Robby, they headed for the bedroom they would now openly share.

They languorously undressed each other, celebrating the removal of each piece of clothing with long, slow kisses.

Much later, when they lay exhausted in each other's arms, Fantasy roused herself enough to speak. "Jesse?"

"Yes, love." His voice rich with contentment, he lightly stroked her arm where it laid across his chest.

"I wish I could have come to you untouched."

Jesse's fingers stilled. "What?"

"I wish I'd been a virgin for you."

Jesse's fingers returned to their gentle rubbing motions. After a long silence, he said, "I don't." Then before she could misinterpret his answer, he continued, "If you had come to me a virgin, we wouldn't have Robby. And you know how I love that boy. I've already started thinking of him as my own son."

Fantasy sighed with pleasure and snuggled closer, a rush of warmth filling her heart.

"Besides, love," Jesse whispered. "In many ways you were as pure as snow, which makes me the luckiest man in the world."

Fantasy didn't say anything, she couldn't. A huge lump had formed in her throat. Jesse didn't elaborate on his comment, but she knew what he meant—never having known a woman's pleasure nor experiencing all the wonderful ways to make love made her a virgin in all but the strictly clinical sense.

"Thank you, Jesse," she whispered when she could speak.

"No need to thank me, Fancy. I love you." Disappointed when she didn't say the words back to him, Jesse sighed and closed his eyes.

Fantasy sensed Jesse's disappointment, but couldn't bring herself to tell him how she felt. His wonderful words about her lack of virginity had destroyed any lingering doubts she might have unconsciously harbored about her feelings. Yes, she loved Jesse heart and soul. But she wasn't ready to chance having her heart trampled again. Though the differences between Jesse and Thomas were too numerous to count, and Jesse had been nothing short of wonderful to her, she just couldn't risk telling him of her love.

As she drifted to sleep she decided to hold her tongue until absolutely certain of Jesse's feelings for her. In spite of her earlier prediction that as a man of honor, Jesse wouldn't abandon her, she had to be certain his profession of love wasn't just an attempt to hoodwink her until his eventual leavetaking for greener pastures. When she was assured of his honesty, she'd say the words locked in her heart.

Chapter 14

Fantasy wiped her palms on her skirt for at least the tenth time in the thirty minutes she and Jesse had been waiting at Pinkham's Stage Line Office.

"Relax, Fantasy. Henrietta is not going to take our son." Jesse's laying claim to Robby sent Fantasy's heart skyward. Glancing up at her husband of one week, she managed a weak smile. She wished they could have taken the honeymoon Jesse promised her. But there was no way they could make the trip with the Williamses' impending arrival. Fantasy prayed she would survive her in-laws'—make that ex-in-laws—visit, and her new family would be intact when Henrietta and Frank left town.

In spite of her anxiety, the prospect of a new life in San Francisco popped into her head. Though she would miss Tombstone, she was eager to take up residence with Jesse in California. Perhaps they would eventually have a brother or sister for Robby. Her nervousness momentarily eased, she flashed a bright smile at her husband.

"Keep smiling at me like that, love, and I just may say to hell with the Williamses and haul you back home."

Jesse's softly spoken words sent a shiver of excitement racing up Fantasy's spine. "I—" The rumble of hooves on the hard-packed dirt street erased her smile and halted the teasing retort she'd been about to make.

Wishing he knew what she'd been about to say, Jesse looked up at the approaching coach.

A cloud of fine white dust followed the stagecoach like a hound hot on the trail of a rabbit as it made its way down Allen Street. The driver hauled back on the reins, bringing the team of horses to a skidding stop. Dust swirling in every direction, the coach continued its rocking, bouncing motion for several seconds then stilled.

An employee of the stage line came through the office door and clumped across the boardwalk. As he reached up to open the stagecoach door it swung open, slamming into his chest and nearly sending him sprawling.

A plump woman in a rumpled, gaudy purple travel suit filled the open doorway.

"Get out of my way, you nincompoop. Can't you see I need some air? How do you expect a body to breathe, cooped up in that stifling stage for hours on end?" She waved an umbrella at the man, just missing his ear as he ducked to avoid her wild flailings.

"Yes, ma'am. Sorry, ma'am." The man retreated another step, trying to get out of the woman's way before she succeeded in doing him some bodily harm. "Here, let me help you," he belatedly offered, reaching up to grasp the hand she thrust in his face.

Stepping onto the boardwalk, the woman turned back to the stagecoach, the movement setting her jowls to jiggling. "Frank! Get yourself out here. Can't you see I'm about to have one of my spells?"

From inside the coach came a muffled male voice. "Yes, dear." A man's gray head, followed by a pair of narrow shoulders, came through the stagecoach door. Stepping onto the boardwalk, he stuck a high-crowned bowler hat on his head and attempted to brush off the dirt covering his well-cut suit. He made his way to the woman, put a hand under one chubby arm and escorted her to the bench in front of the stage line office. "Rest here, dear, while I see to our baggage."

"Don't let those fools crush my hat boxes." She heaved a sigh and plunked down on the bench. Pulling a fan from her handbag, she snapped it open with a flick of her wrist. "My God, how does the poor dear stand this place? It'll be a miracle if my grandson isn't addle-brained from the heat."

Adding the man's name to the woman's mention of a grandson, Jesse's amusement at the couple vanished. Horrified, he turned to Fantasy. The expression on her face confirmed his conclusion. Glancing back at the woman whose attire made her look like an overripe plum, he blew out a resigned breath.

Waving her fan in front of her flushed face, Henrietta muttered in a loud voice, "Where is that stupid girl?"

Fantasy stiffened at the woman's slur, then moved from a shaded area farther down the boardwalk into Henrietta's line of vision. "I'm right here, Mother Williams."

The older woman swung her gaze toward Fantasy, her mouth puckered with annoyance. "It's about time." Glancing around, she added, "Where's Robby?"

"He's home. I told him he could see you later this afternoon, if you've sufficiently recovered from your trip."

"Home? You left my grandson by himself?"

Jesse moved next to Fantasy, slipping his arm around her waist. "Robby is with our housekeeper, Mrs. Williams." Somehow he managed to push down his irritation at the woman's ill manners enough to offer a smile.

Henrietta shifted her beady-eyed glare in his direction. He stood perfectly still while she gave him a thorough onceover. Her nose twitching as if she'd caught a whiff of something vile, she dismissed him with a cold shoulder. Turning to skewer Fantasy with an icy stare, she said, "Who is this man, Fantasy? And what does he mean by 'our housekeeper'?"

Fantasy swallowed, willing her knees not to give out. "This is my husband, Jesse McAllister."

"Your—" The rest of Henrietta's comment went unsaid. Her thin lips forming a perfect O, the fan slipping from her limp fingers, she swayed precariously on the bench. Before anyone could prevent it, Henrietta slid slowly from her seat. With a soft groan she collapsed on the boardwalk in a heap of purple silk.

"Etta? Etta! Can you hear me?"

Slowly Henrietta came out of her swoon and opened her eyes. "I can hear you fine, you idiot. And stop calling me that ridiculous name. You know I hate it." Sitting up slowly on the bed, Henrietta realized her suit jacket had been unbuttoned, her corset cover unfastened. Pushing Frank's hands away from their fumblings with the ties of her corset, she snapped, "What do you think you're doing?"

"Just trying to make you more comfortable," he murmured, dropping his hands from her heaving bosom.

"I can loosen my own clothing. Now, get away from me."

"Yes, dear," Frank murmured. He moved across the room and sat in a chair near the room's only window.

"Where are we?" Henrietta asked after removing her clothes and donning a nightgown she'd retrieved from their luggage.

"We're in the American Hotel. I had you brought here after you had one of your spells." He didn't mention the task had required four of the strongest men he could find to carry his wife the two blocks. "Do you remember fainting in front of the stage office?"

Henrietta's pinched mouth puckered even more. "Of course I remember. I'm not senile. It was after our daughter-in-law told me that man was her husband. That's impossible, she's married to our son."

"Our son is dead," Frank said softly.

A brief stab of pain crossed Henrietta's features. "Yes, I know. That's why we're taking our grandson home to St. Louis. He's all we have left of Thomas, and Robby belongs with us!"

Frank said nothing. He didn't hold with his wife's adamant determination to have Robby back with them. Though he dearly loved his grandson, personally he thought the boy should be with his mother. However, telling Henrietta his opinion on the subject would only start another argument. And he would do nearly anything to avoid another disagreement with his wife of almost thirty years—even go along with her idea of coming all the way to Tombstone to fetch Robby.

Changing the subject, Frank said, "Do you want to rest for a while, dear, or would you like to get something to eat?" He knew his wife never missed a meal without a darn good reason, and it was well after the noon hour.

"What I want is to see Robby."

Frank inwardly cringed at his wife's cross tone of voice, but calmly said, "You will, dear. Fantasy and Jesse gave me directions to their house. We're to be there at four."

"If they have a house, why aren't we staying with them?"

"Fantasy told me they really don't have room for house guests. Both she and her new husband were very apologetic."

"So it's true, they really are married?"

"Yes, Etta, they're married. And very happily, too, if you ask me."

Ignoring her husband's use of the name she detested, Henrietta snapped, "Well, I didn't ask you. I'll decide for myself when we get there." Crawling back onto the bed, she closed her eyes. "I'm going to take a nap. Wake me in an hour."

"Yes, dear. I believe I'll take a stroll around town while you sleep."

Henrietta dismissed him with a wave of one hand, then rolled onto her side and immediately fell asleep.

Unsure whether he should change his plans and stay in their hotel room to soak up the welcome silence, Frank finally decided he'd still prefer the heat of outside. He put on his hat, then slipped from the room.

Jesse shifted in his chair once more, idly drumming his fingers on the dining room table. The Williamses arrived exactly at four and had stayed for supper. Staring at Henrietta Williams, he wondered if the woman ever stopped complaining. She had talked nonstop since their arrival, most of her inane chatter finding fault with everything from the weather to the way Robby dressed.

"Really, Fantasy, you should talk to that housekeeper of yours about her cooking. This roast is much too rare."

Jesse saw the anger flare in Fantasy's eyes and knew she struggled to hang onto her temper. "Actually, Mrs. Williams," he answered for his wife. "I think the roast is perfect." He raised one eyebrow as he looked at her, daring her to disagree.

"Well . . . I . . . I . . ." she sputtered, momentarily at a loss for words.

Jesse noted the spark of amusement in Frank's eyes and decided perhaps the man wouldn't be half bad when his wife wasn't around. In fact, he genuinely liked Frank, though they'd just met. How the man let his wife lead him around by the nose was beyond him. Life was too short to be saddled with a woman like Henrietta. Shrugging off his attempts to analyze this strange pair, Jesse couldn't resist testing the waters by saying, "What's your opinion of the roast, Mr. Williams?"

Glancing quickly at his wife, Frank said, "I quite

agree, Jesse. I've always preferred roast on the rare side. And let's stop this formality. We're family now. Call me Frank."

Jesse smiled his agreement. *Well, well, so Frank doesn't always let his wife dictate to him.* Henrietta's whiny voice pulled him from his musings.

"And you must call me Henrietta." Her false sugar-coated tone made him want to retch.

"How long are you planning on staying in Tombstone?" Jesse hoped his question didn't sound overly rude, but he wasn't altogether sure he could make it through a long visit without wrapping his hands around Henrietta's throat.

"Not very—"

"Now, dear," Henrietta interrupted her husband. "We haven't seen our grandson in nearly a year. There's no need to rush back to St. Louis, is there?" She batted her stubby eyelashes at Frank in a poor imitation of a submissive wife.

"Well, I suppose—"

"Good," she interrupted again. "Then it's settled." Henrietta's meek behavior did a complete turnaround. She was instantly back in control. "We'll stay for as long as it takes—I mean, for as long as we're welcome." She smiled first at Fantasy, then Jesse. The brittle smile emphasized the wrinkles around her eyes and mouth.

Jesse didn't miss the sudden stiffening of Frank's shoulders at his wife's last statement, nor how Henrietta's smile didn't go beyond her thin lips. Wishing he could read minds, Jesse couldn't shake the feeling Henrietta was a conniving bitch of a woman who could very well have something up her sleeve.

Hoping to change the topic of discussion to safer ground, Jesse turned back to Frank. "Fantasy tells me you own a bank in St. Louis."

Smiling broadly, Frank said, "Yes, Williams's Savings was started by my father."

It was obvious Jesse had hit upon a subject dear to

Frank's heart as the man talked at great length about the business he loved.

"I enlarged the building several years ago, and I now employ ten people full time," he stated, pride evident in his voice. "What about you, Jesse? What brought you to Tombstone?"

Keeping his gaze away from his wife, Jesse replied, "I'm in real estate. But my work here is nearly finished. We'll be heading for San Francisco soon."

"San Francisco?" Henrietta couldn't hide her shock.

His gaze brushing possessively over Fantasy, then Robby, Jesse calmly met Henrietta's belligerent stare. "I'm from San Francisco, so that's where we'll be living."

Henrietta fell silent, her mind working furiously. *San Francisco indeed. We'll just see about that!*

Snapping out of her unusual quiet, Henrietta launched into another of her long-winded speeches about something in St. Louis that no one save herself found the least bit interesting. Robby yawned with boredom, and Jesse and Fantasy exchanged sympathetic glances.

By the time the Williamses said their good nights and headed back to their hotel, Jesse's jaw hurt from clamping his teeth together in frustration, and his head pounded with a rip-roaring headache.

He needed his wife's welcoming warmth desperately that night. Through her gentle ministrations to ease the tension in his neck and shoulders, and later her tender loving, the ache in his head disappeared. The reason for his earlier discomfort forgotten, he fell into a contented sleep.

For Fantasy, sleep didn't come easily. Although deliciously relaxed from their lovemaking, sleep eluded her. Having her ex-in-laws in town for an extended visit was going to be even more difficult than she'd imagined. She turned to look at Jesse's profile. Realizing again this wonderful, handsome man was her husband, her heart swelled with pride. They'd only been married a week and in some ways it was still like a dream. But Henrietta Williams was no dream—the woman was a witch straight out of Fantasy's worst nightmare.

Whispering a silent prayer to be given sufficient strength to face whatever obstacles she came up against, Fantasy finally joined Jesse in sleep.

"You almost tipped off Fantasy, Henrietta. You'd better take care, or you'll never get what you want."

"Oh, stop it, Frank. You're making a mountain out of a molehill."

Henrietta and Frank were back in their hotel room, preparing for bed.

"We should forget this whole thing. Fantasy has remarried and Robby seems happy. That's what we wanted—Robby's happiness."

"Can't you see they're putting on some kind of charade for us, so we'll think they're happy and give up our intention of taking Robby back with us?"

Frank turned toward his wife, shock obvious on his smooth face. Unlike Henrietta, the process of aging had been kind to Frank. Although his hair had turned completely gray, he was still lean and relatively fit for a man of fifty-five. "What are you talking about?"

"I think if we pay attention, they'll tip their hand sooner or later. Besides, you heard Jesse say they're going to live in San Francisco. We can't let that happen, Frank." She let down her hair, once the color of honey now heavily streaked with gray, and deftly plaited it into one braid. "We'll never see our grandson again if they move to California. We have to keep our eyes and ears open. We have to get Robby out of this godforsaken place." Pulling back the bedclothes, she got into bed.

"Etta?"

"Hush, Frank. Can't you see I'm exhausted? Now

get into bed." With that, Henrietta closed her eyes and rolled toward the wall.

Shaking his head, Frank finished undressing and slipped a nightshirt over his head. As he lay down next to his wife he wondered if this business of getting Robby back to St. Louis would be the one time she'd push him too far.

China Mary's summons shook Mei-Ling out of the happiness she'd experienced since going to work for Jesse McAllister. Though she knew it would come some day, her knees still threatened to buckle as she walked the several blocks to the Chinese matriarch's home.

"You sent for me?" Mei-Ling asked quietly after bowing politely.

"Aiee. China Mary hear Wing Fong impatient to have money promised him for you. No can stall him any longer."

Mei-Ling's head snapped up, her eyes filling with tears. "You will not stop it?" she asked in a soft voice.

"No stop. You must do as uncle want."

Mei-Ling swallowed hard. "How long do I have?"

"Fong want you to go to Hing Fat in three day."

"Three days," Mei-Ling repeated in a tiny whisper. Three days, and life as she'd known it would end. Unable to speak, she nodded her acquiescence. Bowing again, she walked woodenly from the room.

Several hours later, Jesse heard crying coming from Mei-Ling's bedroom and went to investigate.

"Mei-Ling?" Jesse called, knocking on her door. "What is it? Are you all right?"

After a few seconds, the door swung open. Tears running down her face, Mei-Ling stood in the doorway.

"Mei-Ling? Are you hurt?"

She shook her head, then moved back to her bed and sat down.

Unsure if he should go into her room, the sound of fresh tears finally propelled him forward. Leaving the door open, Jesse entered her small bedroom at the back of his house. He looked around, noticing subtle little changes she'd made to make the room more homey. Extremely uncomfortable about being in her private quarters, his desire to help kept him from leaving.

Taking a step toward the bed, he said, "Mei-Ling, what is it?"

Wiping her eyes, she shook her head again.

Jesse's brows drew together as he silently studied her tear-ravaged face. "If you'll tell me, perhaps I can help."

Mei-Ling drew a deep, shuddering breath. "There's nothing you can do. There's nothing anyone can do."

"How do you know, unless you tell me?" Putting his hand under her chin, he forced her to meet his gaze. "Tell me, Mei-Ling."

She sniffled once, then began speaking in a low whisper. "I received word today that China Mary wanted to see me. She told me I have to leave your house and . . ." She paused to blow her nose.

"Leave? Mei-Ling, I don't understand. Mary has said nothing to me about your having to leave. What's this all about?"

"It is my responsibility to tell you I must leave. My uncle has made an agreement to sell me to Hing Fat, an important businessman in Hop Town. In three days I must allow the sale to be completed."

"Sale? People can't be sold."

"In China, it is very common for the head of the family to sell young women as wives or slaves, or . . . concubines."

"In China maybe, but not in the United States. We fought a war over freeing people from slavery. You should know that, you've lived here your entire life."

"Yes, I know. But my uncle believes in the ancient Chinese ways. He made an arrangement to sell me, and I must obey him."

Jesse fell silent for a minute, digesting what Mei-Ling had said. Finally he said, "Are you to become someone's wife?"

Mei-Ling shook her head.

"A slave, then?" Jesse's anger grew when she shook her head a second time. "Your uncle sold you as a concubine?"

She nodded, then dropped her gaze from the outrage mirrored on Jesse's face.

"You've agreed to this?"

She sighed and gulped down a fresh onslaught of tears. "I have no choice. I must do what my uncle and China Mary say."

After a few more minutes of tense silence, Jesse began pacing the small room. He shoved a hand through his hair, trying to come up with a solution for the young woman's future. Stopping in front of the dresser, Jesse idly fingered the lace-edged doily until something lying on the embroidered cloth caught his attention. His eye's widened. *Dear God, was it possible there could be two of them?* Reaching out, he touched the smooth green stone, then carefully picked it up. He turned towards Mei-Ling, the movement causing the gold chain with its jade pendant to swing back and forth from his fingers.

"Where did you get this?" he asked in a soft voice.

Raising her head, Mei-Ling looked at the necklace dangling from Jesse's hand. "My uncle gave it to me."

"Your uncle? What's his name?"

"Wing Fong. He owns a laundry in Hop Town."

"Yes, I know," Jesse murmured. Louder, he said, "Do you know where he got it?"

"No. He said it belonged to my mother. But I know that's a lie."

"How do you know that?"

"My mother never had anything so valuable. She

told my sister and me many times about how she and her brothers came to America with only the clothes on their backs. There's no way that necklace belonged to my mother. I don't know why my uncle lied to me, but he did."

Jesse clutched the necklace tightly in his hand, now certain it was the same one he'd found in Fantasy's laundry basket—the one she took to Wing Fong's laundry—the one from the stage robbery several months ago. What a strange twist of fate. The physical evidence he needed to tie everything together had been right under his own roof all this time.

After studying her tear-stained face silently for a moment, Jesse made a quick decision. "Listen, Mei-Ling. I don't know what I can do to help you, but I'd like to try."

"Both you and Fantasy have been so good to me, and I appreciate your offer. But I don't think there's anything anyone can do."

"I'm still going to try. You don't object to my trying, do you?"

"No, of course not." She sighed. "I just think you'll be wasting your time."

"We'll see. Mei-Ling, could I keep this necklace for awhile?"

"You can have it. Uncle Fong gave it to me falsely, so I don't want it."

Slipping the necklace into his pocket, Jesse moved across the room and gave her shoulder a gentle squeeze. "I promise I'll do what I can, Mei-Ling, please believe me."

Fresh tears welling in her eyes, she could only nod her head in response.

"Mei-Ling's uncle did what?" Fantasy's shock at Jesse's recitation of his conversation with Mei-Ling was as enormous as Jesse's had been. "You can't sell another human being!"

"Apparently the Chinese haven't advanced to the same level of freedom as here in America. They still condone the selling of each other, even family members, for profit."

"Jesse, you can't let this happen. You can't let Mei-Ling be sold like a . . . like a piece of meat at the market. You've got to do something!"

Jesse chuckled at her impassioned plea. "Yes, I know, love. I've already told Mei-Ling I'll do what I can. She doesn't think it will do any good, though."

"Do you think she's right?"

"I don't know." Jesse sat down on their bed and pulled her down next to him. "I don't think the Chinese will take kindly to one of us roundeyes sticking his nose into their way of life. After all, their culture has been around for a lot longer than ours. But it doesn't matter. I intend to pay a visit to China Mary tomorrow and see what can be done."

Lowering his face, he nuzzled Fantasy's neck with his lips. "Jesse! It's nearly five o'clock. Mother Williams and Frank will be arriving any minute."

"Hush, wife," he murmured softly, his mouth hovering above hers. "We have a few minutes yet." He kissed her thoroughly, leisurely, enjoying her sweetness for several long minutes. Reluctantly he finally broke the kiss. "We'll finish this later, Fancy." His voice was thick with the passion so easily stirred between them.

Her eyes wide, desire thrumming through her, Fantasy nodded her agreement. It continually surprised her how much she wanted Jesse. If anyone had told her when she'd first married Thomas it was possible to desire one's spouse constantly, she would have called such a declaration an outright lie. But with Jesse it was different. From their very first kiss to the first time they'd made love, to each succeeding time they'd made love, everything differed with Jesse. And oh, how she loved him. It had become harder and harder not to say the words while she writhed in the throes of passion. If only she was convinced he could be trusted, that he wouldn't abandon her, then she'd willingly admit her love.

Jack Lawson stretched his booted feet out in front of him and leaned back until the chair's front legs came up off the floor. Stroking his long moustache, he said, "You boys done a good job on our last little undertaking."

The other three men in the room nodded, waiting to hear why they'd been summoned to the Arnette ranch. The four of them seldom met without an important reason.

When Lawson remained silent, Buck Arnette spoke up. "You hear 'bout another shipment of sugar ya want us ta pick up, boss?"

"Yeah, boss. We ain't had any action in a long spell now. I'm itchin' ta get me more of that there sugar," Daryl Arnette added.

"Is that why you asked us to meet you here, *jefe?* Another job?" Ramón García asked in a low voice.

Lawson brought the front legs of his chair down on the floor with a thud. "No, not just yet. Right now, I got something else on my mind."

He scoured each man present with a cold stare. When he was satisfied with what he saw, he said, "We have a problem. Someone is skimming more than their share from the . . ." One side of his mouth twisted in a smile. ". . . sugar sack. None of you would happen to know anything about that, would you?" His smile disappeared, his lips pressed together in a thin line. Once more he slowly moved his gaze from one man to the next. Each of the men he'd never had any reason to doubt met his stare without a flinch, and in turn each answered negatively.

"How'd you find out about this, *jefe?"*

"You remember the fancy jade necklace we got from that woman who put up such a fuss about giving it to us?'' When the three men nodded, he continued. "Well, after I put it in the packet with the rest of the stuff and had it delivered to Fong, I decided I'd like to keep the necklace. I checked with Fong, but he said he'd already sent everything on to be sold. So I sent word to our contact in California not to sell it." He paused again, flicking a piece of lint from one knee of his trousers. "I got word yesterday he never received a jade necklace."

"Who was ya gonna give the necklace to, boss?" Buck asked, winking at his companions.

"Yeah, who's the lucky lady? Anybody we know?" Daryl said, grinning broadly.

Lawson gave the brothers a shriveling look. "That's not important. What matters is who's taking more than his cut." He bent over and carefully brushed a speck of dust from his shiny boots.

"So, boss, ya got any idea who's doin' it?"

Straightening, Lawson pulled a cigar from his shirt pocket and stuck it between his teeth. "I'm not sure, yet," he said, then paused to light the cigar. He drew deeply and exhaled a puff of blue smoke. "But I aim to find out."

"How ya gonna do that? Ya want somebody roughed up?" Daryl's eyes shone with a sadistic gleam.

"Not yet. I don't know who's trying to pull a fast one on us, but I'll figure it out." He drew again on the cigar, then blew the smoke out slowly. Studying the glowing tip, his voice was frigid when he added, "There's only two people who could've taken that necklace. Soon as I find out which one took it, you'll be the first to know."

Chapter 15

"China Mary, I have come to ask you for a very big favor," Jesse said after bowing formally.

The ruler of Hop Town waved him to a chair, then studied him with her inscrutable black eyes for several long seconds. "What big favor?"

"Mei-Ling told me about the arrangement her uncle made to sell her, and I'd like to make an offer of my own."

"You want Mei-Ling for concubine?"

His face burning, Jesse's voice rose to a near shout. "No!" Then more softly he added, "I don't want Mei-Ling to become anyone's concubine."

China Mary fell silent again, absently rubbing the exquisite gold necklace lying on her bosom. "So, what big favor you want?"

"I'd like you to convince Mei-Ling's uncle to forget about the arrangement he made to sell her."

"Mei-Ling his niece, that give him right to sell her. Wing Fong lose face if I say he must change mind."

Familiar with the Oriental obsession of avoiding the loss of face at all costs, Jesse said, "I understand Wing Fong's wish not to have the humiliation of such a situation cast upon his family's name. However, I think there's another solution that will please everyone involved."

Eyeing him dubiously, China Mary asked, "What solution?"

"If Wing Fong will not agree to forget about selling Mei-Ling, perhaps he would consider another offer."

"What offer?"

"I'll pay more than he's already bargained for, double if necessary."

Her eyebrows lifted. "You pay with your money?"

"Yes."

Squinting her eyes, she gave him a probing look. "Why you want help Chinese girl?"

Jesse knew she would ask that question and he'd spent a lot of time thinking about his answer before making this visit. "I mean no disrespect, but I don't hold with the Chinese custom of selling their people. Mei-Ling is a fine young woman, and she will make some lucky man a fine wife. And she deserves better than to end up as a concubine; she deserves a chance to find happiness. I want to make sure she has that chance."

After a long pause while China Mary thought about his words, she finally responded, "I think you speak truth. Mei-Ling fine Chinese girl. But if I ask Wing Fong to do as you say, what I tell man who planned to buy Mei-Ling?"

Jesse rubbed a hand across his jaw. "Is there something else he would accept in Mei-Ling's place?"

China Mary gave a sharp bark of laughter. "What could take place of concubine? Nothing else do same things for master."

"I guess you're right," he mumbled, feeling his cheeks warm again. "But there must be something the man values: money or opium." Although the thought of buying Mei-Ling's freedom with drugs sickened him, Jesse was prepared to do so if necessary.

She nodded sagely. "Aiee, Hing Fat like opium pipe. Maybe he agree to something besides Mei-Ling." Rising from her chair, she pointed toward the door. "Leave now, China Mary send word if I decide to give favor."

Not taking offense at her rude dismissal, Jesse rose,

bowed respectfully then left the room. At least she hadn't turned him down flat. Maybe things would still work out.

The Williamses had been in Tombstone for a week and Henrietta had yet to find a flaw in the fabric of Fantasy and Jesse's marriage. Much to her disgust, her former daughter-in-law and new husband seemed blissfully happy, which only strengthened her resolve to uncover a weakness she could seize and manipulate to her liking.

Returning from an afternoon spent with their grandson, Henrietta entered their hotel room and dropped down on the bed with a groan. "That boy wears me to a frazzle."

Frank frowned at his wife, biting his tongue to keep from pointing out he'd been the one who'd kept Robby entertained all afternoon. "What will you do when we have him all day, every day?"

"Don't be obtuse, Frank. I'll hire a governess to take care of him."

Frank's frown deepened. "You never mentioned hiring a governess."

"That's before I found out how much work there is caring for a five-year-old boy. I don't remember Thomas being such a handful."

"Come now, my dear, Thomas was a pistol of the first sort."

Sitting up on the bed, Henrietta gave her husband a venomous look. "Don't speak about our son like that. Can't you see it upsets me?"

"Sorry," he mumbled, adding, "everything upsets you," under his breath. He took off his suit coat and carefully hung it over the back of a chair. "Etta, I don't like the idea of taking our grandson away from his mother only to have him raised by a governess. That wouldn't be fair to the boy. Besides, I thought our plan was to get both Fantasy and Robby to go back to St. Louis with us."

"That was before we arrived and found out about Fantasy's betrayal of our son. And how many times do I have to tell you to stop calling me that name?" She laid back down on the bed, one forearm covering her eyes.

"What do you mean by her betrayal?"

"Oh Frank, you're such a dunderhead. Can't you see Fantasy should be in mourning, not taking up with, let alone marrying Jesse McAllister."

"Society isn't as strict about the period of mourning out here, Et—uh, Henrietta."

"I don't care. She still betrayed Thomas in my eyes, and she doesn't deserve to raise his son. I intend to raise Robby."

Frank ignored the temptation to remind his wife only moments ago she had announced her plans to hire a governess to see to their grandson's upbringing. Instead he said, "I don't think you're going to find anything wrong with the relationship between Fantasy and Jesse. As far as I'm concerned, we're wasting our time here. I think we should go home."

"No!" Henrietta jerked her arm from her face. Rising up on one elbow, she skewered her husband with a deadly glare. "I hate it here, and the heat is about to kill me. But I'm willing to put up with this horrible place for as long as it takes. And you'll suffer right along with me, Frank." She flopped back on the bed, the springs moaning with protest. "Something will happen to help our plan, I just know it. We're staying."

Hearing the finality of his wife's words, Frank swallowed any further protest. He'd yet to win an argument with Henrietta.

Jack Lawson walked purposefully through the streets of Hop Town. He stopped abruptly in front of the door to his destination and retreated two steps. Looking at his reflection in the building's plate glass window, he straightened his already perfectly tied cravat and adjusted the already perfectly aligned black pearl studs running down the front of his starched shirt. He smoothed his hair carefully and checked to make sure his boots sported their usual high-gloss before entering Wing Fong's Laundry. A tiny bell hooked to the top of the door announced his arrival.

The curtain separating the shop from the back room swung to one side as the owner shuffled through the doorway.

When Wing Fong's gaze landed on the man standing on the other side of the counter his smile of welcome faded. Jack Lawson had only visited his laundry once, just before they'd begun their business arrangement. His presence today didn't bode well. Fong silently cursed his own stupidity. He should have known when Lawson sent a message about the jade necklace the man would not let the matter drop. Trying to hide his apprehension, Fong clasped his damp hands together in front of him and bowed politely. "You honor me by visiting my humble business."

"Do I?" Lawson's words were heavy with sarcasm. He stared at the Chinaman for several minutes, aware Fong's uneasiness grew with each tick of the clock.

Since discovering the presence of a rotten apple in his barrel of cohorts, Lawson had spent a great deal of time thinking about the identity of that "apple." Like he'd told the Arnettes and Garcia, only two people had access to the missing necklace after it left his possession: Wing Fong and Fantasy Williams McAllister.

Through careful consideration, he'd finally concluded the rat couldn't be the former Widow Williams. She didn't know his motive for cultivating her friendship and padding her palm with contributions to her various humanitarian causes. She'd proven an extremely easy mark—running errands for him, delivering robbery loot secreted in his laundry, and bringing the money made from selling that loot back with his clean clothes—without an inkling of how she had been manipulated.

Fantasy McAllister hadn't found out how he'd been using her, Lawson felt certain. If she had, she'd have thrown such knowledge in his face rather than turning a blind eye and pretending ignorance. Even his generosity to her beloved Ladies Aid Society wouldn't allow her to participate in anything illegal. No, if Fantasy McAllister had learned about the real nature of their relationship, she would never have kept it to herself. Somehow she would have tipped her hand; Fantasy McAllister didn't have a devious bone in her body.

So, if his former landlady hadn't taken the necklace, that left only one other possibility. Wing Fong.

Fong's nervous fidgeting brought Lawson back to the present. A smile twisted his lips. "I decided to pay you a little visit, Fong, so you could tell me why you took the jade necklace."

Staring at Lawson's hands resting casually on the counter, Fong wasn't fooled by the man's seemingly relaxed posture. Imagining those immaculately manicured fingers wrapped around his neck, he swallowed painfully. Fong knew there would be no hope for mercy if he denied taking the necklace, then later admitted the truth under torture. He had no doubt Jack Lawson would employ whatever means were necessary to get what he wanted.

Raising his hands in supplication, Fong said, "I beg you see my side, Boss. I not mean to take necklace. It was my niece. She very stubborn girl. She argue with me and I get very angry. I forget self and give her necklace so she obey." Dropping his head, his hands clasped tightly in front of his chest, Fong waited in agonizing silence for Lawson's reply.

Lawson lifted one hand to stroke his moustache. He silently studied Fong's bowed head, wondering if the Chinaman had told the truth. Or maybe his explanation had been an attempt to buy himself some time. "I

want that necklace, Fong. Do you understand me?"
He slapped the counter with his open palm to empha-
size his words. His eyes gleamed with satisfaction when
Fong flinched.

His insides quaking, Fong resisted the urge to shrink
back from his very angry boss. "Aiee," he managed to
say in a choked voice. Humbling himself to get the
necklace back from his niece would be minor, Fong
suspected, to what this man was capable of doing to
him. His Adam's apple bobbed as he tried to swallow
through a suddenly dry throat. "I get necklace."

"When?"

Fong's mind raced frantically. He didn't even know
what China Mary had done with Mei-Ling. But he
would find out. He had to! "I need five day. I give you
necklace in five day."

"Five days? I thought your niece lived with you. Just
take the damn necklace away from her."

Silently calling himself a fool for allowing Mei-Ling
to fall under China Mary's protection, Fong said,
"Niece leave my house. Not know where she went."
Seeing the sudden tic in Lawson's jaw, he quickly
added, "I find her, I promise. But need five day."

After another long pause, Lawson finally nodded.
"Okay, you've got five days. But I'm warning you, if
I don't have the necklace by then, you'll have another
visitor. Someone who takes great delight in making
Chinks squeal like pigs. Have I made myself clear?"

In a strangled voice, Fong whispered, "Aiee, Boss,
very clear."

"Me go see Hing Fat," China Mary said without
preamble as soon as Jesse answered her summons.
"Him bad sick."

"What's the matter with him?" Jesse asked.

A sly smile on her lips, China Mary said,
"Houseboy say wife putting herb in tea."

"You think Hing Fat's wife is trying to kill him?"

"No, not kill. Houseboy say Fat not die. Herb make him no good for pillowing."

Jesse cleared his throat, then said, "What'd he say about Mei-Ling?"

"Hing Fat not buy." She cackled with laughter. "No can wake up male stalk, so him not need new concubine."

Ignoring her joke about Fat's drug-induced impotency, Jesse asked, "If Hing Fat won't be buying Mei-Ling, what about Wing Fong? Does he know about this?"

"Fong not know. I tell you first."

"What should I do?" Jesse asked quietly.

"That depend. You let Mei-Ling go back to uncle and forget. Or you pay price Fong want."

Jesse sat in silence, thinking over what China Mary had told him. Hing Fat was out of the picture, but that still left Wing Fong to be dealt with. If Mei-Ling went back to her uncle, the man would undoubtedly find a new buyer—if rumors about his greed were correct. And more importantly, China Mary would likely refuse to intervene a second time.

"You will allow me to approach Wing Fong and pay him for Mei-Ling?"

"Aiee. If that what you want."

Jesse thought carefully about his response before he spoke. "I'd like you to notify Fong that Hing Fat cannot buy Mei-Ling. I'd also like you to tell him you've found another buyer. But I don't want him to know the man buying her isn't Chinese. Will you agree to do that?"

China Mary nodded once, then said, "Me do. I not say who buy niece. Him only want money to go back to China."

"Even though he'll have to deal with one of the barbarian Americans?" Jesse couldn't resist saying with a smile.

Lips twitching and eyes sparkling with mirth, she replied, "If you have money, Fong not care if you not

Celestial." A full grin splitting her plump face, she added, "You good man, Jesse McAllister, even for barbarian American."

After working out the details of their bargain, Jesse left China Mary's house.

Jesse spent the afternoon at the Tombstone Club with Nick, mulling over the next step in his investigation.

After Jesse told him about his plan to buy Mei-Ling, Nick said, "Our boss may not take kindly to reimbursing you for buying a Chinese woman."

Jesse shrugged. "Could be. If John doesn't think it's a valid expense, I'll pay it myself."

Nick heaved a silent sigh of relief. If his friend hadn't agreed to foot the bill for Mei-Ling's freedom, he would have offered his own money. Easing back in his chair, Nick lazily swirled his drink in a glass of cut crystal. "So what're you planning to do next?"

After a long silence, Jesse said, "I'm going to talk to Mei-Ling. I want to tell her about the agreement I made with China Mary, and I have some questions to ask her about the necklace."

Nick straightened in his chair, pinning Jesse with an intense stare. "You don't think she's involved in this, do you?"

Jesse smiled, his eyes crinkling with amusement. "She might be. Maybe she's the brains behind this whole thing. Maybe she's the leader instead of Lawson. Maybe she—"

"Cut it out, Jesse." Nick's low growl interrupted Jesse's teasing. Gripping his glass so hard his knuckles turned white, he added, "That's not funny."

"Take it easy, Nick. I was just kidding, you should know that. I don't think Mei-Ling is involved any more than you do. But I still need to ask her about the necklace and her uncle. Maybe she knows something that will help us. Then I'll make arrangements to take her to San Francisco."

"San Francisco?" Nick quirked one eyebrow in surprise. "You're leaving town?"

"Just temporarily. I'd planned on making the trip anyway, because I didn't think what I need to talk over with John should be handled by telegram. After I make sure Mei-Ling arrives safely at her sister's home, I'll head for John's office. If he thinks we've dug up enough evidence to make the charges stick, I'll have the sheriff make the arrests as soon as I get back."

"If you . . . uh . . . want to stay here, I could . . . uh . . . take Mei-Ling and talk to John. I mean, you being a newly married man and all."

Jesse bit back the laughter Nick's insightful remark created. "I'm glad to hear you're concerned about the state of my marriage, but Fantasy wants Mei-Ling to have her freedom as much as you and me. Since Fantasy has no way of knowing I have another reason for going to San Francisco, she won't object to my escorting Mei-Ling to her sister. And, because I'm the one supposedly buying Mei-Ling, I think I should be the one to make the trip. But thanks just the same, Nick."

When his friend didn't reply, Jesse continued, "Besides, I need you to keep an eye on Lawson and his gang. They're used to seeing you around town, and if I started showing up wherever they are, they might get suspicious and pull a disappearing act."

Nick poured himself another drink, then said, "You're right, Jesse. I just wanted to . . ." His words trailed off when he lifted his glass and took a sip of bourbon.

"You'll be finished here soon and heading back to San Francisco. It shouldn't be long before you can see Mei-Ling again." Nick's dark eyes appeared troubled when he met Jesse's gaze.

"Yeah, I know." Trying to shake off his strange case of melancholy, Nick's usually engaging smile returned. "So, when are you planning on leaving?"

"In a couple days." Rising from his chair, Jesse added, "After I speak with Mei-Ling, I'll go see her uncle and have a long talk with him about Lawson."

Hearing the determination in Jesse's voice, Nick looked up sharply. "You think Fong knows if Fantasy is a member of the gang?"

"I don't know. But I'm sure gonna try to find out." He reached out to shake Nick's hand. "I've got to get home, Nick. I'll talk to you before I leave."

"Mei-Ling, I've talked to China Mary about your sale to Hing Fat."

Mei-Ling forced herself to remain outwardly calm, though just the mention of Hing Fat's name made her stomach cramp and her skin crawl.

Sensing her sudden fear, Jesse quickly added, "You are no longer going to be sold to him. He's taken ill and can't buy you."

"Ill? But what about when he recovers?"

Jesse reached over to still her trembling hands. "If what China Mary told me is true, he may never recover from this illness."

At her look of confusion, he coughed self-consciously, then said, "Supposedly Hing Fat's wife has been putting an herb in his tea that has taken away his . . . uh . . . desire for—"

Mei-Ling's soft chuckle ended his awkward explanation. Meeting her gaze, he was surprised to find the fear in her eyes had changed to amusement.

Smiling widely, she said, "Hing Li Ma must have finally grown tired of her husband's cruelty. She chose a fitting way to seek revenge. Losing his abilities as a man must be an enormous insult to Hing Fat's male pride, especially if he doesn't suspect his problem stems from a special tea prepared by his wife." More softly she added, "I don't blame her."

"Neither do I," Jesse replied, squeezing her hands in understanding. He released his grasp and stood up.

Moving to the parlor window, he stared at the un-
dulating haze of heat shimmering off the dirt street,
lost in his thoughts.

As if reading his mind, Mei-Ling said, "What about
my uncle?"

Jesse swung around to meet her expectant gaze. "I
plan to go to your uncle and pay him the price he and
Hing Fat agreed on."

"You're going to buy me?"

"Buy isn't the right word, Mei-Ling. I'm going to
give your uncle the money he wants so he can't sell you
to someone else. But you won't belong to me; you'll be
free."

"You'd do that for me?" She blinked several times
to hold back the sudden tears pricking the back of her
eyes.

"Absolutely. Just thinking about how your people
sell each other makes a knot in my gut, and the idea of
me actually participating in such a practice pulls the
knot tighter. But I intend to go through with it, Mei-
Ling. I wish there was another way to get you away
from your uncle, but there isn't."

"Does Fantasy know about this?"

"No. But she won't object. Neither she nor I want
you to be sold. Thankfully Hing Fat is unable to keep
his end of the agreement he made with your uncle. I'll
just take Fat's place, except afterwards you'll be a free
woman."

Mei-Ling broke down then, covering her face with
her hands to hide the flood of tears. Her sobbing made
Jesse very uncomfortable, but the questions he wanted
to ask her kept him in the room.

When she had regained her composure, Jesse sat
down next to her on the settee. "Mei-Ling, I want to
talk to you about the necklace your uncle gave you."

"There isn't anything else I can tell you," she said
between sniffles.

"Perhaps. But I'd like to ask you just the same, if
you don't mind."

At her nod, he said, "You told me you knew the necklace didn't belong to your mother even though your uncle said it did. Do you have any idea where he might have gotten it?"

"No. He had it tucked in a dresser drawer. I never saw it before he gave it to me."

"Did he ever show you any other jewelry?"

"No. He said it was a waste of money. He hoarded all his money so he could return to China. He's never given me anything in the years since I came to live with him. If I hadn't been so shocked when he gave me the necklace, I might have asked him where he got it." She lifted her gaze to meet Jesse's. "Why are you so interested in the necklace?"

After studying her for several seconds, Jesse made a quick decision. "It was stolen in a stage robbery a few months ago." When her eyes widened in obvious surprise, he knew his instincts had been right to confide in her.

"Stolen? You think my uncle stole it?"

"No, not exactly. I don't think Wing Fong was one of the robbers who held up the stage. But I do think he's the man the gang uses to sell what they steal from the stage passengers. Are you sure you never saw your uncle with any pocket watches or other jewelry?"

Mei-Ling shook her head.

"Did you ever see him with a large amount of money?"

A sudden spark flickering in her eyes, she said, "Yes, once. A leather pouch filled with money came in the mail. When I asked my uncle about it, he snatched the bag out of my hands, mumbling something about it being payment for a gambling debt. My uncle has many vices, so I shrugged it off.

"Now that I think about it, I once overheard one of his friends teasing him about never playing fan-tan for fear of losing a few dollars. Except for buying opium, my uncle was very frugal with his money. He planned to go back to China, where he could live like an emperor on his savings. So I'm sure Uncle Fong also lied about the gambling debt."

"When did this happen?"

Mei-Ling's brow furrowed. "It was several months ago, January or February I think."

Jesse nodded. The *cow-boys* had been stopping stages, relieving the drivers of the Wells, Fargo strongboxes and taking the passengers' valuables for over a year. The money Mei-Ling saw could easily have been the profits from one of those holdups.

"Did your uncle ever mention a man named Jack Lawson?"

"Not that I recall. He seldom talked about anyone he knew." She couldn't hide her bitterness when she added, "He rarely spoke to me at all, and then only when he wanted something."

"How about Daryl or Buck Arnette, or Ramón García? Do you remember hearing any of those names?"

Her eyebrows pulled together in concentration, Mei-Ling shook her head, then suddenly her brow cleared. "Wait! I do remember a man named García. I was late returning from my shopping one morning, and in my hurry to avoid my uncle's wrath I bumped into a man as I rushed through the front door. Uncle Fong was livid. He called me an ungrateful sow and ordered me to the back room. Although I didn't get a good look at the other man, I did glance up at him when I apologized for running into him. All I remember is his dark complexion and thick moustache. But I also recall he had a Spanish accent when he accepted my apology, and I'm sure my uncle called him Mr. García when he added his own apologies for his clumsy niece's stupidity." She fell silent and took a deep, shuddering breath.

Jesse silently cursed Wing Fong for the miserable way he'd treated Mei-Ling. He wished he didn't have to face the man, for it would take every bit of his willpower not to box Fong's ears. He had to push his dislike of the Chinaman aside, Mei-Ling's future depended on it.

Mei-Ling's sharp indrawn breath pulled Jesse from his contemplation. "What is it?"

"Something just occurred to me. You don't think I had anything to do with those robberies, do you?" Her features pinched with fright, she stared at him.

"No, I don't think that, Mei-Ling." When she didn't look convinced, he said, "Would I try to buy your freedom, or tell you any of this, if I thought you were mixed up in the robberies?"

She exhaled slowly, then said, "I guess not. You were the first person who didn't treat me like a despicable Celestial. First you, then Fantasy, and then Mr. Trask." Her face flushing prettily when she mentioned Nick's name, she lowered her gaze. "I'm . . . I'm sorry for doubting your intentions."

"Mei-Ling, I'm going to tell you something else. But you have to swear to keep it just between us."

Confusion mirrored on her features, she lifted her face to look at Jesse, then nodded her agreement.

"I was sent here to investigate the ring of thieves I told you about." As her puzzlement turned to shock, he smiled. "No one knows my real reason for being here, except Nick. And now you."

"Nick?" she blurted, forgetting herself and using his Christian name. "You both work as lawmen?"

"Not lawmen exactly. We're investigators, special agents for the same company. I'd like you to promise me you'll keep Nick's part in this a secret as well."

"Of course, I'd never do anything to hurt Nick." Realizing she'd just made another revealing declaration, Mei-Ling clamped her mouth shut.

"Good. I need to ask you to do something else for me. I'd like you to sign a statement about the necklace, how and when you came to have it, and what you just told me about your uncle." Seeing the sudden tensing of her body, he wanted to alleviate any reluctance to cooperate. "There's one last thing I have to tell you.

After I visit Wing Fong and settle the issue of your ownership, I intend to get you away from your uncle, forever. I plan to take you to your sister in San Francisco."

Her mouth dropped open, feeling another spate of tears coming on. Dabbing at her face with the handkerchief Jesse handed her, Mei-Ling whispered, "I don't know what to say, Mr. McAllister, other than thank you."

"Your thanks is enough. That and the statement I mentioned. And I think after all we've been through, you should start calling me Jesse, agreed?" He smiled reassuringly.

Mei-Ling looked into his face. Her first impression of this man at China Mary's weeks before had been correct. Mr. McAllister had proven his kindness time and again. Giving him a weak smile, she murmured her agreement.

"Good. Now, if I get a pen and some paper, will you tell me again about the necklace so I can write it down in your exact words?"

Mei-Ling nodded, then blew her nose. "Does Fantasy know why you're in Tombstone?"

"No, and remember your promise not to say anything to anyone."

"But I don't understand, Mr. Mc—Jesse. Why can't you tell her?"

His mind spinning for a plausible excuse, he finally said, "I'm afraid my wife will think my job is more dangerous than it really is. She has enough on her mind right now with the Williamses in town, without worrying about me, too. For now at least, I think it's best if she doesn't know about my assignment."

Jesse exhaled the anxious breath he'd been holding when Mei-Ling accepted his reason and dropped the subject.

But after he'd painstakingly written out Mei-Ling's statement, let her read it, and watched her carefully apply her signature to the bottom, Jesse couldn't stop thinking about the lie he'd told her concerning Fantasy. The real reason for keeping his wife ignorant of why he'd come to town was a burden he couldn't share with Mei-Ling, and one he wished he could shed. Unfortunately, he had to continue carrying its weight until he could prove Fantasy's innocence.

The next day, as Jesse made his way to Wing Fong's Laundry, his anxiety continued to eat at him. Would this be the day he'd finally find out whether Fantasy was a willing participant in Lawson's gang?

The answer to his question haunted his every step toward Hop Town.

Chapter 16

Wing Fong paced the back room of his laundry with growing impatience. Time was running out. Lawson had agreed to give him five days to get the jade necklace, and already three days had passed.

"That ungrateful Mei-Ling," he muttered. It was his niece's fault he hadn't eaten or slept in the last three days. If she hadn't gone to China Mary, he would have had the necklace when the Boss-man came asking about it, and he could have made up some believable excuse for why he hadn't sent it to be sold with the other jewelry. Then he wouldn't have a deadline hanging over his head. But no, his niece had to make him look like a fool by running from his house when she learned of his agreement with Hing Fat. Slashing his arm through the air, he said aloud, "She should be honored man like Hing Fat want her. Not be upset she not be wife. Bah, stupid girl!"

Not only did he have the problem of giving a necklace—one he didn't have—to Lawson within two days, he still didn't know the whereabouts of his niece so he could retrieve what his boss wanted back. Not wanting to face China Mary directly and admit what he'd done, Fong had begun his own investigation into locating Mei-Ling. Before he'd made any progress, he suffered another setback—a message arrived from China Mary. Hing Fat no longer wanted to buy Mei-Ling.

Even knowing Mary had secured another buyer didn't lift Fong's glum spirits.

His reply to China Mary, agreeing to sell his niece to the new buyer, also asked to see Mei-Ling before the sale took place. For a few hours, hope that his life was not in danger bloomed in Fong's chest. But then his hopes had been dashed—China Mary refused his request.

Fong couldn't concentrate, his appetite dwindled and without opium, sleep became impossible. He smoked enough to ease his body's craving for the drug, but not enough to put him to sleep. He found the prospect of smoking his pipe into oblivion no longer appealing. Keeping a clear head was imperative.

Stopping several doors from Wing Fong's Laundry, Jesse took several deep breaths and rolled his head from side to side to ease the tension in the back of his neck. Unable to totally dispel his apprehension, he chastised himself for letting his emotions reign over his normally detached analytic skills. He hadn't felt such nervousness since his first assignment, for God's sake. But then, he'd never worked on a case where he had a personal stake in the outcome. Hopeful, yet also fearful, Wing Fong knew if Fantasy was a member of Lawson's gang, Jesse resolved himself to learning the truth—no matter how painful. His jaw clenched, he took those last few steps and pushed open the door.

When he heard the bell on the front door of his laundry, Wing Fong hesitated, wringing his hands in despair. Had Lawson returned in less than the five days he'd been given? Fong peeked through the curtain into his shop. A man, another barbarian American, stood at the counter. Filled with panic that Lawson had reneged on his promise and sent someone to extract revenge, Fong considered refusing to face the man, then quickly decided against it.

He pulled the curtain aside and shuffled over to the

counter. "Good afternoon, how Wing Fong help you?"

At his first glance of the Chinaman, Jesse immediately knew Fong was badly frightened. Having spent many years chasing down criminals, he'd become an expert at recognizing the signs of fear.

"My name is Jesse McAllister. I believe China Mary sent word to expect my visit."

Fong's brows shot up. "China Mary? I not know—" His face suddenly brightened. "Ah, this about Mei-Ling. China Mary not say new buyer barbarian Amer—" Fong made a choking sound, then whispered, "Sorry, mean no disrespect. You going to buy Mei-Ling, Mista McAllister?"

The gleam leaping into Fong's eyes filled Jesse with disgust, turning his voice harsh. "Yes, I'm here to discuss Mei-Ling's sale. I told China Mary I would pay the price you and Hing Fat agreed on. I trust she explained that to you."

"Aiee, she tell me." Fong smiled, revealing opium yellowed teeth. "You give me money now?"

Jesse clenched his fists at his sides, longing to wipe the smile off the man's face. Forcing himself to remain calm, he said, "No, not yet. There are some conditions you have to meet first."

Fong cocked his head to one side, giving Jesse a wary look. "Conditions?"

"Yes. First off, I want you to answer some questions about Jack Lawson. Second, I want you to promise me you won't tell Lawson about our conversation. And the final condition is I want you packed and ready to leave town within twenty-four hours. That's when I'll pay you for Mei-Ling." When Fong started to answer, Jesse held up his hand. "Think about it carefully, Fong."

"You work for Mista Lawson?"

"No. My reason for wanting to know about Lawson is a private matter. But let me assure you, I mean you no harm as long as you do as I ask."

Wringing his hands again, Fong stared at the powerfully built American and carefully weighed his alternatives.

If he answered Mr. McAllister's questions and left town before the deadline he'd been given expired, he'd avoid any retribution Lawson might levy on him. And even if Lawson was angry enough to try to follow him, Fong knew places to hide where no barbarian American would find him. Although he had planned on having a much thicker wallet before returning to China, adding the price of Mei-Ling to the money he'd already saved should allow him, through careful management, to live out his days in comfort.

On the other hand, if he refused to cooperate with this man, he would not only lose the money from selling his niece, but he might not be able to locate Mei-Ling in time to get the necklace to Lawson. And if that happened, his life wouldn't be worth a pile of manure unless—

"Where my niece? I want to see if Mei-Ling agree to you buying her."

"Where she is isn't important, and you don't need to talk to her. Why the sudden concern about what your niece thinks, Fong?" Jesse couldn't hide his irritation. "You didn't bother to ask her what she thought about being sold to Hing Fat. All you need to know is this: Mei-Ling is aware I'm here and has no objections." Jesse wanted to add he knew the reason for Fong's sudden interest in Mei-Ling, but halted the words. He'd already said more than he should have.

Fong sighed, his shoulders slumping forward. "I do what you say."

Eyeing the Chinaman carefully, Jesse said, "You're agreeing to all my terms?"

"Aiee, I agree. What you want to know about Lawson?"

"Is there a more private place where we can talk?"

"My home back of laundry. We not be disturbed there."

"Fine," Jesse responded, indicating Fong should lead the way.

Seated in the modestly furnished parlor of Fong's small apartment, Jesse said, "How long have you known Jack Lawson?"

"Maybe one year."

"And how long have you been fencing stolen items for him?"

Fong started at the unexpected question, his complexion turning a strange pasty color. "You lawman?"

"No. Like I said, my interest in Lawson is strictly a private matter. Provided you cooperate, I won't notify the authorities about your part in Lawson's gang." Seeing the sudden widening of Fong's eyes and the twitching of his hands, Jesse added, "Surely you knew Lawson was a thief?"

Fong's Adam's apple bobbed several times. "Aiee. I think he must be when he first come to my laundry. He ask me if I want to earn lotsa money. He say he need way to send secret packages to and from California. I say I know how." When Jesse nodded for him to continue, he said, "Opium come from China in tins that say tobacco. I use same idea for jewelry and geegaws Lawson bring."

With the opening he'd been hoping for presenting itself, Jesse's palms grew damp. "Did Lawson bring the robbery loot to you himself?"

Fong shook his head, his long braid making a swishing sound as it whisked back and forth on his silk jacket. "Him too smart for that. He say landlady bring with laundry. Then I send money back in clean clothes. Plan work good until boardinghouse burn down."

"Was his landlady in on the robberies?"

Fong shook his head fiercely. "No, Lawson say don't talk to Missy Fantasy. He say she not know what she do for him. So I keep mouth shut."

Nothing the Chinaman said could have sounded sweeter. This was the proof he needed—proof his instincts had been correct. Fantasy wasn't a criminal. He wanted to shout his joy, but he couldn't celebrate just yet.

Pulling his thoughts together, Jesse went on with his interrogation. "Who else works with Lawson, do you know?"

"I know two men, Buck and his brother. We meet couple times after fire. Boss-man set up meeting so I get stuff to send to California. Other time to give them money. I never see them before that."

"Do you know a man named García?"

Fong considered the name, his face puckered in concentration. "I know man with that name. He work for Lawson, too?"

"Never mind about him. What was Lawson paying you?"

"I get cut of what sold. Small cut, but still lotsa dolla."

"And you never held out on him?"

Fong's sudden nervousness would have given him away, even if Jesse hadn't already known about the jade necklace.

"Once," he said in a strangled whisper.

Reaching into his vest pocket, Jesse withdrew something and held it out to Fong. "Is this what you took?"

The jade pendant dangling from its gold chain made Fong's breath catch in his throat. Unable to speak, he nodded.

Surmising the reason for Fong's fear, Jesse said, "So, Lawson knows about the necklace, huh? I take it he wasn't too pleased when he found out you'd helped yourself?"

At Fong's pained expression, Jesse added, "Don't worry, Fong, I intend to keep my end of the bargain. I'll pay you for Mei-Ling, provided you keep your end of our little deal. If Lawson's made threats—" Fong's startled gasp momentarily halted Jesse's words. "Ah, I see he has. Well, in that case I'd think you'd be anxious to get out of town. And don't even consider telling

Lawson about me, or I'll make his threats seem like child's play. Have I made myself clear, Fong?"

He bobbed his head vigorously. "Aiee, very clear."

"Good, now how soon can you be packed and ready to leave?"

Fong made a quick calculation. A day wasn't much of a head start on someone as determined as Jack Lawson, but Fong had places he could hide until he could get to California and book passage to China. He would have to leave many of his belongings behind, but leaving town with his cache of money—and in one piece—was more important. "Tomorrow morning I be ready."

Jesse studied Fong silently for several long seconds. Detecting no sign of duplicity, he nodded. "Okay. I'll meet you here at eight tomorrow morning. Once I'm satisfied you're really leaving town, I'll give you the money for Mei-Ling. Do we have a deal?"

"Aiee, we have deal."

His tread lighter than when he'd arrived at Fong's laundry, Jesse left Hop Town to seek out Nick.

"I need you to keep an eye on Wing Fong until he leaves town tomorrow morning," Jesse said after locating Nick at the Alhambra.

"Did he tell you what you wanted to know?"

"Yeah, he answered all my questions. Listen Nick, I don't have time to tell you everything Fong said right now. I think you'd better get over to his place before he changes his mind about keeping his mouth shut. We can't run the risk of Lawson finding out we're on to him."

Nodding, Nick tossed his cigar into a spittoon, then turned to leave. "Sure thing. I'll head over there right now."

* * *

His spirits higher than they'd been in a very long time, Jesse hurried home, his thoughts dwelling on what Fong had told him. Raising his eyes skyward, he whispered a prayer of thanks, grateful he wouldn't have to go ahead with the plans he'd made if Fantasy had turned out to be one of Lawson's cohorts. He bounded up the steps of the back porch, eased the door open and stepped into the kitchen. Spotting his wife sitting in the dining room studying something on the table in front of her, a devilish smile curved his lips.

Fantasy pushed the cookbook away from her with a sigh. Finding recipes Mother Williams wouldn't complain about was a losing battle. Closing her eyes, she dropped her head back, cognizant of the tightness in her neck and shoulders. What she wouldn't give for a back rub. As if her thoughts had conjured up someone to carry out her wish, a hand touched her right shoulder.

"Owww," she squealed, her attempt to twist around in the chair halted by a male voice near her ear.

"Easy, love," Jesse whispered before kissing the side of her throat.

One hand pressed to her racing heart, Fantasy said in a strangled voice, "Jesse! You scared the daylights out of me."

"Sorry," he murmured, his hands working to ease the kinks in her stiff muscles. "You're as tight as an overwound watch spring. Is something bothering you?"

"Nothing that hasn't been bothering me for the last ten days. Ah, that feels wonderful."

Jesse chuckled. "If we had time, I'd give you my complete treatment." He ran his tongue across the nape of her neck, smiling against her skin when he felt her shiver in response. "So, what's Mother Williams done this time?" His voice turned gruff. "She hasn't said anything about taking Robby, has she?"

"No. She hasn't been that bold, yet." Fantasy groaned when Jesse's fingers found a particularly sensitive spot. "Maybe she's decided to let the matter drop—now that I have a husband and Robby has a father. Actually, she hasn't said much of anything to me about Robby's future. I suspect your presence is keeping her quiet."

"Me? How can you say that? Henrietta is most definitely never quiet when I'm around."

Fantasy giggled. "That's true. I meant she's keeping quiet about Robby because of our marriage. I doubt she'll say anything unless she decides we got married just to keep her from getting her way."

Though his wife's comment stung, Jesse withheld comment. He felt certain Fantasy didn't think of their marriage as a sham—at least she'd given him no indication to believe she did.

He continued massaging her shoulders in silence. His earlier exuberant mood over learning Fantasy was not part of Lawson's gang had mellowed, overshadowed by the possible threat Henrietta Williams posed to their future. What if the woman wasn't convinced he and Fantasy were happily married? Would she still try to take the boy from them?

"Do you think there's a possibility she'll make that decision?" he finally asked.

Fantasy shrugged. "She's never asked about how long we've known each other, or when we were married."

"Well, if she does," he replied, his good humor restored, "I'll just have to convince her I swept you off your feet, won't I?"

As the evening progressed, Jesse's light-hearted mood seemed doomed. Not willing to listen to another round of Henrietta's complaints about the food on his table, Jesse offered to take the Williamses out to supper. That's when things started going downhill—fast!

On the short walk to the Can-Can Restaurant, Henrietta had the misfortune of witnessing a fight between two drunken miners in the middle of Allen Street, narrowly missed being bowled over by a team of runaway horses, and overheard a ribald argument between a man and his "lady friend" over the price the man would pay for her services.

Her mouth flattened in a severe line, they arrived at the restaurant. As they were shown to their table, Jesse hoped no other surprises awaited them. Unfortunately, luck wasn't on his side. From the moment Ah Lum, the Can-Can's owner, seated them, Henrietta found fault with one thing after another—her chair was too hard, her tea too cold and her steak too rare. Cursing himself for suggesting this outing, Jesse tried to ignore Henrietta's constant harping. He turned his thoughts to his lovely wife and what he had planned for her when they were finally alone.

As horribly as Henrietta had behaved, Fantasy forgot all about her spiteful former mother-in-law when Jesse closed the bedroom door behind them much later that evening.

"I'm surprised Frank hasn't gone stone-deaf by now," he said, reaching out to unfasten the buttons running down the front of Fantasy's dress. His fingers pushed the fabric apart and brushed over the tops of her breasts beneath her lace-trimmed chemise.

When his mouth replaced his fingers, Fantasy inhaled sharply. In a breathless voice she replied, "Me, too. He's a good man. But I don't know why he puts up with her ghastly behavior. Perhaps it's like the old saying: love is blind."

Jesse grunted, then lifted his head from her bosom. "I suppose it's possible. When you love someone—" He looked deeply into her eyes. "—nothing else matters."

Her cheeks burning, she dropped her gaze to where her fingers worked to unbutton his shirt. The last button free, she grasped the fabric and gave it an impatient tug to pull the shirttail from his trousers. When he stood bare-chested in front of her, she allowed her eyes to feast on his male beauty. Feeling weak at the knees, her stomach quivered with need, a familiar fullness settled between her thighs. She reached out and touched his hair-roughened chest, sending a flicker of desire licking through her veins. As her fingertips glided through the silky hair over hard muscle, the small flame matured into a full-blown fire.

No words passed between them as they quickly undressed, pulling and tugging at their clothes, then carelessly tossing each garment across the room. With a groan of pleasure Jesse pushed Fantasy down onto the bed, then stretched out on top of her.

"Fancy, I've been waiting to make love to you all day," he murmured near her ear, his hands roaming freely over her naked curves.

"Yes, I know. Me, too," came her husky reply. Her hands busily exploring, she reveled in the rock-hard muscles of his thighs and buttocks and the smooth expanse of his back and shoulders. She returned his hot kisses, teasing his tongue with hers and being rewarded with his moan of pleasure. Pulling her mouth from his, she pushed impatiently at his shoulders. "Roll over on your back."

His wife had become more and more aggressive in the privacy of their bedroom—much to Jesse's jubilation—and whenever she took the initiative, he never failed to realize how lucky he was.

He did as she asked and rolled onto his back. His eyes wide with curiosity and delight, he watched her crouch on her knees next to him. The amusement in his gaze vanished when she leaned over and ran her fingers down his chest, over his stomach, and then lower. When her hot fingers skimmed over the pulsing length of his manhood, he squeezed his eyes tightly closed. He groaned his frustration at her continued light touch. At last her fingers tightened around him, bringing a ragged sigh of pleasure from his lips.

Lifting his hips, he matched the rhythm she established with her hand. When a lock of her hair fell onto his thigh, he tensed, the brush of the silky strand across his heated skin arousing him even more. He forced himself to relax, to savor his enjoyment of Fantasy's growing skill as a lover.

Abruptly her hand stilled. For a few seconds she didn't move, the only sound in the room the mingled rasp of their breathing. Then the moist heat of her tongue laved over the tip of his turgid flesh. Jesse's eyes flew open, his body stiffened with shock. "What—?"

Lifting her head, she met his surprised gaze. "Hush," she whispered. "I want to do this. It seems perfectly natural to me." She paused, letting her repetition of the words he'd once used sink in. When his expression didn't change, she asked, "Is there some reason I shouldn't do this?"

Jesse couldn't have gotten the words out—had there been any he wanted to say—so he shook his head. He didn't miss the flare of triumph in her eyes before she lowered her head. He felt his manhood swell even more in anticipation of her warm mouth. When her lips closed around him at last, he couldn't stop his hips from bucking upward in reaction. An animal groan rumbled deep in his chest.

Fantasy used her lips and tongue to bring Jesse as much pleasure as she'd experienced when he'd loved her this way. As an added bonus she discovered her own excitement was greatly enhanced by her ministrations to him.

Not wanting to deny himself Fantasy's sweet body, Jesse held his need in check as long as he dared. When he reached the end of his endurance, he reached up to grasp her shoulders. In a raspy whisper he said, "Stop, love. I can't take a minute more."

Her own desire teetering precariously, she offered no resistance when he pushed her onto her back and immediately settled between her spread thighs.

Biting his lip to keep from shouting his pleasure at

his first thrust, Jesse forced himself to take it slow and easy. When Fantasy tried to increase the pace, he stilled her frantic attempts. "No, love. Take it slow. That's it. Nice and slow."

Following his lead, Fantasy met each thrust of his hips in agonizing slowness. The cadence of her breathing abruptly changed. She gasped then moaned, her nails digging into his back.

"Oh, Jesus, Fancy, I can't wait any longer." With one last thrust, his body shuddered violently.

As Fantasy followed him into the throes of ecstasy, she cried, "I love you, Jesse."

Her declaration made his heart soar, his release all the more satisfying.

Promptly at seven forty-five the following morning, Jesse headed for Wing Fong's Laundry. Nick saw him coming, and stepped from his hiding place.

"Did our boy behave himself?" Jesse asked, stopping next to Nick.

"Yeah. He never left his place, and far as I can tell, he didn't send any messages."

Jesse nodded with satisfaction. "Good." Slapping his friend on the back, he added, "Well, I have an appointment to keep. Go get some sleep. I'll see you later."

Nick yawned, then nodded and turned to leave.

At the back door of Wing Fong's Laundry, Jesse knocked softly. Fong answered immediately, bowing and moving aside for Jesse to enter. Noticing a small covered basket sitting near the door, Jesse said, "You're ready to leave?"

"Aiee. Cousin come soon."

"Cousin?"

"Aiee. Cousin, Hong Wu, live up river on farm. He come to town every day to bring vegetable he grow. I stay on farm for few day, then go to California."

Just then the rattle of wagon wheels came from the

alley behind the laundry. Jesse followed Fong outside and found a pair of scrawny horses harnessed to a dilapidated wagon. A small, wizen-faced Chinaman, with a long braid like Fong's and dressed in the same kind of loose fitting trousers and jacket, jumped agilely to the ground.

Bowing at Jesse, the man turned to Fong and said something in Chinese. Fong replied in the same language, then translated his cousin's words. "Wu say we must go now. Him needed on farm. You have money?"

Jesse waited until Fong threw his basket onto the back of the wagon before reaching inside his jacket. He withdrew the envelope and handed it to Fong. Scowling when Fong took the time to thumb through the money, his lips moving silently as he counted, Jesse snapped, "It's all there. I kept my word, and I trust you kept yours."

The envelope disappearing inside the folds of his jacket, Fong nodded eagerly. "Aiee. I keep word. I go now?"

"Fine."

Fong and his cousin scrambled up onto the wagon seat. Hong Wu flicked the reins on the backs of the horses. The wagon groaned with protest, then lurched forward.

Jesse followed the wagon down the alley and watched the horses turn north. Satisfied Wing Fong was really leaving town, he went to the stage office. With Fong out of the way, Jesse felt it imperative to get Mei-Ling out of town on the first stage so he could return as quickly as possible.

Tickets in hand for the following day's morning stage, Jesse sent a telegram to his boss in San Francisco then stopped at Nick's boardinghouse. He didn't want to disturb his friend's well-deserved sleep, so he left a note asking Nick to come to his house later that evening.

On the walk home, Jesse thought about his impend-

ing trip. Though he didn't relish telling Fantasy, he
knew she would understand the need for him to take
Mei-Ling to her sister. He hated the idea of being away
from Fantasy, especially since Henrietta and Frank
were still in town. If he could wait, he would. But
talking to John Valentine couldn't be put off any longer. Plus it was important to get Mei-Ling out of town
before Lawson learned of her part in the missing jade
necklace. The timing was lousy, but he had no choice.

Nick arrived at Jesse's house just after dark. After
pouring each of them a drink, Jesse led Nick out onto
the back porch where they could talk in private.

"So, when are you leaving?" Nick asked after they'd
settled on the porch steps.

"Tomorrow morning."

"Have you told Fantasy?"

"No. I wanted to tell her this afternoon, but that
magpie Henrietta didn't give me a chance to speak to
my wife privately. It's damn bad luck I have to leave
now, when Henrietta and Frank don't seem to be in
any rush to go back home."

Nick withdrew his cigar case from his jacket pocket
and took out a black cheroot. Rolling it between his
thumb and forefinger, he said, "You never did tell me
what you found out from Fong." Putting the cigar in
his mouth, he put a flaming match to its tip and inhaled deeply.

Fantasy crossed the kitchen, stopping at the back
door. She was just about to ask if the men needed their
drinks freshened when Nick's voice stopped her.

"Did you find out if Fantasy was involved in the
robberies?"

"Yeah, I found out. She was involved all right."
Jesse shifted his legs, his boots clunking on the hollow
steps. "She delivered the robbery loot, then brought

the money back to the boardinghouse, just like I thought." He paused to take a sip of his drink.

Clapping a hand over her mouth, Fantasy backed away from the door. Her eyes wide with shock, a loud buzzing started in her head, blocking out all other sound. She gave her head a shake, trying to quiet the thundering in her ears. As the buzzing faded, she heard the murmur of men's voices then Nick's chuckle.

"Well, Jesse, looks like you'll get that promotion you wanted so bad."

"I hope so. I've worked damn hard to get it."

Waves of pain crashed over Fantasy, hot tears scalded her throat. Biting her lip to hold in a sob, she turned and ran from the kitchen. Inside the bedroom she shared with Jesse, she sat on the edge of the bed, trying to remember Jesse's exact words. Maybe she'd been mistaken, maybe she'd misunderstood. No, she'd heard him distinctly say she was involved in the robberies Nick mentioned, that she had delivered the robbery loot, just like he thought. "Oh Jesse, how could you?" she moaned, wrapping her arms around herself and rocking back and forth on the bed. How could the man who had professed his love think her guilty of robbery?

She tried to summon her anger, but it refused to stir. Only overwhelming hurt and sadness filled her. Hurt Jesse would believe so little in her honesty. Sadness that he actually thought her capable of being a thief.

She should have learned her lesson with Thomas. But no, just like the fool she'd been at seventeen, she'd been sucked in by Jesse's attentions to both herself and her son, his sweet words, his magical lovemaking. To make matters worse, she'd fallen in love with the man. Recalling how long she'd pondered when to confess her feelings, she would have laughed, had her heart not been breaking. How ironic, she'd finally said the words only to learn everything he'd said was a lie—wanting to be a father to Robby, his plans for them to live in San Francisco, his declaration of love. All lies. Unable to control the intense pain filling her chest, a heart-rending sob broke free, then the tears came.

After allowing herself a good cry, Fantasy dried her eyes and blew her nose. Jesse would be coming in soon and she had to think about what she was going to say. It would be useless to pretend she hadn't overheard what he'd said to Nick. She couldn't hide the hurt or the evidence of her tears. Exhaling a long, quivering breath, Fantasy tried to prepare herself for what she had to do. Composure in place, an icy calm shrouding her heart, she sat down in the rocking chair to await her husband.

Chapter 17

Satisfied he and Nick had covered what had to be done during his absence, Jesse told Nick he'd see him at the stage office in the morning, then said good night. As he entered his house, Jesse recalled Nick's offer to get up at the crack of dawn to see him off and chuckled. More than likely, Nick wanted to see Mei-Ling one last time but wouldn't admit it.

Not finding his wife in the rest of the house, Jesse approached the master bedroom. He stopped at the closed door, a grin creasing his face. A tantalizing picture of how Fantasy awaited him flashed through his mind. She'd be sprawled seductively on the bed, gloriously naked, hair spread across the pillow in a wild cascade of auburn waves. Her lips would curve into a beguiling smile when he entered the room, one hand extended in invitation.

His pulse quickening and his body reacting with instant desire, he reached for the doorknob, anxious to learn how close he'd predicted the scene awaiting him. He couldn't help smiling at his line of thinking—his wife had been well named. She was indeed a fantasy, both in name and in actions. Turning the knob, he quietly opened the door.

The sight meeting his gaze didn't resemble what he'd envisioned by any stretch of the imagination. His wife wasn't naked—she wasn't even in bed—and her hair wasn't loose but gathered in a knot at her nape. He received no welcoming smile, no signal of invitation. In fact, the only similarity between the two scenes was Fantasy's presence.

Shaking off his disappointment, he brightened. Perhaps she wanted him to undress her—they'd always found great enjoyment in removing each other's clothes. Confident he'd figured out his wife's plan, he took a step toward the rocking chair.

When she remained seated, hands clasped in her lap, Jesse decided she had to be playing some sort of game. When she didn't acknowledge his presence, his heart did a strange flip-flop. Moving closer, the stiffness of her neck and shoulders erased his warm jovial mood, a chill of dread closing around his heart.

Standing next to her chair, he tried to ignore the alarm sounding in his head. He wished she'd look at him, but she kept her face averted, the lamp burning on the bedside table casting her in shadows. "Fancy?"

Jolted out of her ruminations, Fantasy summoned up her strength and replied, "You can drop the act now, Jesse. And please, stop calling me Fancy."

His brow furrowed at the strain in her voice. "Act? What are you talking about?"

Keeping her back to him, she rose and moved to the window. She stared out over the desert, finding the solace of the Arizona nighttime landscape no longer held its former appeal. Now it only reminded her of how she felt inside—dark, empty, desolate.

After a long silence, Jesse asked again, "Fantasy, I asked you what you're talking about."

"I heard you talking to Nick." She swung around to face him then, forcing herself to meet his gaze. She could see the questions and confusion swirling in his eyes, but she refused to be swayed by them.

When she moved so the lamplight revealed her swollen eyes and reddened nose, Jesse's breath caught in his throat. Dear God, what could have caused her tears? Her words finally sank in, sending a rush of relief surging through him. "If you heard us talking, then you know—"

"Yes," she interrupted, her eyes flashing with their usual fire. "I know you think I'm a thief."

"Wait a minute."

She ignored his request, continuing as if he hadn't spoken. "I went to the back door to see if you and Nick wanted another drink. That's when I heard you call me a thief."

"You didn't hear—"

"I know what I heard." Pinning him with a piercing gaze, she said, "Are you going to deny Nick asked whether you found out if I was involved in the robberies?"

"No, I won't deny that," Jesse replied, his fear returning in a gut-wrenching torrent.

"And did you tell him you know I was involved?"

"Yes, but—" The forbidding look on her face halted his words. *Why the hell couldn't she have heard my next statement to Nick? When I said I knew she wasn't aware of her part in Lawson's schemes.* Fantasy's voice pulled him from his painful thoughts.

"How did you keep a straight face when I accused you of working for Mother Williams? I was so certain you had to be another of her spies I never suspected you were spying on me for an entirely different reason. All that time I thought you were trying to discredit my character, when you were actually trying to prove I'm a common thief." Her voice cracked pitifully. "You must have gotten a good laugh out of silly, little Fantasy and her wild accusations. Well, I see your true stripes now, you two-faced polecat."

"Fantasy, you don't understand."

"Do you think I'm an idiot as well? What more could there possibly be for me to understand? You think I'm guilty of robbery. You used my son and Lord knows who else to find out information about me. You pretended to be interested in me so you could look for the evidence you needed. You even

married—" She pressed the knuckles of one hand
against her mouth to stop her quivering chin. Taking
a deep breath, she swallowed the threatening tears.
"You even married me for the sake of your glory
seeking!"

"Glory seeking?" he nearly shouted. His voice
turned hard. "I didn't come to Tombstone to seek
fame."

"Are you denying you didn't come here to solve the
robberies you and Nick were talking about so you
could get a promotion?"

A muscle jumped in Jesse's jaw. "No, I'm not denying that, only—"

Eyeing him scornfully, she cut him off again to ask,
"You knew Nick before you came to Tombstone,
didn't you?"

"Yes. I knew Nick long before we started working
on—"

"That's another thing," she said, ignoring his obvious frustration at being interrupted again. "Not that it
makes any difference, but just what are you, Jesse? A
sheriff? A marshal?"

"Neither, I'm a—"

Holding up one hand, she said, "On second thought,
I don't care what you are."

Pacing around the room in long, agitated strides, he
shoved one hand through his hair. "Fantasy, if you'll
let me finish a sentence, I can explain."

She sank back into the rocker and sighed wearily.
"There's nothing to explain."

The defeat in her voice was like a vice clamping
around his heart. He inhaled slowly, willing the thun-
derous pounding in his ears to quiet.

"I heard what you told Nick, and you just admitted
you came to town on a robbery investigation. So whatever you have to say doesn't matter. Nothing matters,
except not losing my son."

"I never intended to let Robby be taken from you,"
he said, stung she would even think such a thing.

"I know." In spite of the pain she'd suffered at this latest revelation, Fantasy knew deep in her heart Jesse didn't want to see Robby end up with the Williamses. Though he'd used her horribly, there was no way he could have faked his love for her son. Hoping to utilize that love, she said, "For Robby's sake, I don't want Henrietta and Frank to know there's anything wrong between us."

Stunned with a mixture of disbelief and anger, he stared down at his wife. If she'd only let him tell her the rest of the conversation she'd overheard. Realizing the futility of getting her to listen in her present mood, he nodded his agreement.

Hoping her tattered nerves would withstand the rest of this nightmarish conversation, Fantasy said, "I'll go on pretending we're a happily married couple in front of Robby and my ex-in-laws. And I'd like your promise to do the same. But as soon as Henrietta and Frank leave town our marriage will be over."

The enormity of her declaration struck Jesse like a physical blow. Over? Would she really go that far? Not wanting her to see the absolute terror on his face, he moved across the room. Exhaling an exasperated breath, he replied, "You have my solemn word."

Though he longed to yank Fantasy out of the rocking chair and shake her until the truth soaked into her thick head, he dared not. She had already suffered a terrible shock and wouldn't be receptive to anything he could say or do to clear his name. Perhaps the timing of his leaving town wasn't so bad after all.

Schooling his features into a calm he was far from feeling, he turned back to his wife. "Listen, Fantasy, I'm leaving for San Francisco in the morning." At her startled look, he said, "Remember we talked about sending Mei-Ling to her sister. Well, I thought it would be a good idea for me to escort her. Now that I've settled the issue of her ownership with her uncle, I think it's important to get her to California as soon as possible. I'll be leaving on the morning stage to catch the train out of Benson."

When she remained silent, Jesse lifted one hand to stroke her cheek. She turned her head to one side, avoiding his touch and causing a sharp pang to rip through his heart. "You do understand why I should go with Mei-Ling, don't you?"

She nodded, the former spark of fire in her eyes faded to dull apathy. "Yes, she shouldn't travel alone."

Her listless response sent another stab of pain through his chest. He desperately wanted to erase the hurt mirrored on her face, but knew any overtures on his part to heal the breech wouldn't be welcomed. He could only pray she would be in a better frame of mind to listen when he returned from California. "I'll be gone no more than a week. When I get back, whether you want to or not, we're going to discuss this further."

Fantasy started to protest, then thought better of it and murmured, "Fine." No matter how much they talked, he could never successfully refute her charges. She'd clearly heard Nick's question, and Jesse's answer had been just as clear—it still rang in her ears.

For now, she refused to bring up the subject again. Enough harsh words had passed between them, no need to make it worse than it already was. Though she meant her words about ending their marriage, Jesse's sudden announcement of going to San Francisco had taken her by surprise. And although she agreed he should accompany Mei-Ling, she wasn't ready to sweep him out the door, not until Henrietta and Frank were out of her hair. Still, the thought of Jesse leaving town was strangely disquieting.

She tried to convince herself she should be pleased with the separation—after all, hadn't she just declared her intention to make it permanent? Instead of putting her mind at ease, a depressing question formed and wouldn't go away. Would Jesse really come back, or would he be another Thomas and disappear forever?

Jesse woke at first light, instantly remembering Fantasy's words of the previous evening. A lump formed in his throat that she might not allow him to rebut her charges and would actually end their marriage when he returned from San Francisco. Resisting the urge to shout his outrage at the unfairness of the mess his personal life had become, he rolled over to look at his sleeping wife.

After their heated exchange, he'd been certain she'd ban him from their bed. Yet Fantasy had insisted they share the same room, declaring to do otherwise could prompt uncomfortable questions from either Robby or Mei-Ling.

Surprised by her ability to think rationally about their sleeping arrangements when earlier she'd been so irrational about hearing him out, Jesse had kept his mouth shut. He hadn't wanted anything to cause their last night together to be spent in separate beds.

Jesse hadn't been so pleased with the situation when he slipped into bed and found Fantasy hugging her edge of the mattress and wearing a nightgown—a garment she hadn't worn since their intimate relationship began. Though there had been no doubt in his mind their last night together would be spent chastely, he'd nonetheless been disappointed in her apparent determination to prevent them from touching even accidentally.

He looked down at the weak morning sunlight dancing on the relaxed face of his wife and smiled. During the night, she'd abandoned her side of the bed. Her nightgown hiked up around her waist, she now lay with the soft curves of her bare belly and hips snuggled against him. Unable to resist touching her, Jesse carefully slipped one arm beneath her, then ran the knuckles of his other hand down the side of her face. She shifted slightly, turning her head toward him. He brushed the silky skin of her cheek again, causing her eyelids to flutter upward. Holding his breath, he watched her sleep-clouded eyes blink several times.

"Jesse," she murmured in a thick voice, her gaze clearing to focus on his face.

"Yes, love," he whispered back. When her body remained relaxed and the corners of her mouth curved up in a sleepy smile, he exhaled slowly. He didn't want to give up his last chance to hold her any sooner than necessary. Enjoying the feel of her pressed against him, her next words shocked Jesse out of the peaceful moment.

"Kiss me, Jesse."

Unsure of the intelligence of his actions, he gently touched his lips to hers. She groaned at the contact, wrapping one arm around his neck and pulling herself upward to deepen the kiss.

For several long minutes, he continued to feed his hunger for her in a sometimes fierce, sometimes gentle blending of their mouths. His lungs struggling for air, Jesse lifted his head and stared down into her beautiful flushed face. Left shaken by the intensity of their kiss, his heart swelled with love for the woman in his arms. It had been comparable to the blending of their souls. He wished he could share his thoughts with Fantasy. He wished he could strip off her gown and make long, leisurely love to her. He wished he could erase the hurt he knew she'd suffered the night before. For now his wishes remained unfulfilled.

With a tiny sigh of contentment, Fantasy's hand slid from his shoulder, her eyes drifting closed. Just before she slipped back into the arms of sleep, Jesse could have sworn he heard her murmur, "I love you, Jesse."

"I love you, too," he whispered against her ear, hoping his words penetrated her sleep-fogged mind.

* * *

Nick took the small carpetbag from Mei-Ling's hand. "Is this all you're taking with you?"

"Yes. I packed everything I have." She lowered her head, a blush creeping up her cheeks.

"I didn't mean to embarrass you, Mei-Ling," Nick whispered. Giving in to his urge to touch her, he gently traced the path her blush had taken with his fingers. Her skin was as silky as he'd imagined.

She lifted her head, tentatively meeting his gaze. Seeing only concern in his dark eyes, she said, "I will miss you, Nick."

Fighting his body's intense reaction to her words, Nick smiled. "I'll miss you, too." He cupped her chin in his hand. "Promise me you'll take care of yourself."

A shiver skittered across her skin from the warm touch of his fingers. For a moment she longed to throw herself against his broad chest, to have him hold her close. No one had ever made her feel the way she did with Nick. Drawing on her ability to hide her feelings, she returned his smile. "I will. You must promise me the same thing."

Nodding, Nick moved his hand to finger the black silk of her hair. "I'll come see you in San Francisco." He dropped his hand to his side. "I don't know when for sure. I have some business to finish here in Tombstone, then I'll probably have another assignment. But, I'll visit as soon as I can."

"I will be waiting for you, Nick."

He smiled again, wishing he dared kiss her. She was only seventeen, a mere girl compared to his twenty-seven, yet in many ways she seemed much older. He'd have to settle for a few last minutes of just looking at her.

Jesse watched the farewell between Nick and Mei-Ling from the doorway of the Pinkham Stage Line Office. Checking his watch, he clicked it shut, then approached the couple.

When neither Nick nor Mei-Ling appeared to notice

him, he cleared his throat, then said, "Mei-Ling, it's time to go."

Nick took a quick step back, jamming his hat on his head.

Jesse helped Mei-Ling into the stagecoach, then turned to Nick. Although Jesse's heart was heavy at leaving town with so much unsettled between Fantasy and himself, he couldn't help smiling at his friend. Nick only had eyes for Mei-Ling.

Grasping Nick's arm, Jesse steered him away from the stagecoach. When they were out of earshot, he said, "You look like a calf who's lost its mama."

Nick snapped to attention. "Don't call me a damned calf."

"Don't see why not. As sure as I'm standing here, you've been looking at Mei-Ling with calf-eyes, all sappy like, for a good ten minutes."

Nick flashed his friend a peeved look, but held his tongue. Jesse was right, he probably had acted like a tenderfoot when he looked at Mei-Ling. But, dammit, he'd never felt this way about a woman.

Jesse chuckled. The expression on Nick's face said he was about to take a fall, if he hadn't already succumbed to the power of love. "Like I told you last night, I'll see Mei-Ling safely to her sister's house, talk to John, and be back here as soon as I can. I don't expect to be gone more than five days, a week at the most."

Nick nodded, his gaze drifting back to the window of the stagecoach. He could just make out Mei-Ling's delicate profile in the dim interior of the coach.

"If I'm delayed for any reason, I'll send you a telegram."

Looking back at Jesse, Nick said, "Should I let Fantasy know if you're gonna be gone longer than you thought?"

"No!" Jesse said with more force than he'd intended. He cleared his throat, then said more softly,

"No. I don't think you should see Fantasy at all while I'm gone."

One of Nick's eyebrows lifted. "You're not jealous of me, are you?"

Jesse ran a hand over his face, then blew out a weary breath. "I wasn't going to tell you, Nick. But I guess I'd better." Quickly he explained about Fantasy overhearing part of their conversation and the accusations she made. He left out the part about her plans to end their marriage when he returned. That was too painful to share even with his closest friend.

"Do you want me to talk to her? Maybe I can get her to listen."

"I appreciate the offer, Nick. But I don't think it would help. Besides, with Henrietta and Frank still in town, she has enough on her mind. Talking to you would only dredge up more emotions for her to deal with, and she sure doesn't need that right now. You'd best stay clear of her until I return." Extending his hand, he added, "If I can't get back within a week, I'll also send her a telegram."

Nick gripped Jesse's hand firmly. "Okay, see you in a week." Tipping his hat toward the stagecoach window, Nick flashed a brief smile, then turned and walked down the boardwalk.

Deep in thought, Jesse watched his friend stroll away. A voice behind him jarred him back to the present.

"Going somewhere, McAllister?"

Jesse swung around to find Garland Baxter standing behind him. "Yeah, I'm going somewhere. What brings you out so early in the morning?"

Baxter ran a hand through his hair. "Ran out of money. Had me a run of bad luck last night. I tried to win back what I lost, but . . ." He shrugged. "Before I knew it, the sun was coming up."

Looking at Baxter's rumpled clothes and stubbled face, Jesse said, "Speaking of money, Baxter. I have a question I've been meaning to ask you."

"What's that?" Baxter replied around a yawn, raising up on his toes and stretching his arms over his head.

"When I talked to you after the fire you asked if Fantasy planned to go back to Missouri. And I've been wondering why you thought she'd move back East."

"Her husband's family—" he laughed self-consciously at his faux pas. "I mean, her first husband's family wanted her and Robby to live with them."

Stepping closer, Jesse fixed him with an unblinking stare. "I'm glad you mentioned the Williamses. Just how is it they came to find out about Fantasy's boardinghouse being destroyed in the fire?"

Baxter pulled himself up to his full height, refusing to be cowed by Jesse's superior size. "I didn't cause any harm. I found one of Mrs. Williams's letters at the boardinghouse, asking Fantasy to bring her grandson back to St. Louis. Since you never know when you might learn something such a desperate woman might want to hear, I kept her letter."

Jesse clenched his hands in impotent fists at his sides. Containing his fury, he said, "So after the fire, you wrote to Mrs. Williams?"

Baxter nodded. "I figured she'd want to know about her daughter-in-law and grandson losing their home."

"So what did you get out of it? I'm sure you didn't send word to the Williamses out of the goodness of your heart."

"I needed the money. Lawyers don't make as much as everybody thinks." He tugged on the frayed cuffs of his shirt, then smoothed the lapels of his jacket. "I can't live on my piddling salary."

Jesse wanted to point out his wages would go a lot further if he didn't spend so much time in gambling halls. But he kept his jaw tightly clenched.

"It doesn't matter, though," Baxter continued. "I got wind of a job in Tucson that pays a helluva lot better. I'm planning on heading up that way and see

about it. Can't make any money in this damn town.
Think I'll buy my ticket right now."

Before Jesse could say anything in reply, the stage
driver yelled for all passengers to climb aboard. After
he stepped up into the stagecoach and settled on the
seat across from Mei-Ling, Jesse looked out the window. He watched Garland Baxter make his way into
the stage line office, doubting the man had the price of
a ticket in his pocket. As the stage lurched forward,
Jesse hoped Baxter had told the truth and would be
gone by the time he returned.

Fantasy awoke slowly. The remembrance of a
heated kiss she and Jesse had shared brought a lazy
contented smile to her lips. She stretched, then jerked
upright in bed. The unfamiliar rasp of a cotton nightgown against her skin brought her fully awake. Recalling what had brought about her decision not to sleep
naked as had become her habit, she closed her eyes for
a moment.

Heaving a weary sigh, she forced herself to get out
of bed. Her gaze fell on the note lying on the bedside
table, instantly recognizing the handwriting as Jesse's
bold scrawl. Unable to control the shaking of her
hand, she reached out and picked up the folded sheet
of paper.

She quickly read the three lines, then read them a
second time. The first repeated his insistence they
would talk when he returned. The second asked her to
give Robby a hug and a kiss for him. And the third was
"I love you, Fancy." The signature at the bottom was
a large J.

Feeling the sting of tears, Fantasy blinked them
away. She couldn't give in to a fit of crying, she had a
house to take care of. With Mei-Ling gone, the housework fell to her. Grateful for something to keep her
busy, she moved on lethargic feet to the wash stand.
Reaching for the water pitcher, her hand stilled. A

facecloth hung over the towel bar. Unable to resist, Fantasy's fingers closed over the cloth. Lifting the damp fabric to her nose, the scent of sandalwood wafted up to fill her senses, leaving her slightly light-headed.

"Stop it!" she told herself in a fierce whisper. Replacing the facecloth, she poured water into the wash-bowl, carefully avoiding her reflection in the mirror. She couldn't look at herself for fear of what she'd find lurking in her eyes. Jesse was gone, and that was that. After a quick sponge bath, she dressed for the day.

"What do you mean he's out of town?" Henrietta eyed Fantasy through squinted eyes. "Where'd he go?"

Fantasy had been hoping to avoid this confrontation, but her former mother-in-law wasn't going to be put off. She'd been able to keep Jesse's leave-taking quiet until supper time. His absence couldn't be glossed over any longer.

Trying to remain calm and not let her clamoring nerves show, Fantasy said, "Jesse had to go to San Francisco for a few days."

"San Francisco? When did he leave?"

"On the morning stage."

"The morn—why didn't you tell us sooner?"

"It didn't seem important."

After a moment of silent scrutiny, Henrietta said, "Isn't Jesse from San Francisco?"

"Yes." Fantasy braced herself for what would surely follow. Henrietta could tell her nothing she hadn't already considered on her own. Though she'd had plenty of chores to keep her busy all day, her mind kept wandering into territory she really didn't want to traverse.

"When did you say he'd be back?"

"Probably in a week."

Henrietta's eyes gleamed. "Probably?"

Fantasy found herself wanting to defend her husband's behavior. "He wasn't sure how long his business would take. But he thought he'd be gone for no more than a week."

Henrietta looked at Fantasy for several seconds, then said, "How long have you and Jesse been married?"

"Almost a month," she answered carefully. "Why?"

"Only a month and already he's left you. Tsk-tsk, Fantasy."

"What are you trying to say, Mother Williams?"

"Can't you see I'm just trying to help? I want you to see the truth. Face it, dear, you just don't know how to keep a man. My son left you after a few months, and now your new husband has taken off after only one. It's like I've been telling you, you'd be much better off living with us in St. Louis." Patting Fantasy's hand, Henrietta added, "You don't really think Jesse McAllister is coming back, do you?"

"Of course he's coming back," Fantasy snapped, jerking her hand away and refusing to let Henrietta know the same question had plagued her all day. "Once he's taken care of his business, he'll come back to Tombstone."

Flashing an irritated glance, Henrietta turned and left the kitchen. In the superior tone Fantasy was all too familiar with, the woman's words drifted back to her. "We'll see, Fantasy. We'll see."

HIS WILLING FANTASY

Chapter 18

Jesse paced John Valentine's empty office with growing agitation. Dropping into a chair, he drummed his fingers on the arm.

"Dammit, John," he grumbled aloud, "you knew I was coming and you still left town."

After arriving in San Francisco and delivering Mei-Ling to her sister, Jesse had headed for the corner of Montgomery and California Streets and the Wells, Fargo Company offices. Since he was out of town so much, he normally took a minute to admire the Parrott Building which housed his employer's San Francisco headquarters. But that day, he barely glanced at the structure made of stone blocks quarried in China and assembled by Chinese masons. That day, he had more on his mind than the building's fine appearance.

He'd passed through the Express Department on the main level, then hurried upstairs to the company offices only to be informed John Valentine had unexpectedly been called out of town. No one had any idea how long he'd be gone.

Since Jesse's assignment in Tombstone had been on the personal orders of John and without the knowledge of the firm's two leading detectives, there was no one else Jesse could talk to. He had no choice but to wait.

He'd been cooling his heels for five days now. Five days of endlessly waiting for John to return; five days of increasing impatience to get the business of Lawson's gang settled; five days of itching to head back to Fantasy and straighten out their misunderstanding. Yet each day of waiting pushed that eventuality further and further into the future.

Jesse stared at the note lying on John's desk. The note John left him, expressing his regrets at having been called away on urgent business. Fingering the paper, Jesse frowned. *What was so all-fired important that you'd leave town after I sent a telegram telling you I was on my way? You owe me for this, John. You owe me big.*

The clock on the wall chimed the hour, snapping Jesse out of the stupor of his thoughts. He glanced at the clock and groaned. Six o'clock. Another day spent waiting with nothing to show for it.

Pushing himself out of the chair, he left John's office. On the way to the home he maintained for his infrequent visits to San Francisco, Jesse stopped at the telegraph office. He'd put off sending wires to Fantasy and Nick because he'd hoped to include when to expect him. But since John still hadn't returned, it would be at least another three days before he could arrive in Tombstone. Cursing his luck at picking a bad time for trying to meet with his boss, Jesse wrote out the messages and waited until the telegraph operator sent them before heading home.

Fantasy had hoped after Mother Williams's initial reaction to Jesse's departure the woman would let the matter rest. Unfortunately, Henrietta had different ideas. She constantly brought up the subject, until Fantasy wanted to scream at her to shut her mouth. Of course, she couldn't do that, so she tried to close her mind to her former mother-in-law's neverending reminders. But with little success. Henrietta's continual harping about Jesse's leave-taking and his doubtful return prevented Fantasy from keeping the question of her abandonment out of the forefront of her thoughts. Each snide comment about her inability to keep a man, each hint that she'd be better off in St. Louis, throbbed in Fantasy's head like a nagging toothache. A dull pain which kept her own fears alive and eliminated any chance of easing the hurt.

On the eighth morning of her husband's absence, Fantasy remained in bed longer than usual, reluctant to face another day of Henrietta's barbs. Finally she forced herself to rise, expecting to hear a knock on her front door any minute. Since Jesse had left town, the Williamses made a habit of arriving early each morning and not leaving until well after Robby's bedtime.

She'd just finished putting the last pin in her hair when she heard her son calling from the parlor.

"Momma, I see Gramma comin' down the street."

"Grampa isn't with her?"

"Uh-uh. Gramma stopped out front. She's talkin' to Mr. Baxter."

"Mr. Baxter? I didn't think Henrietta knew Garland Baxter," she mused aloud. "Why would she—?"

"She's here," Robby chirped, interrupting her thoughts.

"Will you let her in, Robby? I'll be right there." Steeling herself for another long day, she gave her hair one last pat and left the sanctuary of her bedroom.

"Good morning, Mother Williams. Where's Frank?"

"He'll be along presently. He went to get his hair cut." Sniffing the air, she said, "I don't smell coffee."

Fantasy wanted to yell she wasn't Henrietta's personal servant, but bit her tongue to still the words. "Robby said he saw you talking to Garland Baxter. He used to be one of my boarders. How do you know him?"

Startled by the question, Henrietta paused in the removal of her hat. "Um, I hardly, that is, I don't actually know the man. I met him one day at the hotel. He told me he used to room at your boardinghouse."

She hung her hat on the hall tree, then added, "Nice young man."

"What was he doing in front of our house?"

"Heavens, I don't know. Just taking a stroll I guess. Anyway, when he saw me he stopped to pay his respects."

"He wasn't coming here?" Garland Baxter had made a habit of coming by every week or so since the fire to inquire after them. Fantasy thought him kind to show such concern. Strange now that she thought about it, he hadn't been by in several weeks, not since right after Henrietta and Frank arrived in—Henrietta's voice pulled her from her musings.

"He didn't mention anything about coming here, dear." Henrietta batted her eyelashes, trying to affect an innocent air.

"I see," Fantasy replied absently, turning to head for the kitchen. "I'll put the coffee on. It should be ready by the time Frank gets here."

After breakfast, Robby took Frank out back to look at his new marble ring, leaving the women alone in the house. Henrietta wasted no time in saying, "Well, it's been over a week and I see Jesse still hasn't returned."

"No, not yet." Fantasy felt like a puppy being punished for an accident he'd had on the floor. Henrietta just couldn't resist the chance to rub her nose in what she saw as Jesse's leaving his wife high and dry.

"I thought he was supposed to send you a telegram if he was delayed."

"That's what he told me." Bristling at Henrietta's lack of subtlety, Fantasy refused to be goaded into stooping to the same level. "I expect he'll be sending a wire soon."

Henrietta turned away to hide her smirk. *Sooner than you think, my dear.* She slipped her hand into her dress pocket, checking to be sure the envelope was still there.

How fortunate she'd made a point of locating Garland Baxter—without Frank's knowledge of course—

after they'd been in town for several days. Otherwise, she wouldn't have known the identity of the man approaching the house on Fifth Street that morning. If she hadn't arrived just then, Baxter would have delivered the telegram to Fantasy. How fortunate, too, it had been Garland Baxter who'd been at the telegraph office when the manager needed someone to deliver a wire to Mrs. McAllister from her husband. Recalling how easy it had been to get Baxter to state his reason for coming to the McAllister house then convince him to relinquish the telegram into her hands, she smiled. He was so easy to manipulate, all because of his gambling habit. Well, she was doing a little gambling of her own, and Garland Baxter was her trump card.

Settling into one of the upholstered chairs in the parlor, Henrietta watched Fantasy sit down opposite her on the settee. "You know, dear. You really should make plans for your future."

Fantasy glanced up from the pile of mending in her lap. "I don't know what you mean. Jesse told you about his plans for us to live in San Francisco when his work is finished here."

"Seems to me, he's already finished it." When the younger woman gave her a confused look, Henrietta added, "Can't you see? That's why he left town; his work was done and he no longer had a reason to stay."

Ignoring the malicious remark, Fantasy said, "I've told you a dozen times, Mother Williams. Jesse said he might be gone a week and he would send word if he was delayed. He probably just—"

Mentally Henrietta finished Fantasy's words, "—got tied up. Will be back as soon as possible," quoting from her quick peek at Jesse's telegram while Fantasy cooked breakfast. Aloud she said, "And I've told you a dozen times, I don't think he's coming back."

Fantasy sighed and went back to her mending. There was no point in arguing. It would only depress her more.

After a few minutes, Henrietta said, "Did you rent this house after the fire?"

"No, Jesse did. Why?"

Henrietta clucked her tongue. "Did he leave you money to pay the rent until he got back?"

Startled by the question, Fantasy's hand jerked in reaction, poking herself with her darning needle. Sucking on her pricked finger, she felt a dull pounding start in her temples.

On the morning of Jesse's departure, she'd found some money lying on the dresser. She figured he'd left it for groceries or other incidentals until he returned. With the trauma of their heated exchange on the night before still fresh, it never occurred to her the rent would be due on the first of the month. She now also recalled having a conversation with Jesse about money soon after their wedding. There was no need for them to open a joint bank account in Tombstone, Jesse had told her, since they would be moving to California soon. The ache in her head intensified.

Seeing Fantasy's reaction to her question, Henrietta pressed her advantage. "Can't you see, dear? The man decided he didn't want to be shackled to a wife and stepson. So he took off, not even having the common courtesy of seeing to your welfare. Instead he left you to fend for yourself." She shook her head, tsking softly. "Too bad he couldn't tell you the truth."

Nothing Henrietta said made more of an impression on Fantasy than her last sentence. The truth. She'd already caught Jesse in more than one lie. Had he lied about coming back to Tombstone as well? Unable to stand another minute in the woman's company, Fantasy stuffed the pile of mending into her sewing basket and rose from the settee. "If you'll excuse me, Mother Williams, I have a terrible headache. I'm going to lie down for awhile."

"Oh, that's too bad, dear," Henrietta cooed, biting her lip to hide her pleased smile. "You run along and rest. I'll just go out back and see what Frank and Robby are doing."

After leaving Henrietta, Fantasy headed to her bedroom. Removing her dress and then stretching out on the bed in her chemise and petticoat, she forced herself to recall every word her former mother-in-law had said.

As bitter as it was to swallow, she had to admit Henrietta had a good point when she brought up the issue of the house. What would she do if Jesse didn't come back? In spite of Henrietta's hints that she would be penniless without Jesse, Fantasy knew otherwise. She'd received her insurance settlement several weeks ago and had promptly deposited the check in her bank account. So there was no question as to whether she could provide for herself and her son. But what would she do with that money?

Several options came to mind, but returning to St. Louis with Henrietta and Frank wasn't one of them. She'd made it on her own before; she could do it again. But not in Tombstone. The town held too many memories, both good and bad, to stay here if Henrietta was right. She'd take Robby and move to another town, maybe in New Mexico Territory. Albuquerque had looked like a nice town when she'd passed through on the way to Arizona. Yes, that's what she'd do if Jesse really had abandoned her.

Fantasy sighed despondently. Her decision did little to ease the pain in her head, or the more severe one in her heart. Balling her hand into a fist, she pounded the mattress in frustration. *What's wrong with me? Why I can't keep a man? Why am I so unworthy of a man's love?* Tears streaming down her face, she could think of only one answer to the questions about her inadequacies. She obviously lacked something a man wanted and needed in a woman, a mysterious something that kept a man around, something she could not provide.

Squeezing her eyes tightly closed, Fantasy willed the

tears to stop. The sisters at the orphanage always said "no use crying over spilled milk." The old adage had little effect on a more serious mishap—her breaking heart.

Later that afternoon, Fantasy found Henrietta at the dining room table reading the *Epitaph*. Rubbing her palms on her skirt, Fantasy cleared her throat. "Mother Williams, I'd like to speak to you for a moment."

Henrietta looked up, her already small eyes squinting even more. "Can't you see I'm reading the newspaper? We'll talk later."

Swallowing the urge to snatch the paper out from under Henrietta's nose, Fantasy replied, "No, we'll talk now. What I have to say can't wait. And, I assure you, it won't take long."

Grumbling something indistinguishable, Henrietta indicated the chair across the table. "All right, what is it, Fantasy?"

"I'd like you to stop talking about Jesse's absence." Raising her hand when Henrietta started to protest, she said, "I know how you feel, but whether he returns still remains to be seen. In the meantime, I don't want to hear any more about it. So, I'm asking you to keep your opinions to yourself."

Henrietta gasped, crumpling the newspaper with her clenched hands. "Well . . . of all the . . . I never—"

"I know you mean well," Fantasy continued, interrupting the older woman's sputterings. "But I really must ask you not to talk about my husband. Please."

Henrietta opened her mouth to make a retort, then closed it again. After contemplating Fantasy's words for a few seconds, she finally said, "Very well."

The tightness in Fantasy's shoulders eased at Henrietta's acquiescence. "Thank you, Mother Williams. Oh, there's one other thing. Please don't say any more about moving back to St. Louis."

"But, dear, I only suggested it because I thought it would be the best thing for Robby. And you, of course," she amended quickly.

Fantasy knew better. Instead of arguing, she said, "Just remember what I said."

Henrietta nodded curtly, momentarily tongue-tied by the unusual spunk Fantasy displayed. She could only hope Jesse wouldn't get back before Fantasy decided she'd waited long enough and packed her bags.

Whistling softly, Nick rounded the corner of Allen and Fifth Streets. When he caught a glimpse of auburn hair, he pulled up short, the tune he was whistling ending abruptly. Swearing under his breath for choosing this route to his boardinghouse, he knew he couldn't turn around and head the other way. Fantasy had already spotted him.

Jesse's warning about staying away from Fantasy ringing in his head, Nick waited for his friend's wife to reach him.

"Hello, Mr. Trask," Fantasy said. "I thought perhaps you had left town. I haven't seen you around."

Nick tipped his hat, then said, "No, ma'am, I'm still here. I don't expect you and I frequent the same kind of places."

"No, I don't expect we do." She hesitated a moment, then said, "I was wondering, Mr. Trask, if you knew when Jesse would be returning."

"Why would I know that?" Nick asked carefully.

"Well, you and Jesse seemed so close . . . and I just . . . well, I thought perhaps you'd heard from him."

"Seems to me, you'd be the one he'd correspond with. You being his wife and all."

Fantasy had no answer for that. She thought she should be the one Jesse would write to, also. But that wasn't the case. After a long silence, she said, "Why did he really come to Tombstone, Mr. Trask? You know, don't—"

Feeling like his collar had suddenly shrunk three sizes, Nick managed to cut her off by saying, "You'll have to excuse me, Mrs. McAllister, but I have an appointment, and you've made me late."

His curt dismissal hitting her like a slap in the face, Fantasy took a step back. "Of course, Mr. Trask. I'm sorry to have bothered you."

Nick pulled his gaze from Fantasy's crestfallen face to glance longingly up the street. He had to get away from her. Yet his conscience made him say, "Forgive me for being rude, but I really have to go." Tipping his hat again, Nick strode off.

Fantasy stared thoughtfully at his retreating back. Though she'd only seen the man a couple of times, he'd always been friendly and extremely polite. Something very strange was going on.

Over the next several days, Fantasy continued her life without Jesse, privately speculating on what kept him away and why she hadn't heard from him. And although her thoughts constantly centered on her missing husband and the unsettling conversation she'd had with Nick Trask, at least Henrietta had kept her word.

As Fantasy applied the broom to the front porch, she smiled. *Maybe Mother Williams has finally realized I'm no longer a child and can lead my life on my own without her interference.* She paused in her sweeping to glance up at the sky. Noting the sun's position, she guessed it must be close to three o'clock. She couldn't believe she'd had nearly an entire day with only her son for company.

Frank had arrived later than usual that morning to say he and his wife wouldn't be joining them. Henrietta planned to stay in bed and rest. The intense August heat of the Arizona desert had finally gotten to her. While Fantasy didn't want to see her former mother-in-law suffer from heatstroke, she couldn't deny she hadn't missed the woman's presence. She had missed Frank, though, and so had Robby.

Hearing the fast approach of a horse, Fantasy shielded her eyes with one hand and turned to watch a horse gallop up Fifth Street, its hooves digging into the dirt and sending up a cloud of yellowish-white dust. When the lathered bay drew even with Jesse's house, the rider pulled back on the reins and brought the horse to a skidding stop. Jumping to the ground, the man strode toward Fantasy. She immediately recognized the lanky blonde as her former boarder, Gil Gunderson.

"Miz McAllister, I'm sure glad y'all are home."

"Gil! What is it?" Fantasy's heart thumped heavily against her ribs at the deep creases on his forehead, the pinched look about his mouth.

"It's Spud, ma'am."

"Oh, dear God. What happened? Is he all right?"

"Don't rightly know, ma'am. I got word of an explosion at his mine. I sent some men out to see how bad it is, then I went to find Doc McKee. He's been called outta town, so I high-tailed it over here."

"I'm glad you let me know, but what can I do?"

"Well, ma'am, you know how Spud feels about doctors. The only one he ever let get within fifty feet of him is Doc McKee. And, well, since he's outta town, I thought, with you workin' for the doc and all, you could tend Spud."

"Gil, I haven't had any medical training. The only doctoring I've done has been assisting Dr. McKee a couple of afternoons a week. The most serious thing I ever helped him with was setting a broken arm. My medical skills are meager at best."

"Yes'em. But Spud would have a conniption fit for sure if I brought anyone 'sides y'all in the doc's place."

Fantasy's brows pulled together, her mouth turned down in a frown. Gil was right about one thing—Spud's distrust of doctors. He always said he didn't want none of the sawbones in town working on him except Dr. McKee if the need ever arose. Fantasy wasn't sure why Spud's low opinion of doctors excluded Dr. McKee. Something had happened before her arrival in Tombstone, but neither Spud nor the doc had ever discussed it.

"Okay, I'll see what I can do until Dr. McKee returns. Does anyone know when he'll be back?"

"Don't rightly know. The sign on his door said he'd been called outta town on an emergency and might be gone a couple a days."

Fantasy sighed. "Well, I guess I'd better get ready." Turning toward the house, Gil's words stopped her.

"Uh, ma'am, on second thought. Spud's mine is a long ways from town, and the only way to get there is by horse." He dropped his gaze, twisting the brim of his hat with his hands. "I don't mean no disrespect, but in spite of y'all askin' me to teach ya to ride the critters, I know ya don't care much for horses."

Fantasy smiled. "Used to, Gil. I can manage now, thanks to your lessons."

His face sporting a blush, he stuck his hat back on his head. "It's a hard ride to the Whetstone Mountains, so if y'all are sure ya can make the trip I'd best get moving."

"I'm absolutely sure." Fantasy's smile faded. "The only thing is, I'll have to find someone to take care of Robby. Mattie and Nash won't be back until the end of the month."

"I thought your in-laws were in town?"

"Former in-laws, and, yes, they are. But Mother Williams isn't feeling well, so I can't ask them." Besides, even if Henrietta hadn't taken ill, the woman's good behavior over the past few days hadn't convinced Fantasy she could be trusted. A leopard doesn't change his—or in this case, her—spots that easily.

"I'd be glad to stay with the boy. Exceptin' I hafta show y'all where Spud's mine is."

After a moment, Fantasy said, "Listen, I have an

idea. Will you try to locate Garland Baxter for me? I'm sure he would be willing to stay with Robby."

"Okay. Y'all get changed and pack whatever ya want to take, but keep it light. I'll go fetch Baxter." He turned to leave, then suddenly swung back around. "What about a horse, Miz McAllister? Should I get Daisy for ya?"

"No, Daisy's too slow. Jesse's horse, Banjo, is at the Lexington Livery around the corner. Could you get him on the way back? Just tell Mr. Crabtree I said it was okay."

Stepping into the stirrup, Gil said, "Sure thing, ma'am. Be back soon's I can."

By the time Gil returned, Fantasy had changed into one of her new riding skirts, packed a small carpetbag and explained to Robby that she had to go out of town for a few days to help an injured miner. Not wanting to worry the boy, she'd purposely kept the miner's identity to herself.

"Did you find Mr. Baxter?" Fantasy asked as soon as she answered Gil's knock on the front door.

Removing his hat and slapping it against his thigh, he said, "Yes'em, I found him. He'll be along shortly." Seeing Fantasy glance over his shoulder at the man standing with the horses, Gil said, "That's Deputy Billy Breakenridge. The sheriff asked him to ride out to the mine with us to investigate the explosion."

Fantasy's eyes widened. "You don't think someone purposely tried to hurt Spud, do you?"

"I shorely hope not, ma'am. But the sheriff wants the deputy to check it out."

Fantasy nodded, then shifted her gaze from the deputy back to Gil. "While we're waiting, I want to write a note to Henrietta and Frank. Come in and have something cool to drink before we leave."

Plopping his hat back on his head, he said, "That's mighty kind a ya, Miz McAllister. But I'm covered with dust, so I'd best stay out here if it's all the same to y'all."

"Well, then I'll just bring the lemonade out here for you and the deputy."

The men had finished their drinks and Fantasy was just finishing her note to Henrietta and Frank when Garland Baxter arrived.

Taking Baxter out of Robby's earshot, Fantasy said, "I really appreciate this, Mr. Baxter. I had no one else I could ask."

"Think nothing of it. You know I like the boy. We'll do just fine."

"I hope I haven't upset your plans too badly. I could be gone a day or two."

"I was supposed to leave for Tucson in the morning. But Gil said you needed me."

"Oh dear, I have ruined your plans."

"Don't be silly, Mrs. McAllister. Tucson will wait for a few more days."

Fantasy stared at him for several seconds, then nodded. "I told Robby there was an explosion at a mine and a miner had been hurt. But I didn't tell him the man I'm going to tend is Spud Fitzpatrick. Learning about Spud's accident would be terribly upsetting to him. So until I return or send word, I don't want Robby told. Is that understood, Mr. Baxter?"

"Yes, ma'am. I understand. I won't say anything about it."

"Good." Holding out a sealed envelope, she said, "I've written a note to Henrietta and Frank Williams, and I'd like you to make sure they get it. They're staying at the American Hotel. I believe you met my former mother-in-law there soon after their arrival in town."

Baxter took the note from Fantasy's outstretched hand, carefully avoiding her stare. "Yes, I did."

Fantasy crossed the room to where her son waited. Bending down to Robby, she looked squarely into his turquoise eyes. "You be a good boy for Mr. Baxter. I'll be home soon, okay, sweetheart?"

Robby nodded, then wrapped his arms around her neck in a fierce hug.

She squeezed the small body tightly against hers, whispering her love for him against his russet hair. Hearing Gil moving restlessly on the porch, she gave Robby one last kiss and hurried toward the door.

Concern for Spud's safety was the only thing that kept her going as she, Gil, and Deputy Breakenridge rode toward the Whetstone Mountains, northwest of Tombstone. Not a mile passed that she wasn't thankful she'd decided to learn how to ride.

After Fantasy's initial lesson with Gil, each time she swung onto Daisy's back the fear clawing at her throat had eased a little more. Now she rarely felt the stirring of her old fright. But the docile mare, Daisy, was nothing like Banjo. Having received little exercise since Jesse left town, the pinto had been skittish from the minute Fantasy stepped into the stirrups. Although he'd behaved himself since they left town, Fantasy held herself stiffly alert in the saddle, prepared for any of the antics she knew the gelding capable of performing with no forewarning.

By the time they'd made the twenty-mile trek across the desert to Spud's mine, she was a mass of aching muscles. Pulling Banjo to a halt next to the other men's horses, Fantasy nearly fell from the saddle. When her feet hit the ground she bit back a groan. Her legs, back, and bottom screamed in protest. It took all her willpower to walk across the camp.

She found Spud in a three-sided lean-to not far from the mouth of his mine. Half a dozen men remained of those who'd arrived from town to help dig out the partially caved-in mine shaft.

Her legs still wobbly, Fantasy approached the lean-to, afraid of what she'd find. Spud lay motionless on a makeshift bed, his breathing shallow. Fantasy swept her gaze over him quickly, noting the deathly pallor of his skin, the large, dark purple bruise on one temple, the numerous cuts and scrapes on his face, hands and arms. As she knelt down next to Spud's prone form, she choked back a sob. "What have you done to yourself?" she murmured, reaching out to brush a lock of gray hair off his forehead. Although the sun hadn't set, she felt a sudden chill.

Inhaling a deep, steadying breath, she pushed her fear aside and began a methodical examination of her patient. When she finished, she sat back on her heels. Staring at Spud's bruised face, she whispered, "Damn you, Fagen Fitzpatrick, you'd better not die on me."

Some time later, Fantasy approached where Gil and the others sat around the campfire. "How bad is he?" Gil asked.

Sitting down next to him, Fantasy accepted a cup of coffee from one of the men, then said, "I couldn't find any broken bones. My guess is, he's unconscious because of the head wound."

"Will he be okay?"

She took a sip of her coffee before replying. "I wish I knew. You never know about head injuries. I've heard Dr. McKee say sometimes they cause only temporary unconsciousness and sometimes . . ." Her voice trailed off as she brought the cup back to her lips.

"Spud will wake up, won't he?"

Fantasy sighed. "I don't know for sure, Gil. Anyone with a head as hard as that old codger's has a pretty good chance of pulling through. I told him time and again not to mess with that dad-blamed dynamite. But do you think he'd listen to me? Not Fagen Fitzpatrick. It's a wonder he didn't blow himself to kingdom come."

Gil smiled. In spite of her unkind words, he knew Fantasy and Spud loved each other like family. As he started to rise, he said, "I'll sit with him for awhile. Y'all get some rest."

"I'm fine. I better get back to him."

Gil studied her for a moment, then finally nodded and sat back down. "Okay, but I'll spell y'all later. In the meantime, I'm gonna try and get some shuteye. It's gonna be a long night. Call me if y'all need anything."

The night passed in a slow blur for Fantasy. Though she allowed Gil to take her place at Spud's side somewhere near dawn, then lay down on the bed of blanket one of the men had fashioned near the fire, sleep eluded her. She stared at the stars winking in the Arizona sky, wondering what else could go wrong in her life.

Much recovered from her indisposition of the previous day, Henrietta and Frank headed for the McAllister house the next morning. Though slightly pale, Henrietta's tongue had suffered no ill effects from her brief illness.

"For pity's sake, Frank, slow down. Can't you see you're walking too fast for me?"

"Sorry, dear," he grumbled, shortening his strides in accommodation. "Are you sure you're up to this? Perhaps you should have stayed in bed another day."

"I'm fine. Stop fussing over me, will you?"

Jerking his gaze away from his wife, Frank clenched his teeth in frustration. He kept his eyes riveted on the street ahead of them, thinking Henrietta certainly ran hot and cold. Yesterday, all she'd wanted was to be fussed over. He'd been at her beck and call every minute—fluffing pillows, fetching ice water, and waving a fan to stir a breeze for hours on end. And now, she snapped at him just because he expressed concern over her health.

A lump formed in his throat. What had happened to the sweet, loving woman he'd met and married so many years ago? What changed the Etta he had fallen in love with into such a harping shrew? Arriving at the house of their daughter-in-law, he pushed his wistful thoughts aside.

When his knock was answered by a man he'd never seen before, Frank's smile of greeting vanished. "I . . . who . . . ?"

Shoving her flustered husband out of the way, Henrietta said, "This is Mr. Baxter, Frank. He used to board with our daughter-in-law. What are you doing here, Mr. Baxter?"

"Come in out of the heat, and I'll tell you, Mrs. Williams." Once the three of them had taken seats in the parlor, Garland Baxter said, "Mrs. McAllister was called out of town unexpectedly yesterday." Handing the envelope containing Fantasy's note to Henrietta, he added, "I believe this will explain everything to your satisfaction."

Henrietta ripped open the envelope and withdrew the sheet of paper. She quickly scanned her daughter-in-law's note, then smiled. "Yes, it explains everything perfectly."

"What is it, Etta?"

Meeting her husband's confused gaze, Henrietta said, "It seems there's been an accident at one of the mines and Fantasy went there to see to the injured. Because I was indisposed, she left Mr. Baxter here with our grandson." Turning to Garland, she added, "You can leave now, Mr. Baxter."

Frank gasped with shock. "Etta! You needn't be rude."

"Oh piffle, Frank. Can't you see I'm quite recovered and fully capable of taking over my grandson's care? I'm sure Mr. Baxter understands." She shifted her gaze back to the man. "Don't you, Mr. Baxter?"

"Yes, ma'am, I understand completely. Robby's playing out back. I'll just get my things, then leave." Rising from his chair, Garland Baxter made a hasty exit from the room.

"Really, Henrietta, I can't believe the way you acted toward that poor man."

"Oh, Frank, Garland Baxter and I understand each other, and he took no offense."

Frank stared at his wife through squinted eyes. "What do you mean you understand each other? Have you met the man before?"

"Yes, Mr. Baxter and I have talked on several occasions." Waving her hand towards the hall, she added, "Now, go play with our grandson. I want to talk to Mr. Baxter privately before he leaves."

"But—"

"Go on, Frank," she interrupted. "Do as I say."

Not liking the turn of events, but knowing he couldn't change them, Frank nodded and left the parlor.

Half an hour later, Henrietta stepped onto the back porch. After her eyes adjusted to the bright sun, she approached her husband and grandson.

Sitting one step below his grandfather, Robby watched intently as the older man painstakingly applied a jackknife to a piece of wood.

Frank smiled at something Robby said, never taking his eyes from his work. He'd done a lot of whittling as a boy and had forgotten how much pleasure he'd derived from transforming a shapeless piece of wood into various animals or, as he was doing for his grandson, a soldier.

When Henrietta stopped next to them, Robby turned his beaming face up to hers. "Look, Gramma, Grampa's makin' me a set of soldiers. We're gonna paint 'em and everything," Robby said, excitement over his new toys evident in his voice.

"Yes, I see. Robby, you run along and play. I want to talk to your grandfather for a minute."

Frowning, Robby said, "But, Gramma, I wanna watch Grampa."

"Robert! Do as I say."

Dropping his head, he murmured, "Yes, ma'am." Robby gathered up the other wooden soldiers his grandfather had already carved, then moved out into the yard and settled under a tree.

Frank rose from the step and brushed the wood

shavings from his pants. "Etta, must you be so harsh on the boy?"

"Harsh?" Henrietta snapped, moving across the porch. "He's only a child, and he shouldn't be around when his elders are talking. Besides, I only asked him to go play somewhere else. What's so harsh about that?" Before he could reply, she continued, "I have something important to tell you. Come inside for a minute." She swept through the door, letting it bang shut behind her.

Rolling his eyes, Frank gave his pants one last brush and followed his wife into the house. Once he'd washed his hands, he sat down across from her at the dining room table. "Okay, Etta, what's so all-fired important?"

Ignoring her husband's use of the hated nickname and his obvious annoyance, she said, "I've been thinking about Fantasy's note, Frank. This is exactly what we've been waiting for."

Frank's eyebrows pulled together. "You're not making any sense, Etta. Are you sure you're feeling all right?"

Henrietta shot her husband an exasperated glance, her lips puckered like she'd swallowed something sour. "I told you, I'm fine. Must I remind you our reason for coming here was to get our grandson out of this godforsaken place once and for all?" When her husband didn't respond, she continued, "What's the matter with you, Frank? Can't you see, this is the chance we've been waiting for."

Chapter 19

Frank gave his wife an incredulous look. "Our chance? You're not saying we should just up and take Robby out of town, are you?"

Henrietta exhaled an irritated breath. "Well, of course that's what I'm saying, Frank. Sometimes I wonder how you manage to run a successful business, when you can't even understand your wife speaking plain English."

Frank's back stiffened. "My bank is not the issue. We're discussing taking Robby away from his mother and going home. Is that what Fantasy wants?"

"Moving back to St. Louis is a very wise decision. Away from all the riffraff in this town. And the awful heat."

"Wise decision be dammed," Frank said, earning a startled look from his wife. "Does that mean Fantasy has agreed to this?"

"You needn't curse, Frank," Henrietta snapped in a haughty voice. Before her husband could open his mouth to reply, she sidestepped his question by asking one of her own. "And why do you find that so hard to believe? After all, she's all by herself with a small boy to think of."

"Wait a minute, Etta. What do you mean 'she's all by herself?' She's married to Jesse now. Have you forgotten about him?"

"Hardly," Henrietta grumbled. Meeting his disbelieving gaze, she took a deep breath. "Oh, come now, Frank. Can't you see Jesse isn't coming back?"

"Isn't coming back? I don't see any such—" He stopped abruptly, staring at his wife through narrowed eyes. "Etta, what have you done?"

Continuing as if Frank hadn't spoken, she said, "Fantasy thinks Jesse isn't coming back; he just used taking that Chinese woman to San Francisco as an excuse to be rid of her and Robby. That's why I know she'll decide—I mean, that's why she's decided to go back to St. Louis. Surely you can see it's the obvious choice."

"I don't know," Frank said quietly. "I'm not so sure Jesse isn't coming back. He struck me as a man of his word."

"A lot you know," Henrietta spouted. "If he's a man of his word, why hasn't he sent a telegram like he said he would? He's been gone almost three weeks now, and Fantasy still hasn't heard from him!"

Seeing the pained look on her husband's face, Henrietta turned away so he wouldn't see her smile. "Go back to the hotel, Frank, and pack our bags. I'll stay here and get Robby's things together." Rising from the table, she turned to leave the dining room.

"What do you plan to tell our grandson?"

Swinging back to her husband, she flashed him a look of annoyance. "I'll tell him his mother has decided to move back East. And since she doesn't know how long she'll be away, she asked us to take him to St. Louis and she'll join us later."

"And what will you tell him about Jesse?"

Henrietta waved her hand in a dismissive gesture. "I'll tell him Jesse will be along later, too."

"But you just said Jesse isn't coming back. You'd lie to the boy?"

Hands planted firmly on her hips, Henrietta pinned him with a fierce glare. "And just what else could I say that a five-year-old would understand? His stepfather is a no-account liar? And the sooner he forgets the man, the better? Really, Frank, use your head."

Frank sighed, rubbing one hand over his face. "I still think—"

"I don't care what you think," Henrietta interrupted, her voice shrill. "We're leaving, and Robby's going with us."

Frank clenched his hands into tight fists on top of the table. Tamping down his frustration, he said, "I just can't believe Fantasy wants us to take the boy back to Missouri. She seemed happy here."

"Can't you see she was just putting on an act for us?" In a conspiratorial whisper, she added, "Don't you see, Frank? Admitting she'd made a mistake by not returning to St. Louis sooner would have been very embarrassing for her. Being called out of town gave her the perfect opportunity to ask us to take Robby home with us."

As Frank thought over his wife's explanation he gradually relaxed his fists. Flexing his fingers to ease the stiffness, he finally said, "Well, I guess that makes sense."

"Humph! I should say it does," she mumbled under her breath. She waved toward the door. "Get going, will you? I sent Mr. Baxter to the stage office to buy our tickets for the noon stage. I can't wait to be shed of this horrid town."

Six hours after the Williamses departed on a northbound stage, another stagecoach pulled into Tombstone and jerked to a halt in front of the Pinkham Stage Line Office.

Jumping down from the still-rocking coach, Jesse tipped his hat brim lower to shield his eyes from the still brilliant glare of the late afternoon sun. He waited for his bag to be tossed down from the top of the stagecoach, then headed toward Fifth Street and home.

Home. He'd begun to think he'd never see the house on Fifth Street again. He'd waited ten days for John Valentine to return to San Francisco. Just when he was ready to say "to hell with it" and leave, John had finally arrived full of apologies and glad he waited. Then Jesse had spent the better part of two more days going over every detail of the Cochise County stage robbery case. Thank God John had been satisfied with the evidence he and Nick had gathered, or Jesse might have resorted to doing his boss and good friend serious bodily harm. As soon as John handed him the official papers authorizing the local sheriff to arrest Lawson and his gang, Jesse left posthaste for the train station.

His thoughts turning from the papers in his inside jacket pocket to his wife, he lengthened his strides. Would Fantasy welcome him, was she still angry, or had his second telegram soothed her Irish temper? He'd labored over what to write in that message, and could only hope the words he'd finally chosen would pay off. He regretted not taking time to send word of his arrival. When John finally dismissed him, Jesse just wanted to get on the first train heading south and hadn't taken time to stop by the telegraph office.

As the adobe house came into view, he picked up his pace, leaping up the steps and calling out as he entered the front door.

No one answered.

Fear pounding in his veins, Jesse searched the house. Fantasy's clothes were in their usual place, the picture she valued so much—the one of her parents—still sat atop the bureau. Jesse sighed with relief. Returning to the parlor, he poured himself a whiskey and sat down to wait.

An hour later, a second drink warming his stomach, Jesse was still alone. Unable to bear another minute in the silent house, he left, heading back to Allen Street. He needed to talk to the sheriff, and perhaps he'd find someone who knew the whereabouts of his wife and stepson.

"Sorry, Mr. McAllister," Deputy Hatch said, leaning back in his chair and propping his boots on the corner of the desk. Through the opened second-story window came the tinny sound of a piano from the Crystal Palace Saloon downstairs. "The sheriff ain't here, he's over ta Bisbee and won't be back 'til sometime tomorrow. Is there somethin' I can help ya with?"

"I appreciate the offer, deputy. But I'll wait for the sheriff to return. Thanks for your time."

"You bet." The deputy withdrew a bowie knife from the sheath on his belt. Humming tunelessly, he began paring his fingernails.

Shaking his head, Jesse left the sheriff's office and stood on the balcony overlooking Allen Street.

For a few minutes he watched the activity below. As usual, the street was packed with men representing every profession in town. Miners, ranchers, and gamblers, plus every type of businessman formed a constant stream of customers, entering and leaving the assorted places of amusement. For a moment, Jesse's attention was drawn to one of the casinos several doors to the west. A crowd had gathered just outside the bat-wing doors, shouting and whooping their enjoyment over someone's run of luck.

When the crowd gave a collective groan, signalling Lady Luck had withdrawn her kindness, Jesse headed for the stairs. After descending to the boardwalk, he checked his watch. Eight o'clock. Rubbing the back of his neck, he looked one way up Allen Street, then the other. He couldn't decide if he should go back home or try to locate Nick. He finally turned west, toward the Alhambra.

"Hey, Mr. McAllister, I didn't know y'all was back in town. How was your trip?"

Smiling, Jesse turned toward the owner of the Texas drawl. "I just got back, Gil, and my trip went just fine. I'm glad I ran into you. You don't happen to know where my wife is, or when she might be returning, do you?"

"Yes, sir, I know where she's at," Gil began, his eyebrows pulling together. "As to when she might be back, I don't rightly know. The accident—"

"Accident?" Jesse interrupted. "What are you talking about?"

Gil's eyes widened. "Y'all haven't heard about the accident? Didn't—"

"No, I don't know about any accident," Jesse interrupted again, his apprehension growing. "For God's sake, man, tell me what happened."

"There was an accident at Spud's mine yesterday. Jake Fisher, an ol' prospector friend of Spud who has a claim near his, heard the explosion. When Jake got there, the mouth of the mine was blocked by a pile of rocks."

"How'd you find out about it?"

"Jake knew he couldn't do much by hisself, so he came right inta town and found me. I told Jake ta hightail it back to the mine with some men who volunteered to help, and I'd be there soon's I fetched Doc McKee. When I got to the mine, Jake said it looked like Spud was tryin' to locate a new vein and the dynamite blew too soon. Can't be sure, though, cuz Spud ain't come to. Least ways he hadn't when I left there late this mornin'."

"Ain't come to?" Jesse repeated, in a daze. "Is that where Fantasy went, to Spud's mine?"

"Yes, sir. Doc McKee was outta town, so I went ta see Miz McAllister. She said she wasn't very good at doctorin', but she agreed Spud wouldn't want anyone else tendin' him. So the three of us rode up to the mine late yesterday afternoon."

"Rode?"

Gil shifted his feet on the boardwalk. "I promised not to tell anyone, but I reckon with Spud gettin' hurt and all, she won't mind if I tell y'all. Least ways, I hope not."

"Tell me what?"

"I've been teaching Miz McAllister how to ride.

She's turned into a right fine horsewoman. She rode Banjo to the mine and never had one bit a trouble."

Stunned Fantasy had turned down his offer then asked another man to teach her to ride, Jesse felt a stab of disappointment. Pushing aside his bruised pride, he said, "I'm sure she won't be upset because you told me." Recalling something else Gil said, his mood brightened. Gil mentioned the *three* of them riding to Spud's mine. Relieved to learn his wife and Robby were safe, he smiled. "I knew she'd do fine, once she got over her fear. Spud told me his mine was in the Whetstone Mountains. How far is that from town?"

"Close to twenty miles."

Jesse turned to look at the purple-streaked sky. "It's too late to make the trip tonight," he murmured. "Guess I'll have to wait until morning."

After getting more specific directions to Spud's mine, Jesse bid Gil good night. He stopped at the Lexington Livery and arranged for a horse to be ready for him at first light. Not wanting to return to an empty house, Jesse wandered around town. Disappointed he didn't find Nick in any of his known haunts, Jesse finally headed back to Fifth Street.

On the walk home, he passed the American Hotel. Realizing he should have stopped by sooner, he went back to the hotel to pay his respects to Henrietta and Frank.

"I'm sorry, Mr. McAllister," the desk clerk began. "But the Williamses have checked out."

Jesse's brows shot up. "Checked out? When?"

"This morning, sir. Mr. Williams came in about ten and said they were leaving on the noon stage to Benson."

"I see. Well, thank you for the information." Jesse started to leave, but the clerk's voice stopped him.

"Um, Mr. McAllister?"

Turning back to the man, Jesse said, "Is there something else?"

"Well . . . um . . . yes. There's the matter of the

. . . uh . . . bill," he managed to finish, his face flushed a dull red.

"Bill?"

"Yes, sir. When Mrs. Williams checked in, she made it plain you'd be paying for their room since you couldn't put them up at your house. And, well, because you were the one who made the reservation, naturally I assumed . . ." The man pulled a handkerchief from his pocket and ran it across his forehead.

Jesse held up one hand. "Say no more." Reaching for his wallet, he said, "I'll take care of it right now. How much do I owe you?"

As he watched the man pull out the hotel ledger, a self-mocking smile twisted Jesse's lips. He'd left himself wide open for this, he realized with perfect hindsight. Apparently there was no end to Henrietta's gall. If he hadn't been so glad to hear the Williamses had left town, he would have been furious at Henrietta's final act of trickery. As it was, the price of a hotel bill seemed preferable to having the woman around. Fantasy would surely be pleased.

Arriving back at his house, Jesse fell into bed with a sigh. He lay awake for a long time, thinking about the news he had to tell Fantasy. He could just picture the look on her face, slightly widened eyes, lips parted with surprise. Smiling at the image, he drifted to sleep.

Deep in the first sound sleep she'd gotten since starting her vigil at Spud's side a day and a half ago, Fantasy was jarred awake by one of the men from town who'd stayed to help.

"Mrs. McAllister? Doc McKee wants ya."

"What? Doc? He's here?"

"Yes'em. He got here 'bout an hour ago, and he said to fetch ya."

She sat up on the bedroll and glanced up at the sky. She'd only been asleep for a couple of hours. "Spud isn't worse, is he? He's not—" she swallowed, unable to finish.

Before the man could answer, another voice said, "He sure isn't dead. And no, he's not worse." Moving into Fantasy's line of vision, Dr. McKee added, "Unless you consider a complaining old coot worse than one that's out cold."

"Complaining? You mean he's awake?"

"Yes. And he's asking for you."

Rushing to Spud's side, Fantasy sank to her knees and grasped his outstretched hand. "I want you to know you scared five years off my life."

Spud squeezed her hand as much as his weakened condition allowed. "Ah, Fantasy, lass. It takes more than a little dynamite blast to do in Fagen Fitzpatrick."

Fantasy shook her head. "When will you learn? Both Doc and I have told you not to use dynamite. You'd better listen this time. Or I'll do you in myself."

Spud chuckled, then groaned when the vibration made the ache in his head worse. "I shoulda knowed I'd not be getting any sympathy from another Irishman."

Fantasy saw the amusement dancing in her dear friend's blue eyes and couldn't hold back her own laugh. "If you don't beat all, Fagen Fitzpatrick. Nearly blowing yourself into the hereafter, then complaining because I don't fall all over you with sympathy." Her light mood sobering, she added, "You truly did give me a terrible scare."

"Aye, I can see that, lass. I'm powerful sorry I gave ye cause to be worrying so. But I found this new vein a gold, and I had to use the dynamite to get it out. Ye should see—"

Placing her finger on his lips, she said, "Shh. We'll talk about it later. Right now you need to take it easy so you can get your strength back. One of the men shot a rabbit and made some broth. Would you like some?"

"Aye, lass. I'd like that."

When she started to get up, he grasped her hand. "Doc said ye took care a me, lass." At her nod, he added, "Doc also said ye done a fine job, that he couldn't a done no better."

"I only did what anyone would do for someone they love."

Eyes damp with tears, he nodded.

Rising, she said, "I'll get that broth."

While Fantasy fed Spud, he plied her with questions about the goings-on in Tombstone during the two months since he returned to his mine. He listened silently to her recitation of the events he'd missed, dutifully swallowing the rich broth she spooned into his mouth. But when she tried to gloss over her recent marriage and change the subject, he shoved the spoon away, making her spill its contents down the front of his shirt.

"Just hold on there, lass. What's that ye said? Ye and Jesse got yerselves married. Is that what yer tellin' me?"

Keeping her gaze on the piece of cloth she used to sop up the spill, Fantasy replied, "Yes, Reverend Peabody married us a month ago."

When Spud started to speak, Fantasy stuck another spoonful of broth in his mouth before he could form the words. He obediently let her feed him the last of his meal, silently studying her face. After she set the bowl down, he said, "Are ye and Jesse not happy?"

Fantasy blinked back the sudden tears before lifting her chin and looking into Spud's face. "I'd—" she had to clear her throat before she could go on. "I'd rather not talk about it right now."

After several seconds, Spud placed one gnarled hand over hers. "Ye know I love ye like yer me own family, lass. If ye need someone to be talkin' to later, I'll be here for ye."

Fantasy nodded, giving him a watery smile. "Thank you, Spud."

"So, what else happened since Con and me left

town? What have ye heard from that evil-spirited mother-in-law of yers?"

Her smile broadened. "That's ex-mother-in-law now, and would you believe Henrietta and Frank are in Tombstone this very minute?"

Spud gave a short bark of laughter. "Get on with ye. Yer pullin' me leg, to be sure." When Fantasy shook her head, his smile faded, his eyes wide. "By all that's holy, they truly are in town?"

"Aye, they truly are," she answered, laughing at the shocked look on his face. "Henrietta and Frank have been here almost a month now."

"And what would make the high-an'-mighty Henrietta Williams leave the lap a luxury to come out to the wilds of Arizona Territory? I'm a thinkin' she's up to no good, that's what!"

"I thought so, too, especially after she sent word she intended to make sure Robby went back to St. Louis with them. Then when she arrived and found out I'd married again, I think whatever plans she'd make went right out the window."

"Don't be underestimatin' that woman, lass. She's a sly one."

"Yes, I know. But I recently asked her to stop talking about how we should move back to Missouri, and so far she's done as I asked."

" 'Course, keepin' her yap shut could be because she's cookin' up another scheme."

"I suppose that's possible. But she was feeling poorly when Gil told me about your accident. She's a terrible patient, so I'm hoping her endless demands plus feeling sorry for herself will keep her mind off any ideas of devising a plan."

"Let's hope so. So you left Jesse and Robby to take care of her?"

A pained expression crossed Fantasy's face. "No. Frank's taking care of her at their hotel. And Jesse's out of town."

"Out of town? Then, who's stayin' with the lad?"

Quickly Fantasy explained what had led up to Jesse's trip to San Francisco and how she'd asked Garland Baxter to stay with Robby.

Spud asked several more questions, then fell silent, mulling over everything he'd been told.

Fantasy fussed with his pillow and tried to smooth the blankets under him. When she saw his yawn, she said, "I'll leave you now so you can rest. Doc says that's the best thing for you."

"What does that old sawbones know?" he grumbled, his eyes twinkling with mirth. "All he's done since I come to is give me hell for usin' dynamite."

Fantasy leaned over to kiss his forehead, then stood up to leave. "I agree with him. Now, you rest," she ordered softly.

"Ye'll be here when I wake up, lass?"

"I'll be here."

The first pink fingers of dawn had just stretched up into the eastern sky when Jesse awoke. He'd been dreaming of making love to Fantasy and would have preferred rolling over and seeking an encore of the pleasures of her flesh in his dreamworld. Then he remembered Gil's words about Spud's accident and came fully awake.

He dressed, packed a saddle bag and was out the door in ten minutes. The sun had just begun chasing the darkness from the sky by the time he was astride a horse and galloping toward the northwest.

Jesse pushed the horse as hard as he dared, but it still took him two hours to reach the Whetstone Mountains. Not being familiar with the terrain, it took another hour to locate the well-hidden path Gil had described which led to Spud's mine.

As he approached the camp, Jesse's gaze went unerringly to his wife. As she stepped from a crudely made lean-to the glow of the morning sun on her auburn hair drew him like a beacon. He stopped his horse in front

of her and dismounted. Never taking his eyes from her
face, he moved closer, aching to pull her into his arms
yet afraid to do so.

"Jesse," she murmured, blinking with surprise.

The sound of his name on her lips and the spark of
joy in her eyes sent a ray of hope straight to his heart.
When her look of welcome instantly changed to cool
reserve, his newfledged hope collapsed. A tightening in
his chest made breathing difficult.

"How's Spud?" he finally asked when he could get
his throat muscles to work.

"He came to early this morning. He's weak, but Dr.
McKee thinks he's going to be fine. He drank some
broth, and right now he's sleeping."

While she answered, Jesse silently studied her. She
looked pale and drawn, her shoulders hunched forward with fatigue. There were creases between her
eyebrows and around her mouth. Large blue smudges
marred the skin beneath her eyes.

"You look tired, love. Haven't you gotten any rest?"
he asked in a gentle voice.

A ripple of pleasure skittered through her body at
his endearment, but she ignored the all-too-familiar
feeling. Keeping her face averted lest she reveal her
reaction, she said, "Not much. I've been too worried
about Spud." *And you!* She bit her lip to keep the
words from spilling out.

She turned toward the camp fire. "Would you like
some coffee? There's a fresh pot, and we have eggs I
can fix if you like."

"That sounds great. I didn't take time to eat before
I left this morning."

After Fantasy fried several slices of bacon, she
cracked three eggs into the thick grease.

Jesse watched his wife bending over the fire, his
throat clogged with love and concern for her health.
Glancing around, he spotted two men at the mouth of
the mine but there was no sign of Robby. Noticing

several occupied bedrolls on the other side of the camp, he decided the boy must still be asleep.

When the edges of the eggs were brown and crispy, but the yolks still soft—the way she knew Jesse liked them—Fantasy turned them onto a metal plate with the bacon and handed it to him. He smiled his thanks and sat down to eat.

After pouring two cups of coffee, she sat down next to him. There were so many things she wanted to ask, but she waited until he finished eating before she spoke. "When did you get back?"

"About six last night," he replied, setting his plate aside and reaching for his cup.

"You got Mei-Ling to her sister's okay?"

Jesse took a drink of coffee, then said, "Yes. Ching-Ling was surprised to find us at her door. But once she got over the shock, she welcomed Mei-Ling into her home."

"Do you think Mei-Ling will be okay there?"

"She'll do fine. Ching-Ling seemed a bit cold, but I think she was sincere when she said Mei-Ling could stay with her."

Fantasy nodded absently, thinking how good Jesse looked. She longed to touch his forearm and feel the muscles contract beneath her fingers, to run her hand along his jawline and feel the roughness of his beard stubble. She did neither, sitting perfectly still. There were also other things she wanted to ask him, but she found her tongue stuck to the roof of her mouth, trapping her questions inside.

While they drank their coffee, a strained silence settled between them. Fantasy's attention was drawn to movement across the camp

Doc McKee rose from one of the bedrolls and approached the fire. After pouring himself a cup of the strong brew, he sat back on his haunches. "How's our patient?" he asked, keeping his gaze on the fire.

"Fine. He's sleeping," Fantasy replied. "That's

what you should be doing. You only laid down an hour ago."

"I'm fine," Doc replied, glancing up for the first time. When his gaze fell on Jesse, his eyes widened. "Well, well. Look what the cat dragged in."

Jesse chuckled. "Good to see you, too, Doc. Although maybe Spud would be better off with a doctor who knows some manners."

Doc McKee flashed a smile over the top of his coffee cup. "I'd be careful what I said, if I were you, McAllister. Have you already forgotten about my promise not to tell anyone about your little accident a few months ago?" Seeing the amusement vanish from Jesse's face, he added, "Don't worry, I gave you my word, and I won't go back on it."

"Thanks, Doc, I appreciate it. But, I am surprised to see you out here. I had the impression you were definitely a city man."

"I didn't get to camp until about dawn this morning. As soon as I returned to town and heard about the accident, I headed up here. Before I arrived, Fantasy was taking care of Spud."

"Then you didn't ride with Gil Gunderson?"

"No. Gil, Fantasy, and the deputy got here the day before yesterday."

"Deputy?"

"Yes," Fantasy replied. "The sheriff was concerned the explosion might have been foul play, so he sent Deputy Breakenridge up here to investigate the accident."

Jesse rose and moved away from the fire. Swinging back to face Fantasy, he said, "No one else rode with you?"

"No. Who did you think came with us?"

"Robby."

"Robby? But I—wait a minute. Didn't you say you got into Tombstone yesterday?" At his nod, she said, "Then, didn't you stay at the house last night?"

"Yes." Her confused expression prompted him to ask, "Why?"

"I asked Garland Baxter to stay with Robby at the house until I got back, but you never mentioned him, so I thought maybe you didn't—" Seeing the sudden blanching of Jesse's face, she asked, "What is it? What's happened?"

"Baxter was the one who sent word to Henrietta and Frank about the fire."

She felt the blood drain from her face. "Are you sure?"

"He admitted it when I ran into him at the stage office the day I left town. He told me he was moving to Tucson, or I would have made sure you knew about what he'd done."

Jumping to her feet, she grasped Jesse's forearm and stared up at him with pleading eyes. "There's more, isn't there, Jesse? I can tell by the look on your face. Whatever it is, tell me."

Holding her shoulders gently, he took a deep breath and said, "When I got to the house last night, there was no one there. No one."

When Jesse's words sank in, her legs started to fold beneath her. He tightened his grip to keep her from falling to the ground in a boneless heap.

"Do you think Baxter is still working for Mother Williams? Do you think he might have taken Robby to her?"

"I don't know."

Trying to shrug off his hands, Fantasy cried, "We have to get back to town. We have to talk to Henrietta and Frank."

"We can't."

She stopped struggling and looked up at him sharply. "What do you mean, 'we can't?' What are you trying to tell me, Jesse?"

He released her and rubbed a hand over his bristled jaw. Finally meeting her frightened gaze, he said, "I went to the American Hotel last night to pay my respects to Henrietta and Frank. The clerk told me they checked out yesterday morning and left on the noon stage."

"Left on the noon stage?" Fantasy repeated in a strangled whisper. As realization dawned she screamed, "Nooooo!" When her mind cleared, she murmured, "She actually did it."

Lifting her head, she turned an anguish-filled gaze on her husband. "Jesse, Henrietta's taken our son!"

Chapter 20

His heart heavy with despair, Jesse wished he could disagree with Fantasy. Unfortunately, it was true—Henrietta had taken Robby. In spite of such a painful turn of events, his wife's statement gave him a surge of hope. She had called Robby *our son*. Did that mean she still loved him? Did their marriage still have a chance? He halted the direction of his thoughts. Before he could seek out the answers to his questions, he had to get Robby back.

"Henrietta and Frank left Tombstone on the Benson stage, so they'll be catching the train from there," Jesse said. Looking at the men who had gathered around when they heard Fantasy's scream, he added, "Do any of you know what time the eastbound train leaves Benson?"

One man, about Spud's age with a stocky yet compact build, stepped forward. Removing his floppy-brimmed hat, he extended his hand to Jesse. "Name's Jake Fisher. The train's supposed ta leave at eleven-fifteen, give or take a few minutes." He slapped his hat against his corduroy pants, smoothed his gray hair with a leathery hand then stuck the hat back on his head. "Durn train's hardly ever on time."

"Eleven-fifteen," Jesse repeated, pulling his watch from his pocket. He opened the cover, then scowled. "That gives me less than two hours. How long will it take to get to Benson?"

"Countin' the time ta make yer way outta the mountains," Jake replied, scratching the gray stubble on his cheek. "I'd say ya could make it in a little over two hours. Ya'd have to push yer horse fer all it's worth, though."

"Damn," Jesse muttered. He fell silent, weighing his chances.

"Please, Jesse," Fantasy whispered. "We have to try."

Her pleading voice and stricken look struck a cord deep inside. "I'll leave right now. Where's Banjo?"

"He's over there," she answered, pointing to the makeshift corral across the camp. "But I'm going with you." She turned to Dr. McKee. "Doc, can I use your horse?"

"Sure thing, Fantasy. I'll have him—"

"Hold on there, Doc," Jesse interrupted. Grasping his wife by the arm, he led her away from the other men. "Listen to me, Fantasy, I know you think you're an experienced rider after a few weeks of having Gil teach you to ride then making the trip up here, but I want you to stay with Spud."

Catching the affront in his voice, she said, "I'm sorry I didn't take you up on your offer to teach me, but it was something I wanted to do on my own. I asked Gil because I . . . I just didn't want to be beholden to you for anything else."

Jesse stared at her for several seconds, silently cursing her hardheadedness. He heaved a sigh, then said, "I still think—"

"I'm going, Jesse. It's my fault Henrietta took Robby." She gulped back a sob. "I should never have left him to come here." Her voice cracked on the last word, tears gathering in her eyes and spilling over.

"You didn't know what Garland Baxter was up to, so don't blame yourself."

Swiping fiercely at her face, she lifted her chin. "I'm going to Benson, Jesse. With you, or without you, I'm going."

Nodding, Jesse gave his wife a weak smile and reached out to brush away the last of her tears. When his thumb touched her cheek, she visibly stiffened, sending a sharp stab of pain through his chest. He longed to gather her into his arms, but made no move to do so. Hiding his disappointment, he dropped his hand and called over his shoulder, "Doc, will you have Banjo and your horse saddled right away?"

"You bet, Jesse."

After Doc McKee and one of the other men hurried to ready the horses, Jesse turned to follow them. Fantasy's hand on his arm stopped him. Staring at her fingers, he made the shocking discovery that in spite of the urgent mission before them, his body was reacting to her touch. Tamping down his ill-timed desire, he met her gaze, one eyebrow quirked in question.

"We will get there in time, won't we, Jesse?"

"I intend to try. If we don't, we'll follow them all the way to St. Louis if necessary. I swear, love, we'll get Robby back." For an instant, Jesse was certain his words caused a flash of something other than fear to flare in the depths of Fantasy's eyes. Just as quickly that something fled, making him wonder if his imagination had conjured up the reaction he longed for.

His see-sawing emotions made his voice gruff when he said, "You'd better go tell Spud we're leaving."

Fantasy looked up sharply. Her brow furrowed, she studied his stern features for a second. Finding nothing to explain his curt tone, she nodded, then turned and headed toward the lean-to.

"Make it quick. We'll be leaving as soon as the horses are saddled."

Seeing Fantasy's back stiffen, her hands curl into fists at her sides, Jesse wished he hadn't sounded so harsh. He wanted desperately to heal the breach between them, yet circumstances wouldn't allow it. Rubbing the back of his neck to ease his tight muscles, he turned his attention to the more pressing problem of retrieving their son. Once they got Robby out of the

Williamses' clutches, Jesse promised himself he would
turn his full attention to accomplishing the even more
difficult task of winning back his wife.

Drawing strength from Jesse's vow to get her son
away from Henrietta and Frank, Fantasy rode stoi-
cally alongside her husband. He set a relentless pace,
yet she kept up without complaint. With each passing
mile, she prayed they'd get to Benson in time. By the
time she and Jesse neared the end of their grueling ride,
the horses were blowing hard, their coats flecked with
sweat and covered by a layer of yellowish-white dust.

At the south edge of town, Jesse motioned for them
to slow their mounts to a walk. The reprieve was short.
The piercing shriek of a train whistle drowned out the
soft clopping of the horses' hooves. His mouth set in a
grim line, Jesse pointed toward the train depot, then
kicked Banjo into a gallop.

Jumping to the ground in front of the Southern
Pacific Train Station, Jesse looped the reins around a
hitching post then raced inside. Sliding to a halt at the
ticket window, he said, "Is that the eastbound train
pulling out?"

The railroad agent, busy sorting a pile of tickets on
the counter in front of him, never looked up when he
replied, "Yup."

"Give me two tickets."

The agent continued his work, still not looking up.
"To where?"

"Dammit, man," Jesse snarled, pointing toward the
railcars moving slowly past the depot. "I want tickets
for that train."

This time the man looked up. "Sorry, mister. It's too
late. Ya heard the whistle. That means she's pullin'
out. There'll be another train headin' east tomorrow."

Reaching through the window, Jesse grasped the
man by his shirtfront and pulled him partway across
the counter. "You don't seem to understand. I said, I

want two tickets for *that* train." Seeing the agent's eyes start to roll back in his head, Jesse released his hold and added in a calmer voice, "Now, how much?"

His Adam's apple bobbing, the man finally worked up the courage to tell Jesse the price of the tickets.

Fantasy ran into the depot just as Jesse stepped away from the ticket window. Waving the tickets, he said, "Come on, we'll have to run to get aboard." Never breaking stride, she nodded and turned toward the door leading to the passengers' boarding platform.

Turning back to the railroad agent, Jesse flipped a gold piece over the glass partition. "See that our horses are taken to the nearest livery, rubbed down and fed. Name's McAllister. We'll be back as soon as we can."

The man halted his attempts to straighten his shirt and tie long enough to deftly catch the coin. He nodded, watched the couple race from the depot, then shook his head. "Ain't never gonna make it."

The train whistle blasted another deafening scream. Steam belched from the smokestack, the engine straining to increase its speed and pull its load out of the station. The last car rolled past just as Jesse and Fantasy reached the end of the boarding platform.

Grasping Fantasy's hand, Jesse jumped down off the platform. He broke into a run on the hard-packed ground, tugging Fantasy along with him, shortening his strides so she could keep up.

Forced to match his pace or risk falling and being left behind, Fantasy was thankful for her riding skirt. A long dress and petticoats would never had allowed her to be so swift-footed. Lungs burning from exertion and sucking in the train's acrid smoke, somehow she managed to stay on her feet.

At last Jesse drew even with the iron railing around the rear platform of the last railcar. He slowed for an instant and pulled Fantasy up next to him. In one fluid motion, he released her hand and grasped her around the waist.

He brought his mouth close to her ear. "Get ready

to jump." When he felt her muscles tense, he lifted her as high as he could and pushed.

Fantasy's feet hit the railcar platform with a resounding thud, then slid out from under her. She sat down on the wooden floor with a teeth-jarring jolt. By the time her spinning senses cleared, she realized Jesse hadn't jumped with her. Scrambling to her feet, she looked down the tracks.

Jesse's efforts to get her on the train had thrown him off balance. His arms windmilling wildly, his stride awkward and wobbly, he struggled to remain on his feet. His efforts proved futile. He couldn't stop his upper body from pitching forward.

"Jesse!" Fantasy's scream was swallowed up by the clatter of the wheels on the metal rails and the hissing and puffing of the steam engine.

As he started to fall Jesse turned his body so his shoulder would take the brunt of the landing. The momentum allowed him to hit the ground with a glancing blow, roll, then spring back to his feet. Having lost only a second or two, he lengthened his strides. Although his lungs felt as if they would burst, he forced himself to keep going. Fantasy needed him! Robby needed him! He couldn't—he wouldn't fail them.

The August desert heat depleting his stamina much faster than he'd anticipated, he summoned one last burst of energy. Finally, he managed to draw even with the railcar. He spared a quick glance toward Fantasy. Feet widespread, one hand clutching the railing, she leaned toward him as far as she could.

"Give me your hand. You can make it, Jesse," she yelled, stretching over the railing even more.

Although her words were snatched away by the wind, Jesse understood her gesture of help and the encouragement reflected on her face. Reaching up, he clasped her hand. Calling on the last of his flagging strength, he threw himself onto the runningboard. He landed on the top step, his boots making a hollow clang on the metal. His legs heavy with exhaustion, he struggled to climb up onto the platform. Banging his shin on the bottom step, he inhaled sharply.

"Jesse, are you okay? Jesse?"

"Yeah. I'm fine," he managed to say between deep gasps. Rubbing his smarting leg, he turned to look at Fantasy kneeling next to him. Her face was pinched, and in spite of her recent exercise, drained of color. "What about you? Are you all right?"

She nodded, the lines of worry on her forehead and around her mouth easing. She shifted off her knees and sat down, wincing as her bruised bottom made contact with the floor of the platform. "I'm just winded."

Rolling over, Jesse heaved himself into a sitting position and slumped against the back of the railcar. Somehow he mustered a weak smile. "Me, too."

Fantasy dropped her head against the railcar and closed her eyes. Thank God they'd both survived their unorthodox method of getting aboard. Her breathing slowing to normal, the stitch in her side easing, her thoughts turned to their reason for chasing down a train. Robby.

After a few minutes of rest, Jesse got to his feet. Once he became accustomed to the train's rocking motion, he reached down to help Fantasy. It took several attempts before her still-weak legs would support her. After brushing off each other's clothes as best they could, Jesse opened the railcar door.

He led Fantasy through two passenger cars before finding the one he wanted. There were only six other people in the railcar. A well-dressed man, his hat pulled over his face, dozed near the front. A young couple and their daughter shared a seat near the middle of the railcar. And two white-haired men sat several rows behind the three passengers Jesse and Fantasy sought.

* * *

"Gramma, I don't wanna go to St. Louis."

"Don't be silly, Robby. Of course you want to go to St. Louis. Didn't I tell you your mother wanted us to take you to our home and she'll come later?"

"Yeah, but—"

"That's enough, Robert. Play with your soldiers."

Sticking out his bottom lip, Robby replied, "But I don't wanna play with my soldiers." He cocked his arm and threw the wooden figure onto the empty seat across from him.

"Frank, get your nose out of that newspaper. Can't you see I need help with our grandson? He's behaving like a spoiled brat. Do you hear me, Frank? Frank!"

Frank's shoulders lifted as he drew a deep breath. Exhaling a heavy sigh, he lowered the paper to look at the woman in the seat facing him. "Yes, Etta, I hear you. What's the . . . ?" His words trailed off, his attention drawn to movement behind his wife. Eyes wide and face blanched, Frank said, "I don't think you'll be needing any help."

Henrietta stared at her husband through squinted eyes. "What are you talking about, Frank? Of course, I need help. Robby must learn to mind me since he'll be living with us."

"I don't think so, Mother Williams," a soft voice said from behind Henrietta's seat.

"Momma!"

Robby's crow of delight brought Henrietta's head around with a snap. "Fantasy! What . . . ? How . . . ?" Her shock prevented her from completing a sentence or doing anything to stop her grandson from scrambling out of his seat and into his mother's arms.

As the import of Fantasy's and Jesse's presence sank in, Frank's face changed from lack of color to mottled with fiery red. Shifting his enraged gaze to his wife, he said in a clipped voice, "Etta, I think you have some explaining to do. You told me Fantasy had agreed to move back to St. Louis. That she wanted Robby to go with us and she would come along later. Isn't that what you told me?"

Henrietta squirmed under her husband's scrutiny. "Yes, that's what I told you. Because it's for the best. Robby should be in St. Louis with us. Arizona is no—"

"Stop it!" Frank snapped. "I don't want to hear any more." Dropping his head back against the seat, he groaned, "Dear God." Closing his eyes, he pinched the bridge of his nose to ease the sudden pounding in his head. "She lied to me. My own wife lied to me," he mused aloud. Henrietta had done a lot of things he disapproved of, but to his knowledge she'd never lied to him. He opened his eyes and looked at her. "How could you do this?"

For once Henrietta remained silent. She had never seen Frank so furious. And she knew if she said anything in her defense, she'd also have to tell him the other things she'd done. Holding her tongue seemed the wise choice.

When Henrietta didn't answer, Jesse spoke for the first time. "Frank, I don't know the exact motives behind your wife's actions, but you're correct about Fantasy. She knew nothing about the two of you taking Robby. She also didn't know Garland Baxter was working for your wife."

"What?" Frank nearly shouted, making Henrietta wince. How could he live with a woman for so many years and not know her, not know what she was capable of? *Because you let her walk all over you. You allowed yourself to live under her thumb.* He took a slow, deep breath. *Well, that's about to change.* His voice was cold when he spoke. "Henrietta, I've put up with a lot of your meddling in all the time we've been married. I've turned a deaf ear to your tirades about what this person does or what that person doesn't do. For years I've listened to your—"

"But, Frank, you don't understand," Henrietta interrupted.

"I was speaking, Henrietta. Now hush up," Frank ordered, carefully folding his newspaper.

Henrietta's eyes nearly popped out of her head at the command. Frank had never talked to her like that.

One of the men behind them sniggered. In a whisper loud enough for everyone in the railcar to hear, he said, "Guess he finally decided to show the rotten biddy who wears the pants in the family, huh, Gus?" He elbowed the man sitting beside him.

" 'Bout time, too," Gus replied. "I'd turn her over my knee for good measure."

The two chortled, then fell silent when Jesse sent them a chilling glance.

Fantasy only half-heard the conversation. She had taken a seat across the aisle from her former in-laws, her attention on her son. Holding Robby cuddled in her lap, she stroked his hair, murmuring to him softly.

Cowed by Frank's sudden show of backbone and mortified at the remarks of the elderly men behind her, Henrietta folded her hands in her lap and let her husband speak.

"Now, as I was saying, for years I've listened to your nonstop prattle, all the claptrap gossip circulating among your circle of friends. But I always believed it was just talk, that you would never do anything to hurt anyone. I believed deep inside you had a kind heart." He shook his head sadly. "That's what I get for not hauling back on your reins before now." He slapped one of his thighs with the folded newspaper. "Well, no more!"

"That's telling her," came a soft voice from the front of the railcar. All eyes turned to the young woman who'd spoken. Her husband glanced up, his face flushed with obvious embarrassment at his wife's boldness, yet he nodded his agreement.

"Yeah, tell her what for," added Gus, earning a guffaw and a slap on the back from his companion.

Ignoring his cheering section, Frank continued, "From now on, I'm in charge." He thumped his chest with one fist. "It will be me, Frank Arthur Williams, who calls the shots, Henrietta. And I don't want any complaints. Do you understand me?"

Pulling her gaze from the look of pure disgust on the faces of the young couple, Henrietta wished she could shrink out of sight. Had she truly become the horrible woman these people believed her to be? She'd never meant to hurt anyone. She just wanted her only grandchild to be near her. Was that—

"Henrietta?"

Frank's voice jerked her out of her ruminations. What she must do was very clear; she'd have to agree with whatever Frank said. If he found out about the other things she'd done, he might do more than yell. A shudder wracked her shoulders. Realizing Frank was waiting for an answer, she nodded.

"And that means with no back talk." When she remained silent, he barked, "Answer me!"

She flinched, then swallowed hard. "Yes, Frank," she managed to murmur.

He studied his wife for several long seconds. Satisfied with her sincerity, he looked first at Jesse, then Fantasy. "I realize now I should have paid more attention to Henrietta's goings-on. For that I must accept an equal share of the blame. I know it's no excuse, but I really had no idea she was capable of the things she's done. It won't be easy, but I assure you, I intend to undo as many of her past transgressions as possible. Believe me, I'll make sure this is the last of her ghastly behavior. Each and every person she's insulted or in some way ill-treated will receive my personal apology. Beginning now."

Straightening his spine, Frank sat stiffly erect in the seat. His voice firm, he said, "I know this is asking a great deal, perhaps more than I have a right to ask. But please accept my apology for what Henrietta has done."

Jesse looked down at Fantasy. "It's up to you. If you want to press charges, you have every right."

Fantasy stared at her former mother-in-law long and hard, the silence broken only by the clickety-clack of the train's wheels. She'd never seen Henrietta like this, meek and quiet. Mother Williams had never given in, not that Fantasy could remember, anyway. She shifted her gaze to Frank. The hard set to his jaw and the nearly feral gleam in his eyes might explain his wife's sudden contriteness. Yet, Fantasy couldn't entirely squelch the feeling Henrietta's acquiescence stemmed from more than Frank's sudden assertion of authority.

"I don't think legal action will be necessary, provided you make no further attempts to take Robby. But if you do anything that in any way looks like you're trying to get my son away from me—" she gave Henrietta a pointed look, "—I won't hesitate to have you arrested. For now though, I'll accept the apology and try to put this behind me."

Frank let out the breath he'd been holding. "Thank you, Fantasy. You won't regret this." Casting a glance at his wife, he added, "As for Henrietta, I intend to personally supervise everything she does. She won't bother you again." He looked wistfully at his grandson sitting on Fantasy's lap. "I'll miss Robby, though. After this, I'm sure we'll never see him again."

For the first time, Henrietta realized the cost of her aborted plans. A tiny moan escaped her mouth and tears sprang to her eyes.

Frank turned to look at her. "Don't go getting all blubbery-eyed, Etta. It's what you deserve, after what you've done."

Jesse and Fantasy exchanged glances. "There's no need to cut you out of our lives forever," Jesse said. "Maybe some day you can visit us in San Francisco. And perhaps we'll get to St. Louis once in a while." He reached down and ruffled Robby's hair. "A boy needs to see his grandparents." Jesse didn't dare look at Fantasy, for fear of what he'd read in her face. He'd just told the Williamses they would be living in California, when he didn't even know if his marriage would survive, let alone if Fantasy was still willing to make the move.

"Jesse's right," Fantasy added. "I don't want to shut you out of Robby's life. But please understand, we need time to get our lives back together."

Henrietta sniffed loudly and Frank surreptitiously wiped at his eyes. Handing his wife his handkerchief, Frank said, "Thank you, Fantasy. You're a special person and a wonderful mother. Though we'll miss you and Jesse, and especially our grandson, we understand. You have my solemn word you won't hear a peep from us. Isn't that right, Henrietta?"

His wife bobbed her head vigorously but held her tongue. A strange look flashed in her eyes, a mixture of fear and new respect for her husband.

"When you're ready to have visitors," Frank said, "we'd be grateful if you'd let us know."

"Of course," Jesse and Fantasy said in unison.

After making sure Fantasy and Robby were comfortable, Jesse said, "I'll go find the conductor and let him know we'll be getting off at the next stop."

Fantasy glanced up at him and nodded. As she watched her husband move through the swaying railcar, her thoughts turned to the future. Although she would be eternally grateful to Jesse for helping rescue her son, she wondered whether her life with Jesse could be rescued as well.

Considering the depth of her pain from all his lies, she didn't think so.

Chapter 21

The trip back to Tombstone from Willcox, where Jesse, Fantasy and Robby got off the train, passed in dismal silence. Jesse rented a buggy to get them back to Benson where he retrieved their horses. Rather than waiting for the next stage to Tombstone on the following day and having to find lodging for the night, he and Fantasy agreed to make the last leg of their journey on horseback.

It was a long, hot, tiring ride. The strain between the two of them made it even more uncomfortable. After watching the eastbound train carry Henrietta and Frank away from the Willcox station, Fantasy had offered her heartfelt thanks for helping reclaim Robby then retreated into silence. Jesse tried several times to break down the wall of coolness she had erected. His efforts didn't cause so much as a crack. Although she answered his direct questions, Jesse knew she did so only out of a sense of obligation. Finally he stopped trying, resolved to wait until they were back in Tombstone. Even the usually talkative Robby, sensing something amiss between his mother and Jesse, said very little. Jesse missed the boy's chatter. He needed something to occupy his thoughts, something besides saving his marriage.

When he pulled Banjo to a halt in front of the house on Fifth Street, the sky was dark as pitch. The trip had taken an entire day and evening, and Jesse was bone-tired. He figured Fantasy and Robby had to be equally worn out.

After swinging from Banjo's back, Jesse lifted Robby down from in front of Fantasy, then grasped her around the waist to assist her dismount. As soon as her feet touched the ground, he dropped his hands. "I'll help you get Robby ready for bed," Jesse said. "Then I'll see to the horses."

Fantasy nodded, too exhausted and drained from their trip and the strain between them to offer any complaint. Though having her husband so close would add to her discomfort, she was grateful for his help.

Fantasy and Jesse stripped Robby of his clothes then pulled a nightshirt over his head without exchanging a word. When Jesse's hand happened to brush hers, he felt her stiffen. Though her reaction to his touch cut him to the quick, he said nothing, stepping back to let her finish putting the boy to bed.

Fantasy straightened from kissing Robby's forehead to find Jesse had slipped from the room. She found him in the parlor, looking out the front window, hands clasped behind his back. Staring at his broad back, she watched his shoulders lift as he inhaled deeply then lower with a sigh.

She must have made some sort of sound, because Jesse abruptly swung away from the window to face her. "As soon as I drop the horses off at the livery, I have an errand I need to run."

"Tonight?" Caught off guard, concern throbbed in her voice. "But, it's after ten and you're about to drop from exhaustion. Can't it wait until morning?"

Jesse's heart leaped to his throat. "No, I'm afraid it has to be tonight. As it is, I've already put it off longer than I should have. I was supposed to do this before I heard about Spud's accident." Before he could stop himself, he crossed the room and reached out to stroke her cheek. His voice dropped to a husky whisper. "When I get back, we have to talk."

Fantasy's eyes widened. Her body reacted instantly

to his touch and the timbre of his voice, her fatigue momentarily forgotten. Chastising herself for responding to Jesse when she should be clinging to her pain, she laced her fingers together in front of her to keep from reaching out to him. She finally replied, "Fine."

Jesse longed to kiss her, but held himself in tight check. Their relationship was much too fragile to risk severing it permanently by giving in to his desire. He settled for one more light caress of her cheek, then dropped his hand. "I'll be back as soon as I can," he murmured.

Unable to make any words pass through her tight throat, she nodded. Several seconds went by before she realized she was still standing in the middle of the parlor, staring at the door Jesse had gone through. Heaving a weary sigh, she forced herself to move.

After giving herself a quick sponge bath to rinse off the travel grime, she longed to crawl into bed. Remembering Jesse's words about needing to talk, she resisted the urge and sat down on the settee to await his return. She fought her sleepiness, but in spite of her efforts her eyes grew increasingly heavy. She finally pulled the pins from her hair and lay her head on the arm of the settee. Intending to rest for just a minute, she closed her eyes.

Jesse slipped in the front door of his house and walked softly into the parlor where a low-burning lamp cast a soft glow around the room. Glancing at the clock, he cursed under his breath. It had taken him much longer to locate the sheriff than he'd anticipated. And by the time the man had read over the papers Wells, Fargo had drawn up asking for warrants to be issued for Jack Lawson, García, and the Arnettes, it was near midnight. After receiving the sheriff's promise not to act on the warrants until the next day so Jesse could accompany him when he made the arrests, Jesse headed back to Fifth Street.

The ticking of the clock and Fantasy's soft breathing were the only sounds in the otherwise quiet parlor. Jesse smiled as he looked down at his sleeping wife. Curled up on her side, one hand tucked beneath her cheek, her hair swirled around her shoulders in glorious disarray.

Unable to resist touching the shiny tresses, he reached down and lifted one auburn lock. The silky curl wrapped itself around his fingers, just as Fantasy had wrapped herself around his heart. For a moment Jesse considered waking her, then decided it would be better to have their talk when they were both rested.

Unbuttoning her shoes and slipping them from her feet, Jesse stretched her legs out on the settee. He wished he could make her more comfortable, or even carry her into the bedroom, but he didn't want to disturb her much-needed sleep. Instead, he brushed her temple with his lips, extinguished the lamp and sought the bed he and Fantasy had shared—the bed he hoped to share with her again.

Sleep came slowly for Jesse. He tossed and turned, unable to find a comfortable position, his mind refusing to quiet for the night. His thoughts dwelled on what he would say to Fantasy in the morning. He hoped when she knew the whole truth, she could forgive his lies. Finally near dawn, his exhaustion won out and he slept.

When he awoke, the sun was already high and he mentally scolded himself for oversleeping. After a quick sponge bath and shave, Jesse pulled on his clothes, thankful he'd told the sheriff not to expect him until noon.

He found Fantasy and Robby in the dining room enjoying a late breakfast.

Fantasy glanced up from her seat at the dining room table to see Jesse standing in the doorway. The sight transported her back to the first time she'd seen Jesse standing in a similar pose—the morning after he'd taken a room at her boardinghouse six months earlier.

Her appetite fled, her senses swamped with other memories as well. Placing her fork on her plate, she tried to keep her voice neutral when she said, "Would you like something to eat? I made flapjacks."

As he stepped into the dining room, Jesse recalled the first morning he'd seen Fantasy and Robby sitting together over breakfast. She'd been just as cool to him then. He'd broken through that cool demeanor once, but could he do it again? Though he'd awoken ravenous, an enormous knot of apprehension chased away his hunger. "I'll just have coffee," he finally said. When Fantasy started to rise from her chair, he waved her back. "Sit still. I'll get it."

He took longer than necessary to fetch the coffee from the kitchen, using the time to compose himself. His future happiness depended on the conversation he and Fantasy were about to have. He had to be in control.

Returning to the dining room, Jesse sat down across the table from Fantasy. Coffee cup gripped between his hands in front of him, his gaze shifted from her nearly untouched plate to Robby devouring another flapjack. One corner of Jesse's mouth lifted. *At least one of us has a good appetite.* Aloud, he said to Fantasy, "Can we talk now?"

Glancing at her son and finding him oblivious to anything other than his food, Fantasy murmured, "Yes."

Jesse cleared his throat, then began speaking in a low voice. "I . . . uh . . . guess I should start with why I came to Tombstone. I'm a special agent for Wells, Fargo. I was sent here from the San Francisco office on an undercover assignment."

Fantasy's eyebrows shot up. "Nick works for Wells, Fargo, too? Is that how you know him?"

"Yes, I've known Nick for six or seven years. We started with Wells, Fargo at about the same time, and he's also a special agent. We've been working on solving the stage holdups plaguing Cochise County for more than a year. Nick came here first, posing as a gambler. Then after he'd found out enough to give us a lead on who was behind the robberies, he sent for me. For obvious reasons, we couldn't reveal our friendship or our working relationship once I arrived in town, undercover as a land speculator."

Jesse went on to explain how Nick had come to suspect Jack Lawson was the gang's leader, and how Jesse started working on finding out the identities of the other men who were part of Lawson's band of robbers.

"Why did you think I was involved?" Fantasy asked, pain still lingering in her voice.

"To be perfectly honest, as soon as I arrived I started wondering if you could be working with Lawson. He lived in your boardinghouse, and I saw you take money from him on my first day in town, so at the time it made sense." He smiled weakly. "Anyway, I didn't have any solid evidence to prove your involvement until I accidentally knocked over one of your laundry baskets."

"My laundry basket? What are you talking about?"

"It was right after I moved into your boardinghouse. A pouch of jewelry fell out of the basket along with the dirty clothes and linens. I recognized a necklace from the description I'd received from the most recent robbery."

"And you thought I put the pouch there?"

"Fantasy, you have to understand how incriminating that looked. It was your laundry basket, filled with laundry from your boardinghouse."

"Yes, I suppose," she answered carefully. "But why would I hide stolen jewelry in my own laundry basket?"

"Wing Fong was working with Lawson. And so was Ramón García." At Fantasy's gasp, he continued, "Wing was Lawson's fence, smuggling the jewelry in tins marked tobacco to California where it was sold. García rode with the gang when they pulled the holdups. That's why Lawson had you deliver things to him."

"Oh God," Fantasy groaned. "You know about the deliveries I made to Señor García, too?"

"Yes. The day I found the jewelry hidden in the laundry basket, I followed you. After you left Wing Fong's, you went to García's Grocery and I saw you hand him an envelope."

"I could have been paying my bill," Fantasy said with false bravado.

"True. Except I knew you bought your groceries from Bauer's over on Fremont Street. And besides, Robby told me Lawson asked you to deliver things for him."

"Robby? Oh, I see," she said dully. "You asked him questions not just to get to know me better, but also to find evidence against me." She rubbed her temples with her fingertips, trying to ease the sudden pounding.

"Yes." Jesse saw her reaction to his answer and added, "I know what you're thinking. How could I use your son to try to prove you guilty of a crime?" He lifted his coffee cup, blew on the hot liquid, then took a sip. "I'm not proud of what I did, Fantasy. Asking Robby questions about you was pretty low. But I had a job to do. And I had to take advantage of any means I could in order to get some answers. Can you understand that, even a little?"

After a long silence, Fantasy finally said, "Yes, I guess I do understand. So, what was in those packages and envelopes I took to Señor García?"

"The packages probably contained his share of the money from the robbery, and the envelopes likely coded messages about their jobs." After another few seconds of silence, he said, "You know, one of the biggest mysteries Nick and I had to solve was how Lawson got out of town to take part in the holdups when he was supposedly asleep in your boarding-house. The fire finally gave me the answer."

Fantasy's brow furrowed. "The fire? How did that prove anything?"

"The fire was the reason Robby told me about the tunnels."

"Tunnels?" Fantasy repeated, then her brow cleared. "Oh, now I understand. The tunnels you and Robby went through to escape the fire." Jesse nodded. "That's how Lawson left without being seen!" Before Jesse could reply, she rushed on, "But how did he know about the tunnels? I lived in that house for nearly a year, and I never knew about them."

Jesse took another sip of coffee, then said, "Lawson was extremely clever and very thorough. He had obviously learned about the tunnels before he took a room with you. Once he'd found a way to sneak out of town, he needed to find someone to become his unwitting accomplice. He chose you. He pretended to be your friend, asking you to take his clothes with the hidden cache of robbery loot to Wing Fong's along with the boardinghouse laundry, and to make deliveries to García."

"No! He was my friend," Fantasy said. "We had so much in common. He was from St. Louis, too. We used to talk about our favorite places there, and he knew about the orphanage where I lived."

"Fantasy, Jack Lawson is from Colorado."

"But, he said—"

"I know, love," Jesse interrupted. "He may have visited St. Louis and or learned something about the city some other way, but believe me, he was born and raised in Colorado. He got run out of Denver for cheating at poker two years ago. Near as we've been able to find out, that's when he came to Arizona Territory."

"But he took such an interest in my work for the Ladies Aid Society."

"That's why I said he's very thorough. He picks his marks carefully, knowing exactly what to do to earn their trust. With you, I'm sure it didn't take him long to find out how much your charity work meant to you. So to earn your trust, he always had a donation ready to keep you from suspecting his true motives."

"True motives?"

"My guess is he figured if he was a regular benefactor to your church's Ladies Aid Society, he would appear to be incapable of any wrongdoing in your eyes." Seeing she didn't look convinced, he added, "Didn't he always ask you to keep quiet about his generosity?"

"Yes, but that could've been because he was being modest. I mean, he was always very generous, and I just thought he didn't want to draw attention to himself."

"It's true he didn't want any unnecessary attention, but not because of modesty. It was his generosity that he didn't want to become common knowledge. Likely, he was more concerned someone would find out and wonder how he could afford so many large donations on a bartender's wages."

A numbness settled over Fantasy. "I was such a fool."

"Don't blame yourself," Jesse said gently. "Like I said, he was extremely clever."

Fantasy listened in silence while Jesse finished telling her how he'd learned the names of the other men working for Lawson and how his investigation continued to point to her as a suspect. After pausing to finish his coffee, he concluded, "The final piece of the puzzle was a jade necklace Wing Fong gave Mei-Ling."

"Can I go outside now, Momma?" Robby asked, breaking the tense moment.

After helping her son wipe his face and sending him off to play, Fantasy spoke. "I can't believe you actually thought I'd be a party to breaking the law, or that you'd marry me thinking I was part of a gang of thieves."

"I married you because I love you, Fancy. As for

thinking you were a thief, it nearly tore me apart when I thought the woman I love might have to face criminal charges. I even came up with a plan if it turned out you were guilty. But the night I proposed I came to realize I knew you well enough to know you couldn't be involved in the robberies. While that realization was a great relief, unfortunately, it also made my job more difficult because then I had even more of a personal stake in its outcome. I became more determined than ever to find the evidence to get Lawson and the others arrested. And in the process, I was determined to clear your name."

"If you didn't think I was a thief, why did you tell Nick you knew I was involved in the robberies?"

"I'm getting to that. It was Wing Fong who finally gave me the last answer I needed. From what I'd already learned, I was certain he knew whether you were part of Lawson's gang, so when I went to see him that's one of the questions I asked. He told me you had no idea Lawson was using you to make deliveries of stolen property. That was the same day you overheard Nick and me talking on the back porch. If you'd listened to the rest of our conversation, you would have heard me tell Nick what Wing Fong said. Or if you hadn't been so hurt and angry when I wanted to explain, I would have told you myself."

Reaching across the table, he grasped one of her hands. "Please understand, Fantasy. I was being pulled in two directions: my love for you and my job. At first, I couldn't tell you the truth because it would have jeopardized over a year of work. Then after you accused me of working for Henrietta and I admitted I wasn't a land speculator, I couldn't tell you my real reason for coming here because you were still a suspect. Please forgive me."

While she didn't remove her hand, she made no move to return the squeeze he gave her fingers. She didn't look up but kept her gaze focused on the table.

"I don't think I can. Not yet, anyway. You told me so many lies, and I'm so confused."

Jesse withdrew his hand and drew a deep breath. "I can accept that. Is there anything else you want to know?"

It took Fantasy a minute to work up the courage to ask, "Why were you gone so long? You said you'd let me know if you were delayed."

"I told you I was going to San Francisco to escort Mei-Ling to her sister, which was true. But I couldn't tell you I also needed to make the trip so I could see my boss, John Valentine. I felt I had enough evidence to have Lawson arrested. But since I came here on John's personal orders, I wanted to discuss the case with him. Unfortunately, he'd been called out of town by the time I arrived, and no one knew when he might return. I had no choice but to wait. Like I told you in my first telegram, I'd be back as soon as I could."

"Telegram?" Fantasy lifted her gaze from the table, her features crimped with confusion. "I never received a telegram."

"Damn," Jesse muttered, raking a hand through his hair. "I should have guessed. More of Henrietta's meddling, no doubt."

Fantasy nodded, her mouth turned down in a frown. "Now that I think about it, I'm sure you're right. With all the to-do she kept making about you not sending me a telegram I should have suspected she was up to something. She—wait a minute. Did you say your 'first' telegram? You sent more than one?"

"Yes. When I decided to wait for John, no matter how long it took, I sent a second wire. I told you I'd been delayed again and would be here as soon as I could. I also said I wanted us to work things out and . . ." His lowered his voice to a soft whisper. "I love you."

Two bright spots of color appeared on Fantasy's cheeks, but she made no comment.

After a long, awkward silence, Jesse said, "I have to

meet the sheriff. We're going to arrest Lawson and the others." Pushing his chair back from the table, he stood up. "I shouldn't be gone more than a couple hours. Promise me you'll think about what I told you while I'm gone."

She forced herself to look at him. The lines bracketing his mouth and creasing his forehead clearly revealed his pain. She wished she could say something to ease his hurt, but she still hurt, too. The best she could do was say, "I promise I'll think about it."

He stared at her long and hard. "I love you, Fancy. As God is my witness, I love you," he said in a soft whisper. With that, he turned and left the dining room.

A few seconds later, Fantasy heard the front door bang shut.

For a long time, she remained at the dining room table, staring at the stone-cold food on her plate. She shoved it away, placed her elbows on the table and cradled her head in her hands.

The conversation she'd just had with Jesse ran through her head again and again. Could she fault him for what he'd done? Had he been wrong to suspect her with the evidence he had? Was there something wrong with a man being so dedicated to his work?

The answer to each question was the same. No. He had only been doing his job, a job he was totally committed to—the kind of commitment she'd made to her boardinghouse. Jesse took responsibility seriously, just as she did. And she could understand how torn he must have been between love for her and dedication to his work. Even so, could she forgive him?

The alternative would be life without Jesse—at best, a lonely, dismal existence. Squeezing her eyes closed, a rush of emotion clogged her throat.

She lifted her head, blinking back tears. More important than believing Jesse's story about why he'd come to town, and understanding why he'd lied, she believed him when he said he loved her. Her shroud of despondency lifting, she rose from the table, cleared away the dirty dishes and rushed into the bedroom.

Once she'd assured herself she looked as good as could be expected after suffering through the emotional turmoil of the past several days, Fantasy checked on Robby. Finding him contentedly playing with his soldiers on the back porch, she returned to the parlor to wait.

She'd just sat down when a knock sounded on the front door.

A thin man with bright red hair and a hawkish nose stood on the front porch, nervously twisting his hat in his hands. "Mrs. McAllister, my name's Elmer Dewhurst. I'm the telegraph operator over at the Western Union office."

"Pleased to meet you, Mr. Dewhurst. What can I do for you?"

He pulled a bandana from his back pocket and ran it over his face. "I'm sorry about this. I hope you'll accept my apologies."

Pulling her eyebrows together, Fantasy replied, "I'm afraid I don't know what you're talking about."

"Oh dear, I haven't given it to you, have I?" Clearly flustered, he stuffed his bandana back in his pants, then pulled an envelope from his jacket pocket. "This here telegram came in for you several days ago. I asked that boy of mine to bring it over here, pronto." A look of dismay came over the man's face. "I didn't find out 'til this mornin' that instead of deliverin' this like I told him, my boy tucked it in one of them pigeonholes of my desk so's he could take off with that bunch of troublemakers he's been runnin' with."

He handed Fantasy the crumpled envelope, then planted his hat back on his head. "I found this when I was lookin' for some new pen nibs. That boy won't do nothing like that again. I whupped him good for shirkin' his duty." Nodding toward the envelope now clutched in Fantasy's hands, he added, "I hope the telegram ain't too late."

Fantasy looked up and gave him a tentative smile. "I won't know until I read it, Mr. Dewhurst. But I thank you for taking the time to bring it over here."

"My pleasure, Mrs. McAllister." Tipping his hat, he turned, stepped off the porch and headed down the street.

Back in the parlor, Fantasy's hands shook as she pulled the telegram from the envelope. She read the date the operator had received it, then dropped down to the message. *Mrs. Fantasy McAllister, Tombstone, Arizona Territory. Another unavoidable delay. Will return as soon as possible. Want to work things out. Love you. Jesse.*

Her voice thick with tears, she murmured, "Oh, Jesse, I love you, too."

"Do you?"

Fantasy gave a startled gasp and whirled around to face the hall. She'd been so engrossed in the telegram she hadn't heard Jesse come in through the back door.

"Do you?" he repeated, stepping farther into the room. "Do you love me?" His throat felt like he'd swallowed the entire Arizona desert.

"Yes, I love you. And I forgive you for lying to me." Holding up the rumpled telegram, she continued, "Mr. Dewhurst brought me your last telegram. He just found out his son didn't deliver it when it came in, and he was kind enough to bring it to me himself."

"Is that what caused this change in your feelings; you learned not everything I'd told you was a lie?" he asked carefully.

"No!" she cried. "Before I read this I'd already decided I believe you, I understand why you couldn't tell me the truth, and that you love me." In a softer voice, she added, "That I love you."

Reading the truth in her eyes, Jesse grinned and closed the distance between them. "Fancy, Fancy. I was so afraid I would lose you." When he tried to pull her into his arms, she stepped back. "What is it?"

"I would like your forgiveness, too," she said, dropping her gaze and fiddling with a loose thread on her skirt.

"Forgiveness? For what?"

"For threatening to end our marriage. I know it was wrong, that I hurt you, but I was so confused and afraid." She lifted her chin and met his gaze, her eyes wide and beseeching. "Please forgive me."

"There's nothing to—"

"Please, Jesse. This is important to me."

After a moment, he whispered, "Okay, Fancy, I forgive you." The joy leaping into her eyes sent an immediate firestorm of desire racing through him. She didn't resist when he reached for her a second time. Pulling her close, he slowly brought his mouth down on hers. His kiss heated and fierce, Jesse tried to convey the depth of his love. Fantasy returned his efforts in full measure.

When he finally lifted his head, his breathing was ragged. He glanced at the clock and moaned.

"What is it, Jesse?"

"I don't think I can wait until tonight to make love to my wife."

Her lips curving into a mischievous smile, she wiggled her hips against the rock-hard evidence of his desire. "Robby doesn't usually take a nap. But since yesterday was such a trial for all of us, I think I can get him to lie down for a little while."

"Do you think you can?"

The hope in Jesse's voice made Fantasy giggle. "Yes, I think I can."

Much later, Fantasy stretched like a recently fed feline then cuddled close to Jesse, her head on his shoulder. "Jesse?"

"Hmm?" he replied, his fingers lazily rubbing her naked back.

"Can we wait until Mattie and Nash get back before we move to San Francisco?"

"When are they supposed to return?"

"The end of the month."

"I don't see why not."

"I'm glad." After a long pause, Fantasy said, "Jesse?"

He smiled against the top of her head. "Hmm?"

"What were you going to do if you'd found out I was a member of Lawson's gang?"

"I was going to take you and Robby away from here, even out of the country if necessary, and start over."

She rose up on one elbow to look at him. "But you were so dedicated to your job."

"I was, but after I fell in love with you, I realized something had been missing in my life—you. And once I'd found you, my job wasn't as important as it used to be. As long as I had you and Robby, I was ready to quit and start over somewhere."

She stared at him for several seconds, then whispered, "Truly?"

He chuckled and gave her bottom a playful swat. "Yes, truly. I came to realize my love for you and our being together meant more to me than anything else in the world. I planned to take you away, then reform you. But when I realized you couldn't possibly be a criminal, I knew I would never have to actually execute that plan as long as I could prove your innocence."

He pulled her down next to him and settled her head on his shoulder. "I'd finally found the love of my life, my wildest fantasy—" he smiled when her giggle interrupted his words, "—and one way or another, I wasn't about to give you up."

Fantasy sighed with contentment, her heart near to bursting with love. "Will you tell me that every night, Jesse?"

"Absolutely, my sweet Fantasy. Absolutely."

Epilogue

Jesse eased down into the hot water, leaned back and rested his head on the edge of the bathtub. Closing his eyes, he sighed with contentment.

He and Fantasy were finally taking the honeymoon he'd promised her. Over a year had passed since they'd left Tombstone and moved to San Francisco. One delay after another had prevented making the trip.

First, Jesse spent several months finding a larger house for his new family. Then his new position as Assistant General Superintendent with Wells, Fargo had kept him extremely busy for several more months. But the major reason for the delay was the birth of Megan Charlotte McAllister in May, 1883.

Finally, when Megan was five months old, Fantasy announced their daughter old enough to stand the rigors of an extended trip.

Their first stop was back to Tombstone to see Mattie and Nash, spending several days getting reacquainted with their friends and newly acquainted with Matthew Edward Sparks, born a month before Megan. Jesse and Fantasy left Arizona Territory with a promise from the Sparks to visit San Francisco soon, making their next stop Silver City to see Nick Trask.

After listening to two days of Nick's grumbles about being stuck on another long assignment, this time in New Mexico, and unable to get back to San Francisco to see Mei-Ling, Jesse loaded his family back on the train and headed for Texas. Jesse and Fantasy stayed two weeks with his parents on the elder McAllisters' ranch near Austin, then boarded another train, this one headed south.

Since Fantasy had taken an instant liking to the ocean, Jesse decided they should spend the rest of their belated wedding trip in Galveston. They'd arrived late in the afternoon and taken a suite of rooms at the recently opened Beach Hotel on the Gulf side of the island. Fantasy was thrilled with the enormous, elegantly appointed room the porter announced as the master bedroom. She was equally pleased with the room Robby, Megan, and the baby's nurse would share on the other side of the sitting room.

Jesse let his eyes drift open, then blinked with surprise. His wife—his naked wife—was kneeling next to the bathtub, a sponge in her hands, a teasing smile on her lips.

After dipping the sponge in the water and working up a lather with a fragrant bar of soap, she began rubbing the sponge over his chest. A groan rumbled deep in his throat. With sure, swift movements, Fantasy soaped and rinsed her husband's upper body and arms.

When she made a move to lower the sponge beneath the water, Jesse halted her hand. "Uh-uh. It's my turn," he said in a raspy whisper. Grasping her arms, he pulled her over the edge of the tub and into the water next to him.

Fantasy's gasp of shock changed to a moan when Jesse's lips nibbled on her earlobe. Plucking the sponge from her hand, he turned his full attention to bathing his wife's lush curves. He knew exactly where and how to touch, and he reveled in her wonderfully wanton response.

Satisfied her desire had reached the same feverish pitch as his, Jesse tossed the sponge across the room. He wrapped his arms around Fantasy's waist and shifted her position until she sat straddling his thighs.

"Fancy. Fancy," he murmured, his hands cupping her breasts, thumbs rubbing the hardened tips.

Fantasy's head fell back, her breath quickening with each brush of his fingers. "Jesse, please."

"Yes, love. Soon," he replied, lowering his head and pulling a taut nipple into his mouth. "Um, sweet. So sweet," he whispered against her silken flesh.

Simple touching soon became more aggressive stroking and petting.

In one swift motion, Jesse lifted Fantasy and resettled her onto his engorged shaft. The joining brought a simultaneous groan.

The water began a rhythmic ebb and flow, spilling onto the tile floor when their frantic movements increased in tempo. Her knees pressed tightly to Jesse's hips, Fantasy suddenly drew a sharp breath. With a high, keening cry, she arched her back and let her climax sweep her away. Weak and deliciously sated, she fell forward onto his chest.

His own release only seconds behind, Jesse lifted his hips one last time, then shouted his triumph.

The water continued to slosh back and forth, slowing its motion with each trip around the tub, just as Fantasy's breathing slowed. At last she lifted her head and whispered, "This is just like my dream."

"What dream?"

"A long time ago, before we ever—you know—I dreamed about us being in a hotel like this, in a room like this." Her voice lowered to a sultry whisper. "In a bathtub like this."

He chuckled. "Did you? And in this dream of yours, did we do what we did just now?" he asked, running his tongue around the outside of her ear.

"I'm not sure."

"You're not sure?" He jerked his mouth away from her neck. "I think I've been insulted."

Fantasy gave him a mock slap, sending more water flying across the room. "I'm not sure because, just when the dream got to 'that part,' I woke up."

"Oh, I see," he murmured, sliding his hands down her back and over the smooth globes of her bottom. He never tired of touching her.

Grasping the back of the bathtub, she pushed away from him so she could look into his face. She stared into the blue eyes flecked with green she loved so much. "Will you make all my dreams come true?"

Jesse flashed her his most charming smile and said the words that had become a tradition between them, "Absolutely, my sweet Fantasy. Absolutely."

Please turn the page for an exciting sneak preview
of Arlene Holliday's next
captivating historical romance
SUMMER WIND
to be published by
Zebra Books
in
May, 1995

Chapter 1

"Would you look at that! See how *la señorita* twit-ches *sus caderillas*," Armando said in a loud whisper. "She is something, eh?"

"*Sí*," Juan, youngest of the three men replied, then added with a grin, "*y los pechos magníficos*. Eh, *compadres?*"

The third man merely grunted noncommittally to his companions' remarks about the woman's hips and breasts, but she had his full attention. Keeping his posture outwardly relaxed, he studied her shapely form and pale blonde hair. As she moved down the boardwalk on the opposite side of Sacramento's K Street, he tried to summon the hatred that ate at him constantly. Instead, a sudden, intense coil of desire gripped his insides. How could he react so strongly to a woman he'd only just seen? The question made him shift uncomfortably in the chair he occupied in front of a miner's supply store.

His jaw clenching with sudden anger, he snorted with disgust at his unexpected reaction to the woman he'd been waiting to see. The woman he'd been sur-prised to learn owned the *Sacramento Argus,* the news-paper whose editorials he'd been reading for six months. At first, he'd found the scathing articles amus-ing. But the increasingly acrimonious writings no lon-ger amused him, prompting his decision to see for himself the owner of a paper which printed such rubbish. He hadn't planned on that person being a woman. There were few women in California, fewer still who owned a business. But it didn't matter; she was just another *gringa* bitch who didn't deserve the time of day.

Yet, he was helpless to keep his gaze from taking in every nuance of the woman. The way the dark green fabric of her dress stretched across her full bosom, hugged her small waist and outlined her shapely hips sent another lick of unwanted desire dancing up his spine. He shifted in his chair again, silently cursing his body's traitorous reaction. Forcing his mind back to the reason he'd been sitting in front of the supply store for over an hour, he watched the woman stop in front of the newspaper office, pull a key from her handbag and stick it into the lock. The corners of his mouth lifted in a satisfied smile. "At last," he murmured.

"Hello, Katelyn," an older woman called from the doorway next to the *Argus,* her voice carrying to where the three men sat across the street.

The blonde's head turned at the greeting, a smile lighting her face. She replied with a nod and a wave, then pushed the door open and stepped inside.

Katelyn. He liked the sound of it. He longed to savor the way it would roll off his tongue, but stifled the urge. Even after she'd disappeared behind the newspaper's door, her image stayed with him. She hadn't appeared to be particularly beautiful, at least not from his vantage point. Her plain features and pale hair were a direct contrast to the sultry, dark-haired beauties he was accustomed to. Yet there had been a palpable sensuality about her that touched something deep inside. A stirring in his soul he hadn't felt in a very long time.

With a grunt of annoyance, he came out of his chair in an easy, lithe motion, his right hand unconsciously seeking the reassurance of the Colt Navy pistol strapped to his hip.

"What is it, *jefe?*" Armando said, starting to rise.

"Nada." Motioning for his companion to remain seated, he stepped off the boardwalk and started across the street. "Stay here. I will be right back."

Armando flashed Juan an anxious look. He already thought their boss *loco* for coming to Sacramento in broad daylight. Yet, *el jefe* apparently thought his reasons worth the risk.

At the sound of the door opening, Katelyn laid down the rag she'd been using to clean print type and called over her shoulder, "I'll be right with you."

Brushing a wisp of hair off her forehead, her nose twitched with distaste. She'd never gotten used to the smell of turpentine, so necessary in the printing business. Putting a smile on her lips, she turned to greet her customer. A tall man lounged negligently against the front counter. Straight, jet-black hair brushed his wide shoulders. He wore a white, ruffled-front shirt and a leather vest. A black silk bandana, rolled and wrapped around his neck several times, was knotted at his throat.

"Good afternoon, sir." She stared up at him, trying to see his face. Only a square chin with a small cleft was visible beneath the shadow of his wide-brimmed hat. "How can I help you?" she prompted when he remained silent.

Deeply engrossed in the newspaper lying on the counter, the man ignored her questions. Pointing to an article with a long finger, the dusky color of his skin a sharp contrast to the cuff of his shirt, he said, "It seems someone who writes for your newspaper has taken a particularly strong dislike of the bandit people are calling *El Buitre.*"

Katelyn's brow wrinkled at his soft, cultured voice. "No one likes *El Buitre.*" Her pronunciation of the Spanish word for vulture sounded so much different than his. He was obviously bilingual. "Is that why you came here, to discuss my articles?"

His head snapped up at her words, the tilt of his hat still hiding his features. *"Your* articles?" he asked in a silky whisper.

"Yes, I not only own the *Sacramento Argus,* but I'm its editor as well." Her spine stiffened in preparation for taking up the all-too-familiar argument about a woman alone in the wilds of California gold country, and worse, trying to run a business. Swallowing the sudden rush of anger, she continued, "I wrote the editorials about *El Buitre."* She nodded to the newspaper spread on the counter between them. "Including that one."

His gaze dropped back to the article beneath his hand. He silently reread the last paragraph. *How can we allow this vile bandit to continue his reprehensible acts of violence against our citizens? When are we going to rise up for what's right and stop this animal? I say the time has long since passed!*

The hair on the back of his neck prickled with the urge to grab the blonde *gringa* and shake some sense into her. He wasn't vile nor violent. And he wasn't an animal. But she'd never believe that. Clamping down on his temper, the initials at the end of the editorial caught his attention. "KAF." He traced the letters with a fingertip. *Ah, Katelyn with a "K."* Aloud he said, "If you are the editor, these must be your initials. I heard someone outside call you Katelyn, which explains the K, and the A stands for . . ."

"Ann." For the first time, she experienced a moment of apprehension. In a town where at least ninety percent of the population was male, a single woman couldn't be too careful. Yet, for a reason she didn't understand, she felt no real fear of this man. "Listen, what's this about? I'm afraid I have other things to do. So if you'd just state your business . . ."

"Katelyn Ann Ferguson," he said under his breath, her name as sweet and tantalizing on his tongue as he'd imagined. "Why do you hate *El Buitre?* Your editorials sound like you have a personal vendetta against him."

Katelyn pressed her lips into a firm line. Her cheeks burning with a flush, she said, "That's none of your business, Mr. Whatever-your-name-is. Unless you have some newspaper business, I'd appreciate it if you'd take your leave."

Straightening to his full height, he tipped his head back and looked down his straight, patrician nose at her. Pulling a coin from his vest pocket, he slapped it on the counter. "I just came to buy a paper. It was a pleasure meeting you miss—it is miss, is it not?"

She nodded curtly, certain her response caused his severe mouth to curve into a brief smile. The startling flash of white teeth against his dark face caused her heart to do a strange flip-flop.

"*Adiós,* Miss Ferguson." He touched two fingers to his hat brim. *"Hasta luego."*

Lips pursed, brow furrowed, Katelyn watched the man tuck the paper under one arm, then turn and stride from the newspaper office. Long after he departed, she stood staring out the front window, her mind filled with visions of a soft-spoken, dark-skinned man. She didn't know his name, nor had he touched her, yet the few minutes he'd spent in her office made her feel as if they had shared an intimate encounter.

Shrugging off the strange sensations hanging over her, she turned from the window and moved back to the type case. She had work to do. The *Argus* was barely holding its own and she had to put all of her energy into keeping it afloat. She didn't have time to moon over a stranger—no matter how he made her feel.

"Are we leaving town, now, *jefe?"* Juan asked when his boss returned from the newspaper office. Looking up at the man he admired, Juan hoped some day he would be as powerfully built. At eighteen, he was nearly as tall as the other man, but he still had a long way to go before he matched the strength of *el jefe.* His grandfather kept telling him he must be patient, but Juan chafed at the wait.

He turned to look at the youth. Juan's narrow face was taut with tension, his dark eyes filled with hope. "No, not yet." At his words, Juan swallowed hard, but said nothing.

"Por favor, jefe, we must leave this place," Armando said, removing his hat and running a hand through his heavily graying hair. "It is not safe here."

He shifted his gaze to the older man. Seeing the apprehension on Armando's round face and how his friend tugged on his long, sweeping moustache, he said, "You worry too much, *amigo mio."* Slapping the newspaper he'd bought idly against one thigh, his gaze strayed to the building he'd just left. "No one knows what I look like. Of all the *gringo* artists' pictures of me, not one has it right. Would you agree, Armando?"

"Sí, jefe, that is true." Pulling on his moustache again, Armando glanced up, then down the street. "But we are *Californios,"* he said in a fierce whisper. "That is reason enough to suspect us. Being here *es muy peligroso."*

After a long silence, their leader pulled his gaze from the newspaper office. "We will not be here much longer, so it is not that dangerous. I have decided there is something else I want to do. But I cannot do it until tonight. Can you wait that long, Armando?"

Armando took a deep breath. *"Sí, jefe,* but the sooner the better."

Katelyn opened the door to the small apartment behind the newspaper office and stepped inside. It was after ten and she was exhausted. She'd spent the entire evening at the city council meeting, trying to talk some sense into those fools about doing something about *El Buitre.* She tried to convince the councilmen they

couldn't keep sitting on their hands, hoping the bandit
would simply disappear. They just listened to her impassioned speech, then replied as they always had: Yes,
something must be done. But what that something was
no one wanted to suggest. Anything, Katelyn thought,
closing the door behind her, would be an improvement
over the lethargic posture they had maintained for the
six months since she'd taken over the newspaper.

Lighting the oil lamp on the parlor table, she started
to turn around when she felt a presence behind her.
Before she could move, a hand suddenly clamped over
her mouth. Another hand jerked her wrists behind her
back and held them captive in a fierce grip.

"I have been waiting a very long time for you to
return, Miss Ferguson," a man said next to her ear.

A scream welled up in her throat, but was stifled by
the gloved-hand pressing more firmly against her lips.
She tried to twist free of his grasp, but he increased the
pressure on her wrists. The next words from the soft
voice halted any attempt to try again. "I suggest you
do not try it, Miss Ferguson. I do not want to hurt you.
But if you make even the smallest of sounds, I will not
hesitate."

Somehow her brain managed to push aside her fear
long enough to analyze the man's voice. It was the
voice that had haunted her all afternoon. The man
who'd come into her office and asked about the author
of the editorials on *El Buitre*. Remembering the
strength she'd seen in his hands and the enormous
width of his shoulders, she went limp against him. She
could never win a physical battle against such a powerfully built man.

"Muy bien," he said at her compliance, then added,
"Now, I am going to drop my hand. When I do, you
are going to gather up some of your clothes, enough
for a few days, then we are going to take a little trip.
You will make no sound. Do you understand me, Miss
Ferguson?"

Her spine stiffened once more at his commands, but she managed to nod her agreement.

Slowly, he removed his hand from her mouth. He released her wrists, but kept his hand pressed to the small of her back. Before she could think of some way to avoid his instructions, she was propelled toward the door to her bedroom. "What's the meaning of this?" she whispered fiercely. "How did you get in here? And what do you mean I need clothes for several days? I'm not going anywhere with you."

He chuckled at her rush of questions. "I see you are a true newspaperwoman. Your questions will be answered in good time, Miss Ferguson. Until then, *silencio*. Now, do as I say and pack a bag." When she didn't move, he raised his voice a fraction to add, "*¡Pronto!*"

Stumped on how to thwart him and strangely not afraid for her safety, Katelyn moved stiffly to her chest of drawers and began pulling out underclothes, stockings, and a nightdress. Dumping them in a pile on the bed, she turned to where the rest of her clothes hung on pegs on the bedroom wall. She arbitrarily selected a handful of dresses, then tossed them onto the bed.

As she stuffed everything into a carpetbag, her mind worked furiously to comprehend what was happening. She'd only met this man that afternoon, so she couldn't imagine what he wanted with her. Holding her for ransom didn't seem likely when there was no one who would pay to have her returned. But maybe this dangerous man didn't know that.

Abruptly, she stopped her packing and turned to face him. "If it's money you want, I don't have much, but . . . but I could get more."

He chuckled dryly. "I do not want your money, *gringa*. Now, hurry up."

Releasing an exasperated breath, she turned back to the bed. On top of her wadded-up clothing, she placed her journal and hairbrush.

As she glanced around for anything else she might

need, he pulled her woolen shawl from its peg on the wall. Shoving it toward her, he said, "You had better take this."

"Why? It's the middle of July, so—"

"Just do it, *gringa,* and do not argue."

"Okay, fine," she snapped, jerking the shawl from his hand, then stuffing it into her carpetbag.

Before she could pick up the bag, he reached around her and snatched it off the bed. His other hand clasping her by the elbow, he nearly pulled her back into the parlor. "Is there someone you should notify about your absence?"

"I—yes, I should tell Jacob Fletcher. He works for me, and he'll worry if I don't show up at the office in the morning. I'll just go tell him right now." When she tried to pull from his grasp, his fingers tightened.

"Hold it. You are not going anywhere. You will write the man a note." Releasing her, he ordered her to fetch pen and paper, then stood behind her at the small desk. "I can read, Miss Ferguson," he whispered softly, running one hand along the side of her neck. "So make it convincing and do not try to tip him off."

Resisting the urge to shiver in reaction to his touch, Katelyn exhaled a frustrated breath. Unable to think of a way to get out of this mess, she complied and wrote a quick note to her close friend and employee, saying she'd been called away on urgent business and didn't know how long she'd be gone. After asking him to tell Grace about her unexpected departure, she closed by telling him to take care of the newspaper until her return.

When she laid down the pen, the man behind her grunted, then picked up the envelope. "Who is Grace?"

"She's a friend of mine. I was supposed to have supper with her tomorrow night. I knew she'd worry if I didn't show up. So that's why I asked Jake to talk to her."

He merely grunted again. "Tell me where this Jacob

Fletcher lives so I can have your note delivered," he said, pulling her from the desk chair and giving her a none-too-gentle shove toward the door.

Swallowing a retort about his high-handedness, Katelyn said, "He has a room in a lodging house on the corner of Seventh and M."

He responded with another grunt. Opening the door, he pushed her across the threshold, then followed her out into the night.

When they reached an alley several blocks from the newspaper office, two men on horseback, leading a third horse, moved out of the protective darkness into the street.

"This is the *something* you wanted to do, *jefe?*" Armando asked in Spanish.

"*Sí*, Armando," he replied in the same language. "I am ready to leave now."

"Does *la señorita* speak Spanish?" Juan asked.

"I do not know for sure. Just to be safe, watch what you say."

"We must leave now, *jefe,*" Armando said.

Katelyn swung her gaze back and forth between the men, wishing she could understand their conversation. Although Spanish was commonly heard in Sacramento, she'd been too busy for the year and a half she'd lived there to pick up more than a word or two. Now she could kick herself for not taking the time to learn the language.

She was startled out of her thoughts by the voice of the tall man next to her. "I trust you will forgive me, Miss Ferguson. I seem to be without an extra horse. I hope it does not inconvenience you overly much, but you will have to ride double with me."

Tipping her head back, she tried to see his face. Although he'd tendered an elegant apology for the state of their traveling arrangements, she couldn't shake the feeling his words were couched in sarcasm. The feeble light the half-moon provided made it impossible to distinguish his features or gauge his mood. "Fine," she finally answered.

The word had barely left her mouth when she felt him move away from her. A burst of hope surged through her. *It's now or never.* She took a step back, then another. When he didn't seem to notice, she sucked in a deep breath, hiked up her skirts and bolted down the street.

Chapter 2

Katelyn heard the snarl of an angry voice behind her, then the pounding of booted-feet. Her lungs burning, she tried to run faster, but her full skirts impeded her progress. She'd gone only a short distance when a hand gripped her shoulder, spun her around and pulled her flush against a hard chest.

"You cannot get away from me, *querida*," he whispered, surprised at how easily the endearment slipped off his tongue. "And besides," he said with a soft chuckle. "Since your home is in the other direction, perhaps you are only playing games."

She wanted to scream at the unfairness of her aborted escape, at how she was badly winded, her heart pounding wildly, and he wasn't even breathing hard. Instead she clung to his heavily muscled arms, struggling to keep herself from sliding to the ground.

Before she could catch her breath enough to voice a protest, she found herself lifted into his arms and carried back to the other men. In spite of his burden, he mounted his horse with ease and settled her across his thighs in front of him. Such proximity momentarily snatched away what little air was left in her lungs.

She inhaled a deep, ragged breath, hoping to steady her nerves. His scent filled her lungs, nearly making her swoon. Not at all what she expected, he smelled faintly of leather, wood smoke and horses. But mostly, he smelled of spice—sandalwood, she thought—and his potent musky, male scent. The combination was extremely heady and made her body respond in ways she couldn't explain.

After the man holding Katelyn gave her note to the smallest of the other men, then gave him what she assumed were his instructions in Spanish, they started out of town. At the first corner, they split up. The man with her note went one way, the others turned in the opposite direction.

Keeping the horses at a walk and sticking to the shadows, the two men moved single file through Sacramento's streets. At the edge of town, Katelyn felt the man behind her jab his heels to his mount's sides, then the muscles of the horse bunch beneath her before lunging forward at a run.

A few miles into their journey, they pulled up and waited. In just a few minutes the third man appeared out of the darkness. After a brief conversation in Spanish, the three men and Katelyn continued their journey.

They traveled for several hours, then stopped along a rocky river bank to water their horses. Katelyn was allowed to relieve herself in whatever cover she could find, but her captor stood not more than ten feet away. She was thankful for the darkness, certain her cheeks were fiery red with embarrassment. Much too soon, he remounted his horse, hauled her back up onto his lap and continued their journey.

After a few more hours of riding, the darkness and the lulling rhythm of the horses' hooves racing over the gently rolling hills made Katelyn's eyes grow very heavy. Still, she fought sleep, determined to watch for something in the passing scenery she could use as a landmark if she had the chance to escape. Keeping watch proved useless in the deep shadows of night. Even the half-moon didn't provide enough light to see anything other than the eery silhouette of a tree, or an occasional glimpse of moonlight sparkling on water when there was a break in the hills.

Unfortunately, the only thing she could be sure of was the road they traveled closely followed a river. But what road and which river? There were several roads leading into Sacramento and more than one river in and around the town.

Being unfamiliar with the California countryside was a definite disadvantage. Not that such a shortcoming mattered much; her sense of direction was nonexistent. Her father had always teased her about not being able to find her way out of a gunny sack without having detailed instructions.

Although filled with growing despair, she finally could not keep her eyes open a moment longer. Giving into her exhaustion, she slumped against the hard-muscled chest behind her. She pressed her cheek against the ruffles of his shirtfront and instantly fell asleep.

When she felt herself being pulled from the horse, she awoke with a start. "What—"

"Hush, *querida,* it is almost dawn, so we are stopping to get some rest. In just a moment you can lie down."

She allowed him to assist her to the blanket one of the other men had spread for her, then curled up on her side. When another blanket settled over her, she whispered her thanks, then feigned sleep. Looking through partially closed eyes, she watched the three men move around the small campsite.

After unsaddling the horses, each man gave his own mount a quick rubdown, then tied hobbles on their front legs. The men spread blankets for themselves near her feet, then sat quietly talking. Katelyn strained to hear their conversation, but caught only snatches of softly spoken Spanish. Though she wanted to remain awake to see if she could learn anything about what the men planned, sleep plucked at her. Exhaling a weary sigh, she gave in and slept.

When she awoke the next time, the sun was high, the sky a clear, brilliant blue. She rose up on one elbow, and looked around. Seeing the sleeping forms of three men just a few feet away, she frowned. So she hadn't dreamed she'd been abducted by a mysterious stranger and his cohorts.

Under the brightness of daylight, she studied the area where they'd camped. They were in a small copse of oak trees on a hill overlooking the rocky banks of a river. The horses stood placidly on the opposite side of the trees.

Yawning, Katelyn considered getting up to look around, but she was just too tired. She rolled over, pulled the blanket over her face, then went back to sleep.

Jake Fletcher stared at the note left for him at the lodging house where he lived. Why in the world would Katelyn send a note, when she could have just left it in the *Argus* office?

More puzzling was why she left town so abruptly. Tucking the note into his pocket, he headed down M Street, then cut north on Third. It wasn't like Katelyn to do something as impulsive as taking off. But then the girl had been working especially hard since her father died. He reckoned she wasn't on a business trip. She probably just wanted to get away for a while and was too embarrassed to tell him.

When Jake turned the corner onto K Street, and the *Argus* office came into sight, his heart rate picked up. Next to the newspaper was the laundry owned by the Widow Grace Barnes.

He slowed his strides, hoping to catch a glimpse of the lovely Mrs. Barnes as he passed the front window of her building.

Recalling Katelyn's note, he stopped. *Durn you, Katie, for asking me to do this.* He pulled the note from his pocket, swallowed hard, then approached the Barnes Laundry.

He pushed open the door, then stepped inside. He

waited at the counter for a few minutes and was just about ready to leave, when a woman came through the curtains leading to the back room.

Jake felt the heat of a flush creep up his face, and silently cursed his nervous reaction to being so close to Grace Barnes.

"Why, Mr. Fletcher, what a surprise!"

"Mrs. Barnes," he mumbled, turning the envelope containing Katelyn's note over and over in his hands.

When he said no more, she said, "What's that you're holding, Mr. Fletcher?"

Realizing he was acting like a schoolboy, he cleared his throat, then said, "It's a note from Katelyn. She says she was called away on business, and she wanted me to tell you."

Grace's eyebrows lifted slightly. "Really? She left Sacramento?" At his nod, she added, "Does her note say where she was heading?"

"No, she didn't say. Here, you read it and see what you think."

Grace accepted the envelope, pulled out the single sheet of paper, then studied Katelyn's note.

While she was preoccupied with the note, Jake took the opportunity to feast his gaze on Grace Barnes. She was just a little thing, not much over five feet tall, with a full, ripe figure, light brown hair worn in a coronet of braids atop her head, and the brownest eyes he'd ever seen. Not that he'd seen her eyes up close very often.

Much to his embarrassment, he always changed whenever he was around Grace. He was a grown man, almost fifty years old for cripes sake. But for some reason, being near Grace made him feel like a tongue-tied boy. Rather than face her possible ridicule, he'd never tried to pursue the widow, but kept their relationship formal whenever they chanced to meet.

Now being so close to the woman he longed for, he felt himself harden from just looking at her. Afraid his condition would become apparent, he turned away.

Pretending to look out the window, his mind filled with images of Grace stretched out on his bed, of making long, leisurely—Her voice jerked him from his daydreams.

"What do you think this means, Mr. Fletcher? Do you really think she left on business?"

Needing a few moments to cool his desire, he took a slow, cleansing breath, then turned around. But seeing the sprinkling of freckles on her nose and cheeks, her brown eyes staring at him, he was instantly hard again. Mortified at not being able to control his physical reaction, Jake finally managed to find his voice. "I'm not sure what to believe. She never mentioned anything about a business trip yesterday, so it doesn't seem likely something could come up so quickly."

"Yes, it is a puzzle," she said, handing the note back to him.

His fingers brushed hers, sending his pulse into a wild rhythm and another rush of desire to his groin. Not able to look at her, he summoned all his strength and said, "Maybe we should get together and discuss this. What do you think, Mrs. Barnes?" He raised his head enough to peek at her face. Her bright smile came as a pleasant surprise.

"Don't you think it's about time we started calling each other by our Christian names? After all, we've known each other for almost three years."

When he nodded, she said, "And, I think getting together would be a good idea. How about supper tonight? I'm a great cook."

He smiled. "I'd like that, Grace." In spite of another rush of heat to his face, he didn't look away. "Is seven okay?"

"Perfect. See you then, Jake."

"Gringa, it is time to get up."

"Go away," Katelyn murmured, then gasped when her shoulder was given a none-too gentle shove. Opening her eyes a crack, she saw a pair of boots next to her. She didn't have to guess who stood beside her, or that he'd used a boot-clad foot to prod her awake. "What do you want?"

"I said it is time to get up. Hurry and take care of your personal needs so we may leave here."

She glanced at the sky. It was now a deep pink, shot with the last of the sun's golden rays. Had she really slept the entire day? Apparently she had, since the sun would be setting in a few hours. Shifting her gaze to the tall man who had issued the order, she looked up at him through narrowed eyes. Feet widespread, arms crossed over his broad chest, he stared down at her from beneath his hat brim. Wishing he'd remove his hat so she could see his face, she bit back a retort, then shoved the blanket aside.

"Would you mind helping me up?" She raised one hand toward him.

After a moment, he uncrossed his arms and reached down to grasp her hand. With one quick jerk, he pulled her to her feet.

"I didn't mean, pull my arm out of its socket," she said, giving him a fuming look. Rubbing her shoulder, she added, "I'm not a—"

"I would not waste time talking if I were you," he said, cutting off her complaint. "We are leaving in five minutes. So, I suggest you take care of your personal needs immediately, or you will have to wait until the next time we stop."

"Fine," she said, shaking out her rumpled skirt, then marching deeper into the stand of trees.

When she returned, she mechanically ate the food he handed her, barely tasting it, but knowing she had to keep up her strength if she was to survive whatever lay ahead.

Again, she rode sitting across the hard-muscled thighs of her captor. Each time they stopped to rest and water the horses, she was allowed to stretch her legs, though ordered to stay close by. After their second stop, they turned away from the river, heading into the foothills of a mountain range. Katelyn thought the distant peaks resembled the Sierra Nevada, which she and her father had crossed on their trip to California. Her spirits lifted at the possibility, then immediately sagged. Even if she was correct, the Sierras were a very large mountain range, and since she had no idea which area they were in, the information was useless.

Still hoping something in the passing terrain would prove helpful later, she continued to watch for some distinguishing landmark. The chaparral-covered hillsides and deep canyons all looked alike in the deepening dusk. As they wound their way higher into the mountains, oak and pine trees mixed with the chaparral. Still, she saw nothing unique enough to remember if she saw it again. From her perspective, they could be going in circles and she'd never be the wiser.

After riding for several hours in full darkness, she grew drowsy from boredom and once again drifted to sleep against the hard chest behind her.

The lack of the horse moving beneath her woke Katelyn with a start. She opened her eyes a crack, then squeezed them closed. The late afternoon sun pierced down at her with a blinding fierceness.

The man holding her shifted in the saddle, rolling her head to the side with his movement. She groaned in protest, bringing a deep chuckle from his chest. *"Un momento,* Miss Ferguson, then you can go back to sleep."

She heard the rustle of cloth, then felt something soft brush her face. The fabric was pulled across her closed eyes and tied securely behind her head. When she lifted one hand to the silk blindfold, a soft voice stopped her. "No, *querida,* you must leave the bandana over your eyes. If you try to take it off, I will have to tie your hands as well."

"Why?" she managed to croak through her tight throat.

"We approach my camp. No one except my men has ever been here, and I cannot risk having someone from the outside know its location."

Katelyn wanted to tell him he had nothing to fear. But there was no point in telling her captor she could never find her way home, let alone back to his camp. He'd never believe her. Sighing with resignation, she dropped her hand and let her head fall back against the warmth of his chest.

"*Bueno,*" he whispered softly, brushing a stray lock of hair off her face. He glanced up to see Juan and Armando staring at him incredulously. He pulled his hand away from the blonde hair as though he'd been burned, his jaw clenching with anger. *Fool! How can I treat this* gringa *bitch with kindness?*

The next time Katelyn woke, the blindfold was still in place and the man behind her was preparing to dismount. With one arm wrapped around her shoulders, the other under her knees, he lifted her off his thighs. Then just as easily as he'd mounted the horse with her in his arms, he swung out of the saddle.

As he removed his hand from beneath her knees, she slowly slid down his body until her feet touched the ground. When he dropped his other hand, her wobbly legs started to buckle. Cursing softly, he grabbed her waist, preventing her from falling. After she'd gained her balance, he moved his hands to the back of her head. His fingers worked at loosening the knotted silk, then the blindfold was whisked from her face.

She blinked at the sudden brightness, trying to clear the spots before her eyes. As she became accustomed to the light her gaze settled on the man standing beside her. His hat hanging down his back by a leather thong, his face was revealed to her for the first time. She sucked in a surprised breath. Never had she seen a more handsome man. But more than his high prominent cheekbones, long narrow nose and square clefted chin, her attention was captured and held by his eyes. Dark as pitch, they glowed with an intense inner fire—a fire she couldn't help thinking was directed at her.

Suddenly some of his words came back to her, filling her with apprehension. His camp. His men. Dear Lord, what kind of man had abducted her? From the scowl on his face and the anger burning in his eyes, she judged him to be an extremely dangerous one. She swallowed her fear, determined not to show even the tiniest bit of cowardice.

"I think it is time I introduced myself," he said in that warm, silky voice she was beginning to know well. After bowing in a gesture of gallantry, he said, "I am Roberto Cordoba, Miss Ferguson. Since you have devoted so much space in your newspaper to me, I thought perhaps we should meet in person."

Her brow furrowing, Katelyn replied, "Roberto Cordoba?" Deep in thought, she repeated the name several times under her breath. Then shaking her head, she said, "The name doesn't sound familiar. Are you sure I've printed something about you?"

He chuckled. "Yes, indeed. You have printed many articles about me. In fact, I have recently learned you were the author of all of them." His voice turned hard when he added, "You have called me every vile name imaginable with that poison pen of yours."

Something niggled at the back of her mind, yet the unlikely possibility didn't bear consideration. There were numerous gangs of bandits in this part of California; he must be the leader of one of them. Then another recollection came back, making her eyes widen with shock. When he visited the newspaper office, he'd been fascinated with her editorials about—Her eyes widened even more. *Oh, my God, was it really possible? Could he be—*

His voice interrupted her thoughts. "Ah, I see you are beginning to unravel the mystery of my identity." He flashed a chilling smile. "Yes, just as you suspect,

Miss Ferguson, you know me by another name. One your fellow *gringos* gave me."

He lifted her chin with his fingers, forcing her to meet his gaze. When he was sure he had her undivided attention, he dropped his hand from her face. Watching her closely, he whispered, "They call me *El Buitre.*"

Dear Readers:

I hope you enjoyed Fantasy and Jesse's story in *His Wildest Fantasy,* just as I hope you were intrigued by the small taste of my next book. *Summer Wind* is about revenge, betrayal, and the incredible passion between two people from opposite cultures with opposite points of view, yet whose love continues to grow regardless of the obstacles before them. Watch for *Summer Wind* in mid-April of next year.

As you read this I'll be working on book number four to be released in the fall of next year. *Dancer's Angel* is about Kit Dancer, a character from my first book, *Wild Texas Blossom,* and Angelina Coleman. Haunted by his past and filled with guilt, Kit returns to El Paso where he meets the lovely Angelina, a woman forced into a miserable situation by an unfortunate set of circumstances. Only after Kit frees Angelina from her predicament, does he learn she is not the kind of woman he thought her to be. She's not only too good for him, she's also the woman he could easily love.

I always enjoy hearing from readers. Please write to: P. O. Box 384, Paw Paw, Michigan 49079-0384.